JAMMY DODGERS

By Robert Grieve Black

2011

A story of Glasgow gangsters and jammy dodgers around the time of the ice cream wars. The characters may at times seem real. You may even feel that you know some of them but it is a work of fiction.

A Jammy Beginning.

1940 November 16th Jamieson Gardens, Glasgow.

The first chill winds of war and winter sucked the last few leaves from the trees and swirled dust and papers round the small Glasgow square. None of the four street lamps offered any light. The pale glow of a half-moon flickered among the moving shadows. The woman's soft moans went unheard in the darkness as she squatted among the bushes in the centre of the square. A few minutes later she stood up, emerged silently from the bushes and scurried down the street. The cold wind tugged at her hair as she disappeared into the night. As the clouds went scudding by, a short break let the moonlight through and anyone watching from a blacked-out window would have seen that she was dark-skinned, perhaps from the Indian subcontinent. She held both hands protectively around her uncovered head.

Her headscarf was still among the bushes wrapped round the tiny bundle that had just entered the world. Glasgow's newest born baby whimpered softly as the wind blew around him and rustled the bushes.

This was all that I ever knew of my real mother. I didn't know who she was or why she abandoned me, ostensibly to die, among the shrubbery of Jamieson Gardens. But from that day until now I have always been blessed by a strange quirk of luckiness. I was what Glaswegians call "jammy", someone who could fall in the River Clyde and come out smelling of roses.

Maggie Robertson lived in Jamieson Crescent a couple of streets behind the "gardens". She was a nurse at Victoria Infirmary and was going to start her shift of night duty. She heard my feeble whimpers but thought it was just the wind and continued on her way. Then something made her stop. She swore till the day she died that she had no idea why but suddenly, she turned back into the square and looked down among the shrubs. I was saved!

She took me to the maternity wing and after a stout battle with the ward sister she left me to be nourished and cherished, for the first few months of my life. She had to go down to Gorbals police station the next morning and explain how she found me. The registry of my birth became something of a problem with no mother, no father, no known relative and thus, neither name nor surname. In fact I was quite a curiosity among those that dealt with me. Remember this was 1940, before the days of mass immigration. The only non-white people that most Glasgow folk had seen were in David Livingstone's "magic lantern" exhibitions or the handful of Sikhs who went from door to door selling clothes from a suitcase. Here they had a chirpy little brown boy who had appeared out of nowhere. Somebody suggested that they call me Jamieson from where I was found and so my birth certificate shows quite simply:

Christian name: *Jamieson*

Surname: *Unknown*

Mother's name: *Unknown*

Mother's maiden name: *Unknown*

Father's name: *Unknown*

Person notifying the birth: *Margaret Robertson*

Maggie didn't just notify my birth, she called in to check on my progress nearly every day and, eventually, she adopted me. That was not easy in those days. She wasn't married and the authorities favoured what they called a stable background. Poor Maggie, whose younger days were dedicated to building her nursing career, never had time nor opportunity to find a husband. Everywhere she turned there was opposition but, as I learned in later life, she was a stubborn body and she decided that this little boy who had dropped into her life was not going to be abandoned to fester in an orphanage just to please the goody-goodies. Her battle lasted the first full year of my life but in the end she won. The adoption was approved and I got a home and a surname.

Another four years elapsed and it was time to start school. I didn't have a "Mammy" like the other kids. I called her Maggie and she called me Jamie. It was never a mother-son relationship; we were always just really good friends. Off I went for my first day at school, a little curly-haired brown boy called Jamie Robertson. You don't get away with a face and a name like that in Glasgow. On my first day one of the bigger lads called me Golliwog. A little lad called Tommy Monaghan rallied to my defence. "You can't call anybody Golliwog," he said, "it's not nice."

"But he looks like the Golly on the jam-jars and his name is Robertson," snapped back the other lad.

"His name's Jamie," said Tommy, defiantly.

"Aw' right, we'll call him Jammy, then," insisted the big lad unwilling to give ground to one of the smaller kids. So I was renamed *Jammy* Robertson and that name stuck with me all my life. Robertson's don't put the famous Golliwog on their jam-jars any more; it's not politically correct. Tommy and I became firm friends and fought each other's battles all the way up through school.

I loved school and hated the schoolwork but all the teachers had a soft spot for the little brown waif and I seemed to scrape through all the tests. In the last year of primary I passed the "11-plus" barrier that allowed me to go to high school but I never excelled at any subject while I was there. I was good at composition and writing essays and even won a prize once. I played football and that was where the "Jammy" name really took hold as I bent a few balls into the net.

When I was about thirteen I took a job in the local Coutts shop delivering newspapers in the morning before school. Coutts, with its familiar green logo, was one of the biggest Scottish chains and had a shop on every important street selling confectionery, tobacco and newspapers. My schoolwork suffered of course, because I was always half-asleep in class but I had money in my pocket without having to ask Maggie. I could go to Rosso's café and pop money in the new jukebox and drink Coca Cola and Irn Bru. It was about this time I got interested in newspapers. Jenny, the girl who sorted out the papers in the morning, was a bit dopey and often put the odd extra copy in my bag, so nearly every day I had a different paper to read. I didn't read everything in depth but learned to skim-read, one day the Glasgow Herald, next day the Scottish Daily Express, or a Mirror or a Scotsman or even the occasional Telegraph. They were all different, not like nowadays where everything is the same bland mush. The front page was usually about some post-war international crisis. British news was about the labour movement, the unions and the welfare state. Scottish headlines were about home-rule for Scotland and home-wins for Rangers and Celtic. Glasgow headlines were usually about crime. These days they sell newspapers with free DVDs and scratchcards. Fifty years ago it was murders and hangings that sold the papers, gruesome headlines and gruesome stories. I scoured the papers every morning and my skim reading skills developed. A standard daily took me fifteen to twenty minutes to absorb from front to back.

I can only remember one big humdinger disagreement between Maggie and me. I won but with the wisdom of age I know she was right. As my fifteenth birthday approached I decided that school and I were not made for each other; I was going to leave and find a full time job. Maggie was furious.

"You've got the brains to do something better," she argued. "You can get the Higher Leaving Certificate and go to university. We don't have any money problems. Take the chance. Most kids don't get the chance."

"But Maggie, you know I hate school." I whined back. "What makes you think I would like university any better? I can't stand the thought of all these years studying things that don't matter. And anyway I don't want to be always taking your money. Please Maggie, don't make me stay at school." I begged.

"So what will you do? The shipyards are all closing. Everything is closing. Where do you plan to get this full time job? What do you actually want to do? Do you know?"

"A newspaper reporter!" I announced proudly. "I'm going to be a journalist."

"And how do you propose to do that, without even the Lower Leaving Certificate, never mind the Higher. You don't even know anybody in the business. Your bum's out the window, Jamie. You're living in cloud-cuckoo-land. You've got to promise me that you won't leave school unless you have a job first. Promise me that!"

It seemed a reasonable compromise so I agreed. She was right of course. I spent the next year chasing the illusive reporter's job, writing letters to all the editors, trying to get past security guards and secretaries to see the sub-editors, watching all the situations vacant columns. In this matter I wasn't quite so "jammy". The following June saw me still stuck at school so I took the first "leaving certificate". I did quite well, which pleased Maggie, and my confidence was renewed that somebody out there was desperately seeking my intellectual talents. No such luck! Television news was starting to upstage the newspapers and the restrictive practices of the printing unions were sucking the blood from the newspaper finances. Nobody was looking for a bright new reporter.

All this time I was still doing the morning delivery round with Coutts and every Friday I skimmed the situations vacant in the Glasgow Herald. I was by now giving up hope of being a reporter and was looking for anything reasonably interesting. In the last week of July it seemed like I might have to go back for another brain-destroying year at school. I really didn't want to go back. That Friday I didn't just skim the adverts; I read every one in detail. One of the small ads caught my eye:

TRAINEE CIRCULATION ASSISTANT.

The position was with the Glasgow Herald, not a reporter like I'd imagined but who knows, perhaps with a foot in the door…? The advert invited letters of application but I decided not to waste time. Direct action was called for so I jumped on the first bus up to the city centre and ran down to the waterfront offices in pursuit of C.J. Brown, Circulation Manager. Someone directed me to his office and I ran up the stairs three at a time. Turning the corner at the top of the stairs I crashed into a rather startled Mr Brown.

"What's the rush, lad? Where's the fire?" he admonished.

"I'm looking for Mr Brown." I puffed.

"Well you've found him but what's so urgent?"

"I want the job." I blurted.

"I suppose you mean the circulation assistant. The advert just went in this morning. Why don't you send in a letter like it asks?"

"No, you don't understand. I want the job. You don't need to waste time reading all these letters."

He looked at me for a few moments across the top of steel framed reading glasses and then laughed. My heart sank. I should have sent a letter like everybody else. Now he thought I was an idiot. He walked over to a door marked C.J. Brown and strode in still laughing. I hung my head, turned and started to walk away.

"Well if you want the job that bad you better come in." he said, still laughing, "Come and tell me about yourself. You might as well since you're here anyway."

He cleared a bundle of newspapers from a chair and invited me to sit down. There was a glint of amusement in his eye and he didn't look quite so fearsome as when he first glowered over his glasses. He then proceeded to quiz me about who I was, where I lived, why I wanted the job and all the usual routine questions. Perhaps I answered them all correctly. Perhaps he liked me. Perhaps he liked the idea of not having to plough through fifty or more applications. Perhaps I was just "jammy". His last question was. "Can you start on Monday?"

"What time do I start?" was my instant reply.

"Ten o'clock, son, but it's best if you are here a quarter of an hour before that so that somebody can show you round."

I raced out of the building even faster than I had arrived and home to tell Maggie the news. I was sitting upstairs on the bus doing a mental re-run of my first ever interview, thinking how clever I'd been, when suddenly the penny dropped. He meant ten o'clock at night. Nobody needs a newspaper circulation assistant at ten in the morning. So what? Who was caring? I had got my foot in the door in the world of newspapers. And anyway Maggie had just started back on night duty so we would be able to have tea together.

Monday couldn't come quickly enough and then, when it did, I spent the whole day skitting nervously around the house. Eventually evening passed to night and I set off for my first real job. Circulation assistant transpired to be hard physical work. It involved getting the bundles of papers from the press, wetting the big destination labels, sticking them on the packs and manhandling them to their relative despatch points. Nearly all of them went to the various John Menzies wholesale depots around Scotland. For the east coast there was a van that took them to Queen Street Station, another van for the city of Glasgow and for the west of Scotland and for London there was an open platform lorry that took them to Central Station. Thinking back now it sounds rather mundane but that Monday night was one of the most exciting of my life. I can close my eyes and remember, the clamour of voices, machines and vehicles: I can smell the mix of fresh newsprint and diesel fumes and I can clearly see the faces of the older members of the team.

I quickly learned the meaning of the word "trainee". It doesn't mean you are going to be trained. It is an excuse for the employer to pay you half as much as the other workers and an excuse for the other workers to dump you with twice as much of the work. There were some encouraging phrases like: "Move yer arse nipper or we'll miss the train". At the two stations we had to push and shove against the postmen who were also trying to get their bags away on time and there was always rivalry about getting the iron-wheeled trolleys to carry the bundles along the platforms and onto the trains. Sometimes if we just had a couple of bundles one of the posties would offer to put them on for us. By the end of the first week I knew most of the people's names. By the end of the first month I was one of the lads and had learned about the quirks, traits and tantrums of this rough bunch of characters who helped feed the country's appetite for news. I doubt if any of them ever read the Glasgow Herald but they were a happy clan who made fun of a fairly drudge job. It wasn't quite how I'd imagined it but it was a great job and I loved the constant deadline pressure that permeated the whole Herald building.

Before I knew it a couple of years had passed. It was still good fun and I was now earning nearly as much as the old hands but it was a dead end alley and as a frisky young eighteen-year-old I had no social life. Like most lads I had already started to enjoy a few pints before I had reached the legal age. Just before my eighteenth birthday I started calling into the Docker's Bar before my shift. The docks and the dockers had long since dwindled in numbers and the Docker's had become the favourite watering hole for the reporters and print workers from the Herald, the Evening Times, the Express and the Record. It was alive with football banter, crude jokes, punter's politics and the jovial hum of pre-press one-upmanship. Many last minute headlines were conjured up as some desperate sub-editor downed the last few dregs of his last pint. I was still reading all the dailies, nowadays in the library, and I got to know a lot of faces to go with names that I already knew by heart.

Jock Corrigan was sub-editor on the crime desk of the Herald's sister paper, the Glasgow Evening Times. He was one of the older reporters; some said he'd passed retiral age but wouldn't hang up his hat. He was a staunch supporter of Rangers and had a line of jokes that were bluer than a "Gers" shirt. He looked like a character out of a Dickens book, as if he really belonged to an earlier century. I first got to know him one night when he was giving me a hard time about my Celtic scarf just before an old firm match. I made some joke about Celtic fans being more select. The Times was more "downmarket" than the Herald. Nearly all copies were sold on the street by the typical, tramp-like, rain-drenched worthies who assaulted peoples' eardrums at the main bus stops and Subway entrances. We became friends when I passed him a rumour that I'd picked up in Queen Street station about jury fixing in a big gangster trial. He followed up, got a two-page scoop spread and bought all my beer for the next week. He knew that I desperately wanted to be a reporter but never misled me into thinking that my chances were anything but slim.

I walked into the Docker's one Friday night and found Jock hugging the bar, looking unusually glum. I thumped him on the shoulder.

"What's up with you Jock?" I asked. "You look like the Gers have just been relegated. What's the matter, no juicy murders? Are they not hanging anybody this week?"

"Aye, Jamie, son. It's me they're hanging! Somebody must've found a pension book wi' ma name on it. They're making me retire, just like that. No choice, no discussion, a bloody gold watch and *thank you, bye-bye*. It's a crime. Isn't it?" and he cackled at his own unintended pun.

"But, anyway, I was thinking," he continued, "Maybe it's not so bad. Could be an opening for you, Jamie."

"What?" I stammered. "No Jock. Somebody's been spiking your beer. There's no way I could go straight in as sub-editor, even if you put in a good word."

"Och! Don't be daft, lad. That's no what Ah meant. Willie Docherty'll get my desk. That's more or less certain. Then Dave Rafferty'll get Willie's place. Sheila Thomson'll start doing Dave's stuff and that'll leave an empty space. No desk, mind you. You wouldn't be sitting in a warm office writing wee stories. Sheila does the Sheriff Court stuff but you keep telling me you want tae be a reporter. You'll never get a better chance. Ah can sneak you in the back door before personnel get around to advertising. You know Willie; he'd be your boss. What d'you say? Ah'll pull the strings. It's not a promise but you're in wi' a good shout."

"Jock, y'old bugger. I could hug you. Yes. Yes. Yes. Pull, shout, do what you have to."

"Ah'll pass on the hug, if you don't mind. Why don't you just fill up my beer glass."?

I heard someone laugh behind me and my heart sank.

"Is this just a wind up, Jock?" I could feel the tears welling up.

"No, Jamie. I wish it was. I don't want to pack it in. What am I going to do?"

I still wasn't convinced that this wasn't one of Jock's wind-ups. I turned round still half expecting to see a row of silly grins but everybody was deep in other conversations.

"You mean I can start now, just like that. No interviews or nothing. I think I'd need to finish the month in circulation with the Herald."

"Leave it with me." Jock said. "I'll clear it wi' the big boys. But, like I said, it's not an absolute promise. The job, as far as I'm concerned, is yours but they might decide to cut back and there won't be a job. I'll tell you for sure on Monday night if I don't die of thirst before then. What happened to that pint?"

So, that was how it all started; Jamie Robertson, crime reporter. Fifty years of grovel and grind, bribery and begging to be the first or the best with the latest news on the low-life (and high-life) of Glasgow. Fifty years watching Scotland's greatest city on the skids. This "Clyde built" city always was a tough place to live and an easy place to die but the second half of the twentieth century saw this great conurbation in abject deterioration. Petty crime, major crime, gangland crime, drug related crime, drink related crime, knifings, shootings, domestic violence, football violence, burglary, shop-lifting, car theft, police heroism and police corruption; check out all the various crime statistics for the UK and the chart toppers all belong to Glasgow, dear old Glasgow town. What's the matter with Glasgow when it's going down and down. Maybe that sounds cynical but you have to be a leather-skinned cynic to survive fifty years in Skid Row. Not just survive, mind you, I was one of the best. I am still one of the best but like old Jock Corrigan somebody came across my pension book. Maybe they noticed that my expenses claims had gotten smaller, now that I'm using the famous bus-pass. Have you ever jumped on a city bus recently? Everybody's over sixty and nobody pays for a ticket.

Maggie is dead now. I miss her a lot as she was the best friend I ever had. In later life she got a bit doddery and went into a home but with me she was always lucid and alert. She kept what she called her "Jamie box", a collection of articles I had published over the years. Everything was neatly arranged in chronological order and I often called on her when I needed to remind myself of a name or a date. Folded neatly on top of all the newspaper cuttings was the scarf that I was wrapped in when she found me. I never married although you will find as you read on that there was one lady who was special.

I have had a fantastic, exciting working life. I've sat on the public benches of nearly every courthouse in Scotland and most of the High Courts in England. I've sat at the crime desk of every major daily in Scotland, done features in all the Sundays. I've met Rupert Murdoch, Robert Maxwell and Beaverbrook Junior and argued with all three about the future of newspapers. I became a regular expert guest on both TV and radio and guest speaker at police and law conventions and universities. Not exactly a celebrity, more just a "weel-kent-face". For the last ten years I've been freelancing and never short of work. It is sad, in a way, that I should have had such a wonderful career filled with great moments at the expense of the unfortunate punters who have fallen by the wayside, but I suppose that's life. I never murdered anybody, never hanged anybody and never sent anybody down for life. I just told the stories.

In real life, though, stories don't fit the standard model of beginning, middle and end. Every story is just one small piece of one long string or, more often than not, several long entangled strings wrapped together in one great intertwining sequence of events. It's not always clear who is guilty, who is innocent, who is the perpetrator, who is the victim even when the jury return a unanimous verdict. The secret for a good reporter is in picking up the loose threads and weaving them into a readable text with logical sequence, conclusion and outcome. That's what the reader wants. That's what society wants. A crime reporter is not so very different from a good detective. The questions nag at you and you look for answers but often what you find are just more questions so you lie awake at night trying to put the ends together, trying to complete the circle that insists on looping backwards taking you down Nowhere Street. And how often do we know that we have put all the pieces into place but we can't substantiate the facts? The reporter can't go to print and the policeman can't prosecute. The evidence is too slim.

And for every good crime correspondent and for every diligent police officer there is always the one case, one crime or one story or one devious character that we couldn't put our stamp on; always the one fish that got away. But inside your head it never goes away. It keeps gnawing away at you and you need to find some answers even if it's just so you can sleep at night. For me it was the Glasgow Ice Cream Wars in the early 1980s. At the time it just made no sense. Happy little vans toured the housing estates selling delicious, soft, ice cream cones, chocolate nougat wafers, fruity lollies, fizzy ginger, iron brew and limeade and other assorted snacks and drinks, each with its own happy jingling chime to announce its arrival in the street. It was one of the nice things in life. Everybody loved the ice cream vans. Lots of people called them "Tally vans" since most of the ice cream was made by immigrant Italian families. Then some evil wizard waved an unseen wand and they started smashing each other's vans, breaking limbs and skulls with baseball bats and shooting out each other's windscreens. The frenzy escalated and it was only a matter of time before someone was killed.

We had the crazy situation where the vans had a police escort round the streets each night. The natural Scots reaction to any serious situation is to hit it with droll ironic humour and so the police escort became known as the "Serious Chimes Squad". But it wasn't really funny. It had tragic consequences for several people and neither the police nor the press came up with any real answers as to why it happened. The easy answer was that it was drugs related but I could never buy that story. Anybody with the slightest knowledge of the "substance abuse" market knows that dealers move the goods around quickly in small quantities with fast cars, bicycles, motorcycles and even skateboards being the preferred modes of transport. Quick to arrive, quick to get away and small amounts that can easily be trashed or thrown away. The idea of a slow lumbering ice cream van trundling around with the night's supply stashed under the freezer bucket just didn't have a real ring of truth.

"A bottle of ginger and eighth of skunk please."

"OK son, here y'are. The skunk's a wee bitty frozen but just rub it between your fingers an' soften it up. An' make sure yer Mammy disnae see it. She's lookin' through the curtains. That's twelve quid. Ah'll throw in the ginger for free."

"Ma Mammy only gave me a pound, Mister, but Ah've got some empty ginger bottles."

No, I wasn't entirely convinced by the drugs theory. As the strange episode unfolded it became clear that several of the heavy players were indeed known drug dealers so there was some link but were they really selling joints, rocks, wraps and fixes from the vans? Of course, one or two hard nuts undoubtedly were and probably still are doing drugs. Desperate people do desperate things but if it had been widespread the "Serious Chimes Squad" would have been able to pick them up like apples off a tree. No, there was something more. Either the ice cream companies or some of the drivers had some ulterior motive in keeping their territory sealed off from competition. It all happened back at the beginning of the eighties.

For the first half of the seventies I was with the old Scottish Daily Express then it closed and we all got wrapped up in the abortive Scottish Daily News with Robert Maxwell. When the Daily News collapsed the iconic art deco building in Albion Street was bought over by the Glasgow Evening Times, I got my old job back, and that's where I was when the ice cream thing kicked off. Then it all changed again when the Herald took over the building. Fed up with all these changes I went freelance and started to do more TV and radio. I started doing more in-depth probes for the Sundays. The Herald building was later sold again and in 2004 it was turned into high-class apartments. I bought one of the black glass-fronted apartments and that's where I now do my thinking and writing.

So now, with time on my hands I have dug out the old files, called up a few old cronies and without the constraints of acceptable evidence I have put together an alternative version of the ice cream clashes. I must, however, make it crystal clear before you read on. Every name is changed and I have adapted many loose connections to fuse this into a story. Do not try to associate any of my characters with anyone alive or dead. As I have already said, searching for answers frequently just brings more questions and, unfettered by deadlines and judicial constraints, I have allowed my imagination to control my typing finger. I have pinned together ends that wouldn't meet and plugged the gaps with creative logic. You will see how I was personally sucked into the vortex becoming part of the story itself rather than just reporting impartially from the by-line.

War breaks out in Ruchazie.

1981 April 17th Glasgow.

A brightly painted ice cream van trundled slowly up the inside lane of the M8 motorway bringing irritated glances from the other rush hour drivers who found themselves having to pull out into the faster lane in the busy evening traffic. Thankfully it pulled off at exit 12 into a slip lane that merged into Gartloch Road. At the wheel was twenty-year-old Steven Quigley, postman by profession. Alongside him in the passenger seat was Miriam McKinley his heavily pregnant seventeen-year-old girlfriend. They were about to get married in three weeks time, hopefully before baby arrived, and the ice cream-run seemed an ideal way to boost their income. They had been allocated a two-bedroom flat in Easterhouse and they were going to need furniture and things as well as all the baby equipment. Besides it was a good way of being together in the evenings, making some money instead of spending it.

Gartloch Road is a long twisting road that starts as the A80 alongside the M8, becomes the B765 as it skirts round the township of Ruchazie, then takes a sideways jump as it becomes the B806 and heads out towards what is now the Glasgow Fort shopping complex. Steve and Miriam just planned to go as far as Ruchazie. Their first pitch was in Gartcraig Road and then down by the church, past the primary school and the community centre. It was a good run, if they got there first, but theirs wasn't the only van chiming round the streets. If there was another van stopped it was best to keep going to the next street and try to get ahead. The competition was fierce; nobody was going to buy two ice creams so it was imperative to be first in the street. Tonight their luck was out and Steve skipped by the Gartcraig stop, clicked on the chimes and moved on into Claypotts Road.

A small group of customers began to gather and the young couple moved into the back to start serving. The van gave a sudden jolt and Miriam was thrown backwards knocking over the sweet rack and landing with a thump on her backside in a pile of Mars bars and wafer biscuits. Steve jumped out to see what had happened and found the rival van had rammed hard into the back of them.

"What the fuck are you playing at?" he shouted at the other driver. "Have you no' got any brakes?"

"Ah'm no fuckin' playin' son," was the response from the grizzly bear that eased menacingly from the other van. "Yer on ma pitch. Fuck off an tinkle yer bell somewhere else."

"It's a free country big fella. We're just doin' the run same as you. Early bird catches the worm an' aw' that. There was no need tae ram intae us."

"How'd yi like this rammed intae yi?" growled Grizzly, pulling a baseball stick from inside his cab. Without waiting for a reply he lunged at Steve and smacked him across the knees. As the young man crumpled he lunged again and brought the bat down hard on the back of his neck. He then turned and thumped both headlights of the young couple's van before stomping off and climbing back into his van. Miriam by now had scrambled out and ran screaming to Steve's aid.

The grizzly bear crashed his gearbox into reverse and backed up till his window was level with Miriam.

"Tell him we're no playin'. It's dead serious. No Frazzini's wagons this side o' the M8. Next time he'll no be the early bird; he'll be worms for the early bird. This was just a friendly warnin' hen. Make sure he understands. Its no a game; it's war"

The Glasgow Ice cream Wars had just begun.

Myra

As a crime reporter I became intrigued by the conflict almost from the beginning and I spoke to most of the small-part players as the drama unfolded; I met with the ice cream bosses and had frequent meetings with the Crime Squad but it wasn't till late 1982 that my interest was really aroused. I was working late one night preparing for a question-answer gig for the radio when the phone rang.

"Is that Jamie Robertson?" queried a gruff female voice.

"Aye, that's me. Who's asking?" I replied pleasantly.

"I need to talk to you." She asserted without answering my question.

"OK, talk away. I'm listening."

"Not on the phone. We need to meet somewhere. It's a big story but I don't want anybody knowing where it came from. Do you know the City Bakeries coffee shop at George Square? We can meet there."

"You mean the Lite Bite. Hey, you know how to treat a fellah." I joked.

She ignored my humour, "What about ten o'clock tomorrow, can you be there?"

"Who could resist such a wonderful offer," I bantered, "But come on, give me a clue. Who am I speaking to? What's it about?"

The earpiece hummed but there was no reply.

"Come on love, I need something to tempt me more than a Lite Bite coffee. Give me just a hint of where we're going on this."

"A million," came the clipped reply. "You want to know about the ice cream battles. Don't you?"

"A million what, love?"

"Ten o'clock tomorrow. Will you be there?"

"OK. How will I know you?"

"Don't worry, I know you," and with that she hung up.

Well, I suppose a million of anything was enough to whet the taste buds of every crime sleuth.

Five to ten next morning I was seated expectantly in CB Lite Bite at George Square. I had taken a cream doughnut to disguise the taste of the coffee. I think they really make the coffee bad in these places so you have to buy something to eat; only in this case, the doughnut wasn't much better than the coffee. Ten on the dot a brusque looking forty-odd-year-old lady plopped onto the seat opposite me. I recognised the face from somewhere in the past but couldn't quite place her.

"Myra Blunt, Security Manager of Coutts Retail," she announced her own arrival. She glowered fiercely, proffered her hand for a ritual handshake and took off to join the coffee queue.

My random-access-memory scoured the old banks of information and scored a hit as she waddled back to her seat, spilling her coffee as she flopped down again.

"Myra Blunt! Bloody Hell, Wee Myra. I remember you now. If you don't mind me saying, you've changed a bit. Wee Myra! You took over my paper round when I left Coutts. Good God! That was a hundred years ago. Did you stay with them all that time?"

"That's right, Jamie, boy! But like you say, I've changed a bit. They used to call me Wee Myra now it's Big Myra, at least that's the most pleasant name I've heard. Security Manager isn't usually the most popular person." She would not have been the most popular person in any situation. The years had not been kind but most of her appearance was self-cultivated. Her hairstyle, her form of dress and her posture all seemed to conspire to make a plain woman distinctly unattractive. "But we're not here to reminisce; I need your help. The bastards think they've got one over on me. They think they're clever but I know it was them. I just can't prove it."

"Suppose you tell me; who *they* are and what *it* was. What's all this about? What about the million you mentioned?" I prompted. She was obviously agitated and seemed unsure about where to pitch in.

"Cigarettes! That's what it's all about: a million smackers' worth of tobacco. You want to know what's behind the ice cream wars. I saw you on the telly the other night. Everybody says they're flogging "Lucy-in-the-sky" but you're not convinced. You've been nosing around for the best part of two years and you still haven't caught a sniff of what it's about. Jamie Robertson, super-sleuth crime reporter stuck up Dead-end Alley. You must be feeling a wee bit like a chocolate teapot."

"Myra, you invited me remember. I've already had to buy my own pishy coffee and now you just want to insult me. I'll ask you again; what's it all about?

"OK! OK! Mr Jammy Robertson. Keep your jam-jar-lid on. I just need to know you're with me," her tone softened and she became more explanatory. "Think about this. Number one: a packet of twenty fags costs about fifty pence. Most kids don't have fifty pence but they want a fag and Jimmy Jingles sells them single fags at five pence each. That's more than double price, quite a nice profit that the tax-man doesn't know about," her chest heaved as she expounded the theory.

"They'd have to sell a hell of a lot of single ciggies, Myra. I know I don't go with the drugs theory but at least it's talking real money. Nobody's going to smack another guy on the head for a five-pence-a-throw selling pitch."

She ignored my negative input and carried on. "And number two: if you've run out of fags you'll pay over the odds. The vans charge sixty pence a packet. And number three: if the cigarettes were stolen in the first place and you've bought them in at half price you're looking at a nice earner. And number four: like I said, the taxman doesn't get his dirty paws on any of this. So there's money in it for the company and for the driver. You think it's only five pence but it soon adds up. An ice cream cone's just ten pence. A Mars Bar is twelve pence. A stick of liquorice is just two pence. Nearly everything they sell on the ice cream vans is just a few coppers. It's not the unit cost that counts; it's the mark up."

"OK. I see where you're coming from but it's still penny numbers. Where do you get your million from? You're still not making any sense."

"What if I told you that Coutts lost a million quids' worth of cigarettes in a heist in 1979?"

"I wouldn't believe you. I know for sure that none of your shops carries that amount of stock. I know Coutts stock controls are all over the place and have been for years. Except cigarettes; they're controlled by computer at head office and no shop has more than two weeks of stock. I did a piece for the Evening Times about a year ago. One of your manageresses got caught with her hand in the till. Every time a customer paid over a pound she just rung in the pence and pocketed the pound. She'd been doubling her wages for over a year before you caught her. She would have got six months at Cornton Vale but she told them that she was pregnant so her sentence was suspended. Her and her boyfriend skipped off and set up a bar on the Costa del Sol. So what I'm saying Myra is that maybe some of them are selling fags that were stolen from a Coutts shop but it still doesn't go anywhere near explaining all the aggravation. And this million you keep on about; I don't understand where you're coming from."

"Aye, that little bitch should have gone down. I put in test purchasers and they caught her three times. It's called *pochling* Jamie. That's a good Scottish word "pochle". It doesn't exist in English, not even the concept. You have pilfering, fiddling, swindling, pinching or half-inching, if you're a Cockney, but everybody knows it's wrong. Pochling, on the other hand, doesn't seem to be considered wrong. In Scotland it's considered one of the perks of the job. If you're a bricky you take home the odd bag of cement to do your neighbour's footpath. I've got a cousin who's the storeman with Royston Electrics in Partick. Do you want a new set of plugs for your kitchen? He'll get you them, cables and all. His wife's a nurse at the Western. She has a first aid box that's better kitted out than an ambulance. The only place I know that has anything similar is in Spain. They've got a thing called *hurto*. In a block of flats somebody pinches all the fire extinguishers. The insurance company refuses to pay up because it's just hurto. They weren't stolen. They just disappeared. Here in Scotland it's more work related. It doesn't matter where you work in Scotland everybody has a pochle. These girls in here; the first day they start they get an official course on hygiene, health and safety. The second day they get the unofficial course on how to bang the tills and get free doughnuts with their coffee."

"Aye, you've got something there, Myra. Do you remember when I left Coutts and went to do the distribution thing with the Herald? The Daily Record guys were always complaining. They put their bundles of papers on at Queen Street and by the time they got to Dundee and Aberdeen a quarter of some packets were missing. The railwaymen all took out a couple at each station along the way. They were entitled; it was part of the job. Hey and *hablas español*. Have you got a pad on the Costa del Sol too?"

" No, I've got a wee studio in front of the Levante beach in Benidorm. That's the Costa Blanca. I go every chance I get and I've been taking night classes. *Hablo un poco*. Anyway, that's not what we're here for. Do you remember Geoffrey Howe's first budget, just after Maggie Thatcher got in?" At this point I was only half listening, trying to picture Myra on the beach. No matter how much I tried I just couldn't visualise her in a bikini.

"You're not listening," she admonished, "I asked if you remember the Tories first budget."

"June 79, who could forget? Howe put a great hype on VAT, as if we weren't paying enough already. He slapped 15% on nearly everything just so he could reward the Tory faithful with income tax cuts. You know the Tories only have three MPs in Scotland. We need our own government. Fifteen bloody per cent. It put about six pence on a packet of cigarettes. That was more than just a pochle. That was blatant robbery"

"Yeah, bang on Jamie, six pence, but it didn't really come as a surprise. Did it? Everybody knew it was going to happen. So the big chiefs at Coutts decided to make a killing. They always buy in more tobacco just before the budget. They know the tobacco tax isn't going to come down but this time they were expecting the big hype so they really loaded up. The tobacco companies were more than happy to play ball. There are six of our shops across Scotland that have too much floor space, most of it upstairs. There's the same space upstairs as there is downstairs and it's not used." She stopped talking to allow me time to digest her words.

"You're telling me they loaded up with tons of cigarettes before the budget but what was the point. They'd still have to pay the tax when they sold them." I wasn't convinced.

"Well, not exactly tons; they're not that heavy, but yes they loaded up and no, the tax didn't apply to existing stocks."

"So they bought in a million pounds' worth."

"Huh! They bought in *four* million pounds' worth. Like I said, there's six shops with space so they spread them around. They put a million pounds' worth into the shop in Newton Mearns."

"Whoa Myra! Hold up there! Coutts never had that kind of loose cash. They've been running tight for years. That's why they got taken over by that big US outfit. Where did they get that amount of cash?"

"Well they wouldn't have needed four million up front; that's the retail sales value. As far as I know they did a deal with the manufacturers so they didn't have to pay until the next year. It's complicated. I think there was some backing from across the water or some arm-twisting. I'm fairly sure they weren't the only ones. But anyway, the store in the Newton Mearns shopping centre is on three levels: the sales floor is on the main shopping level, the middle floor is the staff room, toilets, storeroom and offices and the top floor is just a big empty space. The Divisional Manager has his office in the middle floor. Ten days before the budget three trucks backed up to the rear door and unloaded a million pound's worth. Half a dozen store supervisors rolled up their sleeves and formed a human chain punting them up the stairs. They just shut the bloody door, no mortise bolt, no padlock, and no alarm. They had a cup of tea and buggered off home for the weekend."

"Let me guess. When they came back on Monday the whole lot had gone walkies," I smiled at my glum companion and then grimaced as I sipped the last of the cold, revolting coffee.

"You were always a smart kid Jamie. I've read a lot of your stuff over the years. You've earned your nickname, Jammy. A lot of people would have ended up floating in the Clyde for some of the things you've written. But it's not just luck. Is it? You have the knack. You have a nose for these things," she never broke eye contact as she spoke but she passed a manila folder across the table, "It's all in there, at least everything that I have managed to ferret out of my contacts, but there's a lot I haven't got near to. None of the stock was ever recovered and there's still a lot of it floating around the city. They didn't move it as fast as they thought and some of it must be starting to dry out."

I was starting to get curious, "So, what happened, a break-in? Surely there was an alarm on the main doors?"

"Huh! No! No alarm. I've been shouting about alarms for years but nobody listens. You'd think Glasgow had no robberies. Anyway, it wouldn't have mattered; they had a key. The shop was locked up after trade on Saturday and then they opened for a few hours on Sunday morning just for the Sunday papers. On Monday morning MacAlistair and his secretary went up to double check the boxes against the invoices, the door was open and the empty space was an *empty* space!"

"Who's MacAlistair?"

"He's Divisional Manager, Glasgow West. He looks a bit like Sean Connery with a moustache. He's a tough nut but his bark's worse than his bite. I like him; most people don't."

"Well, I suppose it was just a case of sorting through the keyholders. There wouldn't be many."

"You're not going to believe this part Jamie. Nobody actually knew how many keys were in circulation. Best estimate was about ten."

"Shite, Myra! Your balls must have been in the wringer." I jibed. She just scowled back at me. "Sorry, Myra, just a form of expression."

"No, you're right. Let's say it was my tits in the wringer. It was my patch, my responsibility, but we have clear guidelines. There should only be four keys, the manager, the deputy manager, the lady who comes in early to sort out the newspapers and of course, a copy for maintenance. Just imagine, Jamie, ten bloody keys floating around, maybe even more."

"Who had them?"

"Sandra the manageress, her deputy April, Jess the news girl, Janet the cleaner, Joe McGuinness the Area Supervisor, MacAlistair and his secretary Angela. How many's that? Seven. There's one kept in my office; maintenance have one and, wait for this one. Sandra, the manageress, has to take her kids to her mother's on Saturday mornings and she sometimes gets caught up in the traffic so one of the Saturday girls had a key to get in and open up the shop. A fuckin' sixteen-year-old with the shop keys! Pardon my French but it just defies common bloody sense. And they think; just think mind you; that the last manageress took a set of keys with her on the day she finished because she had to come back to pick up a sewing machine or something. And then somebody thought that there used to be a spare set of keys hanging on a hook in the staff room for emergencies but they seemed to have disappeared. So everybody except Santa Claus had a key and he doesn't smoke anyway!"

"I don't suppose the big chiefs were very happy with your security procedures." I mused.

She glowered at me again for a few seconds before answering, "Jerry Gordon, the managing director, wanted to fire me till I pointed out that it was his decision to put four million quid's worth of stock in unsecured stores without even telling me. So he pounced on poor MacAlistair and he's still trying to ride out the storm."

"OK Myra, so why come to me now? What do you want from me?"

"I want to know how they did it. I know who did it, or at least who was behind it but I can't prove it. Here, there's lots of little bits and pieces in that file, enough to show you where to start looking."

"And what do I get out of it? Is there a reward for information leading to an arrest?"

"Satisfaction is what you get, same as me. I hate loose ends. You're good at putting loose ends together. You can close the circles and round off the rough corners. You want to know what fuelled the ice cream shindig; well here's your chance. I tell you it's all in there. That was a hell of a pile of tobacco and it needed an outlet. The vans are perfect cover for anything they want to shift on the QT but they needed to widen their territory fast. They needed lots of kids buying fags so they started pushing boundaries on the van routes and tried to push the competition off the road."

"You sound pretty sure about all this but answer me one thing. Who are THEY?"

"Read the file big boy. It's all in there. I say it's Danny O'Connor and his motley crew that have the ciggies and they're punting them out through the vans but they didn't steal them; they were the ones that bought them. Like I say, they needed more territory so they started shoving the Frazzini drivers off their patch and young Frazzini kicked back. Now O'Connor is boxed into a corner. He still has a load of the cigarettes left and I've heard that his heavies have started to force some of them into the pubs around the city. They have a stack of them in an old warehouse in Scotland Street, a fuckin' sight more secure than when we had them. But what I really want to know is how they did it. There were three thumpin' great truckloads and they moved them from Newton Mearns into the city in the middle of the night. Somebody must have seen them. Oh, and one more thing. You asked me what I want. I want what's left of them back."

I sat looking at her smoulder. She really looked quite a battleaxe; no doubt she struck mortal terror into the poor girls in Coutts.

"You were a sweet little kid when you came to take up my paper-round all those years ago, Myra. Butter wouldn't melt in your mouth, as they say. A shy wee thing, you were. Now you're cursing like a squaddie. What happened to turn you into an old sour-puss?" I mused.

"Life happened, bright boy. We aren't all jammy like you. Some of us have had to claw our way up."

She stood up abruptly, shoved her chair back roughly and strode out into the Glasgow rain.

Single Ciggies

Back in Albion Street, stretched out on a sofa, with a big mug of real Columbian coffee, I read Myra's file. All the pertinent facts, names, times and places were transcribed in pert order. Any allusions were bracketed to denote them as such, separated from the facts. All her evidence seemed to be circumstantial but you don't spend a lifetime as security manager without developing the hunter's sense of smell. Reading through her notes it soon became clear that anything Myra was alluding to could reasonably be treated as fact, at least for the purpose of further investigation. However this notion about selling single cigarettes to the kids seemed to dominate her conclusions. I decided that it needed checking out.

There are twenty in a pack, ten packs in a carton and fifty cartons in a master case. That's ten thousand individual cigarettes. If a driver sold fifty cigarettes a night it would take about three months to sell a full case and for that he would gross five hundred pounds. Sorry, Myra the sums don't add up. On the other hand, selling full packs at sixty pence to adults might take just a week or so to shift a full case grossing three hundred pounds. So even with twenty vans on the road O'Connor would be lucky to move about a thousand cases a year. The three truckloads would have contained about four thousand cases. I could see how a greedy criminal mind would take a chance on a crazy scheme like that. I could also see that desperation to move the stock would make them do crazy things. If they could frighten competitors off their territory then they would move the stock faster.

Danny O'Connor was a name I knew well. It was a name everybody knew well. He started as a loan shark whose teeth were rather sharp if you didn't pay back your loan on time and was currently becoming one of the big names in Glasgow's ganglands. The sprawling housing estates were full of low-income families struggling to keep up their payments on everything, a ripe picking ground for the loan sharks. Now, it seemed, O'Connor was in the soft fluffy world of ice cream vending. Except, there was nothing soft and fluffy about Danny Boy.

I'd been out round the estates several times watching the ice cream vans both with the police patrols and on my own. I had never seen any of the nasty incidents up close and I'd never seen anything that looked like drug dealing. Maybe it was time to take another look.

I drove out to Garthamlock into a typical Glasgow housing estate where they cultivated four-foot high thistles and decorated some of the windows with wooden boards. Somebody had optimistically called it Coxton Gardens. Most of it has now been demolished and replaced with more modern housing. It was six thirty on a nice spring evening and there were lots of kids out on the street. I parked by the side of the road and rolled down my window. I didn't have to wait long to hear the familiar jingle. A van pulled in alongside the kerb on the opposite side of the street.

O'Connor's Ices, the painted sign proclaimed, *You've tried the rest. Now try the best!*

I called over to a boy scuffing along the street. He looked about eleven or twelve.

"Hey son, would you go to the van and buy me two single ciggies?"

"Why don't ye go yersel' mister?"

"I'm not feeling too good an' he'll be gone by the time I waddle across the road. Tell you what, here's ten pence for the fags an' ten pence for yourself. What d'you say?"

He didn't say anything, just took the money and ran over to the van. A few minutes later he was back, two cigarettes in one hand and an ice cream cone in the other.

"Thanks mister," he chirped as he handed over the cigarettes and then ran off down the street.

I waddled over to the van.

"Twenty Embassy tipped," I demanded.

"That's 65p," clipped the driver as he laid them down.

"That's 10p over the odds," I countered.

"D'you want them or no?" he snapped back.

"I think I'll get them in the Co-op. They charge five pence less."

"Well make up yer mind."

"You know you're not allowed to sell cigarettes to kids?"

"What the fuck is this, twenty questions? Of course I know that. I never sell fags to kids." His tone was becoming distinctly unfriendly.

I produced the two cigarettes.

"What about these two?" I asked. "You sold them to that boy just now."

"D'you know what I think? I think you should fuck off." His arm went below the counter and he pulled out a baseball bat.

I pulled my little Kodak Instamatic from my pocket and snapped a quick shot of our friendly ice cream-man with his weapon of choice and then hastily retreated to the safety of my car.

He crunched the van into gear and sped off with a screech of rubber against asphalt. The van wobbled precariously as it swung round a corner, narrowly missing my young friend munching his cone. I had just experienced my first encounter with an ice cream-warrior and had clearly touched a raw nerve. It seemed like Myra's cigarette theories were worth pursuing. All right, one drop of rain doesn't make a river but I had just witnessed the sale of cigarettes to a kid at an extortionate mark-up plus a 20% overcharge on a full packet and a totally disproportionate reaction from the driver when I questioned him. Definitely worth further investigation.

My next stop was the other side of the river, Scotland Street near the old Broomielaw wharfs. Up onto the M8 and across Jamaica Bridge then back down on the south side, in the late evening it took me just twenty minutes and I drove into Scotland Street just before it turned dark. A warehouse near West Street subway station according to the file but in fact it was an old used-car showroom-cum-garage. Robson Motors said a withering signboard flapping in the wind. The door was bolted and padlocked and the showroom windows were boarded over. The side windows were well barred. An underfed looking Alsatian dog was chained to the fence with enough loose chain to reach as far as the entrance. A hand-painted sign invited visitors to KEEP OUT!

Down the side of the white-painted brick building was a rough driveway littered with old gearboxes, car lights, bumpers and doors. There was just sufficient space to squeeze my Mini down the side of the building under one of the windows. I stepped out of the car to the accompanying yelps from the hungry hound. I took off my shoes and climbed from the bonnet onto the roof of the Mini and gripped the concrete windowsill enabling me to peer in through the grubby window. Through the grime I was able to make out a line of pallets each piled about six feet high with cardboard cases. There was just enough light to see the tobacco company logos.

"Hey! What d'you think your playin' at?"

I looked down at a baldhead sticking out of a dirty mechanic's overall. I'm not sure I would have trusted him with my precious little Mini. The face leering up at me was scarred and shrivelled.

I tried to keep a light tone, "Somebody told me this place was for sale. I'm just taking a look. There's no phone number or anything."

"There's nuthin' here for sale sunshine," he replied gruffly and started to release the dog from its chain. I scrambled down, threw my shoes into the car and jumped into the driving seat in my stocking feet. I gave him a quick wave and made a quick exit. As I swung out into the street a van came hurling into the entrance. We nearly collided as we hurried in opposite directions. I swerved instinctively and escaped with just a slight clip to the front wing of my precious Mini. I looked in the rear-view mirror in time to see the slogan: *You've tried the rest. Now try the best!*

Another coffee.

Two names stood out in Myra's file as worthy of some follow-up: Joe McGuiness the area supervisor of Coutts and Angela McCabe the divisional manager's secretary, so next morning my Mini and me took a trip out to Newton Mearns Shopping Centre. The coffee in the CB Lite Bite here was just as bad as in George Square and the doughnut looked at least two days old. I carried my tray towards the tables. Those that weren't occupied were cluttered with empty cups and puddles of spilled drinks. I shuffled around looking for a clean table. There was one table in the corner where a young man sat alone, coffee in one hand and a Daily Sun in the other. He looked a bit out of place in a neat, navy blue pinstripe suit and dark tie. His mode of dress seemed to clash with his unruly red hair and puffy freckled hands and face. He might have looked OK in a sports blazer and flannels but he didn't match the city gent image.

"Mind if I sit here?" I asked.

"OK, sure, have a seat," he answered without really looking up from the page. He was ardently studying the racing section.

"Have you picked your winner for today?" I queried.

"Slithering Silver, three o'clock at Chepstow. It's eight to one on," he replied, underlining it on the paper.

"Are you going to back it?"

"Aye, ten pounds each way, I think. He looks good, been placed in the last four races but he hasn't been out for a couple of months. The bookies are giving him a good price because they think he's been ill but I think the trainer's just been saving him. The prize money's good and I think he'll go for it. Maybe I should just put the whole twenty on the nose."

"Whoa boy! That's big money you're talking. Ten shillings is my stretch."

He looked up from his paper and eyed me curiously. "I think they call it fifty pence nowadays," he grinned.

"I still think in the old money. You know, I went to buy a packet of fags yesterday and the guy wanted 65p. It wasn't till I got home that I thought: hell's bells that's thirteen shillings. When I started smoking they cost one shilling. Listen, I'm sorry. I'm babbling away here spoiling your morning coffee." I apologised.

"This coffee was spoiled before they picked the beans of the tree," he bantered, "yours looks just as bad and your doughnut doesn't look much healthier," and we both laughed.

"Jamie Robertson," I introduced myself and held out my hand.

He grasped my fingers loosely "Joe McGuiness," he responded.

I couldn't believe my luck: I'd found my man without even having to go looking. "These places are getting worse but I suppose they're handy. Do you work near here?"

"Aye, Coutts just a couple of doors along, area supervisor. This is my office," he laughed.

No point in messing around, I went in with a verbal right hook. "Coutts? They had a big robbery here a year or so back, lost a pile of cigarettes?"

He bristled visibly but held his calm, "No, at least not that I know of."

Well, well, well! Total denial. First scent of the fox! I kept up the pressure. "Yes, about a million pounds' worth. So they tell me."

"Who tells you? A million pounds' worth? That's just plain silly: we don't keep that amount of stock in any of our shops."

I didn't let go, "My source is very reliable. Your bosses bought in a stack of cigarettes as a hedge against the expected jump in VAT rates in the budget. A quarter of them were stored above the shop here in Newton Mearns and they went walkies in the night."

"Your source has got it mixed up with something else, probably one of the supermarkets. Listen!" he stood up, "I have to go, work to do!" He started to walk away but stopped and turned.

"You said your name was Jamie Robertson. You're not *the* Jamie Robertson, the crime reporter?"

"No son. I'm Jammy Robertson, the golliwog on the marmalade jar. Why did you tell me there was no cigarette heist? They were upstairs in the empty space above the offices. You helped to carry them up there. I know that. You know that. So why do you insist it didn't happen? Makes you sound like somebody with something to hide."

He shuffled uncomfortably. "I have to go," he mumbled and scurried out of the café, leaving his paper on the table.

I picked it up and turned to the front pages to catch up with the news but I couldn't concentrate and laid it back down. I sat looking for inspiration in my dead cup of coffee. Strange that he should be in denial. There must have been a police report and an insurance claim. I pulled out Myra's file, checked for the exact date of the robbery and skimmed her notes but I couldn't find any mention of the officer in attendance. Surely it must have been reported to the police. Then it clicked. Something had bothered me from my meeting with Myra. I have an infallible memory for all crimes big and small and I had no memory whatsoever of any mention in the papers and I had certainly never covered the story. Could it really have gone unreported?

I looked up from my despondent coffee cup and spotted a public phone box across the street. My first call was to my old friend John Sinclair in the Scottish Criminal Records Office. As long as a crime is not *sub judice*, that is with currently active court proceedings; the records office will usually provide outline information on any reported crime depending on who you are and who you speak to. I had helped John with information on a difficult case back in the sixties. He later moved to the newly formed SCRO and over the years we exchanged useful titbits. On this occasion his willingness to help was somewhat hindered by a total absence of reference in any of the records. He scanned up to a week either side in case of error but came up blank. It just did not make any kind of sense that a reputable retailer would lose a million pounds of stock and not report it. Myra had a bit of explaining to do. She was undoubtedly a bit cranky but I felt sure she hadn't just been making up fairy tales.

"JS Coutts, good morning, how can I help you?" chirped a soft Glasgow voice at the other end of the phone.

"Myra Blunt, please," I petitioned.

"Can I ask who's calling, please?"

"Just tell her there's a fellah on the line who wants to invite her for coffee in the Lite Bite."

"OK, big spender, hold the line."

A few minutes later the soft voice was replaced by Myra's butch version, "Jamie. Is that you?"

I skipped the pleasantries and pitched straight in. "Did they not call the Police?" About half a minute elapsed without response.

"How about I take you up on the coffee invitation?" she said eventually. "Same place, same time but tomorrow. Can't make it today."

"Myra, I'm not going to go running round after bogeymen. I have some questions that need answered or I just walk away and forget the whole thing. If this robbery took place, how come there's no police record?"

"Tomorrow, City Bakeries, George Square, ten o'clock and I know you won't walk away. It's not your style," and she hung up.

"Ah well," I supposed, "tomorrow it is."

It was pouring rain as I ducked in the doorway of our favourite coffee shop at ten the next morning. I collapsed my umbrella and headed towards the end of the queue.

"Over here!" called a gruff feminine voice. Myra was already seated with a drink in her hand. I went over to join her. "Here, try this!" she invited, pushing over a peculiar looking glass of foam topped coffee. "It's the latest. *Cappuccino* they call it. I think that's Italian for dishwater. Actually it doesn't taste like coffee at all. It's better than the other stuff but only just." Myra was trying to be pleasant.

"Why didn't you call in the police?" I asked, no point in pleasantries and formalities: just ask the questions. It catches people off guard and you get more information from their reactions than from their answers. "Or maybe you've just made the whole thing up. What is it? Are things a bit too quiet and boring at the moment or are you just trying to get back on some colleagues who've pissed you off? You can't just lose three trucks of cigarettes and forget about it. You would need to have an insurance claim and even for fifty quid they'd ask to see the police report"

Myra didn't flinch. She studied the retreating foam on her Cappuccino. "You could lose a fuckin' nuclear submarine in JS Coutts," she snapped, "It was bad enough before the Yanks bought us out. Now they're trying to impose head office controls on an operation that's been managed at branch level for half a century. You don't see the same person in the same job for more than a couple of months."

"So they just wrote off a million pounds. Come on, Myra, d'you think my head zips up the back?"

"They didn't exactly write it off, more sort of lost a couple of pages from the accounts ledger. They couldn't show it on the balance sheet. They couldn't just declare it openly. Imagine the uproar at the next shareholders' meeting. And then, of course, Inland Revenue would have crucified them for trying to evade tax."

"I thought you said that what they were doing was kosher. You said the new tax didn't apply to existing stocks."

"Yeah but…"

"Yeah but what?"

"Well, if you think about it, the whole idea was to sell at the new price and pocket the difference. Otherwise there wasn't much point in buying in great loads in the first place. It's kosher if you sell off your existing stocks at the old price. So the intent was clearly illegal and remember, they still had three million worth in other locations. They had to hush it up and keep their heads down. But that's not all the story. It seems they cut a deal with the tobacco companies so that it was invoiced for before the budget but with six months to pay. That's even more illegal and the suppliers were part of a conspiracy to defraud Inland Revenue. They'd all get ten years apiece if it saw the light of day."

"So how did they cover it up?"

"Well, all retailers have what's euphemistically called shrinkage, shop-lifting, breakage, staff pilfering, bad stock control and so on. They did a bit of creative accounting. You said somebody had pissed me off. Yes, Jamie, they pissed me off big style. They started kicking my arse to squeeze tighter on security procedures. They decided I could magically reduce the natural shrinkage with hourly cash register checks, more test purchasing and other gimmicks. I was supposed to catch more girls with their hand in the till to cover up their own incompetence and dishonesty. I should have blown the whistle at the time but I didn't and now I'm part of the conspiracy. Then we had bogus burglaries in Drumchapel, Byres Road and Bearsden. They were duly reported and all the "stolen" stock was listed so the insurance paid up. And in the meantime somebody has got off Scot free with a mountain of stolen cigarettes. Now we have the new American bosses trying to impose new systems and it's all just one big mess on top of the other. You spoke about the computer control system last time we met. Well guess what? Our pure dead brilliant computer picked up on the stock difference and re-ordered all the cigarettes that were stolen from Newton Mearns, a million pounds worth all at the post-budget price. Nobody knew anything about it till three trucks pulled up in the car park behind the shop. Everybody flew into a great panic and eventually they were all sent back down south."

"OK, so you're pissed off. Why don't you take early retirement? Why don't you just *take the Costa Blanca Plane y Viva España*? Hightail it to the sun and sangria and your *vistas de la playa Levante*. You call me up out of the blue over a year later and ask me to stick my nose in the mess. That's more than just normal pissed off. There's something you're not telling me, something that's not in your neat file."

She smiled. It wasn't a nice big happy smile just a leery grin of satisfaction but perhaps her first smile in twenty years. Her face looked like it might crack.

"I said you weren't just jammy. You've got a nose for these things." She glanced furtively from side to side. "The name that's missing from the file…" she glanced around again and lowered her voice, "It's Horton, Sam Horton."

"And Sam Horton is…? I asked quietly adopting her conspiratory tone.

"Samuel F. Horton is our Property Director. He's been with the company for about twelve years and I've been watching over his shoulder for most of them. I know what he's up to but I've never been able to prove it. You may have noticed that Coutts have been moving into all the new shopping centres that have sprung up: Clydebank, Pollock, Newton Mearns, Falkirk, Stirling. None of the units we take are ideal, either too big or in the wrong place but the bosses want to move away from the old sweetie-shop image. I'm sure he's taking backhanders from the property developers and their agents. Then on the other side we are shedding some of the smaller, more localised shops especially if they have a post office attached. They are difficult to staff and not very profitable for us. But they're profitable for Horton. Most of them are being taken by Pakistani families who can make good earnings with all the family working unsociable hours. Horton signs them up and then he sells them all the shop fittings and things that have been written off in depreciation years ago. The money goes into his own pocket."

"Come on, Myra! This is peanuts we're talking here. Everybody's slipping something in their back pocket. What does he get for the fixtures and fittings: a few hundred quid?"

"I'm just trying to paint you a picture of the kind of man he is. Shut up and give me a chance. Of course it's just peanuts but he's into big plums as well. He's a gangster, Jamie. He's into all sorts of dodgy property deals that have nothing to do with Coutts. He's big buddies with Danny O'Connor. They're both from *Chateaux Lait*. You must have covered the string of post office raids over the last couple of years."

"I know that Danny O'Connor is number one suspect for bank-rolling these raids but what the hell is Chateaux Lait? Sounds like a chocolate factory."

"Come off it, Jamie. D'you no speak *parleama Glesga*? Have you never been to Castlemilk? Listen! O'Connor was bankrolling them but he's been trying to become Glasgow's Mr Big and he has nothing left in the bank to roll. He's been buying up property like it's going out of fashion. Glasgow is going to become the architectural city of Europe so anybody with development land is set to make their fortune. He still puts the team together and the transport and he's the one who stashes the loot and splits it later but I am positive Horton has been behind the last two or three post office jobs and he's the one who's picking the targets. I think he took the job with Coutts as a front. He plays the respectable role nicely and he's on first name terms with all the city councillors but he's a nasty little shit."

"You're a regular fountain of knowledge Myra. We've all been tracking these PO jobs and we know it's O'Connor's mob but there's never anything solid that we can print. I know he's the owner of several pubs. Your guy, Horton, I know nothing about. How come your so certain?"

"Did you take a look at the garage-cum-tobacco-store in Scotland Street?"

"Yes, it appears you were right on that one. O'Connor is the proud owner of Robson Motors."

"No he isn't but you could be forgiven for thinking so. He provides the security and he takes good care of the stock inside but he doesn't have his name on the title deeds. Go to the City Hall and check the Sasine Register. The property is owned by a certain Peter Wallace. Then take a walk round the corner to the register of births, deaths and marriages and you will find that in 1946 Corporal Samuel Frederic Horton married Sandra Wallace. Sandra Horton and Peter Wallace are brother and sister. I am fairly sure you know Peter Wallace."

"You mean Pete the Pimp who works his girls in O'Connor's salubrious bars."

"The one and the same, Jamie boy. Maybe I should take your advice and give up this Security Manager lark, reckon I'd make a half decent crime reporter. What d'you think?"

"I think we both spend too much of our life jumping in muddy puddles. Anyway, you don't really need me. You've got it all sussed out." I pushed the buff coloured file across the table.

She pressed her hand down firmly on mine and pushed it back in my direction. "No Jamie, that's where you're wrong. I do need you. Look at me. I frighten the shit out of everybody and that's how I got most of the information that I have. That's my job;

that's how I am but some of it needs the softly-softly approach. You can go places and talk to people. We need some more concrete proof. I've been on the case for over a year now and it's beginning to slip away from me. Go and talk to Angela McCabe."

"That's the girl who's secretary to what's his name, MacAlistair, the Divisional Manager. I see you have her underlined; what does she know?"

"It's not what you know. It's who you know! Never heard that before, Jamie? Go and talk to her but you'll need to get her away from the office or she'll just clam up like she did with me."

"Where does she live?"

"Her address is in Rutherglen."

"That's nearer than the Mearns. I don't suppose you have her phone number."

"No and there's no point looking her up in the phone book. She's separated from her hubby and staying with her boyfriend. I think you know him. His name's Charlie Frazzini."

I pulled back the file in surprise and knocked the dregs of my cappuccino over the table. This time it was a real smile that crossed her face.

"I thought that would make you jump," she chirped. "Want another cappuccino?"

I didn't even answer that one.

Frazzini and company.

It's amazing how many Frazzinis there are in the Glasgow directory, more than there are of Jamieson. Originally they had all been together in the same platoon when the Argylls took them prisoner at Beda Fomm in Libya in 1941. Half the platoon were either Frazzini or cousins from the same Calabrian village of Villa San Giovanni near Messina. As the valiant Highlanders battled northwards towards Messina their prisoners were shipped back to Scotland to the rapidly swelling prison camp at Douglas Castle in Lanark. At the end of the war the camp was hurriedly evacuated to become a resettlement camp for the Scots who had been prisoners in Germany. Many Italians applied for permission to remain in the UK rather than return to the impoverished conditions at home and in most cases this was granted. So the Frazzini clan spread out around the north side of the Clyde and formed alliances with the already established Italian community. They were cheery, hard-working people and became liked and respected in the Mean City. Many set up businesses, mostly cafés and fish'n chip shops.

Pepi Frazzini adapted Scottish ingredients to an Italian recipe and produced the beautiful creamy Frazzini Ice Cream, at first in the kitchen of a tenement flat in Springburn then later in a purpose built shop just off Sauchiehall Street and then eventually in a small factory unit in the new town of Cumbernauld. He bought a fleet of small Bedford ice cream vans and began tinkling a merry tune around the northeast side of the city. In the summer months the trade was brisk but you can count the sunny days in Scotland on your fingers. He quickly had to adapt to selling sweets, snacks, fizzy drinks and cigarettes.

In the early 1970s Pepi suffered a series of debilitating strokes and grudgingly handed over the reins of the enterprise to his son Charlie. The young Frazzini had just graduated from the Business School at Strathclyde University and quickly set about a major revamp of the business. He bought a fleet of newer, bigger vans and rewrote the drivers' contracts. He offered them the opportunity to franchise the vans and run them like their own business. Ice cream has an incredibly low manufacturing cost and conversely a very high profit so both the drivers and the company could clear a 100% margin. They paid a monthly rental on the vans and were obliged to buy the basic stock items from Frazzinis. Other than that they were free to buy in whatever they wanted from the new cash-and-carry warehouses that had recently sprung up. Charlie kept three vans with salaried drivers to set up or beef up the van routes and the rest were eagerly snapped up by postmen, office workers, students and others who could work evenings and weekends. Charlie's own three drivers were old hands at the game and he used them to push into the housing schemes establishing new routes and building business. With each new route he bought another van and the business really began to take off. His ultimate goal was to have a van in every town and neighbourhood in Scotland. He bought an ice-lolly making machine, which literally doubled sales and profits overnight. But Charlie Frazzini was seriously overstretching himself with credit.

He was also seriously overstretching his own personal position with heavy gambling debts. Another immigrant entrepreneur, George Delavios had fled the Turkish invasion of Cyprus in 1974. He lost his hotels and restaurants, which were north of the Green Line in Nicosia but escaped with enough funds to set up in Glasgow. He quickly saw several gaps in the Scottish catering trade. Delavios Steak Houses appeared in every corner of the city and all the towns in the central belt. He rented several run down "prestige" hotels, repainted them, upgraded the restaurants and soon had the Delavios brand hotel chain. He took a chance on the ambiguity of Scottish law on gambling and put casinos into four of the bigger hotels. Charlie Frazzini was hooked. By the time the authorities had plugged the gap and closed the casinos, our ice cream entrepreneur was deeply in debt to the restaurateur.

Confident that the high profits of the ice cream business would keep him afloat he ordered an aggressive expansion into the northwest corner of the city, into territory that was traditionally "owned" by smaller rivals. He signed up to buy six new vans. Delavios was furious. He assumed that Frazzini was ignoring his debt.

At this point my *alter ego* came into the matrix; James "Jammy" Gillespie. He was a real nasty piece of work. From the age of twelve Jammy Gillespie was a thug. I first had the pleasure of making his acquaintance when he was charged with the murder of his girlfriend. She wasn't too happy with his idea of putting her on the streets "on the game" and was stupid enough to brazen it out with him. He split her skull open with her own high-heel shoe. He was certain to go down for life but the police botched his arrest and his defence counsel objected to the manner in which they had obtained evidence. The judge ordered the jury to acquit him and he walked from the court with the same nickname as me. Years later he escaped prosecution or conviction from numerous situations where he was the obvious perpetrator. He just couldn't be that jammy and the natural conclusion was that he was a police informer and had their protection. On this occasion the girl's family decided to meet out their own justice. Jammy's lank body was found in an alley with several stab wounds. He went off the radar for a few years and some people said he had joined the army or the navy to escape the vengeance of the bereaved family.

Anyway, he came back on the scene in the 70s, rapidly became one of Glasgow's most ruthless thugs and was hired by various "big men" to do their dirty work. Delavios was never a gangland character; that distinction being reserved for native Glaswegians. But he'd rubbed shoulders with quite a few as he clawed his way up to build his empire in five short years. Jammy Gillespie had also accumulated a sizeable debt tab in the casinos and somebody suggested that he could clear his debt with services rendered. He obliged Delavios by visiting Cumbernauld one dark night and smashing the windscreens and headlights of the six new vans in Frazzini's car park. When the night watchman came to investigate he clubbed him unconscious. Gillespie then threw his club (covered in fingerprints) through one of the office windows. The watchman recovered and identified Gillespie from a rogue's gallery of photos. Once again Jammy Gillespie walked free on a technicality. Jammy indeed! Because of the injured watchman Delavios kept quiet about his involvement so Frazzini thought it was one of his competitors trying to cool his heels.

Just when things couldn't get much worse for the Frazzinis Danny O'Connor bought out Davitos on the south side in 1977. Davitos was a fairly localised family business making delicious ice cream. O'Connor bought the business after old Davito died, mainly to get the substantial piece of land around the factory and then

41

decided he may as well give it a go and develop the business. O'Connor was the archetypal Glasgow gangster, a knarled little character who dressed well but never looked well dressed. However he had a hard business head and saw the potential of the vans for laundering some of his ill-gotten gains and for disposing of some of his ill-gotten stocks. The recent series of post office raids had provided him with some bundles of cash that needed to be whitened and some raids had also produced quantities of goods that would be resalable on the vans: chocolate bars, cigarettes, paracetamols and cough bottles. A little more prudent than Frazzini, he gathered some of his loose cash, bought a copy of Loot, a copy of Exchange and Mart, one of Daltons Weekly and headed south to buy up a fleet of second hand ice cream vans. He knew he was going to have to push hard to get his vans out into the housing schemes on the north side, so he contracted hard men as drivers, men who sat in the bookies' shops in the afternoons and were nightclub bouncers or security workers at night, men who could handle themselves in a fight. That's when they started to crunch with Frazzini.

So as 1978 rolled into 79, according to Myra, a million pound's worth of cigarettes were tossed into the cauldron and were seized on by O'Connor who had already overstretched himself just as much as Frazzini. While we may debate till the cows come home about whether or not the ice cream wars were drug related it really boils down to over inflated egos on a collision course. Both Frazzini and O'Connor in very different ways had embarked on a "business plan" that would lead to inevitable conflict. Glasgow thrives on conflict and never far below the surface is the bitter "religious" rivalry that pervades the hardcore thuggery of the Mean City.

The villains are often idolised in spite of, and sometimes because of, their vicious crimes. Robin Hood came from Glasgow not Nottingham. Samson lived in the Gallowgate. William Tell, on the other hand, was definitely not a Glaswegian. If he had been, he'd have eaten the apple and put the arrow through the Austrian. I know these guys and they know me. I've seen them in the dock in the court, through the grill at visiting time in Barlinnie Prison, at the bar of their favourite drinking hole or across the table in their own kitchens. I thought I knew what made them tick. I felt compelled to find out what made hard men go around smashing up ice cream vans. It just isn't part of the Glasgow hard man psyche.

Frazzini's girl.

Charlie Frazzini's number was not in the phone book so I called the Frazzini factory. I'd already met Charlie in my investigations and we'd got along fine. Although he took a tough stance against O'Connor he considered himself to be the victim. At that point I still didn't know about his gambling debts. The switchboard put me through quickly and he agreed to meet over lunch. I think he was expecting to talk about ice cream vans getting smashed up and he was a bit surprised when I asked for Angela to come along too.

"Angela? Well I don't know. That's not so easy. She works out in Newton Mearns."

"Does she work Saturdays?"

"No, the office is closed."

"OK then, why don't we make it Saturday? What about the Alleyway on Byres Road?

"Right! Saturday it is but give me your number in case anything comes up and we can't make it."

Nothing came up and we all made it. The Alleyway was just off the street up an alley. The facia was old brick and the interior done up like old Chicago. The food was authentic hamburgers served as slow-food. Just the place to meet for a discussion about gangsters and a really convivial place for lunch. Charlie, though not exactly a film star, had the natural presence and elegance of an Italian male in his late thirties. He wore a light beige suit, open neck shirt and highly polished crocodile shoes. His long flowing dark brown hair contrasted with Angela's blonde waves. She was definitely a "looker", more than just average pretty in black mini skirt and white blouse with black jacket slung loosely over her shoulders. Up close she looked about the same age as Charlie but from a distance she looked about twenty. Heads turned as we were escorted to our table.

We sat down and scanned the menu. Charlie opened the conversation.

"So what's all this about, Jamie? What do you want to know that we haven't already covered? There's nothing new on the Gillespie front. It looks like he'll just get away with it. We've had a couple of weeks with no incidents on the vans. O'Connor seems to be keeping his head down at the moment. You know a few weeks ago they smashed in one our windscreens. The driver had quite a few cuts to his face. And they're totally brazen about it; *Mr O'Connor says stay out of his territory.* "

"Actually it's Angela I want to speak to, Charlie. I'm afraid I used you to get her here. I don't think she'd have come on her own."

"Why?" he asked.

"Why?" chorused Angela.

"One million pound's worth of cigarettes." I replied.

Angela put down the menu card and looked me straight in the eye, "I thought this was about these silly ice cream battles. What does this have to do with Charlie? Who told you about the cigarettes? What makes you think I can help you?"

"I think we've got things a wee bit mixed up here. I'm the reporter. I'm supposed to ask the questions." I joked.

She smiled, flicked her blonde hair back across her shoulder and looked round the Al Capone style decor, "OK, but since it seems like we're in the U.S. of A. I claim the Fifth Amendment if I don't like your questions."

"Who took the cigarettes? O'Connor?"

She fidgeted nervously and looked sideways at Charlie who nodded as if to say, "It's OK. You can talk to him."

She thought first then answered slowly, "I believe O'Connor has them but he didn't take them."

"You're going to have to explain that," I said. Again she looked to Charlie for his nod before answering.

"I believe they were taken first and then offered round the city looking for the highest bidder. Actually Charlie was offered…" and she tailed off as her boyfriend took over.

"I got a call, I suppose about a week after the robbery, except at that time I didn't know about any robbery. Angela and I had only recently met and she never mentioned it."

"Why not? Something that big!" I interrupted.

"We were told to keep quiet," answered Angela.

"Who told you to do that?"

"My boss, Mr MacAlistair."

"Sorry Charlie, please go on," I signalled for him to continue.

"He offered me a million pound's worth of cigarettes for half their retail value. That sounds a lot but with all the taxes the net mark up is usually just five to ten per cent so it was a good deal."

"Do you know who you were speaking to? Did he identify himself?"

"No. He seemed to know me as if he knew who I was but hadn't met me. He called me Charles not Charlie. Everybody calls me Charlie except my mother and she calls me Carlo. He sounded like educated Glasgow but with a bit of Indian accent. He also sounded a bit agitated. He insisted what a great investment it would be and how he'd been referred to me by a mutual friend. He made it sound more like a piece of real estate rather than a truckload of hot cigarettes."

"Actually it was three truckloads," I corrected, "Why didn't you take up the offer?"

"I'm offended by that question, Jamie. You know better than to ask. We run a clean business and even if I were tempted there were a few good reasons to decline. We have never done a lot in cigarettes and the vans are stocked up with other things that give 100% profit legally. The drivers decide what they carry. They would have started asking questions if I made them carry more tobacco. Secondly I didn't have £500,000; in fact our bank balance is showing a few red zeros after buying the new vans and then having to get them repaired. We didn't have them out on the road so they weren't insured. And number three; we don't have space for holding big stocks of anything. I thought one truck; you say three.

Chick Frazzini runs a clean shop. Anything like that would stand out."

"So you did consider it?"

"Come on, Jamie! I understand the ease and simplicity of using ice cream vans to fence stolen goods in small bulk. There are some that do it but it's the beginning of a long slippery slope where the only way is down. I find the insinuation offensive, as much to my intelligence as to my honesty."

"OK! OK! It's my job to ask provocative questions. I'm sorry if I punctured your pride." I backed off and turned again to Angela.

"You said that O'Connor didn't take them. Who took them then, the supervisor, Joe McGuiness?"

"He's not bright enough to plan something as big as that for himself but I am certain he was there on the night they were stolen. They got a key from someone in Coutts. He's usually one of the first to arrive on a Monday morning. They have a weekly sales meeting and he likes to impress the boss. He fancies himself for promotion to head office or something. Anyway that Monday he was conspicuous by his absence. Mr MacAlistair was in first and then me and about half an hour later we went up to check the invoices and discovered the robbery. The sales meeting started late and even at that our Joe arrived after we'd started, looking rather bleary-eyed."

"You don't like him?"

"Nobody likes him except himself. He has that sneery way of looking at women. I suppose somebody must have liked him because he's married and has two nice kids. He spends half his salary and half his time in the bookies. I've heard that he's in some poker school as well. He works Friday and Saturday nights as a bouncer at the Nut'n Bolt nightclub in Argyle Street." She scowled as she described her colleague.

I interjected, "I know he's a heavy gambler. I've already met him. He backs the horses pretty wildly but none of that means he had anything to do with the robbery."

"The Nut'n Bolt is one of O'Connor's places so there's an obvious connection if O'Connor is involved. And like I said, he was like a half-shut-knife that morning. I found him sleeping across the staff-room table in the afternoon. He'd definitely done an all-nighter and the night club isn't open Sunday nights."

"Maybe his kids were up all night."

"Maybe, but knowing him he'd leave that to his wife. He'd still have his beauty sleep."

"What do you know about his wife?"

"Shamara? She's Asian, a really pretty girl. I don't know what she saw in McGuiness. Her parents have the Kashmiri restaurant in Partick but they broke off with her when she got married. They didn't approve of the marriage."

"You'd make a great gossip columnist, Angela. Do you want me to put in a word for you with one of my editor friends?" I felt I should humour her, softly-softly Myra had said. There was more gossip to be gleaned if I could get her to open up.

"That might be fun," she smiled, "Listen. Can I ask you a question?"

"Why not? Fire away."

"How do you know about the cigarettes and why are you interested now? It's a dead case. The police were never involved and the cigarettes are long gone."

"I know the police weren't called and I know why. I know where the cigarettes went and that O'Connor got them. I know that about half of them are still around and it's not a dead case."

"That's three answers but none of them really answers my question."

"You're as good as this game as me. Actually you asked two questions. I can't tell you how I know but I can tell you why I'm interested. We've been chasing round the streets of Glasgow with the *Serious Chimes Squad* for two years now following these turf wars. It's a very competitive market but even Charlie here doesn't understand what's causing the serious aggravation. The general assumption is that some of the vans are pushing drugs and the violence comes hand in hand with the drug trade but the police haven't found any significant quantity of drugs on any of the vans. This kind of violence belies a sense of desperation. I think that some operators, notably O'Connor, are punting stolen goods from the vans. I think it is connected with the post-office raids of recent times. I think that O'Connor took on this big cigarette heist and got out of his depth. He was overoptimistic and isn't shifting them as fast as he'd hoped. I think it could be just a matter of time before some eager copper comes across his squirrel's nest like I did and then the game's a bogey. I also think that if that doesn't happen and things continue as they are it could get a lot rougher and people could be badly hurt."

"That's a hell of a lot of think!" she pouted.

"That's how a good reporter builds his stories, love, and I'll tell you something else that I think. I think you know a lot more than you're letting on."

I'm not as good at the softly-softly as Myra implied.

"Hey! Back off, Jamie," her boyfriend jumped to her defence, "This is supposed to be a friendly lunch. Angela had nothing to do with it. She's told you what she knows and a bit more on top. You say you know where these cigarettes are. How about you spilling some of what you know or is it just one-sided?"

"They're in an old garage-cum-warehouse in Scotland Street sealed up as tight as a drum with a nasty looking hound to ward off uninvited guests."

"I don't think O'Connor has an old garage in his portfolio," posed Charlie. "In fact I'm fairly sure he hasn't and definitely not in Scotland Street. As you can imagine, I've taken some interest in his exploits since this business hotted up and I know most of his elegant properties."

"The garage belongs to Sam Horton's family." I watched Angela closely as I sprung this little titbit.

"Who's Sam Horton?" Charlie asked and then he jumped visibly as he felt the jab of Angela's stiletto heel under the table.

The lady smiled coyly, "I don't think there's really anything else I can tell you, Jamie. I would if I could."

I put my hands together in a mock-begging gesture, "Just one more question, please."

"Just one?"

"Just one. I promise."

"OK. One more question; ask away."

"How did they move that many cigarettes in the middle of the night?"

She looked at me intently for a good few seconds before answering, "You'll have to move fast to catch that bus, Jamie." Another coy smile and she started to gather her belongings together. Lunch was evidently over and we still hadn't ordered. Some women are touchy. Charlie shrugged an apology as he followed her out the door.

"See you some other time, Jamie," he mumbled.

Walk away.

A few days later I got a call from Hamish Randalson, Editor of the Express. "Morning Jamie, I've got a job you might be interested in." Hamish never phoned unless he had a specific job that he knew you'd be *interested in*.

"Depends Hamish. What do you have in mind?"

"I had a lunch meeting yesterday. I picked up a buzz that some of the Irish troubles are spilling over to our side of the water."

"I don't know Hamish. That's not my beat. I can handle stealing, knifing, wife beating, even the occasional murder but these guys are *fightin' for the land the Saxons rule.* They're from a different time zone. Try young Scott Wilson. He's into all this freedom from oppression kind of stuff. I like the hard news"

"It could be a wee bit ticklish and I don't want any of the young lads sniffing around and getting their heads blown off." Hamish could sound really pompous at times.

"So it doesn't matter so much if old Jamie Robertson gets his head blown off. Is that what you mean." I liked winding him up.

"You know that's not what I mean. It's a question of being level headed but still digging out the story. It's what you've always been good at, Jamie," now the flattery, "you don't ruffle too many feathers but you get the goose plucked." Hamish is also well known for his mixed metaphors.

"And what's the buzz, Hamish, that needs my gentle touch?"

"You know how the IRA are on drugs and drug dealing. Zero tolerance; they keep their patch clean. Anybody tries to market a few joints on the Republican streets is likely to get the full force of a shotgun in some of his own joints. Well it seems that hasn't stopped some silly buggers trying. The Provos confiscate the merchandise but they don't destroy it. They ship it across to mainland UK, a quick trip across on the ferry. With a nice touch of irony their buyers on this side are the Proddies here in Glasgow."

"I thought security was supposed to be tight on those ferries," I objected.

"Well, they're looking for bombers coming over here and maybe guns going over there. The dogs are trained to sniff out explosives. Besides these boys aren't stupid. They find a way."

"I still don't see what you're getting excited about Hamish. It sounds like it could run to a couple of columns on page six or seven, not worth getting my head blown off for. It's a soft feature. You could do it yourself sitting at your desk. Why do you need me?"

"I gather they've been extending the business. This is why I think it's made for you, Jamie. You have contacts on both sides, orange and green. Listen! The whisper is that MI5 have been chasing this one and there's a drugs-for-arms link like the American Contras scandal a few years ago. The Soviets are building up a contingency of "military advisors" in Afghanistan. There's a feed back of poppy seeds that end up with the Moscow gangs. Seems they're prepared to help anybody get guns in return for some logistical help in moving their merchandise. Strathclyde Police have already acted on tip-offs and intercepted significant quantities of quality stuff. The Chief Constable was blowing his trumpet yesterday. So you can see why I need somebody like yourself who can walk on eggshells. I'm really needing a good feature piece of top class investigative journalism, a Glasgow slant on the Irish troubles"

"I don't know if it's for me Hamish. In fact I'm working on something at the moment." Even if I was going to agree, Hamish was a tight-fisted sod when it came to paying for his *top class investigative journalism* so this cat and mouse game could pay dividends.

"That silly bloody ice cream business! That's your idea of a hard news story! Come on, Jamie! You need to let that one go. There's nothing there, man. This is big stuff I'm offering you. I'd settle for one good front pager on it but I'm sure there's more. I haven't lost my nose for these things sitting in my office. What's the matter Jamie? Don't think you can cut it any more in the real world of crime. That stuff's just one up from a school playground fight; two ice cream men thumping each other with a baseball bat. Is this the latest big crime story from the intrepid Jamie Robertson? I say you've lost your bottle old man. What about if I try to get you a place at the Sunday Post?" he was trying to needle me and it was working.

"OK. Double the normal freelance rate and you cover my expenses with or without a story."

"Bugger off! Get me a really good spread and I'll double the rate and cover expenses but no story, no expenses. I'm not paying for you to ponce around the town on that silly ice cream thing."

"You're in the wrong job, Hamish."

"Yes, I reckon I'd be good on the board of Shell or IBM or Ford, running one of these big corporations."

"I was thinking more along the lines of running a brothel you miserable old sod."

"Sometimes it feels like that's what I'm doing. Tell you what Jamie lad, get me a killer front page for Saturday and I'll buy you Sunday lunch at the Boathouse in Balloch."

"OK. I'll take you up on that, if I don't get my head blown off."

"One more thing before you go Jamie. This one didn't come from the Chief Constable. These big drug busts of our *Glesca Polis,* a little bird told me that some of the haul found its way back onto the street. Whoever's dealing it is new to the game. He's pushing pure uncut heroin. Two users have died and two more in serious condition in the Western."

"Now that's more up my street. Why didn't you say so in the first place? I don't suppose you know who that would be."

"I was hoping you might ferret out that little sparkler. Then you'd have two front-page stories. Who knows? We might get a series going. One thing for sure, he must be quite pally with the boys in blue"

My mind quickly switched from ice cream to drugs. Hamish had made a point. Substance abuse and all its rackets is a bit more serious than smashing up ice cream vans. With the phone still in my hand I flicked through my little book of contacts and found the one I wanted.

It didn't pick up instantly but I let it ring for a full minute. Eventually it was answered, "Glasgow Cathedral, Father Drysdale speaking."

"Hello Father Drysdale, can I speak to Father Monaghan please?"

"He's taking confession at the moment. Can I give him a message?"

"I'd like to speak to him when he's free. I'm Jamie Robertson; he has my number. Tell him it's worth a pint of Guinness."

"In that case I'm quite sure he'll call you back, Mr Robertson."

An hour later the phone rang.

"Jamie, my lad, whatever can I do for you? I haven't seen you for a while. Writing about others' misdemeanours doesn't absolve you from your own, you know."

"What about if I bare my soul over a couple of pints, Tommy. I'm putting a story together and I've hit a sticky question so I decided to phone an old friend "

"Well, I'm happy to be your friend, lad, but I'm not exactly a fountain of knowledge."

"I was hoping you might put me in touch with somebody to guide my path."

"Somehow I don't think it's the Good Lord you want me to put you in touch with and you're expecting all this for a measly pint of Guinness."

"I said a couple of pints."

"Your generous to a fault, Jamie. What's your sticky question?"

I gave him the outline just as Hamish had given it to me. Tommy Monaghan, my friend from schooldays, went into the priesthood. It was a connection that worked well over the years. There were many times that he dropped me hints of nasty goings on when he couldn't have gone to the police with information that he'd picked up in the confession box. That's what I was asking from him now.

"I'll see what I can do, Jamie. I think it might be a good idea if we meet where nobody knows us. There aren't many of us who aren't sympathetic to the Republican cause but these are bad bastards Jamie. You'll have to keep one eye over your shoulder. If the Protestant end is involved, they're even badder bastards so you'll need both eyes over your shoulder. I'll find out what I can for you but for Christ sake don't get over involved. What about the bar in the Central Hotel inside the station, six o'clock tomorrow night?" I've never worked out why it is that Catholic priests can swear like troopers and Church of Scotland ministers think *good heavens* and *good God* are blasphemous.

"OK, Tommy. Thanks."

I dropped the phone into its cradle, thumbed through my little book, picked it up again and dialled John McBride, secretary of the Glasgow Branch of the Salvation Army. He was also Grand Master of Lodge 306 of the Orange Order in Glasgow. I knew him more in his role as Chairman of the North Kelvinside Burns Association (Robert Burns not the kind you get messing with fire).

"Hello John, Jamie Robertson here. I was wondering…" I started.

"Jamie Robertson!" he bellowed. "What can I do for you? Where have you been since January? God man, I'll never forget it, the best *toast tae the lassies* I've heard in my life. It was brilliant. Ted Heath wooing Maggie Thatcher reciting Burns.

"*Wee sleekit cowerin' timorous beastie,*

Tha needna' start awa' sae hastie…"

I let him ramble on a bit and then asked the same favour that I'd asked of Tommy Monaghan. His answer was just as positive, just as wary and just as concerned about my health and safety. He agreed to come over to my place rather than meet anywhere in public. When he came to my flat he was even heavier with his warnings than Tommy as he gave me a list of names.

"These aren't normal Glasgow worthies we're talking about Jamie, they're totally ruthless. Violence isn't a human reaction with these people it's a business instrument. It's not just drugs, though that's bad enough. There's guns as well and big wads of questionable money: some of it dirty, some of it fake. It's a filthy business and there's dead bodies too. There are two names that I've been hearing lately in the heroin trade. Both these names came up when I started asking around for you, Danny O'Connor and James Gillespie. I don't know much about O'Connor except what I've heard in stories but Gillespie? Well, I know him personally. Lets put it this way; he was expelled from the Orange Lodge for excessively sectarian views."

So off I went to meet a few of Tommy's flock and John's fluters. I've always felt equally comfortable (or uncomfortable) in Rangers supporters' bars or Celtic supporter's bars but I never go into either wearing my Celtic shirt. Despite the dire warnings the contacts they gave me were surprisingly willing to talk. O'Connor and Gillespie were old enemies but both seemed to have acquired a following of enemies who were more than happy to put the boot in albeit from a safe distance. The Irish troubles still hadn't spilled over into Scotland like they did down south so their menace never really penetrated the Glasgow underworld. There were too many old scores to be settled here. I didn't have to overspend on Hamish's expense account. About twenty quid's worth of beer lubricates enough tongues, enough to give me most of the Scottish side of the story. A couple of faxes to an old colleague, now working at the New York Post, gave me some insight on the international shenanigans with the Provos.

One of John's contacts was quite a bit different. Derek Solent was one of the last of the old fashioned English eccentrics, a Glengarry perched on a head of long blond hair, army fatigue trousers and a ban-the-bomb t-shirt. Now on his third university degree course studying Architecture he already had first class honours in Botany and Economics. He was in fact Dr. Derek Solent having also produced an outstanding thesis on the Buddhist architectural influence in Afghanistan. A true Cockney, born within the sonic reach of the Bow Bells he adopted Scotland as his native home about the same time as Rod Stewart. He was never in any great hurry to complete any of the degrees and between bouts of frenzied energetic study he enjoyed bouts of frenzied energetic support for Scottish independence. He was also a heroin addict. His boyfriend was one of the users who died from an overdose due to the unusually high quality of uncut dope. When I met him both his studies and political fervour were set aside while he launched a one-man campaign to find the clown responsible for his lover's death.

With his sloppy appearance one would be forgiven for thinking he was just another perennial hippy student scraping by on public handouts. In fact in his spare time he was one of the UK's foremost travel writers. As an accomplished author with six books to his credit he contributed regularly to most travel magazines and often worked as a researcher for the BBC on its travelogues. I'd seen him many times but had no idea who he was. If you lived or worked in Glasgow it was difficult to miss this modern day Ben Gunn. My first direct meeting was arranged by John McBride.

"He wants to do a deal with you," said John.

"What kind of deal?"

"He wants to meet James Gillespie. Says he has it on good authority that our friend Jammy was the one who got the goodies from the Police larder and sold them on without milking them down. He blames Gillespie for the death of his live-in lover."

"Sounds ominous. What does he plan to do reform Gillespie or reform his face?"

"Actually you'll like this one. He plans to teach him how to cut the dope; says it'll bring the street price down, make more money for Gillespie and be safer for the users. He calls it a win-win-win situation. He heard you'd been asking around and reckons you're the perfect go-between."

"So what's the deal? What's he offering me?"

"The man's a walking encyclopaedia on the drug routes, where they come from, where they go, who buys them, who sells them, who pays for them and where the money goes. It's all at his fingertips right back as far as the opium wars between Britain and China. I have no reason to doubt that his knowledge is up to date so I think he could be very useful to you. Personally I'd also like to know more about what Gillespie is up to."

So John set up the first meet in the Sally-ally Gospel Hall near Glasgow Cross. We sat around a table with a pot of fresh brewed tea and a tray of home-baked scones. It beat the hell out of a *contratent* with Myra in the Lite Bite. At first I found it impossible to have a serious conversation with this "daft Scots git" speaking Cockney slang and planning to give free lessons to a gangland dealer. When he spoke I was even more doubtful.

"Lets start wif Hawala mate."

I thought this was maybe the latest in Hippy hellos. I repeated "Hawala," hesitantly.

"You must've come across Hawala? Some folks call it Hundi but it's the same fing." He could see the blank look on my face. "OK. Wot about the Chinese chop? Flying money? Starbursts an' boomerangs an' fings?"

I just sat there shaking my head. This guy was clearly crankier even than he looked. I glanced over at John who was looking equally flummoxed.

"Ow the bleedin' heck can you call yourself a crime fighter if you aint got a bleedin' clue mate?" He shoved the Glengarry to the back of his head and succeeded in making himself look like somebody out of the Beano.

"I really don't think there's much I can do to help you," I began. No way would I be the idiot who introduced this weirdo to Gillespie.

"Flippin' right there Bugs Bunny, but you're the best we've got so you'll have to do. Look, I take it you have heard of Swiss numbered bank accounts." This time I was able to nod. Maybe he was coming back down from whatever planet he'd been on. "Right, suppose you ain't got one of them fings; you ain't got the right letters before or after your *cryin' shame*. Listen for every dollar passes through the bank legit' like, there's one passes through the hole in the cheese, right?"

"Right." I agreed. He was the one with a degree in Economics.

"Right, an' if y'aint got money in the bank Frank, what d'you do? Aint too bright to arrive in Kabul or Tehran or Bogotá wif a briefcase full of crispy divers. Wot you reckon Mr Crime Reporter?"

"What did you call it? Hundiwala?"

" No, mate. It's Hawala or Hundi. The Hundiwala is the person wot moves the honey, except he don't move nufin just writes it in 'is book, see. The money never moves so it's impossible to trace. You walk in the back door an' upstairs above yer favourite curry shop an' give the old man yer lolly. He pops it in the drawer like, jots it down in the book an' phones some uver hundiwala friend at the uver end an' tells him to pay out to whoever you're tradin' wif, like. It's the main system for movin' money in India, Pakistan, the Middle East and 'alf of Africa"

"But that must be illegal."

"Hey, McBride. Where the bleedin' heck did you find this guy?" He was becoming a little bit annoyed by my ignorance. "Of course it's flippin' illegal, leastways it is if what your buyin' and sellin' is illegal but it goes way back to the Scribes in the Bible. Reckon that's why Jesus didn't like them; they was fiddlin' the books. Listen, don't mean to be cheeky mate but you look sort of Indian or sumfing yerself. You must know wot I'm talkin' about"

"I can't change the colour of my skin friend. You'll just have to take me as a Glaswegian. That's as foreign as I can claim. Let's just say there's a foggy patch around my parentage."

"Okey-dokey, like I said, wasn't meanin' to be cheeky; just fot you looked like y'ought to have some idea. No offence."

"So what you're saying is that there's a system in place around the world for money transfer without money movement."

"You got it. Now we're talkin' turkey. That me dear friend is the official definition of the unofficial exchange system. It aint illegal although some countries are tryin' to make it illegal but it's obviously open to abuse. They'll never stop it; it's a way of life. The fing is you've got one guy who wants to buy drugs, another who wants to buy missile launchers an' number three is a poor hungry bugger who just wants to buy rice. Hawala connects them up an' A pays B who pays C who pays A, except it's a bit more complicated an' it all works on trust. OK, I know what you're going to say. Between the Republic of Ireland, the seven counties an' dear ol' Glasgow town there aint a 'ole bag of trust but you'd be surprised. Anyway, here's the deal. You get me a meet with this Jammy

Gillespie guy an' you get a crash course on international traffickin'. Okey-kokey?"

"Okey-kokey."

So, next day we sat down round the same table with fresh tea and fresh scones. This time it was just myself, Derek and Gillespie. The gung ho gangster was delighted at the idea of doubling his margin. It was quite an eye opener. Derek told him what to use to dilute the powder, how much to use for different strengths and how they related to the type of user and even the general street price for each level. Then he produced a couple of little packets of powder and showed him how to taste the difference. Mission accomplished, Gillespie was ready to trot off happily so I got in a couple of pertinent questions before he trotted.

"How come you didn't know all this before?"

"It's no ma stock in trade. Is it? But you've got to start thinking about your pension fund these days. This guy comes offering stuff from Belfast, all laid out in little packets. Ah had enough cash to make the buy an' there's no shortage of users on the street."

"Wotabout the uvver stuff wot killed me luvver boy?" asked the Cockney Scot. "You was the one put it in little packets. Where'd you get it?"

"Nobody told me it was pure stuff. Like Ah said Ah'm new tae this stuff. D'you think Ah would have sold it like that if Ah knew Ah could get a bigger profit."

"You ain't answered me question, mate. Where'd it come from?"

"This guy gave me it in return for a favour. Can't tell you his name."

"This favour?" I asked, "It wouldn't happen to be information?"

He shrugged his shoulders uncomfortably, "Just a couple of names and places."

"So, somebody in the police gave you drugs in exchange for information, drugs that they had confiscated from someone."

"Ah don't know where they got them." He shrugged again and walked out. Not quite a confirmation but he hadn't denied their source either.

Derek was satisfied that he'd achieved his purpose so he began to take me on a world tour of Armalites, AKs and Afghan copies handcrafted in the back streets of Kabul: of cannabis, coca and cartels: missile launchers and uncut diamonds. He took me through international crime rings, government intelligence agencies, elite rapid deployment military services, terror groups, charities and questionable corporations. When I walked out into the fresh air of Glasgow's tough streets I had some top quality investigative journalism to offer Hamish.

The IRA started in the 70s with a few old rusty pistols, farmers' shotguns and homemade semtex bombs, the objective being to rattle a few windows and draw attention to the plight of the Catholic minority in Ulster. For a whole complexity of reasons the killing got out of hand. Factions appeared within the organisation and a new hardline group took control both of the movement and of the republican community. In response the Protestants formed their own volunteer defence force and began to retaliate. Both groups felt the urgent need to acquire more modern effective weapons. At this point a small but significant difference comes into play on the question of funding. The IRA have always had a sympathetic ear in the USA where third generation patriots are happy to contribute to the cause. This gave them substantial funds on the other side of the Atlantic. The protestant forces were new on the ground and in any case the protestant community already had political control so they had no sentimental well to tap. They therefore resorted more to criminal activities to swell their coffers. As the years rolled on and the troubles grew this difference affected the manner in which they acquired their armaments. The IRA, who hated drugs and banned them on their own streets, were prepared to act as a conduit for illegal substances between their source and the UK market. The UDA or UFV on the other hand were prepared to participate in the street trading.

So the republicans opened the doors to let the merchandise pass through Erin's Green Isle in exchange for arms from Central America and the Middle East. Payment for the arms passed directly from the USA to American dealers or via Hawala through Dubai to Islamic revolutionary groups. The Protestants formed links with UK gangsters and other mafia style groups and actively pushed the drugs in Ulster and the UK to obtain the funds they needed for guns. In addition there were splinter groups on both sides who were more inclined to do whatever was necessary to achieve their ends and engaged in all manner of criminal activity.

This was 1981 and there is much that we know now but didn't know then. So the piece that I presented to Hamish was substantially lacking in detail. There were very few names to put with the deeds and a lot of what I wrote was speculative. It is amusing now to read it and see how close we came to the truth. Without question there was a Protestant Glasgow gang distributing drugs both here and in Edinburgh. They were connected strongly with a London gang who re-routed much of the merchandise south to Manchester, Birmingham, Newcastle and London. Gillespie was somewhere on the periphery of that gang mostly as an enforcer. Perhaps it was some of those names that he'd provided to the police. There was a parallel Catholic outfit who were less involved in distribution in Glasgow and concentrated more on moving stuff south, often to the same destinations as their rivals. Danny O'Connor's name came up but like Gillespie he was not at that stage one of the main players. They also had contacts within the Muslim community who were not really criminal but aided in the movement of funds. And just a few years previously the CIA had revealed their mucky hands in the Iran-Contras scandal so we couldn't count them or the American Mafia out of the equation.

For Glasgow the sinister aspect at this stage was the movement of guns, which inevitably brought high-powered weapons onto the streets into what we know was traditionally a city of knives and broken bottles with the occasional shotgun. Armed gangsters were a new, frightening concept. Drug usage had been here since the swinging sixties. Consumption had escalated substantially and crime with it but in the beginning it was seen as petty crime. So the two problems were tackled separately. It wasn't till the mid-eighties that the total link of drugs-guns-terror-money-crime really began to sink home and governments and enforcement agencies became fully aware of the cross border trading that could often take place between sworn enemies. The idea that Hezbollah, the IRA and Columbian FARC were in any way connected to turf fights between ice cream vans in Easterhouse was, and to many people still is, pure bunkum. At that time, I must confess, I was in that group too.

I called in to see Hamish on the Friday and he was delighted. As well as getting a good piece to go to print he could now go to his meetings with the city elders looking more informed than the Chief Constable.

"Great stuff Jamie. I knew I could rely on you."

The phone rang. The phone always rang when you were with Hamish.

"Yes. Where? OK, make sure you get a couple of good photos. I'll send down one of the young lads to get a report when it's under control." He turned back to me. "Sorry about that Jamie, a fire down in Scotland Street, an old garage premises but it seems to be creating quite a blaze. One of the firemen injured. Anyway, where were we?"

I was already on my feet and halfway out the door.

Up in smoke.

I tried to enter Scotland Street from the West Street end but it was solidly blocked by a fire tender and two police cars, all with blue lights flashing. There were four more tenders up near the fire, which was still glowing in the dusk of the evening. A cluster of TV cameras and photographers were huddled in conference downwind of the thick acrid smoke. The skeletal form of three extended ladders hung over the burning ruins with three yellow firemen spraying foamy water down on the burning embers.

I spotted Jimmy MacKenzie from the Record, hanging back from the others under a street lamp, scribbling away on his notepad. I walked over to join him.

"Hi Jimmy."

"Hi Jamie."

We sounded a bit like the Francie and Josie TV show.

"Looks like you've got something to write about. Fancy swapping fairy tales?"

"I reckon I've got most of it. You should have been here half-an-hour ago."

"Maybe I've got more than you. I was here a week ago!"

He looked up from his notepad. "You crafty old bastard. What gives?"

"I offered a swap but I can get the detail from the Bobbies over there. They look like the have their hands full so I didn't want to bother them"

"Actually it's quite funny. Apparently this gang comes along all ready to bust in. It's an old car showroom but it's used as a store. I'm not sure whose it is but it's got some cigarettes stored in it. Anyway they're all prepared to kill the alarm but what they don't know is it's trick wired so when the alarm is cut these banks of floodlights come on. So these goons just tip the lights over face down, some on the ground and some on the flat roof, and keep on loading the van. Well they're busy stuffing the loot when somebody shouts FIRE. The lights are these halogen type and they set the roof tar on fire. The burglars jumped in their van and scarpered with what they had. All except one, that is, he kept hauling out boxes of fags and piling them into an ice cream van. He was still there when flashing blue lights arrived. I think he's a friend of yours, name of James Gillespie. The silly bugger actually got caught in the act."

"Where is he now?"

"They cuffed him and put him in one of those cars over there."

"What about the fire? I heard that one fireman was hurt."

"Well, the tarry roof just went up like a light so it was a full blaze by the time the fire engines got here. Flames were shooting out of the roof. The police arrived first. Somebody said there was a watchman so they played the hoses on the main doorway and two fire fighters went in. They were just by the door when some roof beams collapsed and the whole lot came down. One of them got his hands badly burned. Seems he wasn't wearing regulation gloves so he'll get more bollicking than sympathy from the chiefs. The watchman turned up a couple of minutes later. He was in the pub down the road and came out to see what all the commotion was about. Anyway the hoodlums got away with a vanload of ciggies. I don't think there's much else in there. And that's it, now your turn."

I thought for a while before answering. I didn't feel the time was right to hit the presses with my embryo story. I decided on a compromise.

"Listen Jimmie, tell you what. You can have the scoop on this if you keep most of what I tell you under your hat for a while. The story's yours but this is off the record and you can't include any of the names I'm about to tell you."

"You mean Ah can have the lollipop but Ah cannae sook it."

"That's a nice way of putting it. Anyway lollipops are bad for your teeth. What if I throw in another Gillespie story for free? This one you can print if you want."

"Kojak eats nothing else but lollipops," he replied dryly.

"Yeah, but he's an NYPD cop and he doesn't like hotdogs."

"OK. Stop farting around. I get the scoop and you get to keep the Agatha Christie mystery. What's the tale of Gillespie?"

So, I gave him the lay down on the Jammy G. bash in the Frazzini car park and how he got away with it despite the evidence.

"Well, he sure as hell, isn't going to walk away this time. Is he?" his tone was unconvincing, "I mean they caught him red handed and he's sitting over there with the cuffs on. And what about your mystery drama? You were here a week ago. Coincidence?"

"Not exactly. I came looking for the cigarettes. I can't be certain but I'd say there was half a million in there."

"Half a million cigarettes, that's about fifty cases so they probably got most of them."

"No, not half a million fags, Jimmy, half a million pounds' worth. That's about one and a half thousand cases."

"Shite in a bucket, Jamie. You're winding me up," he coughed and spluttered.

"I think that's a smoker's cough you've got Jimmy."

"I think it's a flaming heart attack. Are you trying to tell me that's half a million quid smouldering over there? Hell, that's a big, big ashtray. I imagine you know who they belong to or else you wouldn't be here with your fairy tales."

"I suppose that strictly speaking they belong to Her Majesty's Government. They started as a tax fiddle for JS Coutts but they sort of got lost overnight. This was over a year ago and at that time they were worth about a million pounds. Danny O'Connor acquired them and has been flogging them, as many as he can all over the city, before they dry out."

"I think they've just dried out," he interrupted dryly.

"MacKenzie, you're droll."

"Yeah. It's the Glasgow sunshine. It affects your head. You said O'Connor *acquired* them. You mean he stole them? That's how he usually acquires things."

"It's a bit more complicated. That's what I'm still investigating."

"And that's why I'm sooking lollipops. What are you planning, a big exposé in the News of the World."

"I don't know Jimmy. It's a funny one. I can't get a handle on it but I'm sure it's tied in with all the fisty-cuffs in the ice cream vans. You know O'Connor's got his nose in that one."

"Danny O'Connor in an ice cream van chiming round the houses? Give over! He doesn't sell nougats. He sells nookie and knocked merchandise. I can picture him swinging a baseball bat against some poor bugger's skull but selling ice cream? Never. Check out your info on that one, Jamie."

"No, straight up. He bought…" I started to say but I'd lost his attention. Someone had just stepped out of one of the police cars and was heading our way. As he passed our car he waved in and gave the single finger salute.

MacKenzie spluttered, "Gillespie, Jammy bloody Gillespie. They're letting him walk. They can't, no way. They caught him with his finger in the pie. He can't walk from this one."

He set off in the direction of the police and I followed his disappearing tail. He marched up to the squad car and yanked the front door open.

"Come on, bright boys, you can't let him stroll on this one. You caught him loading cigarettes into a van. He's guilty as hell. Robbery, arson, endangering human life, you can throw the book at him."

"I take it you're speaking about Mr Gillespie?" the sergeant replied smugly.

"You're fuckin' right, I mean Mister Fuckin' Gillespie," Jimmy fumed.

"I think you ought to control your language, Sir," taunted the constable in the other seat; "Otherwise we'll have to do you for breach of the peace." I wasn't sure that he was joking. I decided to step in and cool the situation. There was more smoke coming out of Jimmy's ears than from the smouldering fire.

"Maybe if you could explain to us, Sergeant. We have to catch the deadline and don't want to go to press with the wrong story. We thought you had Gillespie in cuffs. Are you able to tell us if he has been charged?"

"James Gillespie was found loading cigarettes into a van. It was clear that a robbery was in progress and we assumed he was taking part in the robbery. We cuffed him till we could make further enquiries. He claimed that he was passing by, saw the fire and went to try and rescue some of the stock. When we apprehended him he was putting the boxes into an O'Connors ice cream van. We contacted Mr O'Connor and he is happy with that explanation. We therefore had no reason to hold Mr Gillespie. Will that be sufficient for you to meet your deadline?" The two of them sat grinning.

I pulled Jimmy away before he exploded and did something silly. He wandered back to my car just wagging his head from side to side like the dog in the back window.

"I'll give you a lift back to the office so you can get your copy in," I offered.

"Copy? What copy? You mean the BIG scoop? A scoop of ice cream is all we've got. I suppose I have to accept you were right about O'Connor and his new business venture. What do you reckon; have I got a story I can print? GILLESPIE WALKS AGAIN. Do you think we can cover all the five Ws? I'd have to mention the cigarettes and O'Connor but I got that from the coppers so I don't need to honour our deal. Do I? I can't just do another fire in the tinder city. There's twenty fires a day. What is it about that guy? He's an evil bastard and they let him walk every time. They call him *Jammy* like you but that's not natural jammy."

We looked at each other with deadpan faces, absolute silence for at least a minute, and then we both burst out laughing. What do you do in a situation like this; you laugh or you cry? I think we were doing both. We felt incredibly stupid, totally deflated, utterly gutted. James Gillespie is a bit of an urban legend, the guy who never gets caught, hence the nickname *Jammy*. Now we'd just seen it before our very eyes.

I thought again. "OK. You can use it all on one condition. You've got to make it sting. Make it a kicker. They're just making fools of us. I've got a feature going into the Express tomorrow about drugs coming into the city. Gillespie's name came up from several sources but he's not one of the big shakers. I think he's feeding them with names and details and he gets away with murder. His connection with O'Connor is a new twist. I told you at the beginning it's complicated. There's somebody else behind O'Connor. Give it your best Jim lad. Lets get going or you'll miss the magic hour and turn back into a frog."

I took him back into the city centre. He made the deadline and he didn't turn back into a frog. And me? Curiosity was still burning so I went back to the fire scene. I wanted to see the full extent of the damage. They had the fire under control and most of the spectators had dispersed. There was just one fire tender keeping watch and another truck that looked like a fire tender without hoses. This was the salvage truck. The main entrance area had collapsed and the charred remains of some cardboard cases were just visible in the darkness. The salvage team were throwing huge tarpaulins over the rear of the building. That suggested to me that there was a significant part of the building and contents still intact. So neither the fire nor Gillespie's chums had got all of the cigarettes. It's a dangerous job in the Salvage Corps. They often go into the building while it's still burning. They identify the areas that are going to be saved from fire damage and they move quickly to cover things to protect them from water damage. Then when the fire is totally extinguished they cover what's left of the structure with huge weather cladding tarpaulins. Then they claim salvage rights and the insurance loss adjuster estimates the value of their work. If there's a good insurance policy in place they wait happily for the payout. If not they ask the owner to stump up. If it looks like neither is going to pay they come back, remove their protective covers and leave it open to the elements.

So their continued presence indicated that they'd found something worth saving. A large part of the cigarette stock was still intact. I was curious to know the outcome. I seriously doubted that O'Connor had the contents insured; the owner would only have buildings insurance; and I couldn't see O'Connor doling out to the salvage team. It would be interesting to see what happened next. I went home to type up my own report of the evening even though I wasn't going to submit it.

I was awakened next morning by the invasive ring of the phone. It was my student traveller friend, Derek Solent.

"Hey mornin' mate. I'm sittin' 'ere readin' all'bout the big bad world of drugs an' guns an' fings. Bloody good synopsis mate, bloody good. I fot you was a bit fick like between the ears but you copped all of wot I told you an' a bit more besides."

"Morning Derek, sounds like you've got yourself a copy of the Express. Thanks for you kind comments. I must confess the doubts were mutual. I didn't think there was anything under that Glengarry at first and when you started babbling about Hawala I honestly thought you were up there on a happy cloud. Anyway, many thanks for your help. We should get in touch again some time. Oh, by the way, take a look at the Record this morning. The by-line's Jimmy MacKenzie on a fire last night in Scotland Street. You'll find it interesting."

I got up, made breakfast and spent the next hour brooding over my coffee cup. By the third cup I realised what was niggling at the brain cells. Two days ago I spoke to Frazzini and Angela McCabe and told them about the location of the cigarettes. Next day Gillespie and company arrive to clear them out. Coincidence or tip-off? Was Jammy G there on his own account or did O'Connor hire him to set it up like a robbery? He accepted Gillespie's story when the police called him but that could have been just keeping a low profile. I poured a fourth cup and applied some basic logic. Gillespie had no means of selling an enormous pile of cigarettes on his own so he had to be working for somebody. That meant O'Connor or another one of the city's Mr Bigs. If it was O'Connor he was probably double dealing his partner Horton. Frazzini knew because he was the one I'd told but it didn't seem reasonable that he would hire the same bruiser who'd trashed his vans. Logic was pointing its finger at O'Connor. Logic was also pointing a finger at Frazzini or Angela as the ones who tipped him off that we were on his tail.

Some people do crosswords; some people used to do these Rubik cubes; nowadays people have gone crazy for sudokus. I have always enjoyed playing my own little games of logic. My usual score is 75% so I make some mistakes but it gives me an avenue to trot down when there's no clear signpost. I decided that Frazzini had called O'Connor who in turn had pulled in Gillespie. If I was right it would be interesting to see what happened with the cigarettes that were left.

A week later I drove out to take a gander at the scene of the fire. The tarpaulins were gone, the doorway lay gaping open and the perimeter was cordoned off with police tape. I ducked under the tape and walked inside. The entrance area was all charred and a couple of twisted support beams lay awkwardly on the floor. I stepped over them to get a better look at the interior. The ceiling was blackened but otherwise it was surprisingly untouched by the blaze. The cigarettes were all gone. I heard footsteps behind and swung round to see a uniformed constable standing silhouetted in the doorway.

"Are you aware you've just crossed a police control tape? Do you have authority to be here?"

I sidestepped his questions and rebutted him with two of my own. "What happened to the salvage tarps? Where's all the stock that was in here?"

"The tarps were removed by the Salvage Corps yesterday. The other stuff disappeared overnight four days ago. That's why the tapes are there. This is a crime scene. Who are you?"

I flashed my press card. He wasn't impressed.

"I'm sorry, Sir, that doesn't entitle you to cross a scene-of-crime tape. You'll have to leave."

"That's all right; I've seen enough. But listen. Why did they remove the tarpaulins?"

"The lads came back and took them away. We couldn't get a value on the stock from the owner and he didn't have any insurance. The building's insured but it's going to get demolished after this. Then the stock disappeared and the owner refused to pay any salvage so they're within their rights to take them away. I don't envy these lads their job. It's bloody dangerous and they don't always get what's due to them. These tarps are bloody expensive so they don't leave them longer that they have to. Now, I'm sorry but you have to go."

It's refreshing when you meet a police officer like that. He was doing his job. I was doing mine. The salvage boys were doing theirs. He was perfectly entitled to be more officious but he chose to be polite and helpful within the limits at his disposal. The *Glesca Polis* used to have a lot more officers like that. I thanked him and left the crime scene. Time to tackle O'Connor face to face.

A couple of calls established that he was in residence in one of his "classy bars" called Tam's in Maryhill Road. I found a thirty-minute parking space in the street outside. The shabby gold letters on a weathered black sign proclaimed that it was Tam's Tavern. The smaller hand painted letters above the door stated that the licensee was Daniel O'Connor. I wondered what had befallen the unfortunate Tam. It was just after five and the bar had just opened. The barman was stocking shelves and a smartly dressed man was sitting on a barstool with a bottle of Johnny Walker and a glass in front of him. He was clean-shaven with grey receding hair. Despite the tidy appearance he had the look of someone who had done the rounds. We'd met before in a court somewhere. I walked in and greeted him cordially.

"Hello Danny. How's it going?"

"I prefer Mr O'Connor," he replied dryly. "What can I do for you Mr Robertson?"

"Scotland Street?"

"What about Scotland Street?"

"Yeah. That was my question. What about Scotland Street?"

"The bastards cleaned me out. That's what.

"Who cleaned you out, Danny?"

"Mr O'Connor," he insisted, "I thought it was just one of those stories you hear, that start in a pub somewhere, and before you know it everybody believes it. Glasgow's full of Tarzans and Rambos. I thought this bunch was just a joke. Turns out the joke's on me."

"You've lost me, Danny."

"Mr fuckin' O'Connor, please!" He was getting rattled.

"You've lost me, Mr O'Connor."

"The Salvage Gang. You must have heard the stories too. You know how the salvage thing works. If there's something worth saving they hap it up to keep it safe and warm. Well there's a second salvage team that go in when everything's quiet and take the goodies to somewhere safer and warmer. They know there's something worthwhile under the tarpaulins otherwise they wouldn't be there. They know that all the alarms have been disarmed because the firemen switch off the power. So in they come and clean out anything of value. They're a bunch of crooks. The real Salvage Corps are really pissed off because the finger's pointing at them." The righteous indignation would have been justified from anyone other than Danny O'Connor. I couldn't help from smiling.

"Have you reported it to the police? That was a decent stack of ciggies."

"Aye of course I did. *Excuse me officer; somebody's stolen my stolen cigarettes.* How the fuck do you know about the cigarettes anyway?"

"I know everything, Danny Boy. It's my job."

"Listen Robertson. If you don't like the MISTER bit just call me O'Connor. I don't like first names. There's no respect in first names. They're all too cosy."

"OK O'Connor. Who's to say you didn't just move all the fags yourself. That's what Gillespie was supposed to do. Wasn't it? Sam Horton was wanting his money and this was your way of getting him off your back. If they're stolen you won't have to pay him. I imagine he's been getting impatient. After all it's been more than a year."

"Don't talk to me about that arsehole Gillespie. Silly bugger's supposed to be a professional, knows all about alarms and he goes and sets the whole fuckin' place alight. And hey! How come you know about Horton? What's happening in this bloody city? A two-bit reporter knows more than the guy who's getting shafted. OK, smart-arse. I moved the cigarettes myself? Where to?"

"My money says they're in your new place on the south side."

"Listen Clark Kent. I'll square with you though. I don't see why I should but what the hell. My ice cream place on the south side is stacked to the roof with wafer biscuits. My brilliant manager goes and puts three extra zeroes on the order and they arrive by the truckload. Christ knows what I'm going to do with them. I'm still trying to get Askeys to take them back. And OK, yes, that's where Gillespie was supposed to take them but that's history. You can't depend on anybody nowadays."

"Maybe you should nail him to the floorboards. I seem to remember that was one of your more effective means of controlling staff. That got you more respect than dropping first names. Didn't it."

"Ha, bloody, ha! I was acquitted of that."

"That doesn't mean you didn't do it. We all saw the holes in the poor bugger's hands."

"This conversation's finished. Buy a drink or get out."

"Now that's a friendly welcome from the landlord."

"Robertson. Get out, or it'll be your arse nailed to the floorboards."

"OK, Danny Boy. I'm on my way."

The whisky glass smashed off the doorframe as I made my exit.

Logic dictated that my next visit was to Frazzini and I just made it in time. Charlie was getting into his BMW just as I arrived. He saw me, walked over to my little Mini and leaned down to the level of my window.

"If you've come to insult me again, just turn around and go back home."

"How come everybody's so friendly today? I just want to know what you said to O'Connor."

"You're too smart for your own health, Jamie. What makes you think I'd want to talk to that piece of shit?"

"I think they call it the appliance of science or intuitive logic or some other fancy name. To me it's just common sense. I tell you one day about his squirrel's nest and the next day he's looking for a new hidey-hole. It had to be either you or Angela and you've got the biggest ego. I think you called him up to tell him he'd been rumbled just to massage your ego. Did you know it was your friend Gillespie that bungled the removals operation and set the place up in flames?"

"No, I didn't. I think the fancy name for that is poetic justice. Look! I'm just trying to run an honest business, out on the streets selling quality ice cream to the folks in their houses. Along come these thugs, with a criminal record as long as your arm, thumping my drivers and smashing my vans. Then round come the Chimes Squad treating us like we're the bad guys. So OK, yes. It was me that decided to stir things up a bit. I called your friend and gave him a little character assessment. So what? Why are you picking on me? I'm the victim here. I've got enough problems. Get off my back!" Conversation finished, he swung round jumped into his Beemer and screeched off before I had time to think of my reply. *"OK, Charlie, I believe you but I've touched some raw nerve ends. What else is niggling you?"*

Chime and chime again.

Blackhill is one of the most dismal areas of the city. It's got nothing to recommend it; it's just dismal: derelict streets, derelict houses, derelict people. It's hard to imagine anybody wanting to live in it far less fight over it. The events of Christmas Day were particularly strange when viewed in this context. First of all, nobody wants to buy ice cream on Christmas day. They're all stuffed full of turkey, Christmas pies, beer and Irn Bru. So when the ice cream van pulled up on the corner of Walton Street it didn't even have its chimes tinkling. It sat there for ten minutes as if waiting for somebody but nobody came. A Ford Cortina came up the hill a lot faster than the 30mph limit. It skidded to a halt alongside the van and the rear window rolled down. It rolled back a few feet and a shotgun emerged from the window. The rear gunner blasted both barrels into the windscreen of the van and the car screamed off even faster than it arrived.

Freddy Cassidy woke up in hospital with his face full of lead pellets and shattered glass, in extreme danger of losing sight in his left eye. He spent the next three days in intensive care. The doctors removed all the foreign bodies but it still wasn't certain whether or not they could save the eye. The troops in the Glasgow Ice Cream War had obviously not called a Christmas truce.

Freddy was an old acquaintance; I knew him well. I first met him when he was ten years old. That was back in the good old days when the milkmen still made daily deliveries direct to your door. Freddy made a bogey from the wheels of an old pram and placed a wooden box on the back. As a young lad of enterprise he set up his own milk round. He collected the bottles from people's doors before they got up then took them for resale at half-price to the families who didn't get a delivery because they hadn't paid the milkman's bill at the end of the week.

He ran this business successfully for a few months before he was caught. Because of his age he couldn't be formally charged so he had to attend a Children's Panel Hearing where the maximum punishment was a severe reprimand delivered by a toffee-nosed old councillor's wife from Bearsden. They didn't even confiscate his bogey so he just went back next week and took the milk from different houses. The demand was still healthy; all he had to do was change his supply source. My role in the affair was to write a report on the marvels of this new approach to child delinquency. I don't think the Social Work Department liked my report.

In subsequent years young Freddy's exploits provided me with a regular source of good farcical copy as his entrepreneurial skills developed and his respect for authority diminished. When he was sixteen he was caught with his bogey transport once again. This time it was full of ethical drugs that he'd retrieved from the local Chemist's shop. This time he was too big for the children's panel. This time he was sent for two years to Thornliepark Correction Centre near Paisley. This time the reprimand was a little more severe. Regrettably, as with most penitentiary establishments, the improvements achieved with the inmates are that they make them more criminally competent. At the end of two years he was one of Glasgow's growing band of hardmen. His exploits after that were much less farcical. Then somewhere down the slippery slope he discovered the wild world of drugs both as user and supplier.

I went to visit him once he came out of intensive care. He wasn't a pretty sight. I didn't recognise him, partly because his face looked like a current bun and partly because I hadn't seen him for a while. He couldn't see me through the bandages on his eyes and he had difficulty speaking. I left him with the ritual bag of grapes and a packet of jammy dodger biscuits (which seemed a bit silly as it was difficult so see how he'd be able to eat either) and promised to come back in a couple of days.

I went back on the afternoon of Hogmanay and took him a packet of tartan shortbread with a couple of whisky miniatures hidden underneath so the nurses didn't see them. I didn't think it was appropriate to wish him Happy New Year. His face had deflated a little and his right eye was open. I didn't ask about the other one. He was able to move his mouth to speak a little and to swig one of the miniatures. I tried to interview him lightly.

"So, what got you into this mess, Freddy? Were you knocking off somebody else's wife?"

He tried to smile but it hurt. "Naw. They shoot you in the balls fur that, no in the kisser. Naw, Jamie. That was the wife wi' the shooter. Ah saw her pull the trigger just before the blast. It was Jenny Kerrigan."

"You mean you're Gaffer Kerrigan's bum boy and his wife's jealous?"

"Don't be daft. You know Ah'm no wan o' them, an' stop tryin' tae make me laugh. It hurts like hell when Ah move ma face."

"So why does Jenny Kerrigan want to turn your face into a sieve?"

"Ah think she meant tae kill me. Y'know the Gaffer was arrested last week. They nabbed him wi' a boot load o' hash in his E-type Jag. He never handles the gear himself but his carrier smashed up on the M8 an' he had tae move it fast like. Jenny must've thought Ah shopped him."

"And you wouldn't have done a thing like that?"

"Ah cannae say Ah widnae but Ah didnae. Ah hate Kerrigan's guts but Ah'm no a grass. Any silly bugger knows it was most likely Gillespie. He's the Gaffer's right han' man these days but the cops huv him in their pockets. Kerrigan's too glaekit tae see it an' Jenny fancies him."

"Are you working for Kerrigan?"

"Christ no! Ah told you Ah hate the ugly bastard. We did time together. He's a bully an' Ah was the only one that stood up tae him. That's probably why he thinks it was me that grassed him. Gillespie thinks he can take over Kerrigan's patch an' the polis'll help him but they're just givin' him the rope tae hang himself. They'll probably finish up shootin' each other like in High Noon an' O'Connor'll rule the manor."

"So, you're working for O'Connor?"

"Aye. He treats me decent. O'Connor's no as bad as they say but he disnae like you callin' him Danny."

"So I gather. It wasn't one of his vans you were driving."

"Aye it was. He's just bought it second hand an' he's no got it painted yet."

"But what I don't understand is what you were doing out there on Christmas Day, just sitting there like a coconut at the fair.

The police say you didn't have any ice cream in the tub. What were you doing?"

"Ah cannae tell you that Jamie. No offence an aw' that."

"Did you have drugs on the van? Were you dealing?"

"It's no as simple as that."

"It can't be all that complicated."

"No, Ah cannae tell you Jamie. O'Connor treats me decent but he wid nail ma goolies tae the floor. He's no the kind of person that you want tae cross. We're no sellin' drugs in the vans, no tae the punters. You'll have tae work out the rest for yerself."

"Who were you waiting for?"

"Ah don't really know for sure but Ah think it was Gillespie or one of his boozer friends."

He opened the packet of shortbread and started nibbling.

I started to leave and he called me back.

"Hey Jamie!"

"Yes, Freddy?"

"Happy New Year."

Jenny's full maiden name was Jennifer Wilcox. Her family lived in Bearsden, one of the more affluent suburbs on the north west of the city where it begins to open out towards the Trossachs. Her father was in the management staff of British Rail and her mother was a lecturer in the teachers' training college in Bearsden. Jenny was a pretty girl but not particularly scholastic. She left school aged sixteen and began a career as a fashion model and beauty competitor. She was a finalist three years running in Miss Scotland but never the winner. About the age of eighteen or nineteen she drifted away from her cosy middle class family and was drawn to the bright lights and big spenders of the city. A couple of years later she met and married Graham Kerrigan who was her senior by some fifteen years. The Gaffer was delighted to have a pretty young model under his arm and he spoiled her with everything she asked for. For her twenty-first birthday he bought her a hairdresser's shop. Jenny had found her niche.

She changed the name to Jennyfair and with her husband's help she redesigned and refitted the interior and recruited new, younger staff. She hadn't a clue about hairdressing but she did have the flair, the style and the bossy nature to hammer it into a busy, profitable business. Graham (the Gaffer), always the schemer, always the planner, immediately saw its potential and suggested to Jenny that she should expand. Within two years she had a thriving little chain of boutique-style coiffeurs under the umbrella of Jennyfair. Inside each salon Jenny placed a mini-shop of high margin hair-care and cosmetic products. They now had a group of twelve high profile units dotted around the city. Each one had a gross turnover of about £50,000 per year. The accounts rendered to the taxman, on the other hand, showed turnover of double that figure paying out generous director's salaries to Jenny and her hubby. The Gaffer had a nice little money-laundering machine where, along with the hairy heads, his wife helped him to shampoo over half a million pounds each year. The first half million bought them a luxury villa in Marbella, Spain in the *jetset barrio.*

Lots of new, exciting products were coming onto the market so Jenny suggested that they develop the business into distribution as well. Kerrigan decided that it was best to keep Jenny's enterprises completely separate from his other "enterprises" so she made use of some of her father's contacts to locate a vacant archway lockup to rent under the railway near Central Station. The monstrous old arched wooden doors looked rather hideous till Jenny painted them pink and added the lettering in eggshell blue. *JENNYCARE providers of quality hair-care products.* Jennycare was also destined to be a provider of high quality cocaine and hash. The Gaffer now had a perfect clandestine distribution network. Jenny employed her wiggle and sweet smile to secure a good deal from the Ford dealership, a neat little fleet of Ford Fiestas painted pink with the eggshell blue logo across the side. Finding eager sales personnel was easy and Jenny had a new winner.

She now had two extremely profitable legitimate operations, both of which offered her husband a neat loophole for his not-so-legitimate operations. Jennycare quietly distributed some extra packages and the income from these was softly filtered through the cash registers of Jennyfair. Such marriages are made in heaven. Unfortunately, although she loved him dearly, he was never quite able to satisfy her sexual appetite. On Christmas Eve, when one of their little pink Fiestas flipped over the metal barrier on the M8, Jennifer was in bed with one of her husband's rugged young enforcers, the veritable James Gillespie.

The driver/sales girl escaped with minor injuries but the car was rather flattened. It went on the tow-truck to a repair shop called Kwik Recoveries near Glasgow Cross. A large billboard was visible from the motorway with the big black initials KR. These were also the initials of the repair shop owner, Kenneth Reid. Ken was a well-known associate of Danny O'Connor. When Jenny took the phone call she realised that immediate action was called for. She in turn phoned her husband and successfully imparted the urgency of the situation.

"If Reid discovers your two packages the game's up. He'll contact O'Connor or even worse he might blow the whistle to the police. You'll need to get them out of there fast before somebody looks in the boot."

She was now finished with the services of Gillespie and ushered him out. For him this was one of those *jammy* moments. He saw an opportunity to get Kerrigan out of the way, step into his shoes and slip into his bed. He headed for the nearest phone-box and called one of his friends at Strathclyde Police Headquarters.

The Gaffer moved fast. He decided that the only sure way was to go and get the packets himself. In fact he moved so fast that the waiting police car had a perfectly valid reason for stopping him as he made his getaway with the suspect boxes. He was doing over fifty miles per hour in a thirty limit. With Gillespie's tip-off they knew the purpose of his trip so they checked the car and couldn't believe their luck. They caught the legendary Gaffer in possession of significant quantities of marijuana, a Class B prohibited substance. For them this really was Christmas.

Later that day Gillespie called Jenny to console her. He had to make sure she didn't know it was he who had phoned the police so he had his ruse all prepared. He told her that the girl in the car was a girlfriend of Freddy Cassidy, one of O'Connor's men. The word on the street was that Cassidy had called the cops. Gillespie also knew where she would find him and how she could get hold of a shotgun. Next day she asked Gillespie to drive her to Blackhill where she blasted a hole in the windscreen of Freddy's van.

Into the second week of January, Freddy was still in Gartnavel Hospital, in the Kelvinside area of the city. I went to have one more try at quizzing him. The wind had swung round and was blowing the first flutter of snowflakes as I pushed through the swing doors. He had moved to one of the upstairs wards and his mother was by his bedside when I walked in. Iris Cassidy was a rough diamond with a heart of gold. She did her best for Freddy and his two sisters but her best never scored high in the mothering scales. She had been pretty once upon a time but fairy tales seldom come true on the streets of Glasgow. There are several names for her profession; streetwalker is one of the kindest. Despite her best efforts it could not be said that she was successful in motherhood. Here was her son with his bloated face, lying in a hospital bed and the two sisters were no doubt out on the streets following in her footsteps. Iris was visibly angry. Wait till she caught up with the toffee-nose cow that had blasted her son. Maybe her protective maternal instincts could have been put to better use when the kids were younger. I was angry too. Maybe some women should take better care not to become mothers in the first place. Maggie had always been good to me but at times like these I wondered about my real mother.

Freddy still wouldn't budge on further questioning. Street code says you don't grass on friends or employers. The doctors had tried hard to save his left eye but in the end gave up and concentrated on the right eye, which was now OK. He laughed at me when I walked in.

"You're looking a bit more cheerful." I said.

"Naw Jamie, it's yer T-shirt. Ah reckon that's what Ah look like." I was wearing my Iron Maiden shirt with the iconic Eddie skeleton head.

We chatted for a while till the visitors' bell sounded and I walked with Iris to the exit.

"Ah was speakin' tae the doctor. He's lost his left eye but they reckon his right eye is gontae be OK. Ah'm gontae get the bitch," she vowed intently.

"Yes," I consoled her, "It's a messy business."

"Aye, she's gontae be a messy business when Ah get her."

"What was he doing there anyway?" I asked in an attempt to sidestep the revenge issue.

"D'you no know?" she sounded surprised at my ignorance.

"Well, you heard him yourself inside. He won't open up. The most I've got out of him is that he was waiting for Gillespie but that doesn't make a lot of sense."

"It was probably Gillespie he was waitin' for but it disnae really matter. It could've been any of O'Connor's cronies."

"Freddy thinks it was Gillespie who shopped Kerrigan."

"Could've been. Who knows? They're all the same. Y'ever go tae the stock cars?" I shook my head. "You'll have seen it on the telly. They're supposed tae win by drivin' better than the other guy but the bummer that wins just usually pushes aw' the rest off the track or smashes up their cars. Gillespie thinks if he pushes Kerrigan off the track he'll take over. Sees himsel' as Mr Glasgow but he's no got the brains."

"You were telling me why Freddy was waiting for him."

"Wis Ah? Well, y'know. O'Connor has the lads sellin' ice cream because that's what the vans are for but that's no why they're in the street. He uses the vans tae move the drugs."

"Freddy says no. He says he wasn't selling drugs. I've known him quite a long time and if he doesn't want to tell me something he just clams up. He doesn't usually tell me a pack of lies. So if he says he wasn't selling I'm inclined to believe him." I assured her.

"He's tellin' you the truth. At least he's no sellin' tae the punters but he's part o' the relay."

"You're going to have to explain that."

"Oh come off it, Jamie, y'know how it works. The big boy buys the big stash an' splits it down or should Ah say he gets one o' his boys tae break in doon, then one o' the runners carries a load tae the dealer. That's the bit where they have tae move fast. The ice cream van driver is the dealer. He passes it on tae the pushers in bundles o' ten wee packets. He disnae sell it. That's aw' sorted out wi' the boss. The driver's just like a sort of courier, like"

"But the police are watching the vans. How do they keep it under wraps?"

"Hey that's a good one Jamie, under wraps. That's what they call the wee packets o' smack. Anyway that's the easy bit. They put the ten wee packets intae an empty fag packet. The pusher just goes tae the van for a packet o' ciggies like, an' he gets one o' the special packets."

"So what's in it for the driver. It's still quite risky."

"The pusher pays a fiver for the fags and disnae get any change. That's the driver's cut an' he can shift ten packets in a night, easy like, so that's fifty quid a day. That's on top o' what he's makin' off the ice cream. Freddy was doin' alright."

"How come you know all this, Iris?"

She took a cigarette packet from her coat pocket and passed it to me. I flipped it open and saw the little envelopes inside. I passed it back quickly hoping no one was watching and looked at her quizzically.

"Dinnae look at me like that! A girl's got tae make a living. Ah'm no any use for the other business any more. The motor's kind of burnt out."

She didn't realise that my look was not one of criticism, more a look of gratitude. She'd just answered the $64,000 question. I gave her a hug.

She pushed me away, "Hey fella, bugger off! What d'you take me for?" So I buggered off in my little Mini.

Iris set off in the direction of Hillhead subway station. It wasn't long before I (and the rest of Scotland) found out where she went. She stopped on the way to make a phone call in which she established that Jenny Kerrigan was in the Govan branch of Jennyfair and then she went off in that direction on the subway. She marched out of the station into 105, Ross Street and up the first flight of stairs into the swanky hairdressers salon. Jenny was standing behind the reception desk examining some invoices. The invoices scattered across the floor as the raging mother caught her prey by the collar and pinned her back against the wall and dealt her a *Glesca Kiss* (one of Glasgow's famous head butts). Still reeling from the shock Jenny grabbed out and caught the first thing at hand, a pair of hairdressing scissors. She jabbed wildly and one blow caught Iris on her arm. It drew blood and enraged the intruding woman even more. She clutched at Jenny's wrist and twisted it round till the scissors were pointing the other way and heaved all her weight forward. The point of the scissors pierced Jenny's chest and entered her lung. The victim stared in disbelief at the weapon protruding from between her breasts then collapsed on the salon floor with blood spurting from her open mouth. Iris ran out still screaming insults as she went. Jenny died in the ambulance on the way to hospital.

Iris retraced her route back to Gartnavel, first to the A and E where they patched up her wound then back to see her son. She pushed nurses and doctors aside and strode up to his bedside.

"Ah got the bitch," she informed him then turned on her heel and strode out back to the subway and on to George's Cross. The snow was now falling quite heavily. She then marched several hundred yards to Maryhill Police Station and straight in the front door. This snow covered apparition startled the desk Sergeant by announcing, "You'll be looking for me for stabbing that bag o' shite in Govan. Ah'm here tae gi'e masel' in."

By presenting herself at the police station before the arrest warrant was issued she bought herself what the Americans call a plea bargain. Instead of murder she was eventually charged with culpable homicide. Although she had expressed clear intent to kill Jenny, the only two witnesses were her son and myself and neither of us was going to go singing to the police. It was Jenny who first lifted the weapon and first used it and it was still in her hand when it entered her body. Perhaps for the first time in her life Iris considered herself jammy.

The balance of power

Graham Kerrigan was desolate. His arrest really shook him; he thought he was above the law, untouchable. When the two uniforms snapped the handcuffs on him it was a gross indignity. He was accustomed to dismissing inspectors and superintendents with scornful contempt. He was twisted between thinking about whether Jenny would be able to take over for a while or whether it was her who had shopped him. It had all happened so fast. Then word got to him that his wife had paid off the person responsible and he felt ashamed that he had doubted her. Then, a prison warden rattled his cage and announced that Jenny was dead in the same ambivalent tone as one of his mates announced ten minutes earlier that it was snowing. He couldn't quite take it all in. This wasn't happening. The only thing that convinced him of the reality of his plight was the stench of the cell

He was remanded in custody pending trial and taken to Barlinnie prison. The governor allowed him out briefly under heavy guard to attend his wife's funeral. All of Jenny's family were there. All of Jenny's family avoided any form of contact with Kerrigan. At their express request the priest omitted any mention of her husband. What they could never have realised was how much their cold affront rallied his defences and steeled him to the task ahead. He was the Gaffer. That meant the boss. He was used to people doing what he said. If he didn't act now he would lose everything he'd worked to build. He would miss Jenny but there were plenty more fish in the sea. First he had to find out who had really shopped him and square the debt. Then he had to find someone fast who could take the helm in his absence. He knew for sure that he was going down for a few years so he had to act now before his trial. He wasn't just going to roll over and give up. He'd done time before when he was younger and he knew how to work the system. Keep his nose clean, get others to do the dirty work and keep on the sweet side of the screws. He'd lost his wife, lost his liberty and lost a sizable chunk of street credibility but he had no intention of losing the business he had carefully built up. It was time to call in some favours but not from anyone in Glasgow.

Gillespie, meanwhile, was thinking on his feet. With the Gaffer out of the way there was a slot to be filled, who better than himself to fill it? Iris was right; he saw himself as the new Mr Glasgow. The only problem was a lack of funds. If you want to be a drugs baron you need to be able to buy in at the top end. He needed a backer. But Iris was not so right about him having no brains. The fire with the floodlights wasn't down to him. It was one of the younger lads deciding to be smart. His smart thinking with the police had put O'Connor on the spot and he got away Scot-free. He re-thought the whole episode and decided that somebody else must have moved in quickly to get the salvage boys to clear out all the cigarettes. That somebody was probably the person that O'Connor had been trying to double deal. The trail led to Sam Horton's door. Sam Horton must have bankrolled the cigarette caper in the first place. It wasn't the only caper that he'd funded. Gillespie had just thought of the perfect banker.

While all this was taking place I was brought back into the loop of normality by a call from David MacLucas at the radio station. He was ready to go live with a programme idea we had tossed around the year before. It was to be a crossbreed between Crimewatch and Question Time, a mix of guest panel and public phone-in where the central theme was crime versus law and order. I was invited to be the anchor on this new Friday night show. David wanted me to come in to sort out who would be the panellists on the first batch of programmes and to discuss the outline topics. We tossed around ideas for names and settled in the end for "Street Patrol". The next couple of weeks were occupied with planning and calling in our panellists. This part was more difficult than we had imagined. Anyway, we got off to a good start the first week with a lively debate on the increasing number of women prisoners in Scottish remand establishments. The second week we covered the dramatic rise in shoplifting. Our panel was composed of TV presenter, Joyce Wilson; Strathclyde's youngest police Superintendent, Sandra Paterson; Sheriff Peter Anderson; and Yasser Ahmed, councillor and businessman. We had great problems finding somebody to represent the Retail trade. Large retailers can be wary of allowing local managers to speak to the press. Eventually we successfully recruited the fresh-faced new Development Director of JS Coutts, William Chryton.

The show that night got off to a great start when a caller told us how easy it was to go to his local pub and obtain stolen goods at knock down prices. You could go along and place your order for what you needed and it was there next night. The pub in question was called "The Jammy Dodger" in Sauchiehall Street and was one of the best known in the city. The callers were now queuing on the line to share their experiences on air. One woman wanted to know who to ask for in the pub. Halfway through the programme the tone changed as we got a string of angry outbursts from some small shopkeepers. Then we had a call from one particularly agitated shop owner. He had an Asian accent and his ire seemed at first to be directed at Yasser Ahmed.

"What about this Horton fellow? Why is nothing being done to stop him?" the caller demanded.

"Is he one of the people shoplifting to order?" asked the young Superintendent, "If we have specific details we will investigate but it is better if you come to the police station. Or if you prefer we can come to visit you. You can give your name and address in confidence to the programme controller."

"He's not a petty shoplifter. He's a gangster. That's who he is. I want to ask the person on your panel from Coutts. Why do you continue to employ this person when you know he is a criminal? Why is nobody doing anything to stop him?"

I glanced across at poor William Chryton from Coutts. His face had the look of sheer panic. He had no idea how to respond. I turned to my producer and signalled him to cut the call. The relief on Chryton's face was clearly evident as we pushed the discussion back to shoplifting. He was surprisingly quick to recover and explained that part of the remit in his new job was shop layout where high value and high-risk items were strategically located around the shop so as to discourage theft. Cash desk layout and sales gondolas were being redesigned to give the assistants a clearer view of all four corners of the shop. The thieves love blind spots he explained and just a few alterations could enable greater staff vigilance.

The next caller came on and explained how his two neighbours went supermarket shopping each week. Apparently they each took a trolley and placed identical items in each one. Then one went through a checkout paying for the goods. She took the shopping to her car and returned to the shop with her receipt, which she gave to her neighbour. The neighbour pushed her trolley through an unattended cash-point and walked out with an authentic receipt to cover her if stopped. Next caller was a manager from Woolworth's complaining that it was practically impossible to get the Police to prosecute. Sandra Paterson explained that it was the Procurator Fiscal who usually refused to prosecute because the evidence was inconclusive. The thieves often had a valid receipt from a previous purchase, as the last caller explained, or they took items without a price label or they removed the price label. It was thus impossible to say with certainty what shop it was from. Most shoplifters, she claimed, were nowadays operating in gangs and stole to get money to buy drugs. It was a serious and increasing problem but was just one symptom of the continuing drug problem and extremely difficult to get a conviction.

The wind-up signal came and I closed the programme with the usual thank-yous. As we came off air somebody suggested it would be fun to go for a drink in the Jammy Dodger and since it was walking distance from the studio we all agreed. One of the advantages of radio over TV is that the participants can walk into a bar without every head turning. We looked like any other after office drink group apart from Joyce Wilson who raised a few curious faces from their beer glasses. We found an empty table and sat down. Empty is perhaps not the best description; we had to push a clutter of abandoned glasses to one end. Do they not clear tables anymore?

"Maybe we'll see some shoplifted goods changing hands," suggested Joyce with her TV presenter exuberance.

"These things are often a bit overplayed," doubted Sheriff Anderson, "I don't think they really do their business in the public view like that. Sometimes I think the proprietors start these stories to give their bar a bit of a legend."

Sandra Paterson closed her eyes and looked up to the heavens in mock exasperation, "If you care to look over at the table in the corner on your right, Sheriff, the one with the ginger haired girl. I think that's a toaster, a food mixer, a couple of hairdryers, a cassette player and a few other things still in their boxes. Maybe she's getting married and having her show of presents in the pub."

We all turned to look. The girl saw us looking and called to an older woman by the bar. They scooped up their wares into two large bags and were out the door before the bemused Sheriff could muster an answer.

"That was Jenny Harper," said Sandra, "We have pin-ups of her and her family in the station canteen. We might manage to bring her before you one day soon Sheriff. They're a clever bunch; know all the dodges. They're getting bolder and getting bigger. It's a good going family business."

"This is exciting," bubbled the exuberant Joyce, "I don't think I've seen a real thief before, not like that actually doing the business."

"It's thieving, not something to get excited about," reprimanded Councillor Ahmed, "and the people who buy these goods are just as bad as the thieves. It's not a game and it's not just petty crime. The police and the courts need to take it more seriously. That woman Harper is a gangster. I've heard about her before. Why is nothing being done to stop her?"

"That's what the other man said but he wasn't talking about her," recalled Sandra.

"What other man?" asked the Sheriff.

"That guy that got really angry on the programme. He was going on about somebody called Morton. No, it was Horton. He said *He's not a petty shoplifter. He's a gangster. Why is nobody doing anything to stop him?* Then he got sidelined and Jamie rather niftily pulled things back onto shoplifting. But he was really angry and I got the feeling some of you knew what he was shouting about. Is it something that needs investigating? He wanted to ask you Mr Chryton but you didn't answer him. Does this Horton work with your company?"

William Chryton shuffled uncomfortably, "I know Sam Horton and yes he works with Coutts. It's actually a bit delicate. You see, my posting as Development Director in fact sort of relegates Horton in the company hierarchy. The directors of the parent company don't feel that their development objectives are being achieved but he's been in the position for a number of years. They know that the job doesn't receive 100% of his time but I'm pretty sure they don't know of any improprieties. Something like that would have made it easier to move him out."

"Actually," I contributed, "Horton is one of the subjects in a case I have been following recently. It would appear he was a central figure in a million pound cigarette robbery. You will be surprised to learn that the cigarettes belonged to Coutts. I've also heard the stories about him ripping off the people who take over the shops that Coutts have dropped. Most of them are Asian families. What do you have on the matter Yasser?" I asked the Councillor.

"I have had a number of complaints about this gentleman," he replied, "but it's difficult to pin down anything concrete. Coutts' bookkeeping is rather a mess. They don't have full records of these transactions or at least nobody seems to be able to find them. The one occasion that I visited the offices it reminded me of a bunch of kittens chasing their own tails. I couldn't find anybody who'd been more than a few months in their position. I don't wish to sound impertinent Mr Chryton but I think you are the latest member of a not very distinguished club. Anyway the stories I have heard are all basically the same. Several of your shops are in lower grade shopping arcades or in streets that have lost a lot of their passing trade but they can be quite attractive to some of my constituents because all the family are prepared to work the shop. They sign up to take over the let or rental and agree a price for the stock. Then along comes Horton who says they must also pay for the fixtures and fittings and this has to be paid in a separate contract. It seems to me that these items were written off in depreciation many years ago and don't appear in Coutts' accounts so I believe that the money filters into Horton's pocket. It is very annoying but that is not what is really angering my people. About a year or so after taking over the shop it suffers mysteriously from a burglary but the thieves don't break in; they appear to have keys and just open the door and walk in. There seems to be general agreement that Horton is acquiring keys, organising the gang and reaping the rewards from a safe distance. I have never heard anything about a large cigarette robbery but it would fit with the modus operandi. There's no smoke without fire, they say."

Chryton looked directly at me. "Could I ask you a favour?" he asked. "Is it possible for you to put out a carefully worded statement, perhaps a news bulletin outlining the charges that were made on your programme. That would make his position with the company less tenable. I think the board would then be in a position to ask for his resignation. It's not as good as a straightforward prosecution but the evidence is a bit weak for that anyway and perhaps without his office to hide in he might make some move that flushes him out into the open."

I considered his proposal for a moment. "I think he's more likely to disappear into the woodwork but it would put a stop to a lot of his current activities. If you can excuse me for a moment I'll see what I can do." I went to the bar in search of a public phone and called my friend Hamish.

"Hello Hamish. You wouldn't happen to have a little copy space on the front page for tomorrow. I just need a few lines but it's a kicker and you'll have exclusive."

"If you can have it here inside five minutes. We're about to go to press early tonight."

"Have you got a pencil handy? I'll give it to you now. Like I said, I just need a few lines but it needs to be front page."

"OK, fire away as long as it isn't any of your daft ice cream capers."

I gave him a snappy synopsis of the angry phone call and the councillor's back up stories. I held back on the cigarette affair with O'Connor and Gillespie but I insisted that he include the comment, "Why is nothing being done to stop him?" Then with the job done I went back to the table. We finished our drinks; the party broke up and we all went our merry ways.

About a week later I got a thank you phone call from Chryton. Sam Horton had negotiated a severance package and had already cleared his office. As I replaced the phone in its cradle I became aware that I had crossed the line that we journalists constantly tread. Our job is to report events as we see them but what we write can often alter the course of these events dramatically. Horton was now rethinking his career thanks to the few lines that I had published. I later discovered that within a couple of days of being ousted from his cosy job at Coutts he had a visit from James Gillespie looking for a backer who would help him become the city's key supplier of magic mushrooms. It was the opportunity Horton was looking for, one he couldn't resist. No need to dirty his hands, all he had to do was put up £100,000 and keep an eye on Gillespie to make sure he stuck to the agreed pathways. Horton would get a 25% cut every time the pot rotated which ought to be at least once a month. This would fetch him quite a nice pension of £25,000 a month.

There is no doubt in my mind that May 1981 was the turning point in the crazy ice cream war saga and I was one of the prime catalysts. I was not the only catalyst, though, many people and events factored in.

If you watch TV, you will have heard of Kenneth MacAlpine. We are not speaking here of the ancient King of Scotland but arguably the king of Scottish businessmen. Better known as "Ken Mac" he ranks high in the who's who of the British rich list. His first fortune came from a chain of garden centres which he sold to a large seed producer for an eight-figure number. From there he went on to develop the UK's foremost franchise group of kids' soft play centres. He bought out the Italian company that makes the play equipment and MacAlpine Softplay is now developing rapidly across Europe. With a move into the adult market he launched an exclusive chain of city centre golf practice units under the name Kenmac with its tentacles reaching into Japan, the Middle East and the new emerging Chinese markets.

What few people know about Kenneth is that this entrepreneurial empire kicked off with an ice cream van that he bought, second hand, for £400. He was born in Falkirk in Stirlingshire, and lived with his parents in an end terrace house in the little town of Polmont overlooking the Forth estuary and the endless plumes of smoke from the Grangemouth oil refinery and Longannet Electric Power Station. He was a bright kid at school and was destined to become a teacher. At that time Falkirk boasted its own Callendar Park Teacher Training College and Kenneth started his course there in 1973. He was an enterprising lad and took on a variety of weekend and vacation jobs to supplement his student grant. In his last year of study and with the massive sum of

£120 in his savings account he set about looking for a second hand car. It was the spring of 1976 and as he thumbed through the classifieds in the local paper he saw that the Scottish Woodlands group were looking for tree planters for the Easter break. There was a programme of forestation in a large tract of land next to the site of the William Wallace battlefield behind Callendar Park. So off he went to spend his holiday planting Scots Pine and Spruce. The wages were based on the number of trees planted. At the end of two weeks his savings had swelled to £400 and the same week he got his cheque for the student grant. Back in the classified section of the Falkirk Herald he scanned the second hand vehicle section and out it jumped. *Fully equipped ice cream van £400.* There was no real thought went into his reaction. He phoned the seller, went to see it and bought it. Two months later he graduated with a Diploma in Education but there were no teaching vacancies anywhere in the central area of Scotland. Ken went into business as an ice cream man. The summer of 1976 was the hottest on record. Ice cream sales went through the roof. Kenneth made his first modest fortune.

As the summer slipped into autumn several ice cream companies optimistically placed orders for new vans and sold their old ones. Ken bought three and had no difficulty finding drivers in the Thatcher-snatcher cutback era. He wasn't saddled with factory premises like his competitors. He bought his ice cream where it was good quality at a good price: the Frazzini factory in Cumbernauld. In 1978 he bought his first new van and by 1980 he had a fleet of twenty with five more ordered for the coming year. He rented an old boat yard by the side of the canal to park the vans and along with it came a tract of about three acres of land. His tree planting exploits of 1976 had sparked an interest in arboriculture. He cleaned up the parcel of land and filled half of it with coniferous and deciduous seedlings and the other half with young fruit trees and ornamental bushes. In the spring of eighty-one he applied successfully for a trading licence for a garden centre and decided to sell off his ice cream business and expand the garden centre.

His sales technique was simple. He drove one of his vans out to Cumbernauld to the Frazzini depot and offered the package to Charlie.

"I've got twenty-five vans working between the Forth and the Clyde and over into Fife, all making good profits. I want to move over into another business so I won't fart about. You can have the lot for £30,000. I haven't offered the business to anyone else; it's yours if you want it but I need a decision within a week."

"I'll give you the answer now," said Charlie, "a definite yes but I'll need the week to arrange the finance."

They shook hands on the deal. Ken Mac would have the cash to develop his new baby and Charlie Frazzini would take a sizeable step towards being the owner of the biggest ice cream outfit in Scotland. The only problem was for cash-strapped Charlie to find thirty thousand Pounds.

I wouldn't have known anything of these developments if it hadn't been for a chance meeting with my friend Myra. I was at a High Court hearing in the Sheriff Court building in Dumbarton, north west of the city, covering the trial of a local butcher who had murdered his wife and disposed of her body parts in the minced meat that he sold to the local baker to put in his pies. Apparently she had been having an affair with the baker and butcher Joe saw it as justifiable retribution. The jury didn't agree. Myra was at the court for another case to be heard by the Sheriff; a shop manager that she had caught embezzling. Scotland really is the land of entrepreneurs, you know! This lad bought a second hand cash register from the local classifieds and he installed it in the Coutts shop alongside the legitimate version. When he cashed up at night all the takings from the bogus till went in his pocket. His case had been set back by an hour so this gave Myra and I some time for a coffee and a chat.

Fortunately, Dumbarton had one of the new Gregg's eateries with decent coffee and a very palatable range of cakes and pies; a definite step up from the CB Lite Bite although the tables were equally messy.

"I've been meaning to catch you up," declared Myra, "I owe you a big thank you for the piece you did on Horton. That bastard got right under my skin and now we're shot of him thanks mostly to you. I must admit I never thought you took me seriously about Horton."

"I think I owe you an equally big thank you," I replied, "after all you pointed me down a track I could never have seen on my own. It's amazing the stones I've turned since our first meeting with lots of ugly bugs under each one but I've still not pinned down exactly what happened on the night of your cigarette bust. I'm sure Angela McCabe didn't tell me all she knew. I also discovered that you were right about the connection between the cigarettes and the ice cream vans." I told Myra what I found out from Iris Cassidy about flogging the drugs in the empty cigarette packets.

"I knew it!" Myra whooped as if she had just picked the lucky scratch card, "I knew there was a connection but the drug thing is interesting. Neither you nor me were convinced about them peddling drugs but that makes sense. We thought they were just dealing illegal ciggies but using the ciggy packets as a cover for the big stuff, hey, that's nasty territory they're into. Watch your back Jamie. These are big, bad bogeymen."

"Yes, I know," I conceded. "Actually, I've got a bad feeling, Myra. I think it's going to get a lot nastier on these vans. The heat wave of '76 brought a lot of new vans onto the road. It's a tough business out there for the honest Johnnies who just want to sell ice cream. They're already like a pack of dogs fighting over a bone. Throw drugs into the equation and the odds are stacked higher. A few more people are going to get bitten. Freddy Cassidy lost an eye and that's the worst we've seen so far but I can see somebody getting topped before it all ends."

"Is that raspberry-topped or chocolate-topped? Myra cackled at her own morbid joke.

"You've been watching too much Chic Murray," I chastened. "Anyway, what's been happening in your *barrio*, apart from friend Horton?"

"You mean Coutts? It's a bit like you've just said about the ice cream thing. It's going to get worse before it gets better. Our American bosses have taken over the Milligan's chain of shops in the north of England and the Salisbury group down south. Last count we were about six hundred shops. We're changing our name to Coutts Salisbury. I don't know what happened to poor old Milligan but his name got dropped. Six hundred is a hell of a lot of wee shops to manage. It wouldn't be so bad if some of them knew what they were doing but the faces change every other week. Up here in Glasgow there's just me and Tom Sturgeon left from the old days."

"I don't think I know any Tom Sturgeon. Who's he?" I interrupted.

"Old Tom? He used to be one of the Divisional Managers. He covered Fife and the Lothians. He should have been made one of the directors but he didn't like the way things were developing and was daft enough to speak his mind so instead of going up the ladder he hit a snake's head and went down. Nowadays he's just one of the supervisors but he's quite happy just dodging away. And believe me, just dodging away he's worth ten of these bright-eyed new boys. It was him that spotted this guy with the extra cash register. He knew it looked out of place and he gave me a call to check it out."

"Aye. It's the same everywhere these days. The old experienced hands are pushed aside to make way for the fast guns."

"It could be worth your while having a word with Tom. He was on the team that stacked the cigarettes upstairs in the Mearns. Like Angela, he knows more than he's letting on…" She stopped talking as if she was trying to remember something then she looked up abruptly and continued.

"I forgot to tell you. Angela McCabe's not with us now either, another old face moved on. She started with Coutts when she was about seventeen. She's working with Charlie Frazzini now, taking care of the bookkeeping. Rumour has it that Charlie had some kind of breakdown or depression or something and she stepped in to help. He still runs the frontline business side and managing the vans but she controls the purse strings. He's the Captain but she's the First Mate with her hand on the tiller making sure the ship doesn't run aground." She sniggered again at her droll humour.

"You're very metaphoric, Myra," I praised her prose. "Why don't you take up the quill? Maybe you could try your hand at poetry."

"Bugger off Robertson! Shut up and listen before I forget again. Charlie went out and bought twenty-five vans at one shake of the stick. He agreed to take over an outfit from Falkirk last month without checking back with Angela. She had to scramble around looking for thirty thousand quid to back the deal but she managed to dig Charlie out of the hole he'd dug himself. That's another metaphor. Isn't it? Anyway, you know Yasser Ahmed. Don't you? Of course you do; he was on your programme. Well it seems he came up with the goodies on the condition that Charlie's vans buy their lollipops and chewy toffees from his cash and carry confectionery warehouse. You probably know that Charlie usually lets his drivers do their own sourcing but he managed to persuade enough of them to switch to Ahmed's, at least in the short term."

I think Myra might have droned on all day until I reminded her why she was there. "Your case is on in ten minutes. Do you mind if I sit in with you? I might get two lead stories for the price of one."

"Good idea! I'll introduce you to Tom if there's time. He's got to be here as a witness. And then we need to meet up again and really catch up," she said as she scrambled to her feet. She opened her bag and produced a business card, which she stuffed into my hand. " You can give me a ring at my new office."

I glanced down at the card:

MYRA BLUNT

Director of Security

Coutts Salisbury Retail.

Well, maybe they weren't as out of touch as she claimed. Last time I met her she was just Security Manager. Somebody had the sense to see her value to the company. Or maybe she knew something about one of the bosses! Anyway, as luck would have it, I never met her friend Tom Sturgeon that day. It would be several years before our paths would cross again. However I was glad that I stayed. I filed two good pieces that day and proved convincingly to Hamish that I could still cut it in the murky world of crime: *"The butcher who put his wife in the mincing machine"* and *"The shop manager who brought in his own cash register".*

Just helping with enquiries

I love to see my stories in print. Call it egocentric and say it's just work but after all these years I still get a buzz when I pick up a newspaper and find a piece I've written myself. I also like to get the other papers and see how the other hacks have hacked it. I know it's childish but anyway that's what I was doing next morning. All the others had a front-page header with the butcher who butchered his wife and of course it had been on all the TV news the previous night but it looked like I was the only one with the clandestine cash register. No doubt they had all gone shooting off to get their butcher copy in. So meeting Myra was quite providential.

The first phone call that morning was from Hamish, "Morning Jamie. Those were two nice pieces. Just called to say thanks." This was not typical Hamish. He must be wanting something. "You know we never got around to that Sunday lunch I promised you for the Irish piece you did for me. You went bounding off to see a fire somewhere and never called me back. Why don't we make it this Sunday?" Now I knew he was definitely wanting something but I decided to play along. We fixed it for one o'clock at the Boat House.

Next call, from Superintendent Sandra Paterson, was not so friendly and to be honest I was taken aback by her officious tone, "Good morning Mr Robertson. I'd like you to come into the station. We have a matter to discuss."

"OK. What's it about? When did you have in mind?"

"Now. I'd like you to come now please. We'll discuss what it's about when you're here." Her tone was distinctly hostile.

"And if I can't arrange to come right now?" I probed.

"I can send a squad car if you prefer," she challenged.

"This doesn't sound like a friendly invitation. Am I going to be under arrest? Why don't you come and arrest me yourself? I think I might quite like that, Jamie Robertson arrested by the pretty young police Superintendent."

"This isn't a joking matter," she snapped, "I don't plan to arrest you at this stage but it is serious and I'd like your cooperation."

"So why don't we just have a friendly chat over a cup of coffee? Why the formal summons?" I tried to lighten the issue.

"It will be a formal recorded interview. I'll expect you in about thirty minutes," she snapped again. "I take it you know where to come, Central Police Office. Ask the desk sergeant for the Special Investigations Unit."

"Yes Ma'am. Right away Ma'am. But listen, you have to promise I won't get a parking ticket," I teased.

"Don't be flippant Mr Robertson. I did consider a formal arrest but hoped that since we know each other it would not be necessary. Perhaps I was wrong. I can still arrange that squad car."

"OK lass, keep your hair on. If it's that important I'll be there as quick as I can," I snapped back and thumped the phone back into its rest. "Cheeky bitch," I muttered to myself as I fumbled around for my jacket and car keys, "they get a couple of extra stripes and think they rule the city. What the hell's so bloody urgent anyway?"

I remembered there was a big hole in my shirt. My first thought was not to bother changing but I'm scruffy not tatty. A Dennis the Menace sweatshirt was the first thing that came to hand. Somehow it seemed sufficiently inappropriate. The streets were quiet so the drive just took a few minutes. I found a parking space quite near the police station, just as well because I didn't think I could rely on Super Sandra to cancel a ticket. I knew the desk sergeant and tried to quiz him about what she wanted.

"All I can tell you is I reckon you've pissed somebody off big time. It came from above." He showed me where to go to find her office.

> Superintendent S. Paterson
> Special Investigations Unit

I knocked on the door and waited a few minutes before a WPC opened the door and signalled me in. Sandra Paterson stood up and came out from behind her desk. "Thank you for coming, Mr Robertson. I can offer you that coffee you wanted but I'm afraid this isn't just a cosy chat. Mary, can you bring us a couple of coffees? Please sit down Mr Robertson." She proffered a chair.

I decided that my "flippant" banter would get me nowhere so I just took the chair and sat down silently. After all I was supposed to be an expert in interview technique and I knew that if you say nothing it forces the other person to open the conversation. Her opening was direct.

"Do you know Joe McGuiness?"

"I know a Joe McGuiness, yes. I don't know if it's the same Joe McGuiness. We had a coffee and a cosy chat once."

"This Joe McGuiness?" She handed me some photos. The face was puffed up and bruised but it looked like the Coutts supervisor from Newton Mearns.

"It looks like him. I only met him once."

"Are you sure about that?"

"Absolutely sure."

"That doesn't correspond with what I've been told."

I didn't respond.

"Joe McGuiness was your source of information on a large theft of cigarettes from a shop in Newton Mearns as a result of which he has been "punished" by those responsible."

"Joe McGuiness told me nothing. I already knew about the theft before I met him. He insisted that no theft had ever taken place. And for the record our meeting was by chance not by arrangement. Like I told you we just chatted about horseracing over a cup of coffee."

"I don't believe you."

"That's your choice."

"Then who is your source of information? Why have you not informed us about the theft? Why have you not published any story about it?"

"Does the prize money double for each one I get correct?" I couldn't resist taking a jibe at her pompous stance.

"The judge's sentence might double for each one you get wrong."

"I don't understand your antagonistic approach."

"Are you planning to answer my questions? Do you need me to repeat them?"

"No, but I need you to listen to the answers. I have no definite proof that any theft took place. The company didn't report it at the time. Therefore I have not committed an offence by failing to report the little that I know. I haven't gone to press with anything for the same reason."

"You didn't answer my first question."

"That's correct. I didn't."

"You've been in this game long enough to know that withholding evidence is an offence."

"You didn't listen. I said you would need to listen. Do you need me to repeat my answers?"

"You're not being helpful. In fact I would say you are being obstructive."

"You didn't ask for my help. You asked me here for a formal interview. Do you think you need my help?"

"You're not just obstructive. You're a twisted little man. You think you're smart. You think you can just go poking your nose into things just to get a story without accepting the consequences."

"You still haven't listened to my answers."

"Repeat your answers!"

"Repeat your questions." I remembered her questions perfectly but I knew this would throw her.

She shuffled a pile of papers irritably.

"You got your information from McGuiness."

"That's a statement, an erroneous statement, not a question and it certainly isn't one of the three questions you asked me. If you don't remember them I will repeat them for you and repeat my answers. You asked why I haven't reported a theft to the police. I was not involved with any theft and I have no proof that it took place and the company involved did not report that their goods had been stolen. You asked why I haven't gone to press with the story. My investigations are ongoing and as of now I have nothing that I can support with evidence. You asked for my source of information. I have several sources but most of what I know or rather suspect has come from poking my twisted little nose into things that the police are oblivious of. So you are not in a position to insist on knowing my source about a crime that according to police records never took place. I have a question for you. Have you bothered your pretty little arse to check with your own records office for details of this cigarette theft?"

"No, I haven't. I suppose you're about to tell me that it's not on record."

"Wow! An honest answer! Yes, I can tell you that when I checked there was no record of a robbery. That was the substance of the conversation I had with McGuiness. He said that he had no knowledge of any robbery but I am fairly sure he was involved."

"So why did he get his face pulverised?"

"Maybe he was welching on some of his big bets. He puts heavy money on the horses and he's into a poker school somewhere. He's a nightclub bouncer at the weekends so he should have been able to defend himself. Maybe it was somebody he bounced who came back to bounce him. Maybe it was the husband of some lady he's been bouncing on the side. How the hell am I supposed to know? I'm a reporter; I report crime. You're the police officer; you investigate it. Why do you think he got his face remodelled?"

"His wife says the two guys who jumped him said it was a message from Horton and Gillespie. They said it was for grassing to the press."

"Look! Do you want my help or do you just want my scalp? I liked you when we met on my programme. I thought you were a refreshing new face with a fresh new view. You're just like all the other young upstarts on the force but I suppose I should really be saying thank you. Now I have a story to go to press with. I have just been formally interviewed by a senior officer about a hitherto unreported robbery and the vicious attack on a company employee. You have just given me the chance to print the story without the risk of libel."

"You **are** a twisted little man. You wouldn't dare."

"Read tomorrow's papers"

"I can hold you here on any trumped up excuse. You won't get your story out."

"Christ Almighty girl! Don't you know when to shut up? Can I quote you on what you just said? Just imagine the headline: RADIO PROGRAMME CANCELLED WHILE PRESENTER IS HELD BY POLICE TO STOP HIM REVEALING HIS STORY. Back off Sandra! I'm on your side but I'm not prepared to take this shit you're throwing at me. Why don't we start again, informal, off the record? I'll tell you what I think I know."

There was a knock on the door. WPC Mary appeared with a tray of coffees. "Thank you, Mary," said Super Sandra as she dismissed the WPC. "Before we get informal and cosy there's more I have to ask you. How well do you know Samuel Horton?"

"I've never met him," I replied as I reached forward for my coffee.

"Never? You've never met him but you seem to know a lot about him?"

"I know quite a lot about Adolph Hitler but I never met him."

Her hackles went up. It's a lovely expression that. When a tabby cat faces down a rival you can actually see the fur on her back standing straight up. We humans don't really have hackles like the cat but we can't hide it when we are angry. Sandra was struggling to retain her composure. In the end she recovered, ignored my flippancy and plunged on. "And James Gillespie? You're not going to deny that you know Gillespie?"

"Everybody in Glasgow knows Gillespie. He's the original *heid banger* except it's other people's heads that he usually bangs. I suppose you know he's often called Jammy same as me. The kids in school called me Jammy because of my name Robertson. Gillespie acquired the title because he was too jammy to be real every time he was caught by the police. Your lads just let him go every time even when they had enough solid evidence to put him away. But, in answer to your question, yes I know James Gillespie very well. We have met on many occasions. The last time was the night he set fire to the warehouse containing the stolen cigarettes that were never stolen. On that occasion he was apprehended by your officers while still at the scene of the crime. Half an hour later and he was walking free."

"Gillespie is a useful informant. We have him on a tight leash."

"If you really believe that you're an incompetent idiot who should not be wearing the insignia of Superintendent. I am fairly sure that you achieved the rank on merit and that you are very, very competent. So why don't we stop playing these games. Gillespie is a psychopath. He will snap any leash that is put on him and he'll snap the neck of anyone trying to restrain him. You cannot seriously believe that he is under control."

"He's a valuable source of information."

"Bollocks!"

"I beg your pardon?"

"You heard me clearly. I think you understood me. I said *bollocks*. He's feeding you what he thinks you want to hear."

"I can't go into detail but the matter has been sanctioned at a level much higher than Superintendent. Personally I am inclined towards your interpretation of his usefulness but for the moment I have to follow the official line."

"My answer remains the same. Bollocks! A crime is a crime. If the police catch the criminal, they prosecute. That's the law. That's the creed by which justice stands or falls. You can't pick and choose. The purpose and duty of the police is to uphold, apply and enforce the law. I believe the expression is *without fear or favour*"

"You're an arrogant bastard, Jamie Robertson."

"That's the nicest thing you've said to me since you invited me to the party."

"You claim you don't know Horton."

"That's what I said. I know who he is, more or less, but I have never to my knowledge met him."

"And I suppose you've never met Daniel O'Connor either?"

"On the contrary, Danny and I are old acquaintances."

"You mean you are old friends."

I shook my head slowly and smiled wryly, "Danny O'Connor doesn't have friends."

"He has Freddy Cassidy."

"Freddy's just a loyal puppy."

"Freddy's a good friend of yours, I believe."

"If Strathclyde Police were as diligent at prosecuting Gillespie as they have been at prosecuting Freddy Cassidy they'd score more Brownie points."

"You visited him several times when he was in hospital. Were you in any way connected with the subsequent fatal attack on Jenny Kerrigan? Did you know what Iris Cassidy was planning?"

"I knew she was angry."

"Do you know why she was angry?"

"Jenny Kerrigan had just shot her son."

"Why should Jenny Kerrigan have anything to do with a waste of space like Cassidy?"

"Maybe you should be asking Gillespie."

"You're still not being very helpful."

"I'm answering your questions."

"Your answers aren't very helpful."

"Maybe it's the way you ask the questions."

"Have you at any time had any form of association with Daniel O'Connor?"

"I have interviewed him in the course of my work."

"When was the last time you spoke to him?"

"Just before Christmas."

"What was the material basis of your meeting?"

"You mean what did we talk about?"

"I mean why did you meet with O'Connor? What was the purpose of the meeting?"

"I went to speak to him."

"What did you talk about?" She actually cracked a smile.

"You're really quite attractive when you smile, you know." I didn't like this hostile confrontation but she ignored my diversionary tactics.

"What did you talk about?" she repeated, this time without the smile.

"We talked about cigarettes."

"The stolen cigarettes that were never stolen?"

I burst out laughing.

"What's so funny? Do we get to share the joke?"

"Yes, O'Connor was rampaging about somebody stealing his cigarettes."

"I don't understand."

"Well after the fire a lot of the cigarettes were still intact; they were salvaged. Then they disappeared. I thought O'Connor had *stolen* them from himself so he wouldn't have to pay for them but it seems somebody else *stole* them from the burnt out warehouse. O'Connor says it was a sort of phantom gang who go behind the Salvage Corp and I reckon that if Danny Boy doesn't have them it's probably Horton."

"You're beginning to lose me," Sandra frowned.

"You're not so attractive when you frown. I prefer the smiling version."

She continued frowning. "Why do you think Sam Horton would want cigarettes that were previously stolen from the company who have just fired him? You don't suppose he was planning to take them back and say *look what I've found* and they would all love him and give him his job back. You've lost me on this one."

"Maybe I didn't explain this but it's a fair bet it was Horton who set up the original theft. I believe, but can't be certain, that O'Connor agreed to store them, sell them and pay for them in instalments."

"So why torch the place? That doesn't make any sense."

"If your officers had held onto Gillespie you wouldn't need to be asking me all these silly questions. Gillespie was hired by O'Connor to move the boxes to his place on the south side and make it look like a robbery but friend Jammy ballsed it up and set light to the place. Horton isn't stupid; he realised what was going down and hired the phantom salvage gang to get back what was left of the haul."

"How do you know all this?"

"You haven't been listening. I DON'T KNOW ALL THIS," I raised my voice in frustration, "I'm a crime reporter. I go poking my nose into hornets' nests and try not to get it stung. It's all just supposition but you know the name Jammy has stuck with me all these years because I have a knack of getting lucky and sometimes my suppositions turn into good stories. The only two things we know for certain are that there were cigarettes in Scotland Street and Gillespie was there when the place went up in flames. Then some silly bugger let him off the leash."

"What about the Londoner?" she interrupted, ignoring my renewed jibe at the Gillespie affair.

"You mean the train?" I asked, not quite sure what she was getting at, "You think they shunted a wagon onto the tail of the London train and shipped them south? That would get them out of Glasgow but it's a bit far fetched. Wait a minute! You're not going to tell me that you got this *valuable information* from your reliable informant, Gillespie?"

"What the hell are you babbling about?" She snapped, "Who mentioned trains? I asked if you knew the Londoner?"

"Who's he? Or is it she?"

"You don't know?"

"This conversation is becoming ludicrous. No, I don't know anybody called the Londoner."

"Well, well, well!"

"You sound like Dixon of Dock Green."

"Who's he?"

"Forget it. It doesn't matter. Who's the Londoner?"

"Ah! Yes. I get it. Dixon was a Londoner. PC Dixon. It used to be on the telly. What's he got to do with it?

"I said you sounded like him."

"But I haven't got a London accent."

"You haven't got a Glasgow accent either but where the hell are we going with this. You're pissing me around. Who's the Londoner?"

She smiled again, this time a real beamer, "You don't know. Do you?"

"I thought we'd already established that. It seems to be making you happy so it can't be all bad."

The frown returned sharply, "Actually yes it is all bad. Jack Bolton is all bad. He's been up here before and the last time he was here he left a few busted heads lying around. He's apparently never referred to by his real name, just the Londoner. He's an enforcer for the Billet brothers down there and he often handles the big movements of drugs between the two cities. You must have heard of him. He's been up here now for over a week but he hasn't been in contact with anyone who counts, just some of the small time dealers and drivers. I thought you might be able to shed some light."

"Have you asked Gillespie?"

109

"Actually that's what's bothering me. Of all the people he's been seen with Gillespie features more than anybody else. I think Bolton's trying to set up a new dealer network but I'm sure there's another heavy player involved and there's whispers about guns and I think…" The telephone interrupted and I never heard what she thought.

She picked up the ringing intruder, "Good morning, Sir…yes… along the lines of our discussion…I think it could work but I need to be sure…difficult character…yes, you could say that…no, we're still not finished…thank you, Sir." She sat in silent thought for a few moments before she spoke again.

"How's your mother?"

"My mother?"

"Yes. I believe she moved into an old folks home recently."

"Oh. You mean Maggie. Yes she decided herself. Said it was time to accept the inevitable before she set the flat on fire by leaving something switched on. She forgets things but we all do. I think she was wanting somebody to talk to. It's a nice place and the staff are friendly. As far as her health goes she's as fit as you and me."

She looked at me thoughtfully. "You didn't finish telling me how you know Freddy Cassidy."

"You didn't let me finish. Well, you know what it's like in Blackhill?"

"Not really. I've not had the chance to visit every part of Glasgow yet. It isn't a priority. My task is to focus on key elements in the emerging resurgence of organised crime."

I shook my head dolefully. "What the hell is that supposed to mean? You don't really know the streets you're policing. How the hell do you expect to know anything about these people and the crimes they're involved in, if you don't know the places where they ply their trade, where they meet, where they drink, where they fight and where they hide?"

"A superintendent doesn't need to get down to street level. It's a question of effective management."

"And you accuse me of flippancy and arrogance. How do you know what's going on in your factory if you never walk the shop floor? Did you not come up through the ranks?"

"I've earned my rank," she snapped back defensively.

"Tell me about it."

"I didn't apply for this posting, you know. I was selected for the job and offered a transfer from Lothian Police to Strathclyde. It is a special unit with a challenging remit. The selection panel never asked me if I'd been to Blackhill. I'm sorry I don't match up to your more exacting criteria."

"That's not normal procedure, moving people between the forces. It used to be called *jobs for the boys*. I suppose these days it's also *jobs for the girls*. Who do you know in high places?"

"That's an unfair assumption and also totally unfounded. I have no idea why I was selected but it was obviously based on my past performance."

"I imagine you were one of the trendy graduate intake starting at inspector rank?"

"That is also unfounded and you really ought to be better informed. Yes, I joined through an accelerated development programme directly from university but everyone enters the programme as trainee police constable. It took four years before I reached inspector grade."

"What did you study at university? Law?"

"No, but nearly. I took Criminology and Criminal Justice at Edinburgh?"

"And does that help you in finding out who clobbered Joe McGuiness?"

"It helps understand some of the motivations."

"OK. So what do you reckon were the motivations in turning Joe's face to pulp?"

"Well it was a particularly vicious attack, premeditated and planned. It seems to have been a punishment and a warning."

"What did they use?"

111

"Funny you should ask that. I thought it strange when they told me. It appears the attackers used old chair legs."

"I don't suppose your criminology classes covered heavy stick analysis?"

"Maybe I missed classes that day. So hit me with the heavy stick analysis theory."

"Well it's surprisingly basic. If you know what they used to clobber the guy, it tells you quite a lot about who did the clobbering. For example if they used baseball bats they are probably part of one of the new breed of Glasgow gangs, usually into serious robbery and drug dealing, maybe even your Londoner. A pickaxe handle usually implies an Irish connection. Old habits die hard and it harks back to the days when gangs of navvies came over on the ferry to build our roads. If it was cricket bats that were employed that tells you they were second generation Asians. That's usually Indians thumping Pakistanis or vice versa. If it's football related they don't use sticks, just fists, boots and bottles, maybe in extreme cases they use the goal-posts"

She didn't laugh at my football humour, "And old chair legs? What does that tell us? That they worked in a second hand furniture store? Or should we be out round the homes of all known criminals looking for a chair with two legs missing?" She smirked.

"Well in this case, no. It says you should visit Gurney's Bar looking for Willy Gilly and his son Billy."

She laughed openly. "No kidding? I just walk into this Gurney's Bar, wherever it is, like in one of those old westerns where the sheriff walks into the saloon and ask for Willy Gilly and his son Billy. You're winding me up Jamie Robertson. Still some of what you say about the sticks makes sense but you still haven't told me who uses old chair legs."

She was still laughing when PC Mary knocked on the door again and came in to pick up the coffee cups. "Excuse me Ma'am," she deferred politely.

"Thanks Mary," chirped the Super," Listen Mary! Do you know Willy Gilly and his son Billy?" she asked grinning at the young WPC.

Mary's eyes flickered back and fore between her boss and me a couple of times before she answered.

"Yes Ma'am. I wouldn't like to meet that pair in an alley on a dark night."

Super Sandra's jaw dropped. "You mean they really exist? Who are they?"

"You must know Willy Gilly, Ma'am. Everybody knows Willy Gilly. Do you want me to bring you the records file; it's quite big?"

"Yes, well, OK, do that, Mary. Thanks," the Super flustered.

"Willy Gilly's just his nickname Ma'am. His name is William Gillespie. He's a cousin of Jammy Gillespie. Does a lot of the rough stuff for Jammy when the big guy doesn't want to get his own hands dirty. His eldest son's called William too. He's not the full shilling and he just does what his dad tells him. They always go around together and everybody calls them Willy Gilly and his son Billy."

"OK Mary. That's a fair enough synopsis. You can skip the file. I'll see it later."

"OK Ma'am. Eh...Ma'am...Eh. What's a *sunopsis*?"

"It's a ...sort of... Look. It doesn't really matter Mary. Thanks a lot. You've been a big help."

Mary shot me a sideways glance as she slunk out the door. Poor lass didn't look convinced that she'd been a big help.

Super Sandra waited till Mary had gone then turned back to me. "OK, Professor Robertson. Expand your theory with particular reference to chair legs."

"Well the old fashioned Glasgow hard man wouldn't go anywhere near a sports shop to buy a baseball bat, not even to steal one and would definitely have no experience of hard work and pick axes. They get one of their mother's old chairs and snap off the front part leaving the two back legs, just the right size and weight to crack somebody's skull. They're a dying breed but there's still a few around who'll crack heads for you if the price is right."

"So, what's the price for a cracked head?"

"Fifty quid and a pint of beer if it's just a frightener, a couple of hundred if you want the victim to stay down for a while, five hundred if you don't want him to get up again. Willy and his son might have done over McGuiness just as a favour or more likely a favour owed but they'd probably still be looking for their fifty notes. That gives them booze money for a week and ten quid to back a couple of horses at the bookie's. You do know what a bookie's is?"

She ignored my question. "So you're telling me Joe McGuiness is lying in a coma for fifty quid and a pint of beer."

"Well my guess is that it was just supposed to be a frightener but McGuiness put up a fight so Gillespie isn't likely to pay them two hundred for making him stay down longer. And if he dies Gillespie's likely to break a few chair legs over **their** heads. But, like I said in the beginning, he might owe somebody money so there could be a loan shark involved. Anyway, this is supposed to be a Special Investigations Unit with a Superintendent specially drafted in from another force. What's the big interest in a busted head? You get ten or twenty every Saturday night. What's so special about this one?"

She smiled one of her nice smiles, " Nothing special, really. I just wanted to have a chat with you, cosy like, over a cup of coffee." She smiled again, "You can go now."

"Yes, Ma'am." I bowed slightly, smiled back and walked out.

Game, set and match to Super Sandra.

By Yon Bonny Banks

Sunday came round and Hamish called to check that I hadn't forgotten our "lunch appointment". He was definitely up to something. Lunch with Hamish always promised to be a fairly boring affair but on this occasion I was looking forward to it with a mix of apprehension and anticipation. I like Balloch on the Bonny Banks, a quiet, friendly retreat just twenty minutes out of the city. The Boat House was a small hotel and restaurant with a big name. I knew I could expect a succulent Scottish lunch even if the chat might be a bit heavy going. Anyway curiosity hauled me along and I pulled into the car park an hour ahead of our "appointed" time. I staked my pitch in the *staff only* area to get a nice view up the glen and sat skimming the Sundays as a cool drizzle blew in from the loch. I sensed a light tapping on my window and looked up to see a uniformed police officer. No! They can't book you for illegal parking in a hotel car park.

"Morning Jamie," said the voice as I rolled down the window. "What wild, wicked crime are you hacking in a pissing wet car park on the Lord's Day. You should be at home watching the telly."

I didn't look up from the newspaper. I knew the voice instantly. "I could ask the same of you Inspector Sinclair. Have they thrown you out of the Records Office and put you back on the beat?"

"If you could drag your head out of the scintillating Sunday papers you would see that it is in fact Chief Inspector Sinclair and yes, I suppose I am back on the beat in a sort of way. I'm not quite sure why I'm here though. I was summoned from on high and I think there's a free lunch involved. What are you doing here?"

"Meatloaf!"

"Sorry?"

"Bat out of Hell album."

"You're going to have to explain Jamie. My powers of intuition have got a bit rusty with all those years behind a desk."

"You took the words right out of my mouth!"

"Did I?"

" You said: *I'm not quite sure why I'm here though. I was summoned from on high and I think there's a free lunch involved.* You took the words right out of my mouth. I got summoned here as well with the promise of lunch"

"And you reckon we're going to get meatloaf? How do you work that one out?"

"Don't be thick, Sinclair. Have you never heard Meatloaf?"

I'm not a great singer but he was going to need help.

You took the words right out of my mouth

It must have been when you were kissing me.

"Oh! That Meatloaf. Actually he's good. I saw him at the Apollo a few months back. But, Christ, Jamie why can't you speak normal like the rest of us. It's just as well you don't write like that. Anyway I'm getting soaked standing here. Why don't we go in?"

A bow-tied *maître d'* pounced on us as we approached the restaurant door. "Are you with Mr Randalson's party?" He glanced reproachfully at my Glastonbury Pyramid T-shirt.

"Yes," I answered. "Yes," answered John Sinclair. We looked at each other.

"Come this way Gentlemen!" chirped the bow-tie as he whisked us past the main dining room, up a wide spiral stairway and into a private suite. Old Hamish certainly wasn't paying for this. The table was set for ten and a group of four or five had already arrived. I recognised the Chief Constable and one of his assistants.

"I think there's been some kind of mistake," I said to the headwaiter, "I think our reservation is a table for two in the name of Hamish Randalson."

"No mistake, Jamie my lad," the unmistakeable voice of Hamish behind me. "Come and join the others. You probably know some of the faces but there'll be formal introductions later."

I looked around again. With his back to me was Councillor Yasser Ahmed in tight conversation with the Member of Parliament for the south side. Two more walked in that I didn't know and who were either Jehovah's Witnesses or CID officers and I felt sure this wasn't a religious meeting, even though it was Sunday. Their nod to John Sinclair confirmed my observations. There was a shuffle at the door and in walked David MacLucas, my producer from the radio station, chatting briskly with none other than my coffee mate Super Sandra. I was beginning to feel distinctly uncomfortable, a feeling not helped by Hamish's sleeked, conspiratorial smile.

"OK. Gentlemen. Let's be seated," Hamish called the assembled group to order. "Oh! I beg your pardon Superintendent Paterson. I should have said Lady and Gentlemen. I know you're all anxious to enjoy the creations of the marvellous chef but before that I would like to set the mood by asking the Chief Constable to say a couple of brief words about why we are here. Then we'll order the food and we'll introduce anybody that you don't know. After lunch we will have the chance to chew things apart, if you'll pardon the pun."

This was getting too much. It seemed apparent that most of the others knew what was going on and why they were here. "Excuse me interrupting, Hamish, but I am here because you invited me for lunch. This seems more like a meeting of the Police Appropriations Committee. I think I'd prefer just to go home and make myself a sandwich."

The Chief Constable snapped to his feet before Hamish could answer. "I'm sorry if you feel that you have been brought here surreptitiously, Mr Robertson, but there is good reason. Please wait to hear what I have to say," he paused for effect, "before you go home for your sandwich."

Sandra interrupted, "Excuse me Sir," she flicked a glance at her boss, "May I?" He nodded and she continued. "I'd like you to stay Jamie," she smiled, "It will explain our meeting the other day and to be frank, if you don't stay there isn't any real purpose in this lunch meeting."

"In that case I'll stay. Who could resist that wonderful smile? Or maybe we should both slip away for a coffee and a sandwich in the bar and leave the gentlemen here to the formal side of things. You can tell me what all this is about."

"Perhaps this was a mistake," boomed the Chief Constable, "Sandra did say you were flippant, Robertson' but you're just being churlish. Sit down, shut up and listen and if you don't like what you hear then, yes, you can bugger off and we'll find another way of doing this."

"I'll sit down and listen. I doubt if I will shut up. It's not my style. I have faced down nearly every one of Glasgow's hard men. I respect the threat they present but I'm not afraid of them and I'm not afraid of you so don't dare tell me to shut up."

His nostrils bristled and his face puffed with rage. I don't imagine the Chief Constable was in the habit of being interrupted. His silent, hostile gaze bore into my face then growled round the room defying further interruption. "May I begin? He asked but didn't wait for an answer. "Most of you will no doubt know that in addition to my normal duties as Chief Constable of Strathclyde Police Force I am currently Chairman of the Committee of Chief Constables for the Scottish Crime Squad. I think all of you know that the Crime Squad is a unit that embodies all the individual Police Forces of Scotland. It was set up in 1969 to combat the increasing trends in serious crime, series crime and organised crime in particular where its tentacles spread across more than one force, or indeed, south into England or across the water into Northern Ireland. I have been asked to be brief so that necessitates that I also be blunt. The City of Glasgow is the biggest conurbation in Scotland and yet of late the quality and quantity of actionable leads passing from Glasgow to the Crime Squad is pitiful. I have set up a special unit to tackle this problem and appointed Superintendent Sandra Paterson to head up the unit. She was drafted in from another force not recruited from within. The rational behind this move is that she has not been corrupted by the factors that have hitherto prevented Glasgow Officers cooperating fully with the Team Leaders on the Crime Squad." He paused for a drink of water so I chipped in a putt.

"Does Strathclyde Police Force not already have internal anti-corruption measures in place. I would imagine that another layer of scrutiny will make officers less likely to cooperate?"

"Superintendent Paterson's remit does not involve the investigation of other officers, neither on the basis of corruption, nor incompetence nor any other aspect of individual officers' performance. The purpose of the Special Investigations Unit is to sift, sort, identify, analyse and correlate all the significant trends and movements of serious crime across the city for the sole purpose of feeding actionable data to the Crime Squad teams on the ground. We need to shorten the path between information sources and the front line troops.

It has been pointed out to me that you have, Mr Robertson, on several occasions demonstrated remarkable intuition in the direction that crime is heading. It is one of the benefits of viewing things from one step back. Many of us have been plodding the same old beat too long and tend to see things as they were, rather than where they are going. It is also a fact that as serious crime becomes increasingly serious we are becoming more and more bridled with procedural constraints. A well-informed journalist can take a stab in the dark and arrive at conclusions that may well be true but are unsupported by real hard evidence. We don't have that luxury. We are bound by investigative procedures and arrest procedures.

However this is not the key element of our purpose here today. Mr Robertson is also the anchor person on an increasingly popular and successful programme in local radio. This allows him to tap into a crucial source of street level information. Regrettably we have lost much of the contact we once had with the public. It is difficult to chat from a patrol car. I have already approached the management of the radio station with a view to closer cooperation between the programme and our special unit and Hamish Randalson has offered support from his newspaper where particular aspects of crime are especially topical. Again I must be frank and blunt; the general public often want to do what they can to help the victims of crime and to put a stop to criminal activity but they are regrettably, not so keen to talk to the police."

He tipped his reading glasses onto the end of his nose, glowered round the table and returned his glare to me.

"If you have no interest in this venture Mr Robertson, this would be an appropriate moment to slip away for your sandwiches. The rest of us are going to order lunch."

His glower changed to a soft friendly smile. He knew he had me on the hook. I chose to take his earlier advice to shut up and I took a menu card as they passed around. I didn't regret my decision to hang around and I definitely didn't regret my decision to take a menu card. The food was delicious and the programme link-up evolved to be a challenging project. Besides it gave me more opportunity to see Super Sandra with her beguiling smile. None of us realised the extent to which we were breaking new ground nor the extent to which our pioneer project would later be adopted around the country. After lunch Councillor Yasser Ahmed rose to his feet,

"Good afternoon everyone. I think you all know me, Yasser Ahmed. I had the privilege recently to take part in a new radio programme called *Street Patrol*. Also on the programme that evening was Superintendent Sandra Paterson. There was excellent audience participation and we gained substantial insight into current trends in shoplifting. A separate issue also arose and, to cut a long story short, we were successful in putting an end to a dishonest practice in property dealing. Regrettably we did not on that occasion acquire sufficient evidence to pass over for police action. However I understand that the Superintendent has been following up on the case and that there is a significant suspicion attached to the individual concerned in relation to other criminal activities. It would therefore be appropriate that I pass you over to Sandra now and she will shed more light on these dark matters."

Sandra's turn to be upstanding. "Thank you Councillor. Like the Chief Constable I will be blunt and to the point. After the programme that Yasser has just described two things occurred to me. The first was that this was an excellent platform from which to access the *vox populi,* and secondly that the talents of Jamie Robertson go beyond that of presenter/reporter and that in fact he has a deep understanding of the psyche of the Glasgow criminal mind. I put my ideas to the Chief Constable and here we are plunging forward. I must first apologise to Jamie. We gave him some rough treatment the other day but I had to be sure that he hasn't been *plodding the same old beat too long,* in the same way as some of our officers. I think you will all agree that he is not afraid to speak his mind. We need somebody who is prepared to voice his opinion. There will be times that we ask for help on specific matters but we don't want a lapdog presenting the police case. We want to stay in the shadow and we believe it will work best if Jamie appears to be on the side of the people. But I put him through the wringer the other day because I would end up with egg on my face if it turned out Jamie was in the pocket of one of the criminals we are trying to catch. For the record I am now satisfied that he is the person we would like to have on board.

Anyway, here is the proposal. I want to put in place a permanent link between the programme *Street Patrol* and the Special Investigation Unit for which I have responsibility. I have been lucky to recruit onto my team Chief Inspector John Sinclair. I believe that he and Jamie are old acquaintances. I want John to be our liaison, both in the programme preparation and during the time it is on the air and of course to follow up on anything of importance. John has invaluable experience in the collation of information. Crime is one enormous jigsaw puzzle without the corner pieces. Right at the moment it seems as if someone has tipped out the whole box with every piece up-side-down. John and Jamie are both gifted at putting the pieces together.

The good news is that we have secured some funding that will benefit the radio station. As you know CID has a small fund for rewarding information received and it seems appropriate that a part of this should be earmarked for the additional administration costs of the programme. In addition the Scottish Office has agreed to fund a series of *Safe Neighbourhood* advertising spots.

Of course not everybody has their ear glued to a radio so Hamish Randalson has proposed a new section in his newspaper which he wants to call *The Jamie Robertson File*. The plan at the moment is to pick up on random aspects of public safety rather than like the regular weekly spot on the radio. The idea is that Jamie will do a lead feature on a particular case or issue that is causing public concern and invite letters from the readers. OK! OK! I know what you're all thinking. Every crank in Scotland is going to have a field day but it is fairly easy to weed out the crank letters and once again John will work closely with Jamie. We are breaking new ground here and we will no doubt find what works best as we go along.

Before I sit down, I want once more to apologise to Jamie for the way this was put together without his knowledge but Jamie, you will be the anchor man in all this even more than you are at present in *Street Patrol*. I had to be sure, absolutely sure, that you were on the right side of the fence. We are ready to go with this, as of next week, but first you have to agree."

Before I could respond she held up her hand like a traffic cop to stop me answering, only just a little more polite than her boss's "shut-up," and then she smiled straight at me as she continued.

"I have asked your producer, David MacLucas, if he could re-schedule next week's programme and kick off instead with this ice cream war thing and see what the public have to say about it. It seems to be getting nastier and I think there is something deeper that our *Serious Chimes Squad* haven't managed to get a handle on." She smiled again and sat down.

The Chief Constable had got me onto the hook before lunch. Super Sandra had just pulled in the line. But before I plopped meekly into their net I had one question that I needed answered.

"Just one question first. You have explained why you chose me and my programme and your more direct selection interview is fresh on my mind but I would still like to know exactly why you were chosen from another force to lead up this special unit."

"I'll answer that!" the Chief Constable jumped to his feet. "Before becoming Chief Constable of Strathclyde Force I used to give periodic lectures to the trainees at The Scottish Police College at Tulliallan. A number of years ago I was delivering a lecture entitled *Crime Analysis by the Choice of Weapon* to a group on the Accelerated Development Programme, most of whom were young university graduates. There were about forty bright faces nodding politely on every word I said and one young upstart lass with a constant barrage of questions. At the end of the lecture I asked her name. I think she was convinced she'd blown away her chances. I don't like being interrupted, Mr Robertson, because even after many years of public speaking I am extremely nervous. On the other hand I don't mind being questioned. It keeps me on my toes.

When I started setting up this new unit I decided from the beginning that it would work best with someone in charge from outside our own force. So I took the unusual step of contacting my fellow Chief Constables and told them what I was looking for. Sandra Paterson's name was on the list along with her career record. She was, in fact, the only person that was called for interview," he glanced over at Sandra, "I don't believe she knew that."

Something was tickling the hairs on my brain. "Do you mind if I ask you one more question?"

"Not at all. Fire away."

"This lecture *Crime Analysis by the Choice of Weapon*. What was that about?"

"It is a very simple, but often overlooked principle. If you look at the weapon used and consider the immediate circumstances it can often lead you very quickly to a specific group of suspects or even to one individual. I believe you call it *The Big Stick Analysis Theory* or something like that but it applies much wider than baseball bats and chair legs. It is extremely useful in knife crime. Like I said, it is very simple and very helpful but we often forget this in the preliminary analysis of a crime. You may also like to know that, following your interview with Superintendent Paterson, Willy Gilly and his son Billy are currently under the Crime Squad microscope. Contract killings or even contract frighteners are very much a part of the web of crime that we are trying to disseminate."

Well! Well! Well! Super Sandra didn't miss classes that day.

New programme

The following week events just rolled one into the other. We spent most of Monday putting together a guest panel for *Street Patrol* on the ice cream wars. It wasn't difficult persuading the Chief Constable to come on the show. He enjoyed any opportunity to be the public face of the police and never shied away even when the force was under attack. Yasser Ahmed was keen to come on again but since most of the problems arose on the north side of the M8 he agreed to ask his colleague Joe Kelly from Easterhouse. I called Charlie Frazzini as the voice of the ice cream manufacturers and he was delighted to get a chance to air his point of view. We felt it was appropriate to have a van driver on the panel, especially if we could get one who had been the victim of an attack. John Sinclair dug back into the records and successfully made contact with Steven Quigley, the driver of the first attack to hit the headlines.

On Tuesday I had to go and sort out Maggie's things. It looked like she was going to be permanently resident in the home for the elderly. Her flat was rented from Glasgow Council and the housing office were unhappy about a flat lying empty while she was in permanent care. On top of that it just didn't make any sense to continue paying rent. And so I had to go and start clearing out the flat. I spoke to the neighbours in the other flats and managed to find a home for most of her furniture. The girl across the landing wanted the sofas and the beds but her man was in the army on duty in Belfast so I agreed to hold off for a few weeks. The truth was it gave me an excuse to postpone the final closure of the flat. It held lots of happy memories. Most important of course for me was her "Jamie's box". I browsed through it one more time. All the newspaper clippings were still neatly arranged in order but something was missing. The headscarf, the finely woven scarf that swaddled me as I lay beneath the bushes in Jamieson Gardens. It was gone, the only item that existed to connect me with my real mother.

I called in to see Maggie on my way home. She was delighted to see me as usual and chatted away cheerily. I didn't mention anything about clearing out her flat. I knew I'd have to tell her eventually. There was no need to upset her for now. However she did get upset and clammed up when I asked about the scarf. She didn't want to speak about it. Perhaps she'd thrown it out in one of her doddery moments. Best to leave it alone and maybe it would turn up.

I didn't get much crime reporting done that week with all my time spent in the radio studios. By Wednesday we were all set up and prepared for the Friday show. Then, on Thursday evening, the balloon went up. Just round the corner from Councillor Joe Kelly's house in Easterhouse the regular ice cream van tinkled to a halt and began trading. The driver Pat Johnson was an independent with his own van. He was not affiliated to any of the big players but instead bought his ice cream and other supplies where it suited him best. He had been doing the same run for over five years. Lately he'd been getting hassled by one of the Frazzini drivers who was engaging a practice called double-stopping. The bigger companies sometimes tried to force out the independents by stopping alongside them and taking half the trade. This practice obviously made it difficult for the small trader to continue. It wasn't pleasant but it was quite legal.

Anyway, on this particular Thursday evening when a Frazzini van pulled up in front of Pat Johnson he just continued like normal. Suddenly two balaclava-hooded men jumped out, one with a large hammer and the other with a double-barrel shotgun. The lad with the hammer went round the van smashing all the lights and as he stopped to admire his handiwork the other hoody blasted both barrels into the front windscreen. Inside the van Pat Johnson and his daughter Josie were sprayed with slivers of flying glass as the windscreen imploded. By the time the police arrived the Frazzini van was long gone. An ambulance arrived and took Pat and his daughter to hospital while their van was towed to Kwik Recoveries, the same garage as the Jennycare Fiesta had been taken the night Kerrigan was arrested.

This attack, although violent, wasn't by any means unique and would not have been particularly newsworthy except for one thing. It was all caught on camera. Wee Johnny Steele had his birthday a couple of days before and he was proudly patrolling the neighbourhood with his new Kodak Instamatic in his pocket. He was walking by when the two hooded men jumped out so he pulled out his camera and started clicking. Four or five clicks later he knew he had a marketable product in his pocket. He ran home to tell his Mum then jumped on a bus heading for the city centre and the offices of the Daily Record. On Friday morning the Record hit the streets with a full frontal shot of the shotgun blast and the big, bold headline "War on the streets of Glasgow".

I imagine you have all heard the Bangles singing the Prince song *Just another manic Monday*. Well this was Friday and I was singing *just another frantic Friday*. I tried to contact Charlie Frazzini only to find that he'd been hauled in to Central Police Station to explain why one of his vans had so blatantly attacked a competitor, with police officers demanding to know who was driving. Poor Charlie had no idea who was responsible nor why and spent most of the day with police. It looked like we could count him out for the evening show. Young Steven Quigley called up to say he was afraid to take part so we tried to get a hold of Pat Johnson, the driver of this latest attack. He declined but his daughter Josie jumped at the chance to take his place.

"Ah'm no feared o' the bastards," she proclaimed. "Somebody has tae speak out." It was agreed she could represent her father on condition that she toned down the vernacular.

John Sinclair pleaded with the superintendent investigating the case and half an hour before the show Frazzini was delivered to the studios in a patrol car. We had a full panel and were ready to go on air. The phones were starting to ring and with fifteen minutes to go the calls were starting to back up and the lines were getting jammed. A live show means think on your feet, find a solution, get the problem fixed, now! Chief Inspector John Sinclair took the hot-seat to answer the calls, threw off his cap and donned the headphones. He shouted to David Lucas, "thumbs-up means it's a good call worth putting on air, thumbs-down means I'm cutting them off fast and two-thumbs-up means I have a call with valuable information and somebody else has to step in."

"OK," David snapped back, "but I'm putting all good calls on the recorder and we'll feed them in to Jamie with a bit of control." He turned and called over a young technician with instructions to follow John's thumb-code and cut and filter the calls. So that's how we hit the hour and went live. It was supposed to be a live show and it did in fact go out live but the controlled flow of phone calls made a vibrant show more manageable. This later became the standard format for the programme. If any caller was needed for further discussion they were put on hold for a few minutes.

The tension between Josie Johnson and Charlie Frazzini was electric and crackled across the airwaves. Joe Kelly raged indignantly about the rampant violence on his doorstep. Nearly all the calls from the public followed the same theme. Why were the police not doing more to curb the violence and sort out the problems between drivers? About half way into the programme John jumped up making frantic signals that didn't comply with his own thumb-code. The technician realised he had an important caller on the line and signalled to me that he was putting it straight through live.

"It's no Charlie Frazzini," said a gruff male voice, "he's a decent bloke an' he gives the drivers a fair deal. He had nuthin' tae do with what happened last night."

"It was a Frazzini van," I affirmed. "There is no question about that. It's clear from the photos but they are side-on so we don't have the registration number."

"Aye, but that was aw' part o' the plan, tae cause mair trouble," the caller insisted.

"So, who smashed up Pat Johnson's van?" I pushed the caller for more detail. "Who shot at Pat and his daughter?"

There was a moment's hesitation, then, "It was that mad bastard Gillespie, you know, Jammy Gillespie. Ah don't know who was with him. All Ah know is he chucked the Frazzini driver off the motor an' hijacked it. He'll get away with it like usual because he's got the polis in his pocket."

"But I don't understand," I interjected, trying to prompt our caller. "James Gillespie doesn't have any ice cream vans. I'm fairly sure he has no connections with the trade. Why should he want to disrupt the business of an honest trader?"

"He's puttin' the squeeze on everybody. He wants us aw' tae carry his drugs on the vans an' he's puttin' the frighteners on anybody that doesnae play ball. Everybody knows that Pat Johnson told him tae bugger off."

"How do you know all this? Are you a driver yourself? Were you the driver that was thrown off the Frazzini van?" I pushed again.

I had pushed too hard. "Ah've said enough," he answered gruffly and hung up. We had reached our time and the programme was due to end anyway.

I was getting the wind-up signals so I clipped off, "Thank you everybody for your calls. Listen in next Friday and keep those calls coming because that's what makes Street Patrol the people's voice on crime." I eased off my headphones as the advertising jingles chimed in.

The Chief Constable jumped up, "Somebody get me a phone," he shouted.

"Over here," answered the young technician and our chief law enforcer lumbered over, took the phone and started dialling.

"I want Gillespie brought in," he barked into the mouthpiece. "Now! I don't give a damn where he is. Just find him. Any excuse. Tell him he had no lights on his bicycle. Use your imagination." He turned back to the assembled group. "Mr Frazzini, you will appreciate that it would be inappropriate at this stage to offer you a full apology. My officers had to act on the circumstantial evidence. After all it was one of your vans that was used. However please be assured that the matter will be thoroughly investigated."

"That's what your officers have been telling me since this business started. I am one of the victims and each time there is an incident involving one of my vans the finger of blame is pointed at me. I neither need nor want your apology but if this incident is thoroughly investigated that would make a pleasant change. I somehow doubt that the outcome will be any different to in the past. This Gillespie character seems to be something of an escapologist. I do hope you forgive my cynicism."

"On the contrary, I understand your cynicism but there are two sides to every coin. One of your drivers appears to have been evicted from his vehicle last night and the said vehicle was used in a serious assault. It would be helpful if this driver came forward with his version of events. It is not reasonable to expect police help if you and your workforce are not prepared to meet us half way. I leave you with that thought and bid you all goodnight." He ambled over, shook my hand silently and left the studio.

"He is trying to pull things together," said Councillor Joe Kelly. "We all know that Glasgow City has suffered for some time from an ineffective body of police. Back in 1975 the government in its wisdom merged together Argyll, Ayrshire, Lanarkshire, Renfrew and the City of Glasgow. He has a beat that stretches from the source of the Clyde out to the Hebrides. On top of that Margaret Thatcher expects the police to keep a lid on the troubles she has provoked with the miners and other workers' groups. He's a good man and he has some good ideas but the odds are stacked heavily against him."

"The odds are stacked heavily against all of us," retorted Charlie Frazzini as he stomped off out of the studio. He didn't bother shaking hands with anyone.

In the weeks that followed the Chief Constable followed through on his promise. The matter was investigated thoroughly. Gillespie was arrested, interviewed and ultimately charged on five separate counts ranging from breach of the peace to the illegal discharge of a firearm. The Procurator Fiscal wasn't satisfied with the strength of evidence and the case was passed to the Serious Crime Squad. Their enquiries revealed that Gillespie was in fact pressuring both Frazzini drivers and independent drivers to act as carriers in the distribution of drugs. He was also using threatening tactics with O'Connor's drivers to move them of the patch and let his team in. However it was proving extremely difficult to put together a case that would stand up in court. Most of the evidence was hearsay and many of the witnesses were unreliable. Several were known drug addicts and others had a criminal record. Although the van drivers were demanding police action they were in general too afraid to appear in court. At the Chief Constable's insistence and despite the Procurator's misgivings the case went to precognition. The Sheriff ruled that there was insufficient tangible evidence. "Jammy" Gillespie walked free once more. Charlie Frazzini's cynicism proved justified.

He wasn't alone, however. All the newspapers were openly critical of the police. Each paper had front page coverage of Gillespie's release plus an in depth analysis quoting from some of the victims who weren't prepared to appear in court. While Jammy G. had been a thorn in my flesh for quite some time I was more sympathetic to the police. My piece was built around exclusive interviews with some of the key players, the Chief Constable, the team leader of the crime squad, Charlie Frazzini, Pat Johnson and Councillor Joe Kelly. The Procurator Fiscal, Phillip Gardner, declined an interview but he gave me a little inside information and hinted that there might be "further developments" in the near future. Hamish suggested that we follow up with the first "Jamie Robertson File". The response was phenomenal. Letters flooded in. The spelling and grammar required some editorial effort and many of the contributions were scribbled on old envelopes, the back of bookie's lines and Gregg's paper bags but they all pointed in the same direction. The police were not doing enough to stop this crazy "ice cream war".

Six pillars of wisdom.

As the ice cream wars rumbled on Graham Kerrigan languished in Greenock prison awaiting trial. At his first appearance he was charged with possession of a class B substance with intent to sell. He was pleading guilty to possession but not the intent to sell. He had been refused bail because of his involvement in a prison break out in his younger years. The sheriff accepted the police view that he was likely to abscond and not appear for trial. The trial date was set and the Sheriff ruled that the charge be reduced to possession only. Kerrigan claimed that the Cannabis was for personal consumption and although the police and procurator knew full well that he was dealing they had no concrete evidence to back their charges. He had to wait a couple of months for the trial but then just a few days before the due date the court officials went on all out strike. The court schedule was thrown into chaos. Lots of minor traffic offences and the like were simply abandoned with basically a free pardon but more serious cases were rescheduled and the accused persons remained in custody a little longer. When Kerrigan's case finally went to trial he had been in custody for nearly six months.

When the day arrived his case was dispensed fairly quickly. It was in the old Sheriff Court in Brunswick Street, the building that is now the Scottish Youth Theatre. The public gallery was filled with press and others who were keen to see "the Gaffer" get his comeuppance. Possession carried a much lighter sentence than intent to sell but the quantity of drug was substantial and he had previous convictions for other offences. The Sheriff wasn't inclined to be generous. He was sentenced to two years imprisonment. With good behaviour this would in all likelihood be reduced to 18 months and he had already served 6 months awaiting trial. He wasn't exactly a happy bunny. The indignity was worse than the prison sentence but he was a hard nut. He'd done time before and he knew the two years would most likely be just one.

The most important thing for Kerrigan was to maintain continuity and keep his various business enterprises ticking along. By escaping the "intent to sell" aspect he also escaped major investigation into his dealer network and he'd managed to get the

Londoner back up to Glasgow to frighten off any would-be takeover attempts. He'd had to call in a few favours from the lads down south but they had as much to gain as he did from keeping the lines open. He was confident that he could trust them. Revenge would have to wait. Revenge was personal. Freddy Cassidy was just a little piece of dogshit but if you want to stay on top in this game you can't allow a little nobody to shop you to the police. Cassidy would pay the price. Iris Cassidy was different. She was a drug-smacked hooker who was over the hill but she had killed his Jenny. She wasn't just going to die; she was going to suffer. A year wasn't too long to wait. He just hoped she didn't overdose before he got to her.

Iris, meanwhile, had her own trial to attend. Her case would be heard in the High Court before a Judge and a jury of fifteen upstanding citizens. In those days the High Court was in the Saltmarket area, a large imposing building with six great pillars of wisdom supporting the Greek Doric portico entrance. Inside it was an austere edifice offering neither intrigue nor excitement, just sad dull people in sad dull surroundings. It didn't really dispense justice, not true justice. Its function was simply to dispense cases. Its indifference applied equally to victim and perpetrator. Iris was the perpetrator and Jenny Kerrigan had been the victim, at least that's how it was with the case before the court. However among the press and everyone present in the public gallery most of us saw Iris as the victim and Jenny as the aggressor. "The quality of mercy is not strained. It droppeth as a gentle rain from Heaven." Not in Scotland it doesn't. We have lots of rain that droppeth but mercy comes in much lesser quantities.

The police and the Lord Advocate's office wanted to prosecute Iris for murder. The Procurator Fiscal wasn't convinced that they had a substantive case against her. At the judicial review in her first appearance the Sheriff ruled that she should go to trial on the lesser charge of culpable homicide. Today as we sat in court Iris was brought out as the accused to stand trial on this lesser charge but she was still pleading not guilty. I was on her side hoping sincerely that she might get off but I wasn't optimistic and I knew in my heart that she wasn't entirely innocent. However she looked confident and defiant as she stepped into the dock. Iris had received her education at the Glasgow college of Social Security benefits and street survival. Scotland has always been proud of having one of the best education systems in the world but we also have one of the highest drop-out rates. Kids learn the hard way how to survive. You don't need an "A" level in Maths. You need to know how the system works. Iris knew how the system worked. She'd learned the hard way. When she walked into the police station on the day Jenny Kerrigan died she already had her statement prepared in her head.

Her police statement was the first piece of evidence presented by the Advocate Deputy. It was presented as proof of guilt, as proof that she was there and participated in the death of the victim but she had worded it cleverly to diminish blame. The duty sergeant was the first to take the witness stand and he confirmed that he had interviewed Iris and he read her statement to the court.

"My name is Iris Cassidy of 118c Randolph Flats, Walton Street, Blackhill, Glasgow. Today, 12th of January, 1982 I went to the Jennyfair shop in Govan to confront Jenny Kerrigan about why she shot at my son's van and why he lost one eye. Jenny Kerrigan was very aggressive. She must have thought I was planning to hurt her because she grabbed a pair of scissors and attacked me. She stuck the scissors in my arm. I had to try to stop her to defend myself. I managed to catch her arm, the one with the scissors and I twisted it round. Then we sort of fell against each other and she still had the scissors in her hand. The sharp end went into her side and she kind of flopped so I let her go. There were lots of people in the shop to help her so I just walked out of the shop to come home. I went to the hospital to get a bandage on my arm and then I thought maybe she was quite badly hurt because it was in her side so I came here to explain what happened."

As she said, there were other people there and all of them had been interviewed by the prosecution. Unsurprisingly the two that were called as witnesses for the prosecution inclined towards Iris as the aggressor. One was a hairdresser and the other was a customer. Both claimed that Iris came bursting into the shop shouting abuse at Jenny Kerrigan and that Jenny had grabbed the scissors to defend herself against Iris. The hairdresser said that Iris was deliberate in the way she twisted Jenny's arm till the scissors were pointing at Jenny but she couldn't be sure if they had fallen together or if Iris had pushed.

Remarkably nobody had seen Iris headbutting Jenny but defence counsel was going to have to work hard to convince the jury that there was no malice in Iris's actions. Defence counsels in legal aid cases don't usually exert themselves too much. They encourage their clients to plead guilty to get a softer sentence. Iris was pleading not guilty so her counsel was at least going to have to try. She was a young woman QC that I'd never seen before. Maybe the feminine angle would work in Iris's favour but of course the victim was also a woman. As she called her first witnesses it became evident that she had opted for a high-risk strategy. She called both Freddy and Iris obviously looking for the sympathy vote. It was a calculated risk. If she could convince the jury that Jenny Kerrigan was the aggressive party they might ask the judge for leniency due to mitigating circumstances. This could substantially reduce the sentence imposed. On the other hand it could backfire on her. If they were unconvinced and brought a guilty verdict the judge would almost certainly impose maximum sentence. In any case it was extremely unlikely that they would bring in a not guilty verdict. It was not a strategy that I would trust to a young inexperienced QC. I began to worry.

Freddy was the first to be called and Janice Cuthbert QC asked him if he knew why his mother had gone looking for Jenny Kerrigan on the fatal day.

"Because Jenny Kerrigan shot the windae out of my ice cream van an' blinded me in one eye." Freddy's attempts at correct English conflicted with his strong Glasgow twang.

"Why should Jenny Kerrigan do that?" asked Counsel.

"Somebody telt her that I shopped the Gaffer for carrying drugs."

"Who is the Gaffer?"

"That's what everybody calls him. His real name is Graham Kerrigan. He's Jenny's husband. Ah mean he was her husband."

"And was he carrying drugs?"

"Aye. He got sentenced last week."

"So what you are saying is that Jenny Kerrigan fired a shotgun into your van and blinded you in one eye?"

"Aye, that's right."

"And this was because you had reported her husband to the police?"

"Aye…yes…well, no exactly. Ah mean…" Freddy mumbled weakly.

"Are you saying you didn't report him? In that case why did she shoot at your van?"

"Ah didnae shop him. It was somebody else but Jenny Kerrigan thought it was me."

"Why would she think that?"

"It's complicated."

"We really would like to know Mr Cassidy. Let's take it a bit at a time. Did you know that "the Gaffer", as you call him, was in possession of drugs?"

"Well everybody knows that he never handles the stuff himsel' but that day he had tae go an' rescue some stuff because one o' their wee vans was in a smash. It was towed tae Kwik Recoveries an' ma mate works there. There was drugs in the back an' Kerrigan went tae get them an' that's when they nabbed him but it wasnae me that telt because Ah didnae know all this tae the next day. So it couldnae be me that shopped him."

"So if you didn't call the police to inform on Graham Kerrigan, who did?"

"Ah reckon it was Jammy Gillespie."

"Who is Jammy Gillespie?"

"He's the guy that I was waitin' for the next day when ma windae got blasted."

"Yes, well, I see. Yes, I agree. That is indeed a little complicated." The lady QC scratched her chin, shuffled her notes and continued.

"This Jammy Gillespie, why would he want to inform on Mr Kerrigan?"

Freddy grinned sheepishly. "Because he was havin' it off with Jenny Kerrigan. He fancies himsel' with the women and they fancy him. He acts like he's Mr Big. Ah'm no sure about this but Ah reckon he shopped Kerrigan tae get him out o' the picture, like, an' then he tells Jenny that it was me that shopped her hubby. That way he gets Jenny tae himsel' an' he takes over Kerrigan's patch while he's inside. Like Ah said, he fancies himsel' as Mr Glasgow."

"Yes, complicated indeed!" observed counsel as she continued. "How can you be sure that it was Jenny Kerrigan who shot at you?"

"Ah saw her. Ah saw her face at the windae before she pulled the trigger. Ah saw the windae opening an' she leaned out o' the motor."

"And you're sure it was her? Do you know…I'm sorry…did you know Jenny Kerrigan?"

"She used tae be Jenny Wilcox before she was with Kerrigan. She was a model or a beauty queen an aw' that an' her photy was always in aw' the papers an' then when she started aw' these hairdressers an' things Ah saw her on the telly. Everybody knows her…Ah mean knew her. It was definitely her."

"OK. Let's move on. Were you selling ice cream that day when you were shot at?"

"No, Ah was waitin' for somebody."

"Can we be privy to whom?"

"What? Ah don't understand the question," protested Freddy.

"Who were you waiting for?"

"Ah already said. It was Jammy Gillespie." Freddy answered snappily. He didn't like the condescending tone of his questioner even if she was his mother's defence. These lawyers were all the same trying to trip you up with trick questions and make themselves look smart.

"I just want to get this clear," she snapped back. "This Jammy Gillespie that you say informed on Kerrigan is the same person that you were supposed to meet the next day?"

"Aye. That's what Ah said."

"What spite did he have at you? Were you a rival with the women?"

Freddy looked sheepish again. "Don't be daft. Ah'm no in Jenny Kerrigan's league."

"So why pick you?"

"Ah was just the convenient mug. Maybe he knew that Ah had a mate in the garage so he could blame me an' take the suspicion off himsel' an he knew where tae find me."

"So you definitely saw Mrs Kerrigan fire the gun?"

"Aye. It was definitely her."

"Was she alone in the car?"

"No. She was leanin' out the passenger side."

"Do you have any idea who was with her?"

"Gillespie."

"You seem sure about that? Did you see him?"

"No, but Ah know it was him. He was supposed tae meet me an' apart from my Ma he was the only one that knew Ah was there. So it must've been him."

"Thank you Mr Cassidy. I have no more questions."

The judge invited the Advocate Deputy to question the witness.

"Yes, there is one matter." He rose and walked towards the witness stand. "This Jammy Gillespie that you mention. Is that his correct name? Or is "Jammy" his nickname?"

"Aye. Everybody calls him Jammy because he's always jammy when the police are after him. They never catch him or if they do they let him go again. An' even if he goes tae court he always gets off. Everybody knows him. It was him that shot up another ice cream van last month. It was in the news. That was Pat Johnson and his lassie got shot at but no as bad as me. His right name is James but everybody calls him Jammy. He got arrested for that but he'll get off like usual. He's a jammy bugger."

"Very interesting. So his correct name is James Gillespie. Thank you Mr Cassidy. Now why were you meeting him on the day you were shot? I believe you said that you were not selling ice cream that day, Christmas day I believe, that you were waiting there to meet Mr Gillespie. Is that correct Mr Cassidy?"

"Aye. That's right."

"What was the purpose of this meeting Mr Cassidy?"

Freddy shuffled uncomfortably. "He was goin' tae give me a package." He answered reluctantly.

"And this package that you were supposed to receive, what was in it?"

"Ah cannae tell you."

"Oh but you have to tell me Mr Cassidy. You are under oath to tell the whole truth. I will ask you once more. What was in this package?"

"Ah cannae tell you," Freddy insisted.

"Why exactly do you feel unable to answer? Could it be that you are afraid of incriminating yourself? Did the package contain illegal substances? Was it drugs Mr Cassidy? Is that why you are unwilling to answer?"

"Ah cannae tell you," Freddy repeated.

At this point the Judge intervened, "Mr Cassidy, as Counsel says, you are under oath. If you refuse to answer Counsel's questions you will be held in contempt of court. I am not sure where Counsel is heading with this line of questions but for the moment you must answer. You cannot refuse. Do you understand?"

Freddy had gone to the school of life like his mother. He understood perfectly. The Crown Counsel was trying to whittle away at his credibility. His Ma went to challenge Jenny Kerrigan because she'd robbed him of one eye and nearly killed him. It didn't matter what was in the package but if he told the truth the jury would see him as just another drug dealer. He knew the system. He understood the question and knew he had to answer. He looked up at the Judge and replied.

"Ah cannae answer, my Lord. Ah'm no refusing tae answer. Ah honestly cannae answer."

"Why is that Mr Cassidy?" the Judge growled doubtfully.

"Ah didnae receive the package. Jenny Kerrigan blasted ma face with glass an' next thing Ah was in hospital. If Ah didnae get the package, Ah cannae say what was in it."

A ripple of laughter ran round the dull courtroom. The Judge smiled ruefully. He secretly enjoyed these moments when the little man managed to put one over on the learned counsel. He also understood what the Advocate was trying to do with Freddy and that it wasn't really pertinent to the case. He made his ruling on the matter.

"Indeed what you say is true Mr Cassidy. If you never handled this package you cannot in all honesty testify to its contents. I think, Counsel, that we should move on."

"In that case I have no further questions my Lord." He snapped his papers together and slunk back to his bench.

"Very well," concurred the Judge, "Does Defence Counsel wish to call the next witness?"

The next witness was Iris. She looked calm but defiant. Janice Cuthbert QC smiled at her reassuringly and posed her first question.

"Mrs Cassidy, when you went to the Jennyfair hairdressing salon on the 12th of January was it your intention to kill Jenny Kerrigan?"

"No."

"Can you please tell the court Mrs Cassidy? Why did you go?" the QC coaxed.

Iris had been practising this answer all week. When she spoke her voice was soft and caring quite unlike the gruff menacing bark that I remember that day in the hospital as she charged off in search of vengeance. She turned and looked directly at the jury glancing briefly at each one in turn.

"One part of me was angry," she answered calmly and clearly, picking her words carefully. "What mother wouldn't be angry? Jenny Kerrigan tried to kill my son. She didn't manage that but she left him half blind. So yes I was angry enough to want to kill her but the other part of me was asking why. Why did she want to hurt my boy? I think that is really why I went there. I needed to know why. I know that my Freddy isn't perfect but what did he do to her? At that time I didn't know anything about who shopped her man. So I went there to have it out with her."

"What happened when you went into the hairdressing salon?"

"She was in the front shop so I didn't need to go looking for her. I think I started shouting at her. On the way there I had it all planned about what I was going to say but when I saw her it all sort of just came blurting out."

"How did she respond?"

"She grabbed a pair of scissors and came charging at me…" Iris hesitated purposefully.

"Please continue Mrs Cassidy. What happened next?" the young QC encouraged gently.

"Well she took a dive at me and jabbed my arm. She cut me. I grabbed her arm and twisted it round."

"In other words you were defending yourself. Were you not?"

"I had to defend myself. She was trying to puncture me seriously. I managed to twist her arm round behind her and she was trying to push the scissors back round towards me. I pushed her arm back again and she sort of pushed forward and we sort of fell onto each other. The scissors punctured her side. She stopped pushing and was sort of just leaning on me then she fell down on the floor."

"What did you do then?"

"I let her go and everybody crowded round to help her. Nobody was bothering about me so I just walked away. I went to the hospital and they patched up my arm and then I went to Maryhill to the police station"

"Do you regret what happened?"

"After I made my statement they wouldn't let me go home. The next day I had to see the Sheriff and he refused bail because I have previous convictions and one time I didn't appear in court when I should. I've never hurt anybody. These other convictions were for soliciting." She hung her head with appropriate humility as she continued. "I needed money to look after Freddy and his sisters and it was an easy way. I'm not proud of it but I can't change it. So yes, I regret what happened because it took me away from my boy when he needed me. I regret half of my life because I wasn't there when my kids needed me. But if I say that I'm sorry she's dead you wouldn't believe me. The bible says an *eye for an eye* and I suppose she got a bit more than that but she shot at my son when he was just sitting there defenceless. There was a big fuss in the papers and everything last month when Gillespie shot up Pat Johnson's van but Pat and his daughter were in the back and just got some cuts. My Freddy was in the front and he took it right in the face. He's lucky to be alive. So yes, I regret what happened, all of it, but I'm not sorry that she's dead. I didn't kill her. She killed herself."

"Thank you Mrs Cassidy, no more questions."

"Counsel for the Crown, do you wish to cross examine this witness?" asked the Judge.

"Yes, my Lord," replied the Advocate eagerly. "Mrs Cassidy," he growled, "You believe that Mrs Kerrigan was to blame for her own death. Is that what you imply?"

"Yes, more or less."

"More or less. More…or…less," he mused. "Do you mean it was more her and less you or more you and less her?"

"You're confusing me. More or less what?"

"Precisely Mrs Cassidy, more or less what? I put it to you that you went to the Jennyfair salon that day intent on causing harm to Mrs Kerrigan. Whether it was more or less was a matter of circumstance. You believed that she had caused harm to your son and went seeking revenge. Let us not forget also that this shooting incident is very much open to conjecture. Her participation has not been corroborated. Nonetheless you took it upon yourself to meet out justice. In your head she was to blame for your son's unfortunate situation and you travelled from one side of the city to the other to… Let's see how you put it in your own words." He flipped back through his notes. "Ah yes, here it is. You travelled across the city to *have it out with her.*" He flipped the page again for effect and continued, "*An eye for an eye.*" He paused and moved closer hovering over her menacingly. "You left you son's bedside in the hospital, jumped on a bus and crossed the city for the purpose of retribution. Is this not the case Mrs Cassidy?" His chest puffed out with pompous indignation and he flailed his papers in the air.

"No," replied Iris, "You have it all wrong."

"Oh! I have it all wrong. Then tell us again Mrs Cassidy. How was it? In what way do I have it all wrong?" he taunted her.

Iris looked him straight in the eye and answered impishly, "You said I jumped on a bus and crossed the city for the purpose of retribution. That's not correct. I went on the shoogle. You know, the subway. I don't know the buses on that side of the city."

Once again a ripple of laughter went round the court. The Judge lowered his head so we couldn't see his smile.

Counsel for the Crown opened his mouth but no sound came out. He took a few moments to regain his composure. "Very well, Mrs Cassidy. Let's move on. On the day your son was shot at where were you?"

"I was at home. It was Christmas day."

"So you have no way of knowing who fired the gun. Is that correct."

"Freddy told me it was Jenny Kerrigan. I believe him. He saw her before she pulled the trigger. He already told you that."

"But I am asking you Mrs Cassidy. You didn't see any of this. Did you?"

"No but…"

"Thank you Mrs Cassidy," he interrupted, "now can you tell us please? Did you know that your son Freddy was meeting someone that day, someone who was supposed to give him a package?"

"Yes, Jammy Gillespie."

"You mean James Gillespie?"

"Yes."

"And do you know what was in the package? Please remember before you answer that you are under oath."

I watched as Iris glanced towards the other end of the public bench. Daniel O'Connor occupied the last seat. I hadn't noticed him before. He shook his head slightly indicating negative. Iris glanced away quickly and flicked a look at her defence counsel. Again a brief shake of the head.

"No, I don't know what was in the package."

"Mrs Cassidy, I ask you. Do you really expect the court to believe that you have no idea what the package contained?"

Iris was never the brightest button in the box but she knew that it was important to answer this one right. She needed the jury on her side. If she appeared to be lying or fudging she would lose them. That's what the Advocate Deputy was angling for. The package was irrelevant to her guilt or innocence but her answer could affect their attitude to her. Her defence counsel would probably have covered most of the possible questions and prepared her for each but this one was out of the box. Iris was fairly sure that she had the jury with her up to now. They didn't look away when she looked at them. This was a good sign. What she needed now was a smart answer but Iris was not too smart and she had no notes to flip back to but she had a good memory. She remembered one of his earlier questions and took a stab in the dark.

"I have no way of knowing what was in the package the same as I have no way of knowing for sure that it was Jenny Kerrigan who fired the shot. Like you say yourself, I wasn't there so how could I know."

This time the laughter rippled louder in open derision. Even some of the jury were smiling. The Judge bowed his head and grunted loudly to pull the court to order. Again he intervened, "I think we are covering old ground here. I cannot see how this package is relevant to the case even if it contained the Crown jewels. I think it is time to move on. Does Counsel have any more questions for this witness?"

"No, my Lord. The Crown is finished with this witness."

"Counsel for Defence, do you wish to call any more witnesses?" asked the Judge.

"We have one last witness, my Lord. We wish to call Sandra Watts."

Sandra Watts was called and took the stand.

"Please state your name and occupation."

"My name is Sandra Watts an' Ah'm a trainee hairdresser."

"Miss Watts, can you please tell the court who is your employer?" asked the defence counsel, Janice Cuthbert.

"Ah'm on the buroo. Ah lost ma job."

"When was this?"

"Last month."

"And who was your last employer?"

"Jennyfair. Ah worked in the shop in Govan."

"Were you dismissed from this employment or did you leave of your own accord?"

"Ah got the sack."

"Why?"

"They said it was because business dropped since Jenny…since Jenny died."

"Was this the case? Did the tragic events have an adverse effect on business?"

"What?"

"Did the business drop? Was there less business after Jenny died?"

"Like hell! Business was boomin'. Everybody wanted tae come an' see where it happened. People are like that. *Ah got ma hair done in the shop where Jenny Kerrigan died.* No, they sacked me because Ah'd agreed tae be a witness for you, for the defence. It's stupit because Ah'm no bothered. Ah'm just tellin' what Ah saw. They didnae have tae sack me."

"Were you in the shop the day of the unfortunate accident?"

"You've got an awfy funny way o' askin' these questions. D'you know that? D'you mean was Ah there when Jenny copped it?"

"Yes that is what I mean."

"Aye. Ah was sweepin' up the hair."

"What sort of boss was Jenny Kerrigan?"

"She was aw'right most of the time. Sometimes she was nice as nine pence an' other days she was a right bitch."

"What about the day in question, the day she died, the 12th of January. Was she nice as nine pence that day?"

"She was in a foul mood that day. She came in shoutin' an' bawlin' at everybody just after the shop opened. There was lots of whispering between aw' the girls. We aw' knew that somethin' had happened in the last few days that set her off. She was like that aw' week. Then we heard that the Gaffer got arrested so we knew that's what was buggin' her but she didnae need tae be sae crabbit. We were aw' tryin' tae avoid her."

"Did you see what happened when Mrs Cassidy came into the salon?"

"Aye. Ah saw everythin'. Like Ah said, Ah was sweepin' up hair."

"So did you watch it in a mirror or right in front of you,"

"Right in front of me."

"Did Iris Cassidy attack Jenny Kerrigan?"

"It depends on what you mean. She was on the warpath shoutin' an' swearin' at Jenny but she didnae attack Jenny physically, like. That was Jenny. She went crazy, like, an' grapped a pair of scissors."

"And at this point did Jenny take up a defensive position?"

"You're kiddin'. She went straight for the other woman jabbin' at her wi' the scissors. Ah jumped back in case Ah got it instead. She was wild."

145

"How did Mrs Cassidy react?"

"She tried tae defend hersel' an' she caught Jenny's arm an' twisted it, like, but Jenny kept on comin' at her an' then she just sort of collapsed, like. We didnae realise what had happened at first. Then Ah saw the scissors sort of sticking out of Jenny's guts, like, an' then she was bleedin' all over the place. Then she fell on the floor in the middle of the hair that Ah was sweepin'. Everybody rushed forward tae help her an' the other woman just walked out of the door."

"I have one final question Miss Watts. Please think carefully before you answer. Who do you think was to blame for what happened?"

"Ah've thought about that a lot. If the other woman, Mrs Cassidy wouldnae never have come in, it wouldnae never have happened. You know what Ah mean, like. She sort of kicked over the first domino but it was definitely Jenny that started the real aggression. She just sort of flipped an' went crazy."

"Thank you Miss Watts, no more questions."

Crown Counsel was on his feet before the Judge had time to invite him for cross-examination.

"Miss Watts, I put it to you that you were dismissed from your employment with Jennyfair and you saw this as an opportunity to get back at them. That is why your story differs from that of other members of staff. Why did they not notice these mood swings of Jenny Kerrigan? I put it to you that this crazy aggression you describe is just a figment of your very vivid imagination."

"Aye, they all noticed her moods but they're aw' feared. They're feared of the Gaffer an' they're feared of gettin' the sack like me. Ah'm no feared. Ah tell it like it was. An' Ah'm no feared of you wi' your big wig. You cannae put it anywhere because you wernae there. Ah was!"

"Miss Watts, there is no call to be impertinent."

"You're the one that's bein' impertinent. You're callin' me a liar."

QC Janice Cuthbert rose to her feet and interrupted the brusk exchange.

"My Lord, if it please the court. This is all a matter of record. Crown Counsel has all the relevant documents if he chose to read them. Miss Watts received the court summons two months ago while she was still employed by Jennyfair. She was dismissed, like she says, one month later. So the question of trying to get back at her employers like Counsel suggests, is simply unsupported by the facts. I am somewhat surprised at learned counsel's ignorance on this point."

"Indeed." snapped the Judge. "I have these documents before me. What does Crown Counsel have to say on the matter of these documents? Do you in fact have them in your possession?"

There was a frantic shuffle of papers as Crown Counsel consulted his junior lawyer and then he answered. "My Lord, the Crown wish to retract the last question. We have no more questions for this witness."

"I'm glad to here it. Thank you Counsel. In that case does either Counsel wish to recall any witnesses?"

Both counsels chorused in negative.

"Very well. Court will adjourn for lunch and will resume for summing up at 2.00 p.m."

MISTER O'Connor

The Courtroom cleared quickly. I nipped round the corner to the Saltmarket Arms, a rather grubby little pub which turned out to have no food on offer. Never mind, journalists survive on liquid lunches. I ordered a pint of Tennent's lager and a packet of salt and vinegar crisps and shrunk into a corner table to redraft my notes. The beer was good but the crisps were stale. My reverie was broken by the arrival of Danny O'Connor.

"Good Morning Mr Robertson, or is it afternoon. Are you enjoying our cuisine? Wouldn't you like something a little more filling?" Danny was standing there looking positively friendly.

"Good Afternoon *MISTER* O'Connor. What's the occasion? Last time we met you were hurling missiles at me. Now you're all *nice as nine pence* like the last young witness said. Are you a man of moods like Jenny Kerrigan?"

He shrugged his shoulders. "Jenny was alright, you know, just had bad taste in men, first Kerrigan and then Gillespie. Graham Kerrigan's a bad bastard, worse than me. Anyway they were getting a bit too high and mighty. What's it they say? Pride comes before a fall. They thought they were above the rest of us. Now she's gone and he's inside. Life's a jungle and we're just jungle animals."

"The question is, who's King of the jungle?"

"I don't need to be King but I'm sure as Hell not going to be anybody else's pawn."

"Hey, you're mixing metaphors. Have you been taking classes from Hamish Randalson?"

"Mixing metaphors? No son, we don't do cocktails in here just beer and spirits. Hamish Randalson you say. He's a bigger crook than the rest of us and he's a pompous old arsehole. He has dinner with the Chief Constable but he still needs to wipe the snotters off his nose like everybody else. But listen, I asked you a question and you haven't answered. I'm going to have a ploughman's lunch. Do you want to join me?"

"They don't do food just out-of-date crisps." I shoved the packet away in a show of disdain.

"It's on the house. This is one of my places. I can get the barmaid to fix it from the fridge. There's always something for special guests. Do you want some or no?"

"Who could refuse such generous hospitality, if you promise not to throw it at me."

He disappeared behind the bar and re-appeared a few minutes later with two plates. Some lettuce and tomato, pork pie, some cheese and a spoonful of Branston Pickle, quite an acceptable looking ploughman's lunch. I shoved the crisps further over to make way for the plate and tucked in.

After a few mouthfuls I re-initiated conversation. "So, what do you want? Why are you being so nice to me, *MISTER* O'Connor?"

He put down his knife and fork and leaned back in his chair. "Fuck it Jamie, why don't we just use first names? When you say *MISTER* it sounds more disrespectful than Danny. Anyway, like you say, today I'm in a good mood. It's looking good for Freddy's Mammy. What do you think? And he tells me you were around when he got shot at and you were nice to his Mammy. I know you're not on our side Jamie, never will be, but you're a decent sort."

My turn to put down the knife and fork. "OK Danny, now I know for sure you're after something. You're next line is *Jamie, I've got a favour to ask you.*"

He laughed. "Jamie, I've got a favour to ask you."

"Which is, you know that I know all about what was in the package Freddy was supposed to receive and you want me to leave it out of my report on the court proceedings."

"Why do you always have to be such a smart arse?"

"Come on Danny, I saw the exchange between you and Iris and her Counsel. If they're chasing after Kerrigan and Gillespie they're leaving you alone but this is a big ask Danny. This is drugs we're talking about, the distribution of drugs, and you're asking me to keep *schtum*."

"I'm not asking for me. I'm asking for Iris. You can see what the prosecution is trying to do. If she's found guilty today the case will be deferred for sentence. If it comes out that they were dealing drugs she's going to lose all the sympathy that Janice Cuthbert's been getting her."

"You know Janice Cuthbert? I thought she was new around here."

"Of course I fucking know Janice Cuthbert. Do you think she came out of a lucky-bag?"

"Ah, now I get it. That's what you were doing in the public gallery. You're coughing up for Iris's defence. Janice Cuthbert isn't legal aid."

"Janice Cuthbert is a smart young lawyer who has been making a name for herself in Edinburgh. You don't wander over that side very often so you probably haven't heard of her. She's had some good results defending women like Iris mostly in domestic cases where the woman has taken enough beating and decides to bite back."

"I didn't know you were big on women's rights, Danny."

"You don't know fuck all about me Jamie Robertson. You spend too much time with your head stuck up your own smart arse. You just see me as another scumbag gangster. You've got to be hard to survive in this city. Anyway Iris and me go back a long way and Freddy's a loyal worker. I'm just looking out for my own people."

"OK, you're looking out for your own people but if there's too much made of this package it'll get traced back to you so you're looking out for number one as well."

"Aye, OK, something like that, smart arse."

"I think I prefer if you just use first names. *Smart Arse* sounds more disrespectful."

O'Connor laughed. I thought he was going to choke on his pork pie. "You're not so bad yourself, Jamie Robertson. At least you've still got some sense of humour. What about a bit of horse trading? You scratch my back and I'll scratch yours."

"How do you propose to scratch my back?"

"Well first of all I promise not to throw all the whisky glasses at you as you're leaving and then I could throw in a couple of juicy titbits about Jammy Gillespie, something you'd never dream of in a million years."

"Why didn't you say that in the first place? Every reporter in Glasgow would trade his Granny for a couple of good titbits about Gillespie."

"The first part won't really come as any surprise to you. Gillespie is Hell bent on becoming one of the key players in the drugs trade in Glasgow. OK, I know what you're going to say, the pot calling the kettle black. I don't claim to be an angel but I am trying to turn my businesses around and get legitimate. I'm fed up running with one eye over my shoulder but this drugs thing is big money and it rolls in easy. People talk about drug pushers. Nobody's pushing drugs. They don't have to. The demand is there and all you need to do is set up some kind of distribution that keeps you out of the coppers' reach. Some day I might be able to kiss it all goodbye but right now it's just so easy to make big dollars. Gillespie is different. He's starting from nothing so he's having to fight his way in and he's an evil bastard. He hurts people just for fun. He was working for me as one of my mules. Iris probably told you he was one of the lads that runs the stuff to the ice cream vans. The local dealers come and get it from the vans. The police think the drivers are selling the drugs but that's too risky. I suppose one or two of them are but they get a rap on the knuckles if I catch them.

Anyway Jammy Gillespie was just playing me for a mug. He was just learning my set up so he could copy it and now he's got Sam Horton putting up the readies to buy stuff in. The only thing is he hasn't got any vans so he's using his muscle to put the frighteners on the drivers to carry his stuff. Kerrigan's in a different league from us. He's supplying to the posh boys. It's two completely different markets. Gillespie just couldn't resist when he heard that Kerrigan was actually going to be in possession. You can just imagine what went through his mind. With one phonecall he could get Kerrigan put away for a few years and then he could muscle in and take over his wife and his business. I mean, did he really think that the Gaffer would just roll over. I tell you the bastard's crazy. He's a psycho. We can do without his kind. They just make life more difficult for the rest of us."

"So if they find Jammy G. floating belly up in the Clyde I can do a speculative piece on *whodunit*?"

"Ha fucking ha! If they find Jammy Gillespie floating in the Clyde you can do a speculative piece on half of Glasgow. And you can start with all the police officers that don't like the way he keeps getting off the hook. They're not all happy about it you know."

"OK, so like you said, you've confirmed a lot of what I'd already deduced but where's the juicy bits, *something that I'd never dream of in a million years*, that's what you said."

"I was just coming to that. It's all linked up. You need to learn a bit of patience Jamie lad. Have you ever thought how it is that Gillespie survives? It's as if he has a guardian angel watching over him."

"Well, to be honest, yes. I've often wondered what he has. Don't take this the wrong way but I could understand it happening with you. You have money behind you and a bit of clout. You've got the girls in some of your bars that you might use to compromise somebody that yielded to temptation. So if it was *Jammy O'Connor* I could understand that better. No offence."

"No offence taken. I understand what you're saying. Listen, can we continue this conversation on the way back to the court? I don't want to get there and find the public benches full. I don't suppose you do either. We can talk as we walk."

We downed the last of our beers and stepped out into the fresh air of Glasgow. O'Connor continued with the real juicy bit.

"Did you know that he joined up when he was about eighteen?"

"You mean the army?"

"Aye, Blackwatch. He did a stint in the Rhine Army and then he was active in Northern Ireland. He was selected for SAS training and the word is he nearly made it into the squad and then the daft bastard knifed somebody."

"Where did you learn all this?"

"You don't really expect me to answer that. Do you?"

"Worth a try."

"Anyway the important part is that he was court-martialled and got three years in the steamer then he was kicked out of the army. At least that's what his army record shows. The alternative version is that he got a visit while he was in the steamer."

"Sorry to interrupt you Danny but don't you mean the cooler?"

"What's the fucking difference? D'you want to hear this or no? If you want to be smart, see if you can tell us who it was that visited him."

"Graham Kerrigan?"

"MI5."

"You mean the Watchers of PO Box 500, the Spooks, 49 Steps? Hey, come on Danny. You mean they sent him back into Ireland undercover?"

"No. They sent him back up to Glasgow. I know he's become a bit of a legend. Maybe it's just another bit of the legend but my source is reliable. What I've been told is he came out on full army pay at the rank of Sergeant and he's still on the books. He's working for Maggie Thatcher on the streets of Glasgow."

"Does that make any kind of sense? MI5 don't get involved with crime."

"It makes sense if you really think about it. They get involved in what they call internal security. I think they're terrified that the Ulster thing boils over into Scotland. Glasgow's near as damn it 50-50 Protestant and Catholic. When there's an Orange march the centre of Glasgow is closed for a day. It's bigger than anything in Ireland. On top of that, there's a whole lot of Scottish Nationalists who're still chanting about Scotland's oil and they're getting more militant. The United Kingdom needs that oil. We're still paying the Americans for the Second World War. The referendum three years ago was a vote for independence and it was stolen away with the 40% rule. Some of the Nats started a 79 Group and they're shouting about public protest. It was on the telly last night. One of our MPs, Salmond, was talking about, what was

153

it? *Political strikes and civil disobedience on a mass scale.* The other guy Sillars is worse and he's left wing. The Government are paranoid about the Clydeside Reds. Then look at Maggie. She has no real mandate in Scotland. She's closing down the mines and getting up everybody's noses with her *No Lame Ducks* thing that's closing down factories left, right and centre. There's a lot of discontented people in Scotland.

Think it through Jamie. Next year is 1984. That's when Orwell said it would be a police state. Take a look around at what's happening, IRA bombs, Scottish Independence punters, reds under the bed, miners' strikes. What happens when it all comes crashing down? Do you think the Police are going to be able to control the masses? And the army? Half the British Army are Scottish. If the ball burst here, the soldiers are just as likely to join the rebels as they are to back Maggie Thatcher. When law and order isnae there it's us gangsters that'll take control. The people on the street and in the housing estates respect us. So it makes a lot of sense to have the Watchers underground in Glasgow. I just think the person that recruited Gillespie wasnae very bright. That bastard's a bampot."

"That would explain why he made the move to take over Kerrigan's network. There must be lots of yuppies getting their highs through Kerrigan. What a wonderful way to get control of some of the people that matter. Do you know Mister O'Connor I think you should give up this gangster thing and get into politics. You're very well informed"

"Politics? Aye Jamie lad, they're the biggest gangsters of the lot."

We arrived back at the High Court and took our respective places in the public gallery.

Yet another cup of coffee

As the panoply of Scottish Court pageantry filed in I sat on the press bench re-thinking O'Connor's strange revelations. It was crazy enough to make sense but for the time being I resolved to keep it to myself. I wouldn't be the first to make an idiot of myself with an exclusive exposé. It was certainly worth further investigation.

Meanwhile Court resumed and both Counsels delivered their summing up. The Crown Advocate Deputy claimed that only providence had saved Iris from a murder charge. The death of Jenny Kerrigan was the result of Iris's confrontation. The evidence showed that she went to the salon intent on confrontation. Where the accused could have taken action that would have prevented the death and failed to do so, he or she is culpable in the eyes of the Law. Her actions, if not evil, were at the least reckless. She could have stepped back from the affray. Instead she forced the victim into a position whereby self-injury was inevitable. The jury had no option but to find the accused guilty of culpable homicide.

Defence Counsel adopted a less dramatic pose. She didn't tell the jury what they had to do but instead asked them to consider the points of importance. She reminded them that the burden of proof lay on the prosecution. Iris Cassidy didn't have to prove her innocence but she had bravely taken the stand to explain her state of mind at the time of the accident. QC Janice Cuthbert used the word accident emphatically on several occasions and carefully avoided the word victim. The only evidence the jury had on Iris's state of mind and her intentions was that of Iris herself, who openly admitted that she had gone to confront but not to hurt or kill. On the other hand they had one witness who gave direct evidence of Jenny Kerrigan's state of mind. Finally and most importantly was the absolutely incontrovertible fact that from start to finish the weapon that inflicted the fatal wound remained in the possession of the person who was fatally wounded. This was a terrible accident that could have been avoided. Jenny Kerrigan herself could have avoided it. It was difficult to see what Iris could have done under the pressure of violent attack to avoid the outcome other than to stand passively and receive further injury herself. As she closed her notes to finish she looked directly at the jury and said in a quiet emotive voice.

"Members of the jury I beg you to find the accused not guilty and bring closure to this sad event."

The Judge delivered guidance to the jury and charged them with the task of deciding the guilt or otherwise of the accused. He repeated Defence Counsel's advice that it was the responsibility of the Crown to prove guilt beyond reasonable doubt. If they doubted her guilt they must acquit her. He reminded them that they might reach a verdict of guilty or not guilty or of not proven if they felt that there was insufficient proof of guilt. He pointed out that in the event that they found Iris guilty they might feel it appropriate to consider mitigating circumstances such as self-defence and in such case they could recommend leniency. He reminded them that the verdict need not be unanimous. The jury retired to consider their verdict. They returned within twenty minutes.

"Ladies and gentlemen of the jury have you reached a verdict?"

"Yes, my Lord. We find the accused not guilty."

"Will the accused please stand? Iris Cassidy, in view of the verdict reached by the jury you are acquitted and are free to leave the court." The Judge gave Iris a beautiful smile and she turned and smiled back at him as she stepped down from the dock.

The court emptied quickly; the prosecution to lick their wounds, the defence no doubt to get some congratulatory back-patting from O'Connor who must have been well satisfied with his small investment. The press were the quickest off their marks as the hacks ran to the nearest pub to get their stories ready for first issues. My story could wait; no big rush; I was still looking for some inside exclusive. As I ambled thoughtfully towards the street exit I was suddenly propelled backwards by what seemed like a rugby tackle. It was in fact the Procurator Fiscal, Phillip Gardner, rushing down the corridor. I managed to catch hold of the dado board and steady myself before I hit the floor.

"Mr Robertson, my profuse apologies. Are you alright? Life seems to be running on turbo these days. Actually to be truthful it's yourself I'm rushing around in search of. I was hoping to catch you before you left the building."

"You're certainly very persuasive when you want someone to change direction," I puffed, trying to catch my breath.

"I really do apologise. It was my fault entirely. As to your direction, I am quite happy with the direction you are taking, figuratively speaking. I have been following your Street Patrol and it seems to be turning over some significant stones. That's actually what I wanted to speak to you about."

"Well I was hoping I might see Iris and Freddy Cassidy before they leave."

Phillip the Fisc wasn't so anxious to give me a full interview the previous week so I wasn't inclined to bow at his beck and call today. I made to walk away. He grasped my arm.

"Iris and Freddy Cassidy are in my office. That's what I wanted to speak to you about. If you go to room 12, you'll find them there. I have something I must do and then I'll join you shortly."

No point in arguing, off I went to room 12, a small claustrophobic little closet at the back of the court. Iris and Freddy were sitting on two shabby armchairs looking fidgety and nervous.

"Don't worry Iris," I consoled her, "they aren't going to haul you back in there. You are free to leave the court. That's what the Judge said. And, hey! What was it between you and the Judge, big beaming smiles and all that? Don't tell me you know him."

Iris laughed nervously and glanced sideways at Freddy before answering, "I recognised the old bugger and he recognised me. He used to be one of my regular clients back in the good old days. He was a defence barrister at that time, quite handsome in his gowns. He defended me a couple of times but lost both cases. I think he maybe felt guilty about that and enjoyed being the one who let me go today. He's a decent sort, not like the rest of them. It's stupid you know. If a girl gets caught soliciting she gets fined but she can't pay the fine unless she goes back on the street. If she doesn't pay the fine she ends up in Cornton Vale. That's where I was on remand before my case came up. Half of the women that's in there, it's because they didn't pay their fines and most of them have kids. Why don't you do a Street Patrol on that Jamie? All the *dangerous wild women* on the streets of Glasgow."

"There's something in the pipeline about that Iris, but I don't think it'll be helpful to the girls on the street. You know the public view. They want you off the streets so they're quite happy if the police arrest you."

"Aye, I suppose you're right Jamie. Life's just one big shite and we're just the skid marks."

"That's very philosophical, Mrs Cassidy," said Phil the Fisc as he strode in with a folder under his arm.

"Aye, but you and your kind are well supplied with Andrex Soft," snapped Iris.

"You'd be surprised, Mrs Cassidy. The big shite, as you call it, isn't selective where it lands but we still have choices."

"Aye, that's what the man at the housing office said. You have a choice, Mrs Cassidy. Turns out I could choose between a ground floor with rising damp in Blackhill or a top floor with a leaky roof in Easterhouse."

"And you chose the rising damp in Blackhill?"

"Aye, with these Corporation flats, if you're on the ground floor you can get out faster when the whole lot comes down."

"I'm quite sure you'd get out no matter where you were, Mrs Cassidy. You appear to be quite adept at getting out."

"I'm awfy sorry if I burst your bubble today but the jury saw things my way. I'm fairly sure the Judge was on my side too. You would have liked to see me go down for murder. I'm surprised you didn't twist one or two witnesses to say it was me that had the scissors."

"You misjudge me Mrs Cassidy. Like I said we have choices. My recommendation from the outset was that the case should be dealt with as accidental death with no prosecution at all. I was overruled by the Lord Advocate's office. It seems the police are happy to jump on any head they can over this ice cream thing. The public are screaming that they are doing nothing. Actually you made things difficult yourself. It was your choice to go there that day and it was your choice to go and make a statement to the police. Without that statement I don't think the Sheriff would have allowed your case to go beyond the judicial examination. I had the feeling that you would not believe me so I took the trouble of having the relevant documents copied. Here they are; you may read them and I see no harm in your son seeing them but you cannot keep them and, I'm sorry Mr Robertson, but you are not permitted to see them. They are not in the public domain." He passed the letters to Iris who then passed them to Freddy.

"So, how come you're Mr Nice Guy all of a sudden?" Iris asked.

"It's not a question of being nice. The courts were already clogged up with too many cases even before this silly strike we had. The prisons are full of people on remand awaiting trial. You know this yourself. The police wanted you charged with murder, I don't know, perhaps to mark their scorecard. I could see the case was full of holes and all that would result would be a waste of valuable court time. The case was dispatched quickly but it could have gone on for much longer. I have been in this business a long time. Sometimes strange things happen. Perhaps if the charge had been murder the jury might have convicted you. I can say to you honestly now that although I tried to have the case quashed I am of the opinion that you went there that day with *mens rea*. It was your intention to harm Jenny Kerrigan."

"You make it sound as if Iris should be grateful for your magnanimity," I interposed.

"I don't claim that I was magnanimous. It was a question of pragmatism. Life goes on. There are bigger fish to fry. That's why I have asked you all here. I have a proposal to make. Mrs Cassidy, you have no need nor can I imagine any desire to feel grateful to me. However, I would be extremely grateful to you if you would consider helping me. There is something you can do for me which I believe would give you some personal satisfaction."

"You're kidding me. How would I get any satisfaction out of helping you? Unless you're planning suicide?"

"Gillespie," was the clipped reply.

Iris sat up. "Jammy Gillespie?" she queried.

The Fiscal nodded. "He's been jammy for too long. There are a few of us who feel that he has escaped prosecution and conviction too often and too long. He needs to be stopped."

"You want me to stop him? What am I supposed to do? Get him with a pair of scissors. He probably carries a blade and he's a lot bigger than Jenny Kerrigan. You're right, it would give me a lot of satisfaction but I don't think the jury would be so sympathetic next time round. But you said you'll be grateful so maybe you can get me a private cell with a telly and a bath with hot and cold water."

"You have a colourful imagination, Mrs Cassidy, but no, I think that since I'm Procurator Fiscal we are under some obligation to do it within the law. Don't you think?" I think he was enjoying the silly banter with Iris. It can't be much fun being Procurator Fiscal in Glasgow.

He smiled and continued, "What myself and the police need is information. People are afraid of Gillespie but you must have a desire for revenge that might overcome your fear."

"I'm no feared of Gillespie."

"Well just to set the record straight, I very definitely do not want you to go looking for a confrontation with James Gillespie. What I want, like I said, is information, information about his activities and his movements and his acquaintances so that we can build up a case against him with lots of little pieces and who knows, perhaps even catch him in the act. This stupid ice cream war, that's on everybody's mind, has gone on long enough. We need to take Gillespie out of the picture."

"You want me to be a snout, a grass. I'm no a grass."

"A police informant Mrs Cassidy."

"It's the same difference. Why don't you just arrest him for what he did to Freddy? We'll be witnesses."

"Both you and I know that option is dead in the water. Nobody saw him, not you nor your son Freddy nor anyone else. It's not just a case of nobody willing to talk. I really do believe that in the case of the attack on your son there truly and genuinely were no witnesses."

"He's right Mam," Freddy spoke for the first time.

"I said you would be a police informant, Mrs Cassidy. That normally carries some form of remuneration," the Fiscal dangled carrots.

"What would you want me to do?" Iris relented at the mention of money.

"This is where Mr Robertson can assist, if he is willing. I would like him to accompany you to see Superintendent Sandra Paterson at the Special Investigations Unit. He knows her but I don't believe you'll have met her. She is fully up to date on this matter. In fact this whole thing was her suggestion so she can put you in the picture about the finer details."

Freddy spoke again, "O'Connor's no goin' tae be very happy if he finds out we're a pair o' grasses."

Phil the Fisc considered his words carefully before he answered. "I know about Daniel O'Connor and I know that you work for him. I also know what was in the famous package that was tossed around in court today. We're walking a delicate path here, Freddy. You don't mind me calling you Freddy? I am the Procurator Fiscal and as such it is my job to procure evidence. I am aware that many aspects of Mr O'Connor's business fall on the dark side of the line but sometimes in the public interest I have to step occasionally into the darker side. I suggest that if you decide to help us you should be totally honest with your employer. Gillespie is also a thorn in his flesh. I think he would like to see the back of our jammy friend for a while too. Please go and speak to Superintendent Paterson. For the moment that's all I ask. Then if you don't feel happy about it you just say no and we go our separate ways."

Freddy still wasn't placated, "It's no just O'Connor. When you're a grass people always find out. Nobody likes a grass. Bad things happen."

"I understand that much more than you think but Sandra Paterson has some original ideas about keeping things quiet. Why don't you please go and speak to her and take it from there?"

"Alright," Iris agreed, "on condition that Jamie goes with us. I don't trust the police. They've never given me any reason and a few smart words from you doesnae change that."

Jamie was, of course, delighted to go with her, another excuse to see Super Sandra, a chance of pinning down Gillespie and another good story line or at least some meat on the bones of what I had. We bundled into my little Mini and off we went. Sandra welcomed us into her office, a lot friendlier than the last time I'd been there.

"Tea or coffee, Mrs Cassidy, Freddy?" she invited, "I know that Jamie's coffee," she smiled at me. Hey! The ice-lady smiled at me.

"Tea please," murmured Iris hesitantly, "with lots of sugar."

Poor Iris. She had seen the inside of a police station more times than she'd like to remember but she wasn't in the habit of getting afternoon tea. Freddy just nodded as if to say *same as my Ma*. Sandra gave them the kid glove treatment, softly-softly, with idle chatter till the tea and coffee arrived. Then she began to lead in gently, "I'd really appreciate your help Mrs Cassidy. Yourself and Freddy have had a rough time. I understand you think Gillespie was the driver when Freddy's van was shot. This guy's got a lot to answer for."

"Aye, but we can never prove it. That's the story of Jammy Gillespie's life. Isn't it?" sighed Iris.

"I have to be frank with you, Mrs Cassidy, I agree with what you say. There were never any witnesses that day and now there is no real chance of proving he was the driver. We're going to have to get him some other way," she suggested conspiratorially. I have brought in the Serious Crime Squad to try and build up a case against him and they have started to monitor his activities. That is where you can be of real help to us because we need some good, reliable information that will give the investigation more direction and purpose."

"So you want me to snitch," Iris was losing her temerity, "I've never been a snitch. And anyway, you know I've been inside on remand since I punctured Jenny Kerrigan, and we don't have any contact with Gillespie now and Freddy works with Danny O'Connor. Gillespie was working for O'Connor but no any more."

"Yes, I know all that Mrs Cassidy but don't you see? That's the great thing about it. You wouldn't be snitching. Would you? You would just be passing us bits and pieces of gossip, things that you pick up on the grapevine. The same with Freddy. He's bound to hear lots of things about what's going on and he tells you and you pass it on to us." It looked like Sandra was beginning to persuade Iris but then the mention of Freddy backfired.

"No, there's no way I'm getting Freddy involved. He's lost one eye but at least he's still got both his balls. What d'you think'll happen if Gillespie finds out. We already know he's got friends in the police."

Sandra sat down beside her, "He doesn't get involved. Freddy will never have to make contact with the police. I just want you both to listen to little snippets of gossip that you might usually ignore. We want to know what he's doing and who with. Listen I'll give you a couple of examples and you'll see what I mean. I'll ask you some questions and you don't have to answer if you don't want to. OK?"

"OK. Let's hear your questions." Iris was slowly but surely getting drawn in.

"Pat Johnson. His van was shot at like Freddy's. We are fairly sure it was Gillespie that hijacked the Frazzini van. What was the name of the Frazzini driver? I bet you know that."

Freddy couldn't resist, "Everybody knows that. It was Chubby Checker."

Sandra thought he was taking the Mickey, "I beg your pardon?"

"Chubby Checker," repeated Iris, "he's the wee fat guy that checks the wagons in the rail depot at Springburn. He sings in the pubs at night, does Humperdink and Tom Jones and Elvis. What's his right name Freddy?"

"Ah don't know Mam. Ah thought that was his real name. Was it no him that sang Twist Again?"

"It doesn't matter Freddy," said Sandra, "that's just great. You see, you say everybody knows that but we didn't. If we'd known that at the time we would have spoken to this Chubby guy and maybe he would have helped us get Gillespie. Here's another one. You say Gillespie isn't working for O'Connor so who has he teamed up with?"

"It's funny you asking that," said Iris. "Yesterday in Cornton Vale, the other women were asking about Freddy and Danny O'Connor and that and somebody said that Gillespie's in cahoots with Sam Horton and that's funny because no so long ago Danny O'Connor and Sam Horton were the best of buddies. Now he's got Gillespie trying to knock Danny off his perch."

Sandra smiled, "OK, number three. The Londoner. Did you hear anything in Cornton Vale about the Londoner?"

"Not in the Vale but I know who he is. He…"

"No, Mam!" Freddy jumped up. "No, Mam! Gillespie's an evil bastard but…"

"Aw'right son. Don't worry. There's nothing that we can say about the Londoner that he could trace back to us. We've never seen him and he doesnae know us," Iris calmed Freddy then turned back to Sandra. "Mr Gardner said that there would be numeration."

"You mean remuneration. Yes, that's part of the deal." Sandra opened a drawer behind her desk, pulled out an envelope and passed it to Iris. "There's a hundred and fifty in there. That's for the information you've just given. There's the same again if you have something decent on the Londoner. What's his connection with Gillespie?"

"I think Jammy did some work for him in the past but then he went with O'Connor and now he's got his own set up with Horton. He'll no want anything from the Londoner."

"So what's the Londoner trying to set up?"

"The story I've heard is he's the Gaffer's fixer. Kerrigan got nabbed without having time to put things in place. Jenny would have taken control with him running things from the jail but now she cannae and he's no got a second in command. He's got a good business and he doesn't want to lose it so the Londoner's up here to keep an eye on things."

"So why has he been meeting up with Gillespie?"

"Search me. He's probably just keeping his options open. If Kerrigan's operation goes down the pan he might be planning to bring in Jammy G. More likely he just wants to know what Gillespie's up to and then chop his balls off. I hope he does. It'll be better justice than your lot farting about."

"We'll get him, Mrs Cassidy. That's a promise," said Sandra. I looked at her with raised eyebrows. That was a big promise.

Freddy decided to participate again, "Superintendent, you said there was mair money. What if Ah give you a real stotter, something you don't know nuthin about? Mr O'Connor willnae mind because he hates them as much as us. Push it up to four hundred an' Ah'll give you somethin' that'll keep the Crime Squad goin' for a week."

"OK, but it better be good," Sandra really wanted to get them on board. "What's it about?"

"Minicabs."

"Minicabs?" It was Iris's turn to doubt Freddy's *stotter*.

"Aye, Mam. You'll no know nuthin about it. When you were inside, Willy Shotts had a stroke. You know Willy Shotts. Sometimes they call him Six Shots because he's supposed to have a Wild West six-shooter under his pillow. Anyway he's got a whole load of taxis on the south side in the Gorbals and Pollock and Castlemilk. It's no the black taxis like you see in the city. They're no all legal, like, but it's a big business. Mr Shotts had a stroke an' he wanted rid o' the taxi business an' Mr O'Connor was goin' tae buy it. It was aw' arranged except Sam Horton comes along an' puts in a better offer. Mr O'Connor thought Six Shots was bluffin' an' he didnae offer mair money. So Sam Horton's got the taxis."

Sandra looked a bit perplexed. She'd just agreed to pay out four hundred pounds and Freddy's *stotter* wasn't exactly stotting.

"I'm sorry Freddy. I don't really see what this has got to do with ice cream vans and all the violence. It's not even in the same part of the city."

"You're no awfy bright," Freddy replied defensively. "It's taxis. Dae ah need tae spell it out?"

My brain had already jumped three steps and I knew precisely what Freddy was trying to tell her but Sandra still thought he was trying to put one over on her. She turned to me and asked," Jamie, can you help me here. Why am I supposed to be interested in taxi-cabs? OK, so maybe they're not all licensed but that's a problem for Traffic."

"Superintendent Paterson," I gave Sandra her title, "What he's trying to tell you is that you have the potential for a war on the streets that's a lot bigger than the ice-cream war."

Iris was just one step behind me and catching up fast. "Superintendent, where are you from? The planet fucking Mars! The boy's trying to tell you that Sam Horton and our Jammy G. don't need ice cream vans any more. They've got taxis."

"OK I've got that bit. But surely that's going to ease the tensions if they move over to another business." The penny still hadn't dropped with Sandra. I couldn't believe she was being so obtuse.

"Sandra, stop and think," I tried to explain. "We're not talking just ninety-nine cones and trips to the airport. We're talking about *drugs*! Danny O'Connor uses the vans to get the drugs out on the street. Kerrigan's got a dinky little set of Jennycare vans. Sam Horton has just acquired a couple of hundred taxis. Look, I don't want to be insulting, Sandra, but if you can't see what Freddy's telling you, both you and the Crime Squad are just pissing in the wind."

She still wasn't convinced, "But they can't sell drugs from a taxi," she protested.

It was time for Iris to try again, "Superintendent, have we got a promise from you that if we talk up front and honest we've got some kind of deal that you're not just going to arrest me and Freddy all over again."

"I thought I'd made that clear," replied Sandra indignantly.

"Alright, you know about the package that Freddy was supposed to get from Gillespie the day he got shot? Right! It was about five hundred pounds worth of drugs. Gillespie was a mule. The mule takes the drugs to the shifter and he shifts them to the dealers. Freddy was the shifter and I was one of the dealers. When a shipment comes in, the big boys need to break it up and move it fast and they need distribution. Why do you think there's all this rammy with the ice cream vans? The guy that controls the vans controls the distribution in all the housing schemes. But not if somebody else has got the taxis. That'll be even better than the vans because it's in and out quick, no hanging about. Like Jamie says there could be a few battles. Danny O'Connor's no going to take it lying down and there's other people out there trying to muscle in. It's no ice cream cones and sweeties. It's millions of pounds. It's the biggest industry in Glasgow."

Sandra just stood thinking for a while before she answered. She moved behind her desk, pulled out another envelope and counted out the notes. "I realise the significance of what you're saying Freddy. I think we agreed four hundred so that's two-fifty on top of what your Mum has. You can sort it out between you. If what you say is true, it's now even more important that you keep me up to date with what's going on but I don't want you to put yourselves in danger. Here's what I propose if Jamie agrees. You know his programme Street Patrol? Well if you have anything you think I need to know just phone in on any Friday evening. Say you are a friend of Jenny and that will be a sort of code so they know it's you. I'll pay you a hundred and fifty every time you call in, provided there is something concrete. We need some way of paying you. What about if one of our officers just drives by Freddy's van."

"No, none of your officers. They'll blab and everybody'll know about us. Anyway, Freddy's no on the van any more but I think I'll take it on. I need to get myself straightened out and I don't think I'll get a job in Marks an' Spencer's."

"You like to live life on the edge. You better get a bullet-proof windscreen. I'll tell you what. We've got Chief Inspector Sinclair who works quite close with Jamie with the leads from Street Patrol. You would probably speak to him anyway when you phone in so he's going to know all about you. He can drop off your payments. What do you reckon, Jamie?"

"That all sounds fine to me. You're OK with John Sinclair, Iris. I've known him since he was a constable." I assured Iris and turned back to Sandra, " I don't know how you come up with all your ideas, Sandra but I've got a question for you. What would you have done if Iris was found guilty. You've got all this set up as if you knew she'd get off."

Iris was sitting nodding, "Aye, that's what I was wondering too."

"Women's intuition!" smiled Sandra, "Actually it really was women's intuition but not mine. I used to be in Lothian Police, like you know. My last post there was related to domestic violence. I met a very bright young QC called Janice Cuthbert and we've kept in touch. She doesn't lose many cases and she was confident about yours, Iris. If you had been found guilty she was sure that mitigating circumstances would have got you a light sentence and with the time you've already served in remand the judge would have let you go free on licence. Either way she was certain you'd walk free today. If we women stick together Iris, life isn't always such a big shite."

"Aye, alright but I'm only doing this till we get Gillespie. I'm no going to spend the rest of my life as a copper's snitch. That's just as bad as being a street hingoot."

"I accept that," confirmed Super Sandra.

Iris, Freddy and I squeezed back into my Mini and I took them home to the rising damp in Blackhill. I left them hoping things would turn out better for them but I'm afraid I'm a defender of Iris's big excrement theory. They were still in O'Connor's clutches and even on a nice day he just used people. Sandra was expecting them to produce information on Gillespie but if O'Connor's source was right and Jammy G. was in fact a government watcher, he would not slip so easily into the net. Maybe I was getting in too deep myself. The Cassidy's were not unique. I returned to the comfort of my flat on the riverside.

On Street Patrol.

Street Patrol was becoming a popular Friday night show. Audience figures were excellent and the phone-in participation was better than we ever expected. Then 1983 saw the first episodes of Taggart, that larger than life hardman Glasgow cop. Lots of people began to think that maybe we could make some impact on street crime. I was invited by ITV to switch to a television version and I had no doubt that it would work OK but it wasn't for me. I had done some TV work before but I was convinced that the real success of the radio version lay in total anonymity. More than half of the calls we received were from public phone boxes. Everybody has an opinion. Everybody loves to talk. Everybody likes their minute on the air. Nobody wants to talk to the police. Iris and Freddy had just proved it. Half of the Bobbies in Glasgow had tried to find the name of the Frazzini driver who was hurled out of his van the night of the Johnson shooting. Everybody in the ice cream trade knew it was this lad Chubby Checker but nobody told the police. Charlie Frazzini, himself, must have known but said nothing. Our little Friday programme gave people a voice. Through the initiative of the Chief Constable and Sandra Paterson the police were listening to that voice. It's strange but we nearly missed the biggest success we ever had because Sandra wasn't really listening. A caller came on the line with a gold nugget of information when Sandra was taking the calls and she nearly passed it up.

We were doing a session on credit card fraud. This was the eighties when ATMs had just appeared. At this time most people called them cash-machines while others thought there was a "wee man" in the wall giving out the money. Credit cards started to appear but they still hadn't taken hold. In the high-street shops a credit card transaction was enacted with the aid of a heavy imprinter gadget that slid back and fore. You laid the credit card in the machine, then a triple-copy sales voucher, then pushed a roller across the voucher to imprint the card. Then you wrote in the sales details by hand and if the transaction was for more than fifty pounds you had to phone the issuing bank for authorisation. The process took anything from two minutes to two hours depending on how many other people were phoning for authorisation.

Everybody in the banking sector saw it as the way forward, converting the world to plastic money. Joe Public wasn't quite so convinced. The banks decided to convince us.

Some of the big banks embarked on a major campaign to equip all their customers with a credit card whether they asked for it or not. They posted a shiny new (unsigned) card to their regular customers. All the customer had to do was sign acceptance on the form provided and return it to the bank. Then you signed the back of your card and it was ready to use. You could now go out and spend about double your monthly salary. The interest rates were quoted as monthly rates to make them look attractive. Lots of people took up the offer and the credit card started to become one of the main methods of payment.

The trouble came when these cards never reached their intended destination and ended up, instead, in the hands of a fraudster. Thousands were stolen from the Post Office sorting rooms and later offered for sale on the black market. As long as they never exceeded the fifty pounds transaction limit the bogus cardholders could scoop up two or three hundred pounds worth of merchandise. Cards stolen in one city were quickly shipped to another city to be sold and used, making it difficult to trace the cards.

Credit charges began to appear in the accounts of bank customers who had never received the card. Naturally they went screaming to their local branches demanding explanations and refunds. The banks, having invested millions of pounds in the new systems, didn't want to admit defeat so they underwrote the losses and appealed to the police for urgent help. It was the type of assignment the Serious Crime Squad was intended to tackle. The major retailers were asked to help in intercepting stolen cards and a cash bonus was paid to any alert member of sales staff who helped in confiscating a stolen card. At the insistence of the police the banks stopped the practice of sending unsolicited cards. It began to look as if they were getting on top of the situation. Then the problem of widespread drug abuse swept the country and with it a dramatic increase in petty crime. Bag snatching and purse snatching quickly doubled. Lots of ladies' bags and purses now contained a bona fide credit card. The cards were traded for drugs and then once again passed on to another part of the country to be used to buy merchandise that could in turn be traded for cash. The banks went back to the police for help, this time insisting that it was a police problem. Pressure mounted on the regional crime squads to cooperate nationally and come up with a solution. This time it was Glasgow that came up trumps, thanks to Street Patrol.

It was a Tuesday and we were busy preparing for the Friday programme. We were going to cover the more topical issue of drunk driving, breathalysers and losing your driving licence. It was a contentious issue and the debate was sure to be heated. Everybody agreed that the problem had to be tackled but nobody wanted to lose their licence for just one extra drink. We had particularly scheduled this one around John Sinclair's holidays. We expected a large phone in level from our audience but nothing important or interesting for the police so we didn't need John. So it was something of a surprise when he called me that afternoon.

"Are you not supposed to be on holiday?" I asked.

"Holiday!" he answered dryly, "Aye, that's a nice thought. The wife's got me redecorating the kitchen."

"OK, now I see. You want to come in on Friday to escape from the wallpapering. No problem, that's what's great about radio. Just come in with your painter's overalls. Nobody'll notice." John always came to the radio studio in uniform and cracked endless quips about my garish T-shirts.

"Jamie, do you never get tired of your own silly jokes?"

"Never, John. Life's more fun on the flip side."

"I would call it the flippant side and it might be fun for you but not for the rest of us who have to listen."

"Hey, Hey, Hee, Hee, get off of my cloud! What's bugging you? Sounds like more than just the wife wanting a new kitchen."

"OK, sorry Jamie. Aye, you're right. It's the Chief. He's shouting and bawling about this credit card thing. You know he's already got a bee in his bonnet about the lack of leads we pass to Crime Squad. He's got a big meeting of all the Chief Constables in London next month and I think he wants to impress. So the bottom line is he's asked me to ask you if we can do a Street Patrol on credit card fraud. Maybe we could get a couple of phone-in leads."

"No problem at my end John. The week after next, how would that suit? You'll be back off holiday then."

"How about Friday this week? That's the other thing Jamie. You know how the Chief is trying to up the public image of the police. He sees our job as fighting crime and keeping the streets safe for people to go about their business. He says it's not our job to go around *arse wiping* for the Government. He's not against the drink driving campaign, in fact he's all for it, but he says it's going to set us back ten years with the public. So he's not mad keen on you covering it and stirring up debate about it in your programme. He says it'll just increase the negative view of the police. I have to say I agree with him. What do you think, Jamie? Could you re-schedule Friday?"

"Bugger off, John. Have you got any idea how much time and effort goes into putting a guest panel together. You just swan in, sit on your arse and take phone calls. We've only just got it all in place and you're asking me to call up all the panellists and tell them it's changed. You can't do that to people."

"Who have you got on?

"We've got Alistair Douglas, Chairman of Scottish Brewers and Johnny Talbot, the Rangers striker who lost his licence a couple of weeks ago. For the police we've got Jack Stirling from traffic. I think you know him."

"Well Johnny Talbot didn't just lose his licence, you know. He was pissed as a monkey the night he was stopped and when they took him into the station he'd lost his wallet. Whoever took it hit his credit card next day for over a thousand quid. He had a high credit limit. I think he might prefer to talk about that. I can talk to Jack Stirling for you and I'm willing to use my charm on Alistair Douglas if you give me his number. On top of that the Chief's been selecting his own panel. He's got the Chairman of the Bank of Scotland. They do Barclaycard/Visa up in Scotland. And he's got the Scottish Regional Manager of Curry's TV shops. The Royal Bank of Scotland are planning a big push on Access cards and it seems they offered to do a radio advertising campaign if we do a special on the credit card problem. They're making noises about sponsoring Street Patrol for a year. Check it out with David and see what he says. I'll call you back in half an hour. Have to go, I've got a sheet of wallpaper just fallen on top of the bird cage."

"What are you doing with a bird cage in the kitchen?"

"The dog barks at the bird all the time, if we keep the cage in the living room."

"What a menagerie! Family life? Sometimes I'm glad I'm still single."

"Aye, they don't call you Jammy for nothing. I'd love to take up your offer of coming in my overalls but what if I tempt you with some icing on the cake. If you agree to the change I'll persuade Sandra to come in and take my seat. I've seen how you look at her."

"OK. You have a deal. I'll talk to David. I don't imagine he'll turn down the sponsorship thing. Enjoy your painting."

He didn't answer but there was a distinct crash in the background before the phone clicked off.

I spoke to David. Friday was quickly re-shuffled to talk about credit card security. Johnny Talbot, the footballer, was more than happy to switch subjects and remain on the panel. David got Telfer Adamson, the Dean of the Business School at Strathclyde University to join in. Jack Stirling, the traffic cop was swapped for his brother Alan who was one of the team leaders in the Crime Squad. Add to that the Chairman of the Bank of Scotland and the Regional Manager from Curry's and we had a very competent panel. The Chief Constable spoke to the Chairman of Scottish Distillers to excuse the last minute change.

Friday came along and Street Patrol went on the air. John was still wrestling with his wallpaper but he had, as promised, persuaded Sandra to sit in for him. It's a pity we weren't on TV. She was looking radiant. The calls were slow to come in at first but as people started to realise that they weren't alone in being ripped off, more people rang in. We took ninety-three calls from folk who had lost cards or had never received their card in the first place and all of whom had subsequently been charged for purchases they never made. They were all quite angry and were blaming the banks, not the police. We only had one call from a member of the public who offered a lead on the fraudsters. Sandra nearly missed it.

"It's about my boy," said a distraught mother's voice, "He was doing well at school and everything. He was a good lad till he got involved with drugs. At first it was just a couple of smokes with his schoolmates but then he started into the hard stuff. His behaviour changed. He began stealing from my purse and I knew we had a problem."

Sandra started to cut her off. "Hello love. We understand your problem but we're not doing drugs tonight. We're doing credit card fraud."

It was quite common to get calls that were not related to the question in hand and we had a procedure in place to handle it.

"We'll be doing drugs again in a few weeks. For the moment I'm going to pass you over to a colleague who'll take your details and he'll put you in touch with a counsellor who can help you deal with the situation. Just hold on a second and I'll put you through."

"No! No! Wait! You don't understand. I know it's credit cards you're doing. That's why I called." Sandra caught the urgency in the mother's voice and stayed with the caller.

The woman continued, "The thing is he stopped taking money from my purse a few weeks ago but his moods were still the same and I felt sure he was still doping. He had to be getting money from somewhere so I took a look in his room. I found two credit cards with other people's names and there was a box with about twenty new music cassettes still in their wrappers. I think he's using the cards to buy cassettes and then he's probably selling them cheap to his friends."

"Do you have any idea where he got the cards?" asked Sandra.

"No, I've got no idea and he's my boy so I can't go to the police but I'm terrified he gets caught. He's not a bad boy. What can I do? You've got to help me."

Sandra signalled frantically for help in taking the calls. She did a "thumbs-up" sign with both hands, which was the signal we'd agreed for a caller who was giving good information that we didn't want to go out on the air.

"Would you like someone to go out and talk to you at home?" Sandra prompted.

"Aye, maybe, but it would have to be in the morning when Davy's at school."

"What about Monday morning? Is that OK for you?" Sandra pushed.

"Aye, Monday's fine. Thank you. Do you want my name? It's Kathy Coulter. You'll need my address. Won't you?" She filled Sandra in with address and directions and agreed on 10.00 a.m. Monday.

"Can you send Jamie Robertson? I don't want the police. I won't help you if you send the police. I don't want Davy to get into more trouble."

"OK. I'll get Jamie to go. Don't worry. If there's any problem with that we'll ring you on Monday morning."

All this was going on while I continued to conduct the programme on air so I didn't know about my Monday meeting till we came off air and Sandra brought me up to speed. Anyway, I had nothing on for Monday so there was no problem.

"I'll come along too," said Sandra.

"But I thought she said no police."

"She doesn't need to know who I am. I'll keep quiet. I'll dress in civvies and you can just introduce me as a colleague and she'll think I'm from the radio too."

"You're devious Sandra Paterson," I chivvied.

"Don't you think beguiling is a nicer adjective?"

"Much nicer and I do agree that you are beguiling but in this instance devious is more accurate. You agreed with this woman that there would be no police. You agreed on my behalf and I always stick to my word."

"You've heard what they say Jamie. Unlike poles attract." She smiled, a beguiling smile. On Monday morning we went together to see Kathie Coulter.

The Coulter house was in Milngavie just north of the city. It was a detached bungalow in a quiet residential street, definitely not a poor family. Sandra was as good as her word. She kept quiet and let me do the talking and the mother never questioned who she was. She took us to the boy's room and showed us the cards and the cassettes. I asked Sandra to jot down the numbers of the cards and we returned to the living room.

"We really want to help you Kathy but you've put us in a difficult situation," I explained. "We have now witnessed a real crime situation and you don't want to involve the police. For lots of reporters that wouldn't present such a problem but in my programme I work very closely with the police. If I don't report this I am technically a party to the crime. We need to find a way round this."

"Davy would never forgive me if he knew that I reported him. There must be another way." Kathy Coulter was now crying.

"There is maybe a way," interrupted Sandra. She flashed me a look that said *I know I'm supposed to keep quiet but we need to bag this one.*

She moved across the sofa to sit closer to the mother and continued, "What if we could guarantee that Davy will not be arrested? We could get a couple of officers to speak to him as he comes out of school and he would never know that you gave us the tip."

"But how can you guarantee that they won't arrest him. I was listening to what they said on the programme and they sounded desperate to catch somebody." Kathy was pleading.

"Well first of all Street Patrol has an excellent relationship with the police and that includes some senior officers. They will listen to what we say. They are desperate to catch the gangs who are trading these stolen cards. Your Davy is more of a victim than a culprit even though he is very much breaking the law. He is a small fish and they want to catch the big sharks. We have taken a note of the card numbers. We can run them through the credit card company and they will tell us what purchases have been made recently. If the officers present Davy with this information he'll never suspect it was you who gave him away. They'll lay it on heavy and give him a fright and in all probability he'll tell them where he got the cards. After that it will all click into place and the police will go after the big boys."

"You have to promise that Davy will be OK," begged the mother.

"Look at me Mrs Coulter," demanded Sandra, "I give you a solemn promise that Davy will not be charged. If we don't get that undertaking we will not send any officers. What I can't promise is that he'll be OK. You need professional help to deal with his problems. What does his father say?"

"His Dad knows about the drugs but he doesn't know about the credit cards and things. I haven't told anybody. I've been going crazy with worry."

"You know it was me you spoke to when you phoned on Friday?" asked Sandra.

"I thought it was the same voice but I was pretty uptight and I don't remember much of our conversation. You were going to pass me on to somebody else."

"Well I'd still like to pass you on to that somebody else. She has a lot of experience in helping families in your situation. I have to be honest and say that if Davy has been using heroin or cocaine you are going to have some difficult months and that's assuming he's willing to accept help."

I said nothing. I was not in a position to make the kind of promises that Sandra was making.

Sandra asked to use the phone. Kathy acquiesced hesitantly. Sandra called in the card numbers and asked for a transaction check. With things in motion we took our leave of Davy's mother and headed back to town and Sandra's office. The transaction list was waiting for us as we walked in.

Sandra picked up the sheet of paper. "OK. We have a list of eight separate purchases with places and dates. It's time to squeeze the little bugger's balls." I cringed instinctively. I was growing fond of her but she could be quite an aggressive lady.

"What about your promise?" I reminded her.

"I sometimes keep my promises," she replied smugly, picking up the phone. A few minutes later two black leather jacketed ruffians walked in, close cropped hair and looking like they hadn't shaved for several days.

"Jim Taylor and Rusty Wallace," presented Sandra, " you both probably know Jamie." They leaned across to shake hands and the smell of beer nearly knocked me off my chair. So much for the rules about drinking on duty. Sandra explained the situation to them and emphasised that she didn't want the boy arrested.

"Don't worry Ma'am," said the Rusty one, "we don't go around arresting school kids. It's not good for the image." There was a certain logic in his assurance.

"Ok, boys. Thanks for your help on this one. If you find out anything you can take it to the rest of the crime squad and start acting on it straight away. I won't be running the case but drop in and let me know how it goes."

Can I trust you?

The two "scruffians" departed and we sat talking for a while. We chatted about how the programme was going and how successful or otherwise we'd been with follow-ups and of course friend Gillespie inevitably entered the conversation. Suddenly her face went serious and she looked at me.

"Jamie, can I trust you?" she blurted out.

"We had quite an exhaustive discussion on that topic in this same office not so long ago. I thought we'd cleared the air on that one."

"No, I don't mean like that. I mean can I trust you as a friend? It's a bit like Mrs Coulter. I need to tell somebody something that mustn't go any further but once you know you will be under a moral obligation to tell. I have to ask you to trust me and I have to be able to trust you. You have to promise not to tell anybody."

"Please don't tell me you're a lesbian. I don't want to know."

"No, Jamie, I'm not gay."

"So what's the big mystery?"

"You haven't promised."

"I can't promise not to tell something that I don't know. Maybe you're just going to have to trust me as a friend." I laid my hand on hers. "Maybe you're going to have to trust me as more than just a friend."

She went rummaging in her handbag. I thought she was going to cry so I handed her my handkerchief. She waved it away and continued rummaging. She produced two pieces of paper which she handed to me. They were bank statements, one for the last three months and one for the same period of the previous year.

"What am I looking for?"

"Payments into my account, apart from my salary that is."

"There's £189.50 every month for last year and the same payment this year has gone up to £400. I take it that's your flat in Edinburgh and that you have it rented out. The name of the payer was Ronald Lee. Now it's Sonia Lung. Is Ronald Lee not the guy that's got all the Chinese restaurants? What does he want with a flat in Edinburgh? You've hiked the price quite a bit. Have you not? Four hundred's a bit steep. Anyway, what's the problem?"

"That is the problem. Four hundred is very steep and I never asked for that much. That kind of price can get you a posh flat in Merchiston. Mine's in Gorgie. And yes Ronald Lee has several Chinese restaurants. At least three of them are rented from a gentleman called Sam Horton. I think you know him. Two Chinese girls rented my flat when I moved to Glasgow. They said they were students and that the rent would be paid by a family friend from Glasgow. Then just a few months ago they started paying this ridiculously high rent. I didn't put the price up and I didn't even notice till last week."

She rummaged in her bag again and produced a small card. It was the kind you see in shop windows advertising flats for rent and puppy dogs for sale. This card wasn't offering puppy dogs for sale. It offered oriental massage by a student from Hong Kong. Her name was Sonia and there was a phone number.

"That was in the newsagent's window two doors up the street in Gorgie." Sandra explained, "I went there last Wednesday."

"I suppose you've checked out the number."

"I checked with BT and it's registered at my address. I phoned the number and got an answering machine, a sweet little voice offering *velly chamming body massage fo' good plice*." She stomped back and fore nervously and then grabbed her bag again. She pulled out another two papers and threw them at me as if they were contaminated.

One was a newspaper cutting from the classified ads with similar wording to the shop window card. The other was the ubiquitous warning notice made up of letters cut from a newspaper, the kind you see in films. In all my years as a crime reporter it's the only one I've ever seen. It would have been comic if it hadn't been real.

"Go back to Edinburgh. You are not welcome in Glasgow. Bad things happen in Glasgow. The Chief Constable would like to see your bank statement. This is a warning from friends of Gillespie."

"Wow!" was the extent of my intelligent input.

"Now you understand why I want you to promise that you won't tell anybody," She looked at me pleadingly. "This would ruin my career. Even if they believe that I'm not accepting kick-backs, I'll go down as an incompetent idiot, allowing myself to be compromised."

"I promise not to say a word to a living soul but I also promise to do everything in my power to make you sort this out yourself now before it gets completely out of hand. You don't have to be Einstein to know what's going on. Why don't you get them evicted? No, it isn't that easy. Is it? But did you not have a clause in the contract about not conducting any kind of business?" I looked up at her hopefully. She shook her head.

"What about your old colleagues in the Lothian force? Surely they could pay these girls a couple of *friendly* visits." This time I shook my own head. "Not really a practical solution. We need to get that advert stopped. I imagine it's from the Evening News. Is it? I know the editor, Tommy Grierson. I'll give him a call. You need to go back and check the other shops in the area and pull down any other cards."

"Could you do that for me? The advert I mean. Get it stopped. It is the Evening News."

"It'll just take one phonecall. I don't need to go into detail. I'll just say it's displeasing the police. He knows me well enough. I don't understand how it slipped through in the first place. They don't usually run ads like that"

Two minutes later it was done. We were too late to stop that evening's edition but from next day the advert would be cancelled.

"Thanks Jamie. That's one part sorted. I can get my sister to do a round of the shops to take down any cards. The thing that worries me most is that they have my bank account. Just imagine if they pay in a few thousand pounds. How would I even try to explain that away? You can see why I asked you to keep this to yourself. You can't tell anybody especially any of your colleagues in the press. They would just crucify me with a story too good to refuse."

"You've just given me an idea," I said. "There is a way to beat this but it's very high risk."

"It's already high risk," she sighed. "I'm willing to consider any way out. What do you have in mind?"

"Well, you've just said it. It's a great story but we have to turn it around and go on the offensive. The way I see it you need to kick the ball into touch now. There's only one way to do that. Publish and be damned, as they say. Except I don't think you need to be damned. You could end up getting praised if we get all the angles lined up straight. The first thing you have to do, no matter what you say, is go to your boss and show him the papers you've just shown me. Then tomorrow morning you need to speak to your bank and have every penny that you have received extra all placed in a holding account. When that's in place we go public with a full front page disclosure. With my name on it the public will come out on your side. A *Jamie Robertson Exclusive* has more credibility than the Holy Scriptures. The final step is to initiate legal proceedings to have these girls evicted and then sell the bloody flat. It'll always just bring you problems. A police officer is always compromised if he or she has any source of income other than police salary. You're not just another bobby on the beat. You're a rising star. You have to be squeaky clean."

"I love you Jamie Robertson!" She planted a big sloppy kiss on my cheek. "Like you say it's high risk but what the hell? If it works I'll come out as the people's heroine. It's not going to be easy telling the chief, though. He thinks the sun shines out of my bum."

"Listen Sandra. What I said about accepting a second source of income. Do a little research among the officers some time. How many are taxi drivers on their day off? How many are security advisors? How many used to be joiners or electricians and still do moonlighters on the side? That's just the good guys. Then there's the darker side, the ones who accept pay-offs. It's not always money, sometimes just free drinks or free meals, free girls, free holidays. The Chief Constable knows this and that's the principal reason he brought you in from outside. It doesn't matter how much your bahookie shines, if you're compromised now you cease to be any use to him. You can't just run and hide. Even if you don't want it plastered on the front page you still have to tell a more senior officer. You can't avoid that. In your place I would go right to the top, no point in messing around."

"Wow! Just like that, I go and tell him that his favourite toy is broken. He'll wipe the floor with me. He went out on a limb with this Special Investigations Unit."

"Well, it depends how you sell yourself Sandra. You can be the person who tells him his favourite toy is broken or the person who knows how to fix it. Lay it on thick like layers of marmalade. You're prepared to put everything on the line, front page in a mainline newspaper risking total humiliation. Remember he picked you from the list of runners because he saw you as a winner not an *also ran*."

"I hear where you're coming from. I'm not sure I like being compared to a racehorse but he is looking for a different approach. This, sure as hell, is a different approach."

"Of course you also have an ace up your sleeve."

"I have an ace up my sleeve? That's a laugh. The way I see it I'm holding both jokers."

"Exactly, and who do you reckon are the two jokers. Who's behind all this? Who put the Chinese hookers into your flat? Who put the money in your bank account? *Who put the ram in the rama lama ding dong*? It wasn't Charlie Brown."

"Well that's obvious, Horton and Gillespie."

"And who put Gillespie into Glasgow's great melting pot of crime?"

"He put himself, with a little help from people like Horton."

"That's not exactly how I heard the story."

"What's this? Another *Jamie Robertson Exclusive*."

"What if I told you he's an undercover agent working for MI5?"

"Yes, and Mickey Mouse is a CIA agent. I'd say you've been reading too many action man comics. Come on Jamie. Where did you pick up that little gem?"

"Well let's go with the horse-racing idioms and call it an odds-on bet. I can't prove it and you would find the lines of communication blocked if you tried to check yourself but your Chief Constable has a direct line to the Metropolis. Ask him to check, in fact, insist that he checks."

"What do I do if this all goes pear shaped? The chief might just decide to call in internal investigators and I would be suspended pending the result. We both know what the result would be. I'd be out on my ear."

"Well, you could marry me and become a happy housewife."

"D'you know Jamie? I could think of worse things than being Mrs Jamie Robertson but you know me. I'm a career girl." She touched my hand softly. "We can be good friends. Maybe you'd like me to show you sometime that I'm not gay."

"OK, career girl you can show me later. Right now you have to go upstairs and fight your corner. What you just said a moment ago is right. The moment you tell your boss he's obliged to call in the investigators but he can't do that till tomorrow. So we have to bring it forward and get into the paper tomorrow. That gives you the edge in any investigation. I did say this was high risk. If you get me a typewriter I'll start on a first draft while you're away and the chief can have a chance to veto what's in it."

She picked up her phone. "Hi Mary. I need to speak to the Chief Constable urgently. Can you check if he's still in the building and get him to wait? And can you send in a typewriter to my office now please."

A couple of minutes passed and Mary came in pushing a typist's trolley. "The chief is still here Ma'am. He's waiting for you upstairs but he says to hurry."

"Wish me luck." Sandra said and walked out the door behind Mary.

I sat down at the typewriter and started writing. I found myself singing quietly as I clicked away:

Who put the ram in the rama lama ding dong?

Who was that man?

I'd like to shake his hand.

He made my baby fall in love with me.

She was gone about half an hour. When she returned the Chief Constable bustled into the room with her. "Good evening, Mr Robertson. We appreciate your help. Sandra has put me in the picture. This could be a crucial moment in what we are trying to do. We can't have people going around thinking they can just pop police officers into their pockets. It's not just corrupt; it's down right wicked. Where's it going to end? We have to nip it in the bud. I like your idea, full frontal attack. I also agree with what you say about the urgency of the matter. Now that Superintendent Paterson has informed me I am obliged to invoke an internal enquiry but I can't do that till tomorrow. So we only have a very small window of opportunity. Can you manage to get a front page story out for tomorrow morning?"

I pulled the second page from the typewriter and handed him my two-page draft article. He scanned it quickly.

"Can you add a direct quote from myself commending the boldness and bravery of Superintendent Sandra Paterson. And can you add to that quote, *Police work is becoming more and more challenging every day with clever criminals trying to outwit the law while individual officers are increasingly shackled by procedural constraints. The only way ahead is to fill our ranks with officers who face up to the challenge with boldness and integrity and refuse to be outwitted by these dangerous elements.* I want it to be clear from the outset that I stand 100% behind her."

"Do I have your permission to publish the threatening letter?"

"Definitely. The whole point is that the officer concerned has taken the right course of action. We must demonstrate that she has been threatened but not compromised. Sandra, can you make sure that Mr Robertson has a good photograph of yourself. In uniform is best. I'll leave you both to get on with it. I have a meeting and I'm already running late but I'm glad you came to see me. You don't need to clear the final draft with me. Just go ahead and do your best."

As he turned to leave the two crime squad "scruffians" burst in. A cloud of beer odour wafted in ahead of them. The Chief Constable bristled noticeably. With no pardon or excuse me they just barged in chirping with their success.

"We got the name of the person who sold the cards to our Davy lad. Would you believe he bought them from the ice cream van that's parked inside the school ground at lunch time?"

"That's the stolen credit cards, Sir," Sandra enlightened her Chief. "We got a good lead from Street Patrol on Friday. Oh! God! I've just realised. That boy's mother thinks I'm a radio station employee. She's going to see me in the paper tomorrow." She turned to Rusty the red head. "What did you do with the boy?"

"Like you said. We put the frighteners on him. We took him home and laid it on heavy with his mother, told them that this time we were letting him off with a warning."

The Chief Constable caught on quickly to the conversation. "I take it this boy Davy was your lead from Friday. He had stolen cards and you're letting him go with a warning?"

Sandra stepped in to defend the detectives. "It was on my instructions, Sir. I could see no other way forward. She refused to help if her son was going to be charged. We desperately needed a lead on where these cards are being traded. I asked the lads here to go squeeze the information out of this boy and then go light on him. If he'd clammed up we could have got him sent to Young Offenders for a year or so and we'd be no further forward." She turned back to the swirl of beer odour, "Who's the owner of the ice cream van?"

"It's one of Danny O'Connor's. We don't have the driver's name but we'll go along and grab him tomorrow."

The Chief Constable headed towards the door and turned back round just as he opened it, "You say this van is parked inside the school grounds?"

The two detectives nodded, "Yes Sir!"

"That's not permitted. These ice cream vans are just a total pest especially when they're parked at a school but they definitely can't park inside the school grounds. I'd like you lads to do a full report on this and have it on my desk for ten tomorrow morning. I'll have a word with the Director of Education. Anyway I'm off. Good night to you all. Excellent work."

I got together my draft copy, Sandra's photo and her bits of paper and set off for the Editor's office. I got my front page and it hit the streets next morning with the bold headline:

THUGS TRY TO TRAP ONE OF GLASGOW'S TOP COPS

Below this was a half page photo of Sandra smiling proudly in uniform. Both radio and TV covered the story in the midday news. The Chief Constable got congratulatory phone calls from the Secretary of State for Scotland, the Procurator Fiscal, several senior judges and from the Chiefs of the other Scottish Constabularies. Sandra was totally vindicated and it was decided that no internal investigation was required.

With regard to the credit card investigation the van driver was apprehended and was singing lots of names in the hope of getting a lighter sentence. When questioned about parking in a school playground he claimed that he'd paid the Head Teacher fifty pounds a month for permission to park. The Head Teacher was suspended from his post pending an enquiry. Regrettably there was little that could be done to prosecute whoever had tried to set up Sandra. We knew it was Horton and Gillespie but proving it was not going to be easy. Arresting Gillespie would only lead to another humiliating release.

In the afternoon the Secretary of State for Scotland had a mysterious change of heart and slapped a D-notice on the story of Sandra's bogus bribery. Despite what most people believe, there is no legal obligation for the media to comply with a D-notice but convention usually rules so there was no mention in the evening news. But both Sandra and myself were delighted with this knee-jerk reaction from the Government because it effectively confirmed that Gillespie was on their payroll. The Chief Constable, on the other hand, went berserk. He spent the rest of the day calling every Member of Parliament in Scotland. How dare they send an operative into his patch without informing him and setting ground rules? He demanded and got an interview with the Secretary of State down in London, later in the week, together with the head of MI5.

On the Wednesday I got back into the old routine and with a lot of help from the others at the radio station we got back on track for the next Friday programme. We already had the plans in place for the drink driving debate so with the Chief Constable otherwise engaged it seemed a good moment to get it out of the way. It turned out to be a lively, entertaining debate and as we wound up I decided to go home and have a quiet night in front of the telly. However this was not to be. Sandra phoned and caught me just as I was leaving the studio. The Chief Constable would like us both to join him for dinner at the Great Western Hotel, his way of saying thank you for a job well done. It would have been churlish to refuse.

We had a private booth in the corner of the restaurant. He did indeed thank me profusely for my help but it soon became clear that his true motive was to quiz me about Gillespie's connection to MI5.

"I'm not so naïve that I don't see the need for special investigators but it appears they placed a particularly disagreeable character on my patch without so much as a by-your-leave. It's obvious that they had some influence among some of my officers. Otherwise he would not have escaped justice so often and for so long. He really pushed things beyond the limits of reason. I ought to have been kept informed but someone decided that his cover would be more authentic if only a few carefully chosen officers knew. Anyway I have done a review of my executive staff. One of my Assistant Chief Constables will be moving to the Borders. Until the post is filled Sandra Paterson here will be taking over his duties with the rank of Chief Superintendent. Her main responsibility will be liaison with the Government agencies and with Special Branch in the other Constabularies. John Sinclair will take over the work of the Special Unit but will not have any change of rank for the moment. That will come in due course. He will continue to work with you on Street Patrol."

I wondered why he was bouncing all this of me. "I assume you are telling me all this in confidence. You don't want another front pager for tomorrow?"

"Good God, yes. It is all in the strictest confidence, at least for the moment while my officers have time to digest the changes. Next week you can print what you like. But tell me, don't you think it is ridiculous that you should have known about this dreaded Gillespie figure while the Chief Constable remained in ignorance? You don't have to answer that. Ignorance has never sat comfortably on my shoulders. That's where you people in the press have an important role to play. Some people say ignorance is bliss but that's a load of bollocks. I believe in openness." I could tell he was leading somewhere so I let him roll on.

"You knew about Gillespie, about his army career and how he was recruited. Would you be willing to disclose your source? It won't go beyond this table, I promise you. I'm just intrigued that it slipped by me. Did John Sinclair know?"

I chose my words carefully, "John Sinclair worked for many years at the Police Records Office but the office was really unnecessary. John is a walking encyclopaedia of offences committed in the Strathclyde region. There is very little that he doesn't know. He would have a mental list of all the offences that Gillespie committed and escaped from. The John that I know would have made it his business to find out why. I would say that he probably did know but like all the other less senior officers he didn't see it as his place to question orders from above. How were these officers to know that you were in the dark? But I think your question really is, did John Sinclair tell me." I paused for his clarification.

"Yes, I suppose that was my question."

"John and I have never discussed whether or not Gillespie was MI5. My source would never be considered a reliable source. The truth is that when I told Sandra on Monday it was with tongue in cheek. I was not absolutely sure. She needed some more ammunition to confront you and I felt sure you would check it out. As things happened they stuck a D-notice on the story and at that point I knew there had to be a reason."

"You have cleverly avoided telling me who told you."

"Sorry. It's the habit of a lifetime, difficult to break. It's no big secret. I was told by Danny O'Connor. That's why I had reason to doubt it but the more I thought about it the more I thought it might be true."

Sandra stepped into the ring. "You told me you had no connections with Danny O'Connor. When did you have this cosy conversation?"

"It was the same conversation when he told me that he had paid for your friend Janice Cuthbert to get Iris Cassidy off a culpable homicide charge." If I had hit Sandra on the head with a brick I don't think it would have had such an effect. She was visibly stunned.

"Why didn't she tell me?"

"Well I call it the habit of a lifetime because I don't have a legitimate excuse but I think she can call it client confidentiality."

"Welcome to the world of the ill-informed, Chief Superintendent," the Chief Constable said dryly, "both you and I seem to be a couple of steps behind this O'Connor fellow. I take it we are speaking about the same O'Connor that you mentioned on Monday night who has his people selling bogus credit cards."

"Amongst other things," I agreed, "Danny O'Connor will sell you just about anything and if he hasn't got it he'll find it for you. I don't have *cosy connections* with him like Sandra suggests but I have followed his career for twenty years. He's what you might call an honest rogue. He's a gangster, no question, and not the kind of person you want to cross but if he tells me something it usually turns out to be true. He told me that James Gillespie was in the Black Watch and that he was kicked out of the army for assaulting someone with a knife just as he was about to pass out into the SAS. O'Connor reckons he was picked up by MI5 and sent back to Glasgow to blend himself into gangland."

"For what purpose?"

"O'Connor thinks it's to keep an eye on Scottish independence groups but I suspect it has more to do with arms movements and the Glasgow connections with the dissident factions in Ireland."

"None of this explains why my office should be kept in the dark."

"Well, I'm only guessing here but I think they set out to create a larger than life character, a sort of Ned Kelly. With the audacious things he gets up to he has half of the Police force hell-bent on catching him while the other half are surreptitiously letting him go. He's not the biggest gangster in Glasgow, not by a long shot, but he has become the most talked about and everybody's afraid of him even the other gangsters. But he's become a sort of urban legend so he has achieved the level of notoriety that could give him the cover he needs to go underground. Like I say, this is all just guesswork on my part."

"I'm not prepared to tolerate this state sponsored thuggery no matter who is behind it nor what their motives. Ireland has it's own set of problems. Nobody wants to see the IRA getting the upper hand and I believe that the UDA is no better. However if you look carefully at the situation, the number of deaths over there in the last couple of years has started to fall while here in Glasgow the rate of homicides in on the increase. My job is to police Glasgow and the wider area of Strathclyde. What we need is a purge on crime and more importantly a purge on organised crime. The last thing we need is home-grown gangsters. I have made my views clear to the Secretary of State. I think you will both be interested in the outcome. I have to point out Mr Robertson that the D-notice remains in place so what I am about to tell you must not go into the public domain."

"If what you tell me is something that I don't already know I will respect your decision," I conceded, "but with regard to anything that I already know or have already deduced I am free to make my own decision on whether or not to comply with the D-notice."

He studied me intently for a moment before continuing; "I think I am ahead of your friend O'Connor this time. MI5 have decided to cut Gillespie loose. He no longer operates under their protective umbrella. It seems that this decision had already been taken and implemented. You may recall, Mr Robertson, that Superintendent Paterson, as she still was at that time, questioned you about any knowledge you had of a person known as the

Londoner. You apparently had no knowledge of him or his activities. It seems that he too is an undercover operative of MI5 and is deeply embedded in the London underworld. He was Gillespie's controller. In a strange sequence of events he came up to Glasgow recently to baby-sit the business empire of a certain Graham Kerrigan who, as you know, was sent down for the possession of drugs. Apparently he came to the conclusion that Gillespie had gone native. In any case there is now absolutely no impediment standing in the way of Strathclyde Police catching and prosecuting James Gillespie."

"So what you are saying is that you can now go ahead and clobber him but we can't report it because of this D-notice?"

"The D-notice applies to the incident involving the attempt to discredit one of our officers. There was a fear that Gillespie's true identity might be revealed and by association so would that of Jack Bolton, the Londoner. There is a real fear that organised crime is becoming a bigger monster than we can handle. It has tentacles that reach into the Metropolitan Police and, as we know, into our own force. Manchester, Liverpool and Birmingham are all affected too. That, I am told, is why MI5 have been embedding officers inside the criminal gangs. No doubt they are watching arms movements to dissident groups where the occasion arises and probably also some factions here in Scotland but it is the widespread organised criminal element that is coming under close scrutiny."

"And you are happy to go along with all this?"

"No, I am not. I thought I'd already explained my position on what I call state sponsored thuggery. Of course there are times when we need to put officers undercover and we have our own Special Branch for especially sensitive situations but to have officers going out behaving as gangsters, cracking skulls, dealing drugs and trying to corrupt honest officers and living off the spoils of crime, no. We need to have a line that can't be crossed. Most of all we need to have clear guidelines for the officers who are placed in the field, for those controlling them and for communication between senior officers so that we all know what the hell is going on in our own backyards."

"So, if you now go out and catch Gillespie for cracking skulls or dealing drugs or robbing post offices or whatever, these situations will not be covered by the D-notice."

"That is precisely what I am saying."

"And these guidelines for control and communication?"

"Somebody has to take the lead in these things. It might as well be Strathclyde. I'm hoping Sandra will bring some fresh light into the tunnel. I think 1984 might be an appropriate year to put some guidelines in place."

Time rolls on.

The crime squad started to piece together a list of people and places that traded stolen credit cards. Nearly every person caught seemed happy to grass on somebody else in the hope of a lighter sentence. One by one the outlets were closed down and the pertinent list of names and places was passed to other forces throughout the UK. Nothing is foolproof and nothing is forever but it would be fair to say that the police had got to grips with the problem. The banks were happy with the results and felt encouraged to reinvigorate their expansion plans. They stopped sending unsolicited cards and set up a single call centre where customers could report lost cards faster. Nobody managed to pin down Danny O'Connor, however. As always he was never directly involved. Some individuals in his vans and bars were arrested and convicted but he had never personally handled any cards and nobody squealed his name in court.

The Head Teacher who took the bribe to have a van in the school playground was dismissed and got a job driving the ice cream van of the driver who had bribed him and was now in custody for selling dodgy credit cards. The City Council followed up with clearer guidelines on the parking of vans near schools. Over the years they had amassed a sizeable file of complaints and they seized the opportunity to take action.

Iris Cassidy took her driving test and passed first time so she was able to take over Freddy's van. When I spoke to her she assured me that she was clean from all drugs and was only selling legal goods from her van. She had smartened herself up and Danny O'Connor seemed to have renewed a romantic interest in his old flame. Nevertheless, the arrangement she made with Sandra only lasted a short time. John Sinclair wasn't happy about it and Sandra had moved on to her new posting. I don't think Iris ever called in any significant information to John. In the end it just kind of fizzled out as other events took over.

Graham Kerrigan was likely to be released in the autumn of 1984 but nobody was sure exactly when. Tensions were heightening as the day approached. The Gillespie Horton taxi enterprise blossomed and they abandoned their push into the ice cream market but their enhanced mobility strengthened their grip on the market for drugs and their battle with O'Connor intensified. Neither of the two was yet competing directly with Kerrigan who still controlled the top end of the market but Gillespie had already tried once and was likely to try again. The taxis gave him a much wider reach while the ice cream vans were limited more to the poorer housing schemes. The total drugs market was rocketing in size and with a year out of circulation Kerrigan just managed to mark time so now his lesser percentage share was shrinking. He wasn't likely to take that lying down. As summer slipped into autumn the temperature was in fact rising in the mean city.

In the previous few years both Danny O'Connor and Sam Horton had used their ill-gotten gains to acquire a portfolio of property around Marbella on Spain's Costa del Gangster. In the seventies, as Franco got older and his grip on the dictatorship diminished, millions of pounds slipped in illicitly. The banks and cajas were happy to open accounts of *pesetas convertibles* where a small portion of the money was deposited. Many houses and apartments weren't listed in the official property registers and those that were, showed up at a fraction of their market value. Wads of bank notes simply passed across the table. Anyone selling a property would openly declare how much he wanted in *negro (black money)* and how much in *limpio* (clean money). O'Connor and Horton had lots of *negro*. It was a time when property values doubled every four or five years and nobody ever asked where the cash was coming from.

Danny O'Connor had several properties and one in particular with six bedrooms, plush gardens and large figure-of-eight pool, perched on the mountainside overlooking the Med but Iris wasn't invited to join Danny in Spain. He had younger señoritas in Marbella. He promised to take her for a holiday at the end of the summer. One of his favourite pastimes was fishing and he kept a caravan permanently parked at Loch Lomond. He hadn't been for some time so he invited Iris to the Bonny Banks for a week in September. It wasn't quite like the beaches of the Costas but it was a pleasant escape from Blackhill.

They planned to stay till the Saturday but on Friday night one of O'Connor's bar managers was fatally stabbed while trying to break up a drunken brawl. Freddy, who was minding shop for Danny, panicked and drove Iris's van up to the Loch to report things to the boss. Danny decided to go back into the city and left Freddy to look after his Mam in the caravan. Danny had a well stocked drinks cupboard and mother and son went on a binge. Freddy fell asleep on the sofa and Iris rolled off to bed. At some point during the night they had some uninvited guests. Witnesses would later offer conflicting versions of what they saw but the caravan went up in flames and both Iris and Freddy perished in the blaze. By the time the fire service arrived there was little left but the charred shell and two charred bodies. There was very little material for the pathologists to do a post mortem but they were able to say that Freddy had received at least one blow to his head which cracked his skull.

Several other residents of the campsite came forward and it was established that two men were seen running from the caravan about a minute before the blaze. One of them was carrying what looked like a baseball bat. One of them left footprints in the mud which were later identified as Hush Puppies. Some witnesses said the men wore balaclavas but one woman was adamant that they were dark skinned. In the circumstances the police decided that the balaclavas were most probably the case. The question arose as to whether the target was the Cassidy's or if the real target was O'Connor himself. The two most likely perpetrators were Gillespie or Kerrigan. But Kerrigan was still in prison so he couldn't have done it himself. Anybody who knew him would agree that although he had promised revenge for being caught and jailed and for the death of Jenny, he would have done it himself not by proxy. That left Gillespie but his motive was unclear. Was he trying to kill O'Connor or Iris or Freddy? Some others suggested that Iris was double crossing O'Connor and he had faked the fire and the attack as an opportunity to get rid of her.

Then the police had a breakthrough. Two regular drinkers in Gurney's Tavern recounted that the night of the fire James Gillespie was seen passing money to Willy Gilly and his son Billy. The same two witnesses claimed that the father and son were back in the bar two nights later and were overheard saying that they hadn't planned to kill the Cassidy's or to torch the caravan but just to give them a beating and a warning to stop making accusations about Jammy Gillespie. The police jumped on this new evidence and went in search of Gilly and Billy. It didn't make sense to me for Jammy G to have done this in September. Iris was quite vociferous about Gillespie at her trial but she never passed on anything to Street Patrol or to Sandra and had been quiet ever since the trial. I checked out the names of the two witnesses and found that they both had ice cream vans and it all seemed very convenient that the alleged conversations took place in one of O'Connor's pubs. I became convinced that Danny Boy had decided to get rid of the Cassidys for whatever reason and used his cronies to foist the blame onto Gillespie. I did a little further checking and discovered that one of the said witnesses had been caught trading stolen credit cards and was currently on bail awaiting trial. The other name didn't produce any immediate links so I asked around. It turned out that this was the real name of "Chubby Checker", the country western singer who was evicted from his van by Gillespie the night of the attack on Pat Johnson.

I went to the funerals of Iris and Freddy with Sandra. We had started going out together and I have to admit that an evening at the cinema followed by a curry at the Koh-i-noor was preferable to a morning at the crematorium. I was curious about how the priest would handle the eulogies and was pleasantly surprised. He dwelt mainly on family ties and family values neatly avoiding the fact that Iris's family never saw her when they were kids. When she wasn't out hooking she was blind drunk or mind-blown on skunk. My sympathies lay with Freddy. I liked the lad. He reminded me of the Dylan song *There but for fortune go you or I*. I often think that if Maggie hadn't come along when she did and I hadn't died of hypothermia, I might easily have become a *street wean*. There was quite a large gathering of mourners and a healthy cluster of news photographers. The BBC and ITV were there to film the passing cortege. If Iris weren't dead she would have hid round the corner out of sight. I wondered who would get her flat with the rising damp and remembered that I still had to sort out Maggie's flat. We left the crematorium silently, hand in hand.

Sandra didn't speak until we reached the car. "I promised her I would get Gillespie," she reproached herself, "and now it looks like Gillespie got her first."

I didn't answer.

"Did you hear me?"

"I heard you."

"You didn't say anything. Do you blame me? You think I should have stayed in the Special Investigations Unit and concentrated on catching Gillespie. Do you think that thought hasn't occurred to me? Would it have made any difference?"

I put a comforting arm round her but still didn't answer. I didn't feel like a confrontation. I knew that sooner or later I would have to confront the devil and go head to head against the current line of investigation. I knew that arrest warrants had been issued for the three Gillespies but so far they hadn't been found. A search warrant was also in place and the police, in all probability, were in Willy Gilly's flat now. I wasn't sure what they hoped to find. It didn't make any sense to me that Jammy Gillespie has asked his cousins to do a hatchet job on Iris or Freddy. A few months ago, yes but not now.

"You're very quiet, Jamie. What are you thinking?"

"I was thinking about Maggie's flat," I answered with half-truth, "I need to get it finally emptied and wind things up. I've been putting it off. I'm surprised the council haven't been more pushy. Maggie won't be going back and I started to clear things out but I've let it drift."

"You've never told me much about your young life. How old were you when she adopted you?"

"I was about one year old when the adoption was finalised but she cared for me from the moment I was born."

"What about your mother? I mean your real mother."

"What about her?"

"Where is she? Is she still alive?"

"Maggie found me under a bush in Jamieson Gardens. That sounds funny. Doesn't it? That's what parents tell their kids. *We found you under a bush in the garden.* Except in my case it's true. The only thing that I knew about my parents was that at least one of them was Asian. Glasgow kids don't usually have such a nice suntan. Anyway Maggie found me, took me to the hospital where she worked and then after a fight with the authorities she became my official mother. She's a lovely person, getting a bit screwball now, but one of life's gemstones."

"That's a sad story. I had no idea."

"Yes, I don't tell many people because it always sounds sad and soppy but I'm not sad about it. I consider myself very lucky. Glasgow has a predominance of Freddy Cassidys. When I first started school one of the other kids nicknamed me Jammy and I've always been jammy. Now I've got you, I've got jam and butter."

We both spontaneously burst into a chorus of *The Jeely Piece Song*.

If it's jeely jam or butter

If the breid is plain or pan

The odds against it reachin' earth

Are ninety-nine tae wan.

Passers-by were watching us and laughing. It's not every day you see a Chief Superintendent in uniform striding down the road hand-in-hand with an Asian guy in a donkey jacket and a T-shirt of Mr T from the A-team, singing the *Jeely Piece Song*. It didn't feel like we'd just come from a funeral. It felt good. I put my arm around her again and we walked on towards the car park.

"Jamie, I've got something I need to tell you."

"I'm listening."

"I might be leaving Glasgow."

"Back to Edinburgh for a quiet life?"

"No, down south. I've been offered a job at Scotland Yard."

"You're definitely on the fast track. How did this come about?"

"Do you remember the night we had dinner in the Great Western and the Chief Constable was speaking about guidelines for liaison between MI5 and Special Branch and the senior Constabulary Officers?"

"I remember what happened when we went back to your flat afterwards."

"Yes, you would. Wouldn't you? But listen, this is serious. He moved me into a temporary slot that was previously filled by an Assistant Chief Constable and since then I have been working a lot with the people at Scotland Yard. Now the Assistant CC job has been filled by David MacDougal and as from next week I take over his job as divisional commander of the north east. In the meantime I have also been short listed for the newly created post of Special Branch Liaison Officer at Scotland Yard. They say short listed but I think it's just a formality. I think I made a good impression."

"You can't do both jobs. Can you? What are you going to do?"

"I've spoken to the Chief. The new liaison thing won't be in full swing till the beginning of the year and he's agreed to let me go to the planning meetings. For the next few months I take over the north east division giving the boss time to move somebody else up."

"So, it's three months *watchin' schemebos getting' bongoed on Bob Hope then off tae the big smoke*"

"Any chance of getting that in English?"

"No chance, they say that three months is enough to learn a language with total immersion. It's time you learned the *Glesca patter.*"

"That's why I think I'm more suited to the job in London. It's not so up close and personal. The north east division takes in all the housing schemes that have been involved in these ice cream wars, quite a rough area from all accounts. Do you have any advice for a greenhorn?"

"You're only going to be there for three months but it could make or break your career. It's a tough area to police. That means the people who police it need to be tough. That means they're not going to take too kindly to a fresh-faced career girl telling them how to do it. Let them get on with the job. They've been there a long while and they'll be there when you're gone. Just look and learn."

"Funny, that's exactly what the Chief Constable said."

I couldn't tell her what I really thought. Policing a city like Glasgow is a bloody tough job. There were men and women who had worked these streets for years. It wasn't the place for a career girl collecting brownie points. Just as well it was only for three months. As long as she didn't ruffle any feathers it would pass without her causing too much damage. I had fallen in love with her and she had lots of qualities I admired but she would never be one of the Glasgow Scoobies. She would be better off in an executive job down in London but that gave me a problem. I didn't want her to go.

She interrupted my thoughts. "There is one good thing. I'll have one last chance to keep my promise to Iris Cassidy. The north east division takes in the eastern side of Loch Lomond where she was murdered so my team are in charge of the investigation. I have three months to put Gillespie where he belongs."

"Maybe you'll be able to rein in the detectives in charge of the case."

"Why would I want to do that? Their doing a good job so far. They just need some encouragement and a clear sense of direction."

"Aye, that's what I mean. I'm afraid their clear sense of direction is a wee bitty clouded. Somebody pinned Gillespie's name on the board and it's the only name they see. I think a wider perspective is called for. They're going to waste valuable time chasing after Gillespie when he's not really in the frame."

"Jamie! I don't believe I'm hearing this. Like I said, I promised Iris. Gillespie is going down for this. These two other Willy and Billy cousins of his are going down too. These two did it and we can get James Gillespie for conspiracy. We have a search warrant for their flat and warrants for their arrest so it's just a matter of time till they're picked up."

"And if you don't find anything in their flat?"

"We'll find something."

"Sandra, I hope that just means you're feeling optimistic. I don't really want to consider what else you might have meant."

"Look Jamie. Gillespie's a thug. You know and I know that he's responsible for smashing people's property and people's heads. If we could pin him for everything he's done he would need to be Methuselah to serve out his sentence. We have witnesses who heard them conspiring to rough up Iris. We need something tangible to place them at the scene. Come on, Jamie, you can't have moved over to the Gillespie camp. He's evil. We have to stop him and this is the best chance we'll ever have."

"I like you very much, Sandra. I have done since I first met you. I like your flair, your positive approach, your determination to get things done and all this quite apart from your obvious attraction as a woman. If you abandon your own high principles you will become a different person. If you fabricate evidence or encourage your junior officers to do so you will have crossed a line and there's no way back. If you and your team are convinced it was the Gillespies then you need to search until you have concrete evidence. Personally I don't believe it's there to be found. I hate Gillespie as much as anybody and you know how much it has riled me in the past when he was allowed to walk free."

"This afternoon we'll have the result of the search. Let's just wait and see what we find. Then we still have to find the Gillespies and bring them in for questioning. For the moment it's an ongoing investigation."

We went for lunch and the conversation switched to Sandra's move down south and what it would mean for our relationship. I knew there was no point in trying to persuade her to stay. She would follow her own star and my practical side felt it was a good move even if my emotional side disagreed. After lunch we went our separate ways and then I saw her again in the evening in a more formal setting. She was sitting in at a press conference alongside the Chief Inspector leading the Loch Lomond fire investigation. CI George Fraser introduced himself and his new boss, Sandra Paterson, and proceeded to update the assembled reporters on the state of progress.

"We now have three suspects in custody, William Gillespie senior, his son William Gillespie junior and a cousin James Gillespie. The two Williams have been charged with the murder of Iris Cassidy and Frederic Cassidy. James Gillespie has been charged with conspiracy to murder Iris and Frederic Cassidy. All three have been remanded in police custody and will appear in the Sheriff Court tomorrow.

"It may also interest you to know that the father and son William Gillespie were arrested on the island of Arran around three o'clock this afternoon. An arrest warrant was issued yesterday and they were apprehended by local police as they emerged from a bookmaker's office. James Gillespie was apprehended in Gurney's Bar in Glasgow. He resisted arrest and one of the arresting officers received a head-butt resulting in a broken nose. As a consequence James Gillespie has also been charged with resisting arrest and aggravated assault. In addition a search warrant was issued yesterday for the flat currently rented by William Gillespie senior. The search was undertaken this afternoon and officers removed two chair-legs that were clearly adapted for use as weapons and a pair of shoes of the brand Hush Puppies. They also removed two black balaclava type hoods. These items have all been retained as possible evidence."

So we all trooped along to the Sheriff Court the next morning for the first appearance of the three accused. The courtroom was packed with press. The Sheriff reviewed each of the accused quickly, ruling that for each one there was a case to answer and that they should remain in custody without bail. Jammy had blown his chances of bail when he gave the unfortunate constable a *Glesca kiss* and for Willy Gilly and his son Billy the police maintained that there was a risk that they would intimidate witnesses. The Sheriff agreed and all three went back to the local nick.

I now had my hands firmly tied. I couldn't declare my misgivings publicly. I was convinced that Danny O'Connor had bribed or threatened the two witnesses who claimed to have seen and heard the exchanges in Gurney's Bar before and after the fire. The police were happy to take these two at face value for two reasons. There was a lot of public pressure to find the perpetrators and James Gillespie was currently Glasgow's "most wanted" gangster. I was not surprised that the police had found the two adapted chair-legs, after all this was Willy Gilly's stock in trade. As for the balaclava hoods, every hoodlum in Glasgow has one. However I was extremely dubious of the Hush Puppies. The hearsay evidence would not be enough to convict the Gillespies. The police needed some strong corroborative evidence. Even these shoes were not conclusive. It would be interesting to see what further gems of "truth" evolved. But I could not express these doubts publicly. The accused had gone before the Sheriff and the case was now quite definitely *sub judice*. Any comments that I or anyone else made now could be seen to influence the outcome and we would be held in contempt of court. In any case I couldn't go barging in accusing the police just as Sandra was taking over her new division. Perhaps she would recognise that her Chief Inspector was a little over-zealous. Perhaps I was misreading the signs and the police had the right people in custody. I would just have to wait and see. In the meantime there was nothing to stop me making my own enquiries.

Gurney's Bar was where Danny O'Connor seemed to hang out these days. From the outside it wasn't unlike Tam's Tavern where he pelted me with whisky glasses. I reminisced as I walked in the door. He wasn't going to be over-enamoured with my current line of questioning either. Nonetheless, when I called him earlier, he agreed to talk and this is where he chose to meet. I came straight to the point.

"I want to talk about Iris and Freddy."

"It's a funny business," he replied, "I still can't get my head round it. If Gillespie was after me he would have come himself and he wouldn't have stopped. He would have come after me again. If he was after Iris or Freddy he would have done it just after her trial. That's when she was mouthing off about Gillespie driving the car when Jenny Kerrigan did the hit on Freddy. He would have tried to shut her up then not now. Somebody's trying to put him in the frame and he doesn't fit."

"Come on, Danny. It's me you're talking to. You've stitched him up like a mail bag. What I don't understand is what Iris did to piss you off. I thought you and her had something going and Freddy was your collie dog licking at your shoes. I'm pretty sure she didn't grass you up to the police. So what happened? Did she refuse to call you *Mister* O'Connor?"

"You've got it all wrong, Jamie." He looked at me with sad eyes. "I didn't top Iris. I was falling in love with the old hag. She was what I needed. She didn't piss me off. She understood me. I think she's the first person I've met that I really felt comfortable with. She didn't make any big demands. We had a nice week at the caravan."

"So why are you trying to stitch up Gillespie?"

"What is it with you, Jamie? When you get an idea in your head you don't fucking listen. I didn't set fire to the caravan and I didn't get anybody else to do it. I don't believe Gillespie did it and I don't think he got anybody else to. And I know what you're going to say. That just leaves Kerrigan but he couldn't have done it because he's still in Bar-L and he wouldn't have put out a contract on them because he would want revenge for himself."

"Then who did it?"

"I'm fucked if I know, Jamie. I've thought of every angle and there's nothing makes any sense. I think maybe they just picked the short straw. A couple of bampots came along that knew it was my caravan and thought there might be something worth taking. Except they didn't expect to find anybody there and Freddy rumbled them in the dark. There's a paraffin lamp. Maybe it just got knocked over. Or maybe the two silly buggers knocked over the lamp themselves and all this other stuff about Hush Puppies and things is just a whole pile of shite that some young Scooby invented. D'you know the post mortem said they were pissed as newts? What wasn't roasted was pickled."

"Danny, the two key witnesses are regulars at this bar, *your bar*, and one of them drives one of *your vans*."

"And that fat bastard over there tuning his guitar is Chubby Checker, the other witness, and he's about to start singing in this bar, *my bar*, like he does every week but I didn't tell him to go singing to the bluebottles."

"So what the hell is going on?"

"When you find out come and tell me."

Chubby Checker strummed a few chords and burst into song. The punters swayed in time and joined in the chorus of Humperdink's "Ten Guitars". He was actually quite good. A hush fell over the bar when he started singing Elvis's "In the ghetto". It's difficult to know if a singer brings business to a bar. If the singer's good they stop drinking to listen or join in. Chubby was obviously very popular. The punters swayed and clapped again as he crooned through Lena Martell's "One day at a time". I was beginning to enjoy the show when Danny nudged my ribs.

"Let's go through to the back room. I can't hear myself think." The music was making him maudlin and he didn't like to be seen as a softy.

"OK," I agreed, "but I want to talk to him before I go."

Danny spoke to the barmaid as he passed by, nodding in the direction of friend Chubby. We moved through to a small office behind the bar and continued our chat.

"You've nearly got me convinced, Danny, but you've got a lot to gain by putting Gillespie out of the way."

"The only way to put Gillespie out of the way is with a double-barrel shotgun. Don't think it hasn't crossed my mind often enough. Anyway him and Horton are out of the way. They don't bother me any more."

"Explain."

"Do you know about Six Shots the taxi man?"

"I heard he had a stroke. That wasn't exactly a stroke of luck for you. Pardon the pun."

"Aye, I thought he'd lost his marbles but the old bastard was still in the game. He sold his taxi business to Sam Horton. I thought I had it in the bag. Anyway Gillespie's squad do their stuff now in the taxis and that's taken the heat of the Tally-vans. And talking of Tallies you won't have heard about Charlie Frazzini."

"No but I think you're just about to tell me."

"Well he didn't have a stroke but he had next best thing, a bout of nervous depression. Don't blame me. It was his own doing. In fact I was his saviour. He was hitting the poker schools hard and he was on a big slider, downhill all the way. Our honourable councillor Yasser Ahmed started to get worried about the money he lent him and began giving him a hard time. Angela McCabe was threatening to leave him if he didn't get straightened out. She came to me and asked me to buy out Frazzini. So, to cut a long story short, Ahmed now has his money back and Angela and Charlie are soaking up the sun in their new villa in Mijas with two hundred million pesetas of spending money. Everybody's happy and O'Connors vans have the freedom of the city. Actually I've decided to change all my vans to the Frazzini name. It's more authentic. It was supposed to be a surprise for Iris. You know, it means I won the ice cream war that you all talked about but I'm going to miss Iris. She brought out the good side of me."

"OK. I'm listening to what you're saying. The fire had nothing to do with you and it wasn't you that set up the Gillespies. What about the two witnesses? You have to admit it's quite a coincidence that they say it was here in this bar that they saw the Gillespies."

"Not really. If I was going to rename Gurney's I would probably call it Glasgow Gangsters. Everybody comes here. Your pal from the Record comes here regular. He just sits and listens to the chit chat and goes away with his exposés on Glasgow Gangland. Joe Public thinks there's all these gangs and everybody has their own territory but that stuff's from the 1930s and 40s. The planners fucked it all up when they built the big housing schemes. There's lots of guys now just hire out when there's a job to be done or go to the highest bidder. If I had somebody that needed a really good tankin' I would just as likely get Willy Gilly if he was in the bar that night. Jammy Gillespie usually comes in on a Friday night. We put on the radio and listen to that chocolate teapot on Street Patrol. If Jammy had to pay off one of his men he's as likely to do it here as anywhere else. Willy and Billy damn near live in here when they're not in the bookies. Anyway, Elvis Presley's nearly ready for his break through there. Why don't you go and ask him?"

We went back into the bar to strains of "Love me tender".

He strummed his last chord and Danny waved him over.

"Listen Chub, this here's Jamie. He wants to talk to you. Don't worry I can vouch for him. He's a reporter, you know, the guy that does Street Patrol. He wants to talk about you being a witness against Jammy G but it's all off the record. He can't report what you say. He's no allowed once they've charged somebody."

"So why're you asking?" he looked at me as if to say *what's the point if you can't write anything?*

"I've been keeping tabs on Jammy Gillespie for years. I want to be sure that it's cast iron this time. They haul him in, go through the motions and then they let him go. What happened the night of the fire?"

"It was a Friday night. Ah was down tae sing that night and Ah got here early. Somebody turned on the radio tae listen tae your programme. It was about the girls that hawk their mutton on the street. There was a lot of banter going on and Jammy Gillespie said something about…ah cannae…this is sort of difficult." He began to dry up and was obviously embarrassed.

"Come on," said Danny, "spit it out!"

"Ah'm sorry Danny. It was him that said this no me. OK? He said that Danny O'Connor was going out with a clapped out hooker. Then he said something about it no lasting or it wouldnae be for much longer or something like that. That was when he gave the money tae Willy Gilly. Willy gave some of it tae Billy and he went tae the bar for a round of drinks."

"How much was it?"

"Christ, Ah don't know. Ah couldnae go an' count it."

"But was it a bundle of notes or just a few quid for the drinks?"

"Ah don't know."

"Did they say anything?"

"It was all sort of pub banter most of the time but then Gillespie said, "she's needing her mouth shut for her."

"And you think he meant Iris Cassidy."

"Ah don't know. There was a woman on Street Patrol, you must remember, she was prattling on about people rights and keeping the streets clear of prostitutes. He might have meant her but Lizzy Carter said Ah've no tae mention that in the court."

"Who's Lizzy Carter?" asked O'Connor.

"Dinnae get mad Boss. It was just a wee thing an' it's sorted now. D'you mind when Gillespie chucked me off the Frazzini wagon an' ah didnae go tae the polis. Frazzini just rented us the vans an' we had tae pay the insurance an' road tax an' things. Well ah didnae have any insurance. When it all blew up in the papers an' everything about Pat Johnson getting shot up an' aw' that I kept ma heid down. Then somebody telt them it was me an' they sent Lizzy Carter. She used tae be in school wi' me, now she's in the polis. She said she would let me off but Ah had tae get insurance the next day an' she said Ah owed her one. She came back the other day an' said that Tommy Riddrie had geid them evidence an' she needed me tae corroborate it. Then she telt me it was about the big shite that bounced me off ma ane van. Ah havnae said anything that isnae true, just put a wee bit lipstick an' mascara on it?"

"Tommy Riddrie is the other witness, right?" I asked for clarification. "I believe he's on bail waiting for his case to come up for flogging dodgy credit cards."

Danny O'Connor answered, "Aye, Tommy's alright but he's been hitting the big H and he's all over the place. If this Lizzy Carter wobbled her tits at him he'd say what she wants especially if she's promised to have a word in the Sheriff's ear."

"What about the other bit, when they were back in here after the fire?"

"Aye, Willy an' Billy were goin' on about it servin' her right. Big Willy said the bitch deserved it an' then something about the fire being an accident."

"Did he say it was an accident or it could have been an accident?" I asked.

"What's the difference?"

Danny heaved a sigh, "Aye, like you say son, what's the difference?"

"Can I ask you a personal question?" I asked.

"Well, Ah thought aw' this was personal but on you go."

"How can you sing and run an ice cream van? They're both night jobs."

"My wee brother does the van on the nights Ah'm singing."

"And you work in the rail depot during the day?"

"Aye but how d'you know that. You've just met me."

I avoided his question. "If you have three different jobs how come you couldn't pay for the insurance on the van?"

"Ah could pay for it, nae problem. It was just that we bought a couple of dugs. Ah'm no the only wan. Half o' the vans are no insured. Wi' aw' the vans that were smashed the insurance companies hiked the premiums. Ah was going tae pay it but Ah got the chance o' the twa dugs."

"They must have been expensive dogs."

"Aye, twa greyhounds. They're beauties." He looked at Danny. "Can Ah go back tae sing?"

"Aye," Danny sighed again, "off you go lad. Grab a pint at the bar as you go by. Tell Hazel it's on the house." He turned to me. "What about you Jamie? Another pint?"

"Aye, OK. I'll get the bus home. It wouldn't look good if they nabbed me for drink driving."

"So what do you reckon?" he asked as he came back with the two pints of beer. "Maybe the Scoobies have got him this time but they're going to need something a bit stronger than that yodelling lump of blubber. Any half decent defence counsel is going to tear him apart and they're going to say Tommy Riddrie just agreed to spout about Gillespie to lighten his own sentence. I told the silly buggers these cards would just be trouble."

"I don't know. There's a little worm wriggling around inside my brain. The whole thing doesn't hang right. You know they got Al Capone for tax evasion not for all the crimes he committed. That's fair game. Maybe they'll get you the same way some day. Another year or so and Spain will be in the EEC. You'll have to find a new laundry. But, anyway, I'm fairly sure this thing hasn't got the Gillespie stamp on it. We'll just have to wait and see what comes out at the trial."

"Do you want my advice? Forget it. Iris is gone. We can't bring her back. If the Scooby Doos in Blue stitch up Gillespie it's no more than he deserves. He should have gone down years ago. On the other hand if they let him go again it'll be no different from what it was before. Somebody'll catch up with him some night in a dark alley."

"What about justice?"

"Justice? What the fuck is that? I give up on you, Jamie Robertson. The story is some woman found you under a bush. I say you're from another planet. You've been playing Clark Kent nearly as long as I've been playing Robin Hood. Tell me once, just once in all that time, that you've seen justice. It's no about justice it's about how much you can pay for your brief. I've told you before, it's a jungle, the survival of the fittest. Does your girlfriend know you're poking your nose around in her number one case? Stop being an arsehole Jamie. Take the bus home, put your feet up and watch the late night film."

As I left Gurney's Tavern the punters were joining in a chorus with Chubby singing Bonnie Tyler's *It's a heartache*. I took the bus home, put my feet up and watched a film. The film was rubbish and I fell asleep on the sofa. When I woke up in the morning I decided it was time to go and sort out Maggie's flat. It would give me something to do instead of worrying about Glasgow's crime rate. Maybe Danny O'Connor was right. It seemed funny that he was saying the same thing as Sandra.

Rough justice.

The day of the trial arrived. Sandra was now down south taking up her new post. The High Court was still as austere as the day that Iris stood in the dock accused of causing the death of Jenny Kerrigan. Now the three Gillespies were called in to stand accused of causing the deaths of Iris and her son. The millwheel keeps on grinding. The main charge against Willy and his son Billy was that they had caused the deaths by setting fire to the caravan where the victims were sleeping. The charge therefore was murder. They were also charged with conspiracy to murder or cause bodily harm. James Gillespie was charged with conspiracy to murder or cause bodily harm. He was also charged with resisting arrest and assault on a police officer. For good measure they tagged on a charge of aggravated assault and theft of a vehicle. Chubby Checker had overcome his earlier reticence and was prepared to accuse Jammy G of the attack on Pat Johnson but they obviously had no evidence about the attack itself. The big surprise was when he was additionally charged with the illegal possession of a firearm and discharging the firearm with intent to cause injury.

I was intrigued by the way that the charges were presented. If the father and son were found guilty of murder there was an assumption of guilt also on the third conspirator, James. If they were not found guilty of the murder there was still a chance of conviction on the conspiracy charge for a lesser offence. The alleged conspiracy took place in the pub whereas the actual murder took place at the caravan. It was a subtle distinction intended to secure maximum total sentence even if the main charge of murder failed. The four additional charges against James Gillespie were thrown in for good measure but I felt more comfortable that he might in the end go down for things that he had definitely committed. It was going to be a long trial.

The jury were sworn in and the first week was spent just laying out the events and the charges. The witnesses called were the pathologist, the police attending the scene of the fire, the fire officer and four caravan site residents who confirmed that they had seen two hooded men leave the scene one of whom was carrying what looked like a stick or a bat. Large photos were pinned to a board to show the burnt out caravan, the two charred bodies and several shoe prints. The pathologist confirmed that Freddy had a cracked skull which was a recent wound and that he had detected fresh blood on the outside of his head but that both had died from smoke inhalation. A forensic expert was called to confirm that the shoe prints were of Hush Puppies.

In the second week most of the witnesses were police officers presenting the statements they had taken from Tommy Riddrie and Chubby Checker (real name Robert Williamson) and describing what happened and what was said by each of the three accused during and after their arrest. The two officers who collected the two Williams from Arran recalled that Billy seemed regretful about what had happened saying that Iris and Freddy weren't supposed to die, just get a warning. William senior told Billy to shut up and wait for their lawyer. Although the two policemen were adamant about what the Gillespies said, neither had taken formal notes of the conversation. Later, back in Glasgow at the police station and in the presence of a lawyer William senior insisted that the money he received from James Gillespie was from a private bet that he won. We saw Chubby's friend Lizzie Carter explain confidently how she took statements from her two hearsay witnesses. Chief Inspector George Fraser described the process of collecting evidence from the homes of the accused and the numbered items were placed before the jury. The Crown Prosecution continued laying out the map of the course their case would take. They indicated that a substantial part of the evidence they would produce would indicate a history of bad feeling between James Gillespie and the Cassidys and a history of collusion between the three accused.

They were as good as their word and the trial rolled on through its third and fourth week. Several extracts were read out from the trial of Iris where both she and Freddy named James Gillespie as the driver of the car in the shooting of Freddy. The judge interrupted proceedings to rule that he would permit this evidence only as evidence of possible motive. He instructed the jury to disregard this as evidence of any previous attempt to harm the Cassidys. Nevertheless a photograph of Freddy's bandaged face was pinned to the board. I was surprised the judge permitted such a flagrant breach of his own instructions. There were several points throughout the trial where the judge limited the relevance of evidence but allowed it to go ahead. The cumulative effect of several small snippets would inevitably push the jury towards an assumption of implication in the crime. The prosecution didn't break the rules but they clearly pushed out to the limits making the most of what they had, cleverly weaving their case against the accused. The defence were hamstrung on these little snippets because questioning them would only emphasise them. This inhibited their ability to highlight flaws in the prosecution case. It seemed to me that the judge allowed a lot of trivialities that did not constitute real concrete evidence.

Anyway, I had to take time out to prepare the radio show and other pieces of work so I couldn't attend the trial every day. It seemed to drag on forever and public interest began to wane. Eventually they arrived at the summing up and even that took two days. I was beginning to feel sorry for the members of the jury who had to listen to hours of both counsels drolling on with frequent interruptions from the judge to remind them of the rulings on relevance and context. Then at the end the judge took three hours himself to instruct the jury on points of law, repeating the obligatory: "The burden of proof is on the prosecution. They must prove guilt beyond reasonable doubt." The jury were out for a full day considering their multiple verdicts. It took about twenty minutes to read out their decisions.

> William Gillespie Senior:
>
> Conspiracy to murder: guilty (majority decision)
>
> Murder of Iris Cassidy: guilty (unanimous decision)
>
> Murder of Frederic Cassidy: guilty (unanimous decision)
>
> William Gillespie Junior:
>
> Conspiracy to murder: guilty (majority decision)
>
> Murder of Iris Cassidy: guilty (unanimous decision)
>
> Murder of Frederic Cassidy: guilty (unanimous decision)
>
> James Gillespie:

Conspiracy to murder: not proven (majority decision)

There was a chorus of disbelieving gasps and utterances around the court. Was Jammy G off the hook again? The judge called the court to order and the process continued.

Resisting arrest: guilty (unanimous decision)

Assault on a police officer: guilty (unanimous decision)

Illegal possession of a firearm: guilty (majority decision)

Discharging a firearm with intent to cause injury: not proven (unanimous decision)

Aggravated assault: guilty (unanimous)

Theft of a vehicle: guilty (unanimous)

The court erupted with cries of derision and cheers of delight. Nobody seemed sure what had happened. The judge ordered the public benches to be cleared. We learned later that sentence was to be passed in two weeks time and in the meantime all three remained in custody. As I was leaving the court I caught sight of Sandra. I waved and she came across to speak.

"I didn't know you were back up in Glasgow. You should have phoned."

"It was a last minute thing. The trial went on forever and I thought I wouldn't make it. I wanted to come back up to see the team to congratulate or commiserate."

"So which is it?"

"Which is what?"

"Congratulations or commiserations?"

"Why don't we go somewhere for a drink and catch up? I'll be about half an hour."

"OK, but not around here. What if we make it an hour and meet at the restaurant in Central Station Hotel? I'm hungry. I imagine so are you."

"OK. See you there in an hour." She planted a kiss on my cheek and bounced off.

One hour later we sat munching traditional cod and chips with a pint of beer.

"So, was it congratulations or commiserations? You didn't get the big man."

"Jamie, last time we met you were dead against this trial, with your purist views of Scottish Justice. I've asked you twice before if I can trust you. This time I'm not going to ask but you must accept that what I now tell you must be taken on trust and not repeated. It is not for public consumption. I didn't pursue Gillespie out of a vendetta. It had a lot of personal elements but they were all coincidental. I was following instructions."

She took a folded up newspaper page from her bag and unfolded it on the table in front of me.

"Do you recognise this?" she asked.

"Of course. It's the piece I did for Hamish a year or so ago." I checked the date on the page.

"You understand how the wheels turn, the circular flow, money, drugs, guns?"

"The principles, yes. I've never actually come across it."

"Yes you have but you weren't to know. You know that James Gillespie is ex-army. You probably don't know that his family are not from Glasgow. They're from a small community called Bilston Glen in Mid Lothian. It's a mining town. I've told you before that in the Lothians force I was involved in domestic violence. One of the men that I successfully prosecuted was a shot firer in the mine. He thought his wife was cheating on him so he strapped a stick of gelignite between her breasts and lit the fuse. The poor woman went crazy. A neighbour, who was also a miner, heard the commotion and ran in and snapped off the tail of the fuse before it exploded. The neighbour got a police commendation for bravery. The husband got five years for attempted murder. His name was Gillespie, a cousin of our James. When the *friends of James Gillespie* set up that caper with my flat it was very personal."

"Anyway just recently James Gillespie or "Jammy" as you call him has been trying to break away from Sam Horton and set up on his own. He has been selling guns and explosives to the UDA and sometimes trading them for supplies of drugs. My new job with the Met is, intrinsically, about liaison but I was also asked to help sort out Gillespie. They knew what he was doing but had nothing solid. A decision was taken at a very high level that he had to be taken down at any cost. I think the man we call the Londoner was in favour of just eliminating him, James Bond style but that was overruled."

"Wow! You're not the quiet wee lassie that I thought you were. I understand what you're saying but I still can't go along with what you've done. This is an officially approved miscarriage of justice and you are one of the main players. Are you telling me the judge was in on all this as well?"

"I imagine he was kept in the picture. You probably noticed that a large part of the prosecution case was just little bits and pieces of innuendo that whittled away at the jury's doubts but weren't really admissible evidence per se. The Judge really ought to have kept them in line and he didn't."

"Yes, I noticed that. I couldn't understand why he was letting it go. What about the two cousins? They're going down for a murder that they almost certainly didn't commit."

"They are what the Americans call collateral damage, innocent victims of the war, except they aren't totally innocent. They're a wicked pair of thugs. Everybody's happy to see the back of them."

"I'm afraid I don't see it that way, Sandra. Anyway, what about your main target? He got off again. So what did you gain?"

"He got off the murder charge but he'll go down for a good few years on the other charges. Mission accomplished. We've plugged a significant gap in the supply of weapons into Ulster."

"And the real murderers? They just stay out there on the streets like it doesn't matter?"

"Who knows? Maybe there wasn't really any murder at all. Their livers were floating in alcohol. That wasn't given too much importance at the trial. Maybe they were just blind drunk and fell about the place. Freddy banged his head and knocked the lamp over. Anyway I'm trusting you not to go stirring things up."

"Well Sandra, you can trust me. I will keep all this under wraps for the time being. But the sad thing is that I can't trust you any more. You are not the person that I fell in love with."

I pushed aside my uneaten food, stood up, kissed her on the cheek, went by the desk to pay our bill and walked out into the Glasgow rain.

It's a heartache, nothing but a heartache
Hits you when it's too late. Hits you when you're down.
It's a fool's game, nothing but a fool's game.
Standing in the pouring rain, feeling like a clown

I stood staring into the street oblivious of the rain streaming down my face. Perhaps it was tears. I don't know how long I stood there. Then I pulled myself together, went and bought a bag of chips with lots of salt and vinegar from the Blue Lagoon and walked home eating the chips.

As time goes by, towards a new millennium.

Well, that was the story of Jamie and Sandra. Many years would pass before we met again. That also was the story of the ice cream wars. It was a strange episode and as I said in the beginning I was left with more questions than answers. James Gillespie was sentenced to a total of twelve years in prison. Willy and Billy received the mandatory life sentence. A few years after their conviction they appealed for acquittal on the basis that the original trial was flawed and that several key parts of evidence had been fabricated by the police. Their appeal fell largely on deaf ears. It bothered me because I knew that they had been *stitched up* but I held to my promise to Sandra not to disclose the true nature of events. My conscience pricked.

I met up again with Myra Blunt from Coutts. She was substantially displeased with how things had panned out.

"I gave it to you on a plate Jamie and what did you do with it? Sam Horton and Danny O'Connor are still lording it over the city and they're a damn sight richer than when I passed it to you. I thought you had the balls to do something with it. You were too busy playing games on the radio while it all just slipped through your fingers." I knew she was right. My conscience pricked.

Graham Kerrigan was freed from prison and quickly clawed back control of the yuppie end of the drugs market. Sam Horton and his taxi drivers solidified their grip from the city centre westwards on both sides of the Clyde. Danny O'Connor controlled most of the large housing estates between Paisley and Cumbernauld. Other younger players also muscled in to fill the gaps. The ice cream war was over but a new, more serious wave of stabbings and shootings took its place as the young bucks wrestled for control of the lucrative drugs market. Glasgow slipped deeper into the abyss surpassing all its previous crime records exponentially. Horton and O'Connor now lived most of the time in Spain. It was safer than the streets of Glasgow. Graham Kerrigan built a house on the edge of the Campsie Hills. It was like a fortress with alarms, CCTV, floodlights and dogs.

Things changed in my life too. I began to lose interest in Street Patrol. John Sinclair sat in for me a couple of times and seemed to enjoy it so I asked him to take over. He felt he'd been passed over for promotion in the Chief Constable's reshuffles. I think the Chief believed that John could have warned him about Gillespie's MI5 connection and he never forgave him. John felt stuck in a dead end so he was happy to take early retirement and the full time presenter's job on the radio. Then Maggie died. She just passed away quietly one night in her sleep. I went to the care home to collect her possessions. I was hoping the missing headscarf would be tucked into a section of her handbag but it wasn't there. I spent a few days on a downer. It wasn't just the scarf that was missing. Maggie herself was now missing. It left a big gap and for a time added to my general lack of contentment.

I was now totally freelance. My despondency passed, the years passed and other events occupied the headlines. The Irish troubles continued for some more years and then frittered out with a succession of on-off peace talks. Old sworn enemies sat round the table looking for a slice of the cake. Then came the Lockerbie disaster and the debacle of *Scottish Justice* that followed. A few years later the horrific shootings in the school at Dunblane sucked in every crime reporter in the country. After that I became less and less involved in direct reporting and much more behind the scenes doing planning and research for television. The ice cream wars faded into distant memory. Sandra and I never got back together. We exchanged Christmas cards and I enjoyed seeing her climb in rank. She went on to be Commander at the Met then a spell as Deputy Chief Constable in one of the English counties then back to London in some clandestine post that didn't seem to have a title. I never met anyone else and remained an eligible bachelor.

James Gillespie served his time. Sam Horton no longer needed him so he had to start again from scratch. He went back to dealing arms. The conflict in Ulster had not fully subsided but the Loyalists attempted a ceasefire in 1991 and again in 1994 and now the UDA were trying to sell off their arms instead of buying them. They needed funds to hold their organisation together. Around this time Glasgow, like all cities in Britain, saw a move away from knives and baseball bats towards guns as the means of settling gang disputes. Jammy G was happy to oblige as a go-between trading guns from across the water. It seemed like he was jammy once again but it wasn't long before Danny O'Connor's predictions came true. Gillespie was found dying from six bullet wounds in a derelict piece of land near Garthamlock. The sixth bullet was fired into his rectum. Why did I see this horrific violence as a kind of natural justice and yet could never bring myself to agree with Sandra's phoney murder case?

The world has totally changed during these last twenty-odd years especially in the field of news reporting. People don't sit in silence any more. Internet has changed all that. Some people post their opinions in forums. Some people tweet and some people blog. Some take photos on their cellphones and send them flashing around the world on Internet. Imagine what might have happened in the ice cream wars if we'd had camera-clicking cellphones to capture the van-smashing. It's not just the technology that has changed. The new technologies have enfranchised the people. People question things more. The news is no longer just the viewpoint of the reporter. I like the change even if it has squeezed some of my colleagues out of their jobs.

One thing has remained constant. The newspapers still do Hatches, Matches and Dispatches. There is still the obituary column. That's where I read about the death of Sam Horton. He died in a car crash in the south of Spain. There was press speculation that it wasn't an accident, that O'Connor's men were involved. I had no wish to attend his funeral but in retrospect I might have learned a few things to avoid complications later. That's also where I read about the death of Myra Blunt in June 2007. I went to her funeral and found myself standing next to a well-dressed man with silver hair. I felt sure I had met him briefly at some time in the past but I couldn't quite place him. Maybe it was in a trial, perhaps as a witness. He must have noticed me staring. As we walked away from the crematorium he turned and held out his hand to shake.

"You're Jamie Robertson, if I'm not mistaken. I nearly met you once. Myra wanted me to talk to you but I don't know what happened; it never seemed to materialise."

"You will have to excuse me." I apologised, "I should know you. I recognised you and I have a niggly feeling your surname is a fish. I don't think it's Salmon and I'm fairly sure it's not Kipper or Herring." We both laughed.

"I'll give you five out of ten. It's Sturgeon, not so easy to remember."

"Tom Sturgeon?"

"Now you've got it."

"Yes, it's coming back now. You worked with Myra. I saw you in court in Dumbarton. You discovered the shop manager who installed his own personal cash register. Myra wanted us to have a chat but we both had to rush off somewhere. God man, that must be over twenty years ago."

"Was it as long ago as that?" he mused. "Yes, I remember now. Myra wanted me to talk to you. She thought I could help you with some of your investigations. She made it sound very mysterious. What were you investigating?"

"Myra came to me with a story about a big robbery of cigarettes from Coutts. That was in the late 70s. She was sure you knew something about it but wouldn't speak to her. Anyway other events took over and I never had the chance to follow it up with you."

"You must be talking about Newton Mearns. Good God, yes! That was a strange one. Did you find out anything in your investigations?"

"We tracked down where the cigarettes went but I never managed to get a handle on who took them in the first place. Sam Horton, Coutts' property director, was definitely involved but he wasn't hands on. Whoever it was needed to have big transport. I never cracked that bit."

"Did you speak to anybody from Coutts?"

"Hey! Now you're testing the memory cells. McGuiness. Yes, Joe McGuinness. He got badly beaten because somebody thought he spilled the beans but he never gave me any information. In fact, he denied that any robbery ever took place. I checked with police records at the time and they had nothing."

"Aye, it took place alright. McGuinness was one of the bunch that humped the boxes up the stairs to the makeshift storeroom on the Friday. So was I. There were half a dozen of us running relays. When we came back on the Monday somebody had cleaned the place out. Take it from me. There was a robbery. Who else did you speak to?"

"Charlie Frazzini's girlfriend, Angela. What was it? Angela McCabe. She didn't give me anything that I could work on but she did confirm that the robbery took place. There was something she was holding back. That was where you came in, actually. I told Myra that Angela knew more than she was saying and Myra said that so were you. She was sure you knew more."

"I didn't know. I just felt it in my bones. I think you probably know what I mean."

"I know what you mean. Angela said something strange before stomping off in a tantrum. She said something about me catching a bus. It didn't make sense but she was sort of smirking when she said it and, like you say, I felt it in my bones. She knew something."

"Ah yes, Angela, a very pretty young woman. Yes, she was a bit stroppy but we all liked her. She was a good friend of McGuiness's wife. Oh! Hell, the memory cells, like you say. What was her name? Shamara. That was it. She was Asian. You say that Angela mentioned buses? That's interesting. I had a theory, you know, about how they did it. I think Myra knew this and that would be why she told you to talk to me. There wasn't anything I could put my finger on but you know when you get that tingle up and down your spine. I'm usually right about these things. I don't suppose you're still interested. Mind you, there's a sequel, something more up to date that got me wondering."

"I should have dug you out at the time. Yes, I'm still interested. Listen, there's a Frankie and Benny's near here. Let's get a bite to eat and talk about the good old days."

My little Mini had long since died. I now have a dinky little new style Fiat 500, so we jumped in that and drove across the other side of the motorway. The traffic was heavy so we didn't resume our chat in earnest till we were seated in the restaurant. Tom Sturgeon cackled mischievously to himself.

"Aye, so we were talking about stroppy Angela. Her and Shamara McGuiness were friends. Shamara's family were from Bangladesh. Some of her cousins worked on the buses and they used to do odd jobs, as well, for O'Connor. You know who I'm talking about? Danny O'Connor? Aye, of course you do. Well, anyway, there were three brothers. I think two of them were drivers and the oldest one was a mechanic. I know this sounds crazy but at the time I was convinced they took a couple of the buses out of the depot in the middle of the night and used them to transport the boxes of cigarettes. Even at that, it must have taken a couple of trips. There was a fair old pile of smokes in that top floor."

I was sitting nodding. "You know, that doesn't sound so crazy. The whole bloody episode was crazy. Somebody took the cigarettes and they needed big transport. You don't get much bigger than a double-decker bus. But would they have got it in to the back of the shop?"

"I checked that and yes, there were no bridges or anything. The back doors of the shopping centre are just a hundred yards from the main bus route."

"That would explain why McGuinness got his head smashed in. They nearly killed him. When Myra got me involved she knew where the cigarettes were and I went snooping around. They probably thought it was poor old Joe that told me."

"Aye, and there's more to it but it's all just hearsay, shop gossip. There was a funny story that one of the buses took a detour. The brothers weren't convinced that O'Connor would pay them what he promised so they took a slice off the top. There was another friend of the family who was quite willing to buy some cheap ciggies. I believe you know him. He used to be a city councillor, Yasser Ahmed, a real paragon of virtue."

"The twisted, hypocritical old shite!" I exclaimed causing a few heads to turn. "You know, I always thought he was too goody-goody to be true."

"The thing is, there was such a pile of tobacco that a few boxes weren't missed. Actually, there was so much that they had problems shifting them. I thought Sam Horton was involved. O'Connor didn't have the money at that time to bankroll a big heist. Hang on! I've got it! Tarkham. That was the family name. Shamara Tarkham but, of course, to us she was Shamara McGuinness. The old grey cells are still working."

"I really do wish I'd taken up Myra's suggestion and spoken to you. I never really got to the bottom of it and Myra always thought I'd let her down. Why didn't you tell Myra about your suspicions?"

"That was a funny old time at Coutts. Everybody had to watch their backs. I was a divisional manager and I shot my mouth off too often. I didn't agree with all the sudden changes they were making. I was moved down the ladder. I still kept my DM's salary so it was just a case of stay out of sight and keep my nose clean till retirement. And then, it was all just gossip, hearsay and hunch. I couldn't go around accusing people. The company decided not to report the theft. Stirring things up would have just ruffled a lot of the wrong feathers. Myra was different. Her job was all about ruffling feathers and she didn't care which bird got ruffled. She was a funny old bird herself. Nobody liked her because of her job but the problem in Coutts was that nearly everybody had their hand in the till. Myra and I both hated that so we got along OK. How did you come to know her?"

"I used to do a paper round in Coutts when I was still at school. When I got my first real job Myra got my paper round. I was fifteen and she was about twelve or thirteen. I spent my last few days showing her what to do. That seems like a long time ago. Thanks a lot Tom. You have filled in a lot of blank spaces. But you said there was a sequel. I'm intrigued. What was that all about?"

"Aye. What the hell? Half of them are probably dead now anyway. These Tarkham brothers, I heard different stories about them. They left Glasgow not long after that. It seems they did quite nicely building up a business somewhere in the Middle East. I'm not sure where exactly. There was bad blood between them and O'Connor. I reckon he didn't pay them for providing the buses. I don't know exactly what it was. He was starting to get involved with the ice cream thing. They were involved in some way with that. And then there was a funny thing." He stopped suddenly as if he was trying to remember something. I waited a couple of minutes then got impatient.

"What was funny? Do you mean funny-strange or funny-ha-ha?"

"Strange, very strange. I saw them. I saw two of the brothers."

"You mean you saw them with the buses taking the cigarettes? But you just said it was all hearsay and gossip."

"No! No! You don't understand. I saw them again back here in Glasgow." His eyes seemed to be looking somewhere into the distance.

"Is that important?"

"Aye, maybe I should have told somebody. It didn't seem important at the time but I thought about it later. I thought about phoning in to one of your programmes but it never came up so time drifted on and I forgot about it till just now talking to you. I think you would consider it important."

"Why?"

"It was a Friday afternoon. I saw them in a car in Partick, along Dumbarton Road. Then on the Saturday it was all over the news, the fire in the caravan at Loch Lomond. It was O'Connor's caravan and two of his friends died in the fire. I remember thinking; *maybe it was supposed to be O'Connor that was in the fire.* Then I thought, *no Tom Sturgeon, you old fool. You're putting two and two together to make six.*"

"Are you sure it was them you saw?"

"I'm sure enough to put a fiver on it with Ladbrokes but I wouldn't like to stand up in court and swear on oath."

"How did you know them? Did they have some connection with Coutts apart from Shamara?

"Shamara's family had an Indian restaurant in Partick. It was always a favourite haunt for Coutts supervisors for Friday lunch. The cousins often filled in as waiters. You know how it is. All the family help out. We got to know them quite well. I'm fairly sure it was them I saw and they recognised me."

"And you say they are in the Middle East but you don't know where?"

"No, it could be Saudi or Dubai or Abu Dhabi, Bahrain, one of those places. I'll tell you who would know. Angela McCabe."

"Aye, but she's gone off to Spain. O'Connor might know but he's in Spain too."

"Does it matter now? It was a long time ago."

"You're going to laugh, Tom, but I don't like loose ends. Yes, it was a long time ago but I still wake up sometimes in the middle of the night trying to put the ends together. The Gillespies are due out soon but they've served a sentence for a crime that many of us believe they never committed. You have given me a clue to follow. It might lead nowhere but I'm going to have to check it out. I just need to find out where this Tarkham family went to."

"Well, good luck. I'm not sure I've done you a favour." Tom toddled off chuckling to himself. After a few steps he turned round still chuckling and said. "Maybe I should have been a crime writer like you. You don't like loose ends, you tell me. Neither do I. It can bug me for days sometimes when there's something I can't get in place. It's bothered me since I heard about it. Do you think Councillor Ahmed would have been on the take? Do you think maybe he was just doing the boys a favour when he took the cigarettes off them?" He chuckled again. "No, that's a daft question. Don't answer it. Anyway, listen! That's not what I was really thinking. I just had a wee flash of inspiration. If Yasser Ahmed helped the Tarkhams back then, he probably knows where they went. What do you think?"

"What do I think? I think that wasn't a wee flash of inspiration. It was a big one. All I need to do now is find the honourable councillor. He must be well retired by now. Thanks again, Tom and yes, I think you'd have made a good reporter."

I went back home and put on the percolator for a cup of fresh Columbian roast coffee. With the smell wafting through the flat I dug out the phone directory and sat down on the sofa. I was surprised to find six Yasser Ahmed's in Glasgow but luckily there was only one Yasser Ahmed O.B.E. I circled the number and went to rescue the coffee before it stewed. My impatience got the better of me and I picked up the cordless phone in the kitchen, returned to the sofa and started dialling. I recognised the voice instantly. Yasser was delighted to hear from "an old colleague" and invited me round for morning coffee next day. We could catch up on old times. How wonderful it was of me to call.

Clyde View City apartments are located between Glasgow Green and the new Financial District. Everything is in walking distance, St Enoch's underground station, Central Station, and Argyle Street shops. Yasser Ahmed greeted me like a long lost friend and escorted me to a large open lounge with plush leather sofas in front of huge panoramic windows overlooking the Clyde and the Islamic Centre on the other side. He was eager to talk about old times and the wonderful contribution he had made to his home city. He wasn't so eager to talk about the Tarkhams. I tried three or four different ways to ply them into the conversation and each time he used his well-honed political skills and neatly side-stepped. In the end I had to stop pussy-footing and ask directly.

"Councillor Ahmed," I gave him his dignified title. I'm sure he would have liked Sir Yasser but an O.B.E. doesn't carry an automatic knighthood. "It is great to talk about the good old days but I looked you up specifically to ask you if you could help me locate the Tarkham family. I only need you to tell me which part of the Middle East they went to and I can find them from there."

"Why do you need to speak to them so urgently?"

"It's not urgent. I'm sorry if I gave you that impression but you know me. I'm impatient. When I decide something it has to be done yesterday. I'm writing a book about Glasgow in the 70s and 80s and the Tarkhams are particularly interesting because they emigrated at a time when most Asians were immigrating. I thought it would be a different perspective."

"Yes, I see what you mean. Several members of my extended family came over here in 1972 when they were expelled from Uganda. The Tarkhams settled in Glasgow about the time of the Second World War, so they were some of the first. Yes indeed, very interesting. I see no harm in telling you they are now in Dubai, doing very well from all accounts. They have built up a rather nice little transport business over there. I'm quite sure you can Google it. Isn't that what everybody does these days. Their business name is

Tamaku. I'm really sorry but I can't furnish you with their address but I'm sure you'll have no bother finding them. Are you into all this googling and emailing? My wife is never away from the thing but it's beyond me."

"Oh yes, Councillor. I think Google was invented just for me. Thanks for your help. I'll have no trouble finding them, I'm sure."

His wife managed to drag herself away from her PC and brought in a lovely spread of coffee and cookies. She asked if I liked "our" Islamic Centre across the river and was amused to discover that I was Catholic. "But you look like one of us," she smiled, "Where are you from?"

"Well, if you look across the top of the Islamic Centre you can just about see what's left of the Gorbals. Just beyond that is Cathcart and in between the two is Queens Park. Somewhere in there used to be Jamieson Gardens. That's where I'm from." I said, pointing across the river. She smiled again, looking at my Celtic shirt and Bay City Rollers type tartan scarf.

"Yes, I can see the Glasgow connection. At least the accent is a bit more authentic than Rod Stewart. It was nice of you to come to see us. Yasser misses all the bustle and meeting people. I like things quieter but it's lovely to have a visitor."

She was obviously pleased so it eased my conscience about the real purpose of my visit. We sat chatting over coffee for about half an hour till I politely took my leave. I was impatient to get home to go googling for the Tarkhams. I decided that the business name might show up easier so I typed in *Tamaku Dubai*. It came up on the first page *Tamaku Transport* and also on the first page *Tamaku Retail*. When Yasser Ahmed said they had a *nice little transport business* it was something of an understatement. They had trucks, taxis, buses, an executive jet and a couple of helicopters. The retail section was a small chain of high class outlets in shopping malls and classy hotels. I clicked on their email contact form and completed the details saying more or less the same as I told Yasser Ahmed. The reply came back the same afternoon. They would be delighted to entertain a writer from Glasgow to show of their achievements. All I had to do was get myself to Dubai and they would arrange a pick-up from the airport.

A family gathering.

One week later I was on my way with Emirates Airline, a direct flight from Glasgow to Dubai in a window seat. Just over seven hours later with a moonlit sky we skimmed over the Jumeirah Palm Complex then out across the desert for a few miles before curving back round towards the city with the skeleton of the world's tallest structure, Burj Khalifa, twinkling in the night sky. True to their promise the Tarkhams sent a car to meet me at the airport and escort me to my hotel. I had booked a Sheraton online in the centre of the city, on the edge of the Creek. We agreed that next morning they would collect me and show me round their empire.

Next morning the city traffic was gridlocked. We spent about one hour in visits to their various depots and five hours getting between them although they were only a few miles apart. I was thankful for the air-conditioned limo. My guide was Masood, the eldest brother and in the course of the morning I met the other two, Rasheed and Naseer.

"Have you seen the Jumeirah Palm, Mr Robertson?" Masood asked as we drove out along Al Sufouth Road. We had just passed the iconic Burj Al Arab Hotel shaped like a giant sail over three hundred metres high. The traffic had quietened as we drove along the seafront.

"I saw it from the air last night. It was dark but quite impressive."

"We have a little house there. My family invite you to have lunch with us. You can meet everybody and find out everything you need to know. The Palm is still not finished but already you can see that it is a marvellous construction. It's a little like the Tarkham family. When we came here we were nothing and the Jumeirah Palm was just a little piece of the sea. Now we are looking good but still not finished. It's very different to Glasgow, don't you think?"

"From the little I've seen this morning I would say that Dubai is an incredible city but it doesn't have a heart. After fifty years being ripped apart by the Corporation Clowns, Glasgow still has a heart. Don't you miss that?"

"The Tarkham family didn't experience much of Glasgow's heart. We have no regrets about coming here. There are a few things we miss but there are compensations."

We arrived at the famous Palm and cut down to the houses on the lower branches. Each house has its front garden with pool and rear garden with boat mooring. There were a number of vehicles already parked with the logo Tamaku Transport on the side and a couple of Mercs and Beemers. Their driveway was full of vehicles and they spilled out onto the roadway. It seemed that the whole family had assembled to welcome me, the three brothers and their wives, their sons and daughters and their spouses, lots of kids and a wizened-looking old lady that I took to be the great-grandmother, mother of Masood, Rasheed and Naseer. From the moment I arrived they bombarded me with questions about Glasgow, the new Scottish Parliament, Rangers and Celtic. It was strange to be sitting in a foreign country with a family so obviously Asian and listening to so many Glasgow accents. I actually heard someone say *pure dead brilliant*. It's an expression that is often applied to things that are really quite mundane. Here in Dubai their lifestyle was pure dead brilliant. I felt the familiar pangs of conscience, invited into this wonderfully happy and successful family and my only purpose was to burst their bubble.

Everybody was speaking in this beautifully accented English, even the kids, all except the old lady who seemed to be speaking quietly in Urdu.

"You must be hungry," said Masood's wife. "You are having lunch with us. Aren't you?"

I'd already caught glimpses of the food being laid out and I was now catching the wafting spice odours. The pangs of guilty conscience niggled but not enough to stop me saying, "Oh, yes. I'd be delighted."

We sat down around an enormous rectangular table, about twenty people in all, men on one side, women and kids on the other side and the old lady sitting at the end. The other end was set but nobody sat there.

"So, Mr Robertson, what can we tell you about our humble adventures?" asked Masood, "and please don't be shy. Eat up! He watched my awkward fumblings eating with one hand. "Would you find it easier with a knife and fork?"

"No, thanks. I'm fine and this is all delicious."

"OK. Fire away! What would you like to know?"

"I was wondering about your business. It's transport, I know, but you seem to have everything covered. I don't know why but I expected just a fleet of buses but you have trucks, limousines, even air transport."

"Buses, yes and mini-buses and taxis. This is a city on the move, like you no doubt saw this morning. Most of the business comes from moving workers around Dubai but we also do a daily bus service to the other Emirates. It's a weird set up. We take the passengers from here to, let's say Abu Dhabi or Muscat but we can't bring anybody back. Our bus comes back empty and the people have to take a mini-bus back. Each Emirate protects its own share. We also service the executive market with chauffeured limousines, a couple of choppers and a Lear jet. You'd be surprised but that isn't the most profitable part of our business. There's a lot of idle time when we don't have so many executives wanting to move around. The real money maker is the trucking side. We are quite literally selling sand to the Arabs." He laughed and the others joined in.

"How do you mean?" I enquired.

"This whole Jumeirah Palm Tree is made of sand. They dredge it up from out at sea. The first part is just dumped in place by the dredgers but once they get above sea level the dredgers have to dump it down the coast and we truck it into place. It's just truck after truck after truck, millions of tons of the stuff. Our business is like Dubai itself, built on sand."

"I saw that you also have a retail wing."

"Indeed we have. That's the ladies' side. They have the shops, not Paki shops I must tell you. We have a Toys-R-Us franchise and a couple of Body Shops. Nothing grubby, all top class. We have a boutique of Indian saris and one of ladies' headgear and a really naughty one of somebody's secret. I can never remember the name."

"Victoria's Secret," came the answer from the female side of the table.

"Thank you ladies. Anyway, Mr Robertson, that's our humble business."

"It sounds like your humble business is quite a big pie. I imagine you have a few stories to tell. How did you get started? You weren't in business in Glasgow?"

"We came here from Glasgow in 1982. My brothers and I worked on the buses. Rasheed and Naseer were drivers and I was a mechanic, foreman mechanic actually. I suppose when we came over here it was a natural move into buses. It's hard to imagine a city with no buses but the city was much smaller then. We started with a few old Leylands but then we got a great offer from Mercedes and it all blossomed from there. Mother and Naseer are the accountants. Rasheed is the one who chases new business. I just make sure it all keeps ticking along."

"So you started from scratch, with nothing?"

"We had some savings. We were planning to open Indian restaurants in Glasgow, one each, so we had a little capital laid aside. We all had a second job to make extra cash."

"Would that be when you worked for Danny O'Connor?" I asked. The question just slipped out unplanned. It got a reaction.

"What? What? How? How do you know about O'Connor?" Rasheed struggled to find the right question. All the others went quiet. A hush of suspense hung over the table. I changed the subject quickly.

"What about the company name, Tamaku? Why not Tarkham?"

It was Naseer that answered. "That was my contribution. It's a family joke. Tamaku is the Bengali word for tobacco."

"You mean you transported tobacco. But Masood says you started with buses. Did you transport tobacco in the buses?"

"Not in Dubai." The answer came from a young voice down the table accompanied by a chorus of light sniggers.

"This is intriguing," I enthused. "Did you use the buses in Glasgow to move tobacco around?"

"There was one occasion," conceded Naseer.

"That would have been the cigarettes that went a small detour from Coutts in Newton Mearns to Danny O'Connor's little squirrel's nest in Scotland Street." In for a penny, in for a pound. It was time to apply a little pressure.

"Who the Hell are you? We were led to believe you were doing a book on migrant families. You are not a writer. What do you want?"

"I am a writer, I promise you. I'm surprised you didn't run my name through Google." There was a shuffle and one of the younger lads shot off to a laptop PC on the sofa.

"Here it is, Jamie Robertson. He's a crime writer."

"Why have you come here? What is it you really want?" asked Masood. You are like a Campbell in the house of MacDonald. We welcome you into our home; you eat our meat and what now? What is the real evil purpose of your visit?"

"I am sorry that I abused your hospitality. I am just looking for answers to questions that have plagued me for half of my life."

"And when you have the answers, what will you do?"

"That depends very much on the answers."

"Very well. We did bits and pieces of work for O'Connor mostly with his second hand clapped out ice cream vans. On one occasion we moved a large quantity of cigarettes for him in Corporation buses at night. We were never paid what was promised. It was many years ago and the company never reported the theft. They had their own ulterior motives. So the case is dead. You have your answer."

"Did you know Sam Horton?"

"Of course I knew Sam Horton."

"How did you come to know him?"

"You don't know. Do you? You have just been guessing all of this."

"I told you I am looking for answers."

Masood looked ruefully at his old mother and asked something in Urdu. She nodded hesitantly. He continued speaking, "Sam Horton used to be my father-in-law. My first wife was Sandra Horton."

"Sandra Horton, the model?"

"The very same. Horton never liked me. I wasn't good enough for his precious daughter. He wasn't exactly the bright shining citizen himself. Was he?"

"I don't know. You tell me."

"It was Sam Horton who set up the cigarette thing. We were supposed to get a better cut than we got. We took the cigarettes to an old sort of garage workshop. Six trips it took. The lads in the bus depot thought I'd taken a bus out to test and taken a nap somewhere. There were tons of the things. They didn't manage to sell them on as fast as they hoped. We kept asking for our money but it never came. Horton started to get nasty and Sandra and I began to drift apart."

"What about Angela McCabe? Where did she fit in to this?"

"Angela? She didn't. Well I suppose she did in a way. She was Sandra's bridesmaid at our wedding. I think she maybe told Sandra about the great pile of tobacco and Sandra told her Dad. He had access to a key and well, I think you know the rest."

"So you admit it was you who took the cigarettes?"

"Yes, it was us. We aren't proud of it. We are an honest family. We are well respected here. You make us sound like common criminals."

"But isn't that what you are? Would you be so well respected if the people here knew how you started?"

"It would ruin us. We have a legitimate business here in Dubai that we have built with many years of hard honest work. You cannot publish any of this story. It would serve no purpose."

"On its own, no, you are right. The story is dead."

"So, we can trust you to keep quiet."

"It's not that simple. You went back to Glasgow, you and Rasheed. You set fire to a caravan by the side of Loch Lomond and you walked away leaving two people to die and you left two men to be falsely accused and imprisoned for their murder. The two people who died were friends of mine. That story isn't dead. You'd be surprised how much public interest there still is in the case."

"How, in the name of Allah, do you know all this? Nobody knows it was us."

"Somebody told me once that it doesn't matter what you do, it always comes back to bite you."

"We didn't plan to kill these people. We went to get O'Connor. When a man came at us in the dark we thought it was him. Rasheed hit him with the stick and he fell over. He knocked down a lamp and it set fire to the place. We didn't know there was a woman there. We panicked and ran."

"You ran away and left them to burn to death."

"No! No!" shouted Rasheed. "Masood has told you, we didn't know about the woman. We thought the man was O'Connor. Would you have gone back into a blazing caravan to save Danny O'Connor? Answer me honestly. Would you?"

"No, in all honesty, I don't think I would, but what did you hope to achieve anyway? You had started your business here. Did you just go to kill him because he didn't pay you for the cigarette job? That doesn't make sense."

It was Masood's turn to speak again. Once more he checked with his mother in Urdu and once more she nodded. "Take a look at the top end of the table. There is a very important member of our family not here. My father lies buried in a bed of concrete under a block of flats on Glasgow's waterfront. He was murdered by O'Connor because he owed him money. I don't know all the details, something about a house in Spain. My father was never in Spain in his life so I don't know what it was about."

"How do you know it was O'Connor?"

"He made sure we knew. He said that was the penalty for double crossing him and the same would happen to us if we didn't clear out. So we took what we had and came to Dubai."

"Why didn't you go to the police?"

"We went to the police when he disappeared but they never found any trace. There was no body. They said he had probably gone to Pakistan or Bangladesh. They closed the case and said sorry."

"Well I said I was looking for answers. I certainly have some now."

"And you said that what you do will depend on the answers. What will you do?"

"Two men are serving life sentences for the murder of the two Cassidys in the caravan. They are father and son and the father will probably die in prison. They were never fine upstanding citizens but they were innocent of the crime. I think this has to be put right. Many years ago I separated from the woman I thought I loved because she was the senior police officer responsible for their conviction. I was sure at the time that some of the police evidence was dubious. Now I have the chance to prove that I was right. I have no option but to publish the truth."

"Stop! Stop this now. I will hear no more of publishing the truth." It was the little old lady that I thought spoke no English. "What is the truth? What does it look like and who is really interested anyway?"

I was a bit taken aback by her sudden outburst. "I have spent years digging into the cigarette theft and the caravan fire. I spent many sleepless nights trying to put all the pieces together and now they are all falling into place. I will return to Scotland and publish what I know."

"This must stop now, Jamal." She was staring at me with piercing eyes. "You do not have all the pieces. There is one important piece, my son. You cannot publish any of this."

"I'm sorry lady. I understand your worry but I think you are a little confused. My name is Jamie, not Jamal. Despite my appearance I am not one of your people. I see no reason not to expose the true story."

"You are wrong. There is good reason. Listen to me, your name is Jamal and you will not tell anyone your story because

Masood, Rasheed and Naseer are your brothers." I just stood looking at her unsure of how to handle a raving old lady.

"Yes, look well my boy. Your given name was Jamieson because you were found beneath a bush in Jamieson Gardens in 1940. This was later shortened to Jamie and I believe you are sometimes also called Jammy because people think you are lucky. How do I know these things? Because I am your mother. I have always called you Jamal because you are Bangladeshi."

Masood must have thought his mother had gone senile. "Mother, listen to me. I am Masood and these are Rasheed and Naseer. We are your sons. You do not have any other sons. This is Jamie Robertson. I am sorry that we upset you by bringing him here today. I think perhaps you are a little confused."

She turned her piercing stare on Masood. "I am not confused. Do you think a mother confuses these things? I gave birth to a little boy in the bushes of Jamieson Gardens in Glasgow on the 16th of November 1940." She turned back to me. "Tell me, Jamie Robertson. What is your date of birth?"

"I was born on the 16th of November 1940," I answered meekly, "in Jamieson Gardens. I was wrapped in a scarf and abandoned there to die."

"You were not abandoned. I wrapped you in my hijab and put you under a bush to protect you from the wind. I didn't know what to do. I was just fifteen years old. I left you there to go and find my sister. I couldn't take you home. My people would have killed me. Your father and I were meant to be married but it was the beginning of the war and he was on a merchant ship somewhere in the Atlantic. When I returned with my sister you were gone. Somebody had taken you."

"So you just forgot about me and got on with your life."

"I have never forgotten about you, never. Maggie kept me informed about you when you were young and when you were older I followed your stories in the newspapers. I never forgot about you."

"You knew Maggie! Why did she not tell me? Who was my father? Is he still alive? Why did you never contact me? Who are these three? You say they are my brothers."

"Good heavens, so many questions! Come let us sit on the sofas. Masood, Rasheed, Naseer, please come too. I have never told you this before." She beckoned her sons and moved towards the sofas. The rest of the family gathered round too, eager faces anxious to hear the family secrets.

"Your father's name was Jamal. He was a sailor and he jumped ship to stay in Glasgow in 1935. That was the year of the great British Empire Exhibition in Bellahouston Park. My sister and I were both in service working with a British family in Bengal. They came to Glasgow with the Indian representation and they brought us as maidservants for the trip. Jamal, your father, got a job working on the construction of the exhibition. When the exhibition ended the family were posted to Jamaica and they just abandoned us in Glasgow. I can't remember how Jamal found us but he took us to join a small group of Indian immigrants living in an old tenement block in Partick. I can remember every night it was difficult to sleep because we could hear the clang, clang, clang of men working in the shipyards.

Jamal went away again to sea and I never saw him again till 1939. We fell in love and although I was still young all our friends approved. We were going to be married that summer. Then there was a fight with some white boys and I think one of them was badly hurt. Jamal said he had to get away. There was an Indian ship in the docks that was bound for America so he signed up and promised to return. About a month after that I realised that I was pregnant but I daren't tell anybody. I desperately hoped that he would return before our child was born. However that was not to be. I didn't find out till after the war that he perished at sea when his convoy was attacked by German U-boats.

I was just fifteen years old and I was very afraid. I had a very slender figure and I always managed to arrange my sari so that nobody noticed as this little child grew inside me. I decided that I would have to go to a hospital on the other side of the city so that nobody would know. I was going to Victoria Infirmary that night but I never arrived. My labour pains started when I left the Subway station and I still had to walk the rest. Finally Mother Nature took over and you were born in the street with the wind whistling round my ears. I wrapped you in my hijab and placed you under a bush and went back to Partick to find my sister. When we returned you were not where I left you. Margaret Robertson, a true angel from heaven, found you and took you into care."

She stood up and moved to the end of the table beside the empty place. She turned to her sons and continued.

"Then I met Mahendra. He didn't know and I could never tell him. We married and had three beautiful sons but I could never forget the little bundle that I left there in the cold. I searched until I found Maggie Robertson. I made her promise never to tell anyone. Our people are obsessive about family honour. It would have cost me my life, of that I was sure." She turned again to me. "You had an excellent mother in Maggie and it would have broken her heart if I had taken you away. It was best to leave things as they were and that is what I ask of you now. Leave things as they are. My sons, your brothers, are good men and they have all this wonderful family as you see. What's past is past and cannot be changed. Go back to Glasgow and look for some real crime to report. It isn't exactly in short supply. Or better still just put your feet up and enjoy your autumn years. Come back to see us again some time and leave your notebook behind. We are your family. You will always be welcome."

"This is all quite a shock," I murmured. "How do I know what you say is true. It is difficult to take in."

She didn't answer. Instead she walked out of the room leaving a silence that echoed round the table. Nobody moved or spoke. A couple of minutes passed and she returned with a small box under her arm. She walked up to me and handed me the box. It was quite heavy, made from mottled grey marble inlaid with gold. On the lid was a cursive letter "J".

"Open it!" she commanded.

I raised the lid slowly and almost dropped the box when I saw the contents.

"Now do you believe me?"

There were tears in my eyes as I answered. "Yes, I believe you are my mother." I took the hijab from the box. It was the one that was missing from Jamie's box.

"So, my son, now you know why you cannot go back and tell the world your story. It will destroy your own family."

I looked at this frail old lady, still struggling with the realisation that she was my mother. I should have rushed over to her and held her close. That is surely what a son should do.

Instead I answered, "I'm not sure. It's not that simple," and I fled from the room, out of the house and into the street. I walked about a mile through half-constructed roadways with the tears stinging my eyes, looking for a way out. Eventually a car came by and stopped. The window rolled down and Naseer looked out.

"Come, Jamie. I will take you back to your hotel."

I accepted his offer. We sat in silence as we drove along the sea front road, neither of us knowing quite what to say. Eventually he broke the silence.

"Mother is over eighty years old. Her heart is not good. It will kill her if you insist on making my brothers stand trial for murder. I knew that something had happened but they would never tell me what it was."

"Your mother… my mother," I stuttered. "What is her name?"

"She is Sanchita, Sanchita Tarkham."

"It sounds Spanish. What does it mean?"

"It is a Bengali name. It means treasure."

"What is she like?"

"She looks frail and her heart now is weak but her character is strong. After our father died she held the family together. We would not have achieved what we have without her guiding hand."

"I think I would like to see her again before I go back to Glasgow. Will you tell her that?"

"I will tell her. When do you return?"

"My return flight is the day after tomorrow."

"This has all been a terrible shock. I imagine for you too?"

"It's just terribly confusing. I have spent all my life hating the woman who could just walk away, leaving me like she did. Now

I have met her I don't hate her but I can't just change and suddenly love her but she is my mother."

We arrived at the Sheraton hotel. He drove in to the front entrance and about six young porters pounced on the car door.

"I will tell her that you would like to see her."

"Thank you."

I walked into the hotel with my head swirling.

Up the Creek

I went for breakfast next morning. I didn't have much appetite but the dining room overlooked the Creek and I occupied my mind watching the boats go up and down.

"That is the old Dubai you can see out there. When we came here there wasn't much more than the Creek."

I turned round to see my mother beautifully dressed in a green sari. She was wearing the hijab from the box. I stood up. We looked at each other silently for a short time then she held out her arms. I pulled her to me gently and held her close.

"Be careful son. I'm quite breakable."

I let her go and pulled out a chair for her to sit down. A waiter appeared from nowhere to offer her tea or coffee.

"Tea please," she replied and turned back to look at me. "You wanted to see me. Well, here I am."

"I needed to see you. I couldn't just leave without seeing you again."

"Have you thought about what I asked of you?"

"I have thought of little else."

"And have you decided?"

"I still don't know. It isn't just black and white like it's supposed to be."

"Nothing is ever just black and white, my son. Surely you of all people know that. You have spent your life reporting on the flotsam and jetsam of your city."

"I thought this time was different. I thought I had found all the answers."

"I have to tell you a story. I cannot tell you all the details and what I tell you must never be repeated. When we were still in Glasgow my husband, Mahendra, was involved in a transaction with Daniel O'Connor. For reasons that I cannot tell you he had to stop the transaction but he was having problems getting O'Connor's money back. It was a large sum of money. Daniel O'Connor was needing the money back quickly. I don't know but I think he had to pay for supplies of illegal drugs that he was selling on the streets. He sent two men to persuade Mahendra that he needed to return the money fast. They used sticks and beat him so hard that he died. O'Connor took his body and buried him in a construction site in a lump of cement. The two men who killed my husband were a father and son called William Gillespie.

"My sons do not know all this. They only know that O'Connor was responsible because he didn't stop with Mahendra. He threatened to come after my boys if his money was not returned. There are other things that I am not able to reveal but it wasn't just Allah who was looking after us. The money was tied up here in Dubai. I knew this and I persuaded my sons to come here. They believe that the business got off the ground because of a generous offer of credit from Mercedes but that is not exactly true. The money was unfrozen and was passed on our behalf to the Mercedes company to buy vehicles.

"Then one day Masood and Rasheed had this crazy idea that they would return to Glasgow and avenge their father's death. They made a terrible mistake and two innocent people died in a fire. I knew nothing of this till they returned and they confessed to me about what had happened. Then we learned about how the police arrested the Gillespies. They charged them with these murders and they are still in prison now. You tell me that you want to set them free and in order to do this Masood and Rasheed must confess. I cannot let you do this. Please tell me that you will let sleeping dogs lie."

I shook my head in disbelief. "Good God! It just doesn't stop. Just when I get my head around one thing you tell me something more incredulous."

"Believe me son, the whole story is more incredulous than you could ever imagine. But believe this also. You will not tell the world your story. I will not let it happen."

"Can we stop talking about this? I wanted to see you again before I leave. You know all about me. I know nothing about you. What did you do after I was born?"

"Are you finished eating?" She asked and I nodded, yes. "Well, why don't we take a stroll along the quays. We can talk as we go."

We exited the hotel on the Creek side and walked towards the boats lined up along the quays.

"After you were born my sister and I found work at the Grand Central Hotel. It was easier than you might think to get a job. It was wartime and lots of women were working in the armaments factories or joined the women's forces. We were both chambermaids and were there right through the war years. You probably know that the Indian army was very much involved in the war. Some of them fought in the desert campaign alongside Scottish troops. Anyway about 1942 there were some officers stayed in the hotel. I remember they were HLI, the Highland Light Infantry Regiment and there was a very handsome Indian soldier who was batman to one of these officers. We met one day in the corridor and he spoke to me in Urdu. He was not from Bengal but from a city called Secunderabad near Hyderabad. His family were Muslim and they all spoke Urdu. We only exchanged a few words. You can imagine my surprise when he came back at the end of the war just to find me. He wanted to marry me but we didn't really know each other. He said that didn't matter because our people usually had arranged marriages and didn't know each other.

"I couldn't tell him that I was promised to another man. I never heard from your father after he left in 1940 but he was the father of my child and I could not consider another man. There was an agency of the War Office in Buchanan Street where people could go to find out about members of their family who were missing in action. Somebody told me that they also did merchant seamen. I was not his next of kin but I had a lot of his personal papers and the man was very helpful. He seemed to accept that I was Jamal's wife and he looked in all the lists. That was when I discovered that Jamal was dead. That was also when I decided that I had to try to find you. I went to the Register of Births and Marriages and found an entry for a little boy called Jamieson. I went to the Victoria Infirmary and somebody told me where to find you.

"I went to see Maggie Robertson. She was very happy to meet your real mother but I could tell she was terrified that I was going to take you away. I told her about Mahendra. We talked about it for a long time and we agreed that you should stay with her and that we had to keep it all secret. We kept in touch over the years mostly by letter at first and then sometimes we agreed a time to phone from a call box. I went to see her once when you were about ten years old and she showed me some photos.

"Mahendra and I married in 1946 and he was demobbed about two months later. At first he wanted me to return to India with him but there was a lot of unrest beginning between the Hindu people and the Muslims so we remained in Glasgow. I forgot to say, his name was Mahendra Tarkham. Anyway Mahendra got a job working in the kitchens of the Grand Central and he also started a sort of travel agency. There were lots of people coming and going at that time and he had contacts who could buy train tickets in India and send them to the UK. Later his brother, Maladhar, came with his young wife, Mallika. They had one little girl called Shamara and we had three boys. You now know the three boys. Maladhar was working in the kitchens with my husband. He was a wonderful cook but of course at that time the Grand Central Hotel did not serve Indian food.

"In the 1950s the hotel was not doing so good and a lot of people lost their jobs. Mahendra and Maladhar both had driving licences for heavy goods vehicles that they got in the army so they went to work on the buses. Mahendra expanded his little agency and he also did insurance and things like that. In 1965 he rented a small shop in Partick and stopped working on the buses. Maladhar was saving all his money and my husband gave him a small loan and he started one of the first Indian restaurants in Glasgow. It was an instant success. Mahendra hated cooking but he helped his brother to keep the accounts and things like that. I had the three boys so I was what they call a full time mum. We had a good life till my boys and my husband got involved with Daniel O'Connor. Then everything started to fall apart. I thought about going to see you to ask for your help. I think I wish now that I had done that but we make our choices and we have to live with them.

"You have to make a choice now and you will have to live with it but so do I. You are making me choose between you and the rest of my family."

"How do you mean?" I asked.

"If you will not promise me now, before you leave, that you will not publish anything about my boys, I will be forced to take steps to stop you. Please don't make me do that."

"That sounds very sinister. Are you going to recruit the help of Danny O'Connor?"

"There are people more powerful than Danny O'Connor."

"I cannot promise before I go. This has all been a big shock and I need time to think."

"My son, I am an old woman. Time is not a luxury that I can afford."

"Then we must both make our choices. By your own words you tell me that you chose to leave me, not once but twice. What difference will a third time make?"

She didn't answer. She took a cellphone from under her sari and flipped it open. "Naseer, can you come and collect me. I am finished here."

The car arrived by the kerbside. She looked at me with eyes that were sad but hard. "Goodbye my son. May Allah be with you."

Naseer came round to open the door and help his mother into the car. He shook my hand firmly. "Goodbye my brother. Somehow I feel we will meet again. I hope it will be a happier meeting."

Welcome Home

It's not much fun at the best of times walking round a city on your own. Dubai is not a walk round kind of city. I certainly was not in a walk round kind of mood. I wandered to the mouth of the Creek and took one of the old wooden ferries across to the old souk. I felt like Henry Cooper must have felt the night he was thumping Mohammed Ali and the referee stopped the fight because his eye was bleeding. I had won the fight but now I was disqualified on a technicality. I think it's the most despondent I have ever been and I felt a long way from home. Worse than that, Dubai has no pubs. Gurney's Bar sounded very attractive. It was Friday, the Muslim version of our Sunday and there were thousands of people out on the street just hanging around. The really strange thing was they all looked like me. The Arab people keep well out of sight. It's just the Asian immigrants who wander the streets.

I went back to the hotel and sat on the bed zapping through the TV channels. I dozed for a while and woke up to a BBC voice chatting about Glasgow. I sat up to listen.

"A blazing car has been driven into the main terminal building at Glasgow Airport. Two men have been arrested. Early reports suggest a connection with recent failed bomb plots in London. Prime Minister Gordon Brown has chaired a meeting of COBRA emergency committee. The airport has been evacuated and all flights suspended."

I turned the sound down to try and de-fuzz my brain. This couldn't really be happening. I was going to be stuck here. I made a cup of coffee in the coffee-maker. They only had little packets of decaf. It was revolting. I found some miniatures in the mini-bar. I selected a cognac and sat down on the bed again to plan my strategy. I phoned down to reception and asked them to connect me with Emirates Airline. A few seconds later I had a chirpy how-can-I-help-you young lady who listened sympathetically to my plight. She confirmed that flights to Glasgow were suspended but seemed confident that it would not affect tomorrow's flight. I was to come to the airport as normal.

Her optimism proved worthy. Despite the TV drama the attempt had failed and the airport re-opened. On the Saturday my flight take-off was delayed two hours but we left Dubai punctually at the rescheduled time. I couldn't sleep on the flight and by the time we touched down in Glasgow I was feeling like I'd been on a weekend binge. I wasn't prepared for the reception. It was like a war zone, guns everywhere, dozens of police in body armour carrying Glock submachine guns at the ready. They lined the route from the plane to the border control point. The queue edged forward slowly as each passport was scrutinised by an immigration officer and two plain-clothes police. I arrived at the desk and handed over my passport.

"One moment please," said the border controller and he turned to the detectives, "Jamieson Robertson." Two machine pistols prodded my ribs and within seconds I was surrounded by uniforms and guns. My insides did a flip and I think I wet myself. It is not a pleasant experience to have two guns in your gut.

"Come this way Mr Robertson. Leave your bag. Somebody will bring it. Keep your hands where we can see them." The two pistoleros nudged my belly and I nodded my intention to comply. They led, pushed and prodded me to a door marked United Kingdom Border Control and nudged me into a seat. On the other side of the desk was a man about retiral age, silvery blond hair, dark suit, crisp white shirt and tie. He seemed vaguely familiar.

When he spoke the voice didn't match the suited gentleman, "Well Jamie, wot the fuck you been up to matey? Been a bad boy. Aint ya? I fot you was retired."

It was Derek Solent, the scruffy punk who used to wear the ban-the-bomb T-shirt and Glengarry hat.

"Who the Hell are you?"

When he spoke again he'd dropped the Cockney twang. "You know perfectly well who I am, Jamie and I know who you are. You must remember me."

"I remember you perfectly but my question was who are you?"

"I represent Her Majesty's Government."

"In what capacity?"

"In an official capacity."

"You can't possibly think that I am a terrorist."

"I know you are not a terrorist. I know everything about you. Your detention has no connection with the incidents here yesterday."

"My detention? You are telling me that I am detained. Why?"

"I think the common expression is *detained during Her Majesty's pleasure*. I know that is usually reserved for people going to prison but it serves in your case as well. You represent a serious security risk if allowed to go free."

"You're crazy."

"I believe that was your appraisal of me last time we met. I think it would be wise if you became more cognitive of the situation you are in."

"I have no idea what you are ranting about. In what way do I represent a security risk?"

"Britain has a complex network of counter terrorist resources. It has been decided at a very high level that you pose perhaps the most serious threat to these resources at this moment in time. It is not within my brief to discuss the matter further until I am accompanied by another senior operative who will be arriving shortly from London. Until then you will be detained here at the airport. Would you like anything to eat or drink?"

"I demand my right to call somebody."

"I'm afraid you do not have that right."

"The person I want to call is a high level member of British security services in London."

"Would that person happen to be Sandra Paterson?"

"Yes, it is some time since we have been in touch but she will vouch for me. But how did you know?"

"I told you. I know everything about you. There is no need for you to call Sandra Paterson. She is already on her way. She is the other operative I mentioned who wishes to be here before I formally interview you. Now, would you like something to drink?"

"I don't suppose there's any chance of a decent cup of coffee?"

"There's every chance. I will make it myself. I believe you like Columbian?"

I started to feel that the world was spiralling out of control. What in God's name was going on? I did a mental re-run of everything I had written in the last couple of years. Since the New York 9/11 incident I had become acutely aware that I had a "security risk" face and I was accustomed to the extra frisk and bag check. It was annoying but understandable. This wasn't a case of mistaken identity. He knew exactly who I was. I thought again about TV items I had researched but my remit was always the crime angle not terrorism. Maybe Sandra would get it sorted out but there was something ominous there too. Why had she chosen to come all the way up from London? Then it hit me like a twenty ton truck.

I will be forced to take steps to stop you. There are people more powerful that Danny O'Connor.

This had something to do with my mother.

There are other things that I am not able to reveal but it wasn't just Allah who was looking after us.

There was no other explanation. That conversation was yesterday in Dubai and today I am detained at gunpoint as a security risk. But what could that wizened old lady have that would make the people at this end jump? I would have to wait for the arrival of Sandra to find out. I began to wonder what she would look like now. Would she still make chest flutter and my legs go wobbly? I laughed inwardly at the thought. My chest was already fluttering and my legs wobbly. Where the Hell was this leading? I had two more hours to wait. In the meantime I had Solent's coffee. It was actually rather good.

When Sandra walked in the door my chest fluttered and when I stood up my legs wobbled. She was still a very attractive lady, very polished looking in grey pinstripe suit, slim and elegant, neatly coiffeured hair. What should I do? Hug? Kiss? Shake hands or curtsey? She saved me in my fluster by planting a Spanish type kiss on either cheek.

"Hello Jamie. Nice to see you."

"It's lovely to see you Sandra but could we not have fixed a dinner date or something."

"Oh, Jamie. You haven't changed, still flippant in a crisis."

"I don't have a crisis. Except I've been kidnapped by a crazy Cockney punk who now looks and talks like John le Carre and makes rather nice coffee. He seems to think you can cast some light on my crisis. Why don't you ask him to make you some coffee?"

"I already have. He'll be in shortly then perhaps we will cast some light. How are you?"

"Well apart from all this nonsense I've just had a rather unsettling experience in Dubai."

"I know."

"I know you know but I don't know why you know."

"John Sinclair always said you had a peculiar way of expressing things. At least you're not singing me rock songs."

"John Sinclair was an honest copper."

"I imagine that implies that I'm not."

"If the cap fits…"

Derek le Carre broke the building tension by coming in with a tray load of coffee.

"Derek, can you take over here and tell Jamie exactly why he is here. We always end up bickering like an old married couple."

"Certainly Commander. Well, Jamie, where do we start? First of all, everything we are about to discuss carries a DA-notice, Official Secrets Act and Counter Terrorism Act. Put simply it means we can keep you here till we're fed up looking at you and if or when you walk out that door you will never whisper a word of our discussion to a living soul. Commander Paterson has told us that you will never comply with this so short of sending you to Guantanamo Bay we had to come up with a compromise. She seems to be under the belief that by coming up here and asking you personally to promise silence you will comply her wishes."

He looked over to Sandra inviting her to speak. She just nodded him to continue. He spread open his fingers on the table in a gesture of deep thought.

"OK. Let's cut to the chase. Sanchita Tarkham is a crucial link in our information network in counter terrorist activities. If you cast your mind back to when we met in Glasgow about 1980 I introduced you to the world of Hawala."

"I remember our discussion."

"My own initiation into this wonderful world of commerce was with the help of Mahendra Tarkham. He operated a kind of travel agency and did insurance and also import-export documentation for the growing number of immigrants. I was intrigued by what he told me, did lots of research and became something of an expert on the subject of Hawala. In 1982 I was asked to help MI6 with a matter that had been triggered by a tip-off from Mahendra Tarkham. He was suspicious of a large movement of funds that he had been asked to make on behalf of Daniel O'Connor, whom I believe you know. I have to cut a long story short here but it went something like this. O'Connor received funds from the IRA. He asked Tarkham to transfer the money by Hawala via Dubai to Morocco where it was exchanged for marijuana. The marijuana was then shipped to Spain. In Spain the hash was passed to an offshoot of ETA who turned it back into cash. A portion of the cash was to be placed as a deposit on a villa that O'Connor was buying. The bulk of the cash went into the coffers of ETA. It is not clear exactly how but members of the ETA organisation had intercepted a consignment of ground-to-air rocket launchers sent by us to the Mujahidin in Afghanistan to shoot down Russian helicopters. ETA would place these rocket launchers inside a large freezer which was legitimately for O'Connor's newly acquired ice cream business. O'Connor then had to keep the toy guns in store till they were picked up. Have you followed all that?"

"The Moroccans get cash for their hash. ETA have friends in Spain who turn the hash back into cash. When they have the stash of cash they send some rocket launchers over to Scotland to be picked up by the Provos. Danny boy gets a deposit paid on his new villa and a new freezer for his ice cream. I imagine your new friends in MI6 were a bit perturbed at the idea of the IRA having British rocket launchers to bring down British planes. Come to think of it I'm not too happy about that idea either given that I've just flown in over the Emerald Isle."

"The Hawala transfer was intercepted in Dubai. The Provos were pissed off that the Brits had rumbled them but they didn't blame O'Connor. They just told him there was a hold up with the money. Danny being Danny, he decided to lean on his Hawala dealer to get the money moving. He hired two friends of yours by the name of Gillespie to rough Mahendra up a bit and they went over the top. Mahendra died and O'Connor disposed of the body. By the time MI6 found out what had happened there was a block of flats on top of poor old Mahendra. They asked me to help the Tarkham family. I spoke to Sanchita, your natural mother, and persuaded her to move with her family to Dubai. The cash was released to her to start up a new life on the condition that she agreed to continue her husband's Hawala business in Dubai."

"And my frail little old mother is now one of your key informants in Hawala money movements."

"Sanchita is now our number one informant on money movements which in fact makes her our number one informant on terrorist activities and major international crime activities. Her information has underpinned about 90% of all major crime busts and about 75% of all terrorist interceptions. The lady is irreplaceable. Commander Paterson would you like to take over at this point and explain some of the MI5 involvement?"

I interrupted before Sandra could speak. "I thought you said MI6 not MI5."

"If you allow Commander Paterson she will explain."

Sandra thanked him and took over. "You will no doubt remember our last conversation in Central Station many years ago. You were so high and bloody mighty about the black and white sides of justice. I tried to tell you that James Gillespie was being taken out of circulation because of his arms dealing. What I didn't tell you was that I was also under instructions to ensure that his two cousins went down as well. In fact they were the prime targets not

Jammy Gillespie like you thought. I didn't lie to you because at that time I didn't know the whole story.

"In the liaison post that I had just started my contacts were all MI5 but the pressure to put away the Gillespies came from MI6. Very basically MI6 are responsible for handling threats that come from outside the UK while MI5 deal with threats of terrorism or destabilisation that come from within. In addition, as you know, every Police force in the country has a Special Branch whose task is to deal with every kind of threat at a more local level. At that time it was a bit of a pig's breakfast with each group frequently treading on the other's toes. After our Chief Constable stirred the pot about James Gillespie working for MI5 the Government responded and a new office was created with the unfortunate name of IDLE (the inter departmental liaison executive). I was one of a team of six who had to bring all the departments into line and cooperate more.

"I wasn't officially started in the post, you'll remember, still baby-sitting Glasgow North-East Division and I had some meetings down south. In one of those meetings I was given very clear, precise instructions about what was to happen with the Gillespies. I didn't really have to do anything. The north-east team had already done the groundwork and I just had to rubber-stamp it. I didn't know then that Willy Gilly and his son Billy had murdered your mother's husband. Would you have walked out on me that night if you'd known? You're an awkward sod. I think you probably would.

"Anyway Masood and Rasheed went home to Dubai and told your mother that they had killed O'Connor. She contacted Derek Solent here and asked him to make sure it was smoothed over. He came to me and I had to tell him that they had in fact killed Freddy Cassidy and his mum. Someone in MI6 came up with the idea of covering it up by charging the Gillespies. It solved several problems. Your mother was eternally grateful and doubled her efforts at keeping us in the Hawala loop. We obviously have a network of informants but Dubai has become the main hub nowadays. It's a bit like Lloyds of London. If there is a big movement of funds then lots of little hundiwalas work together. Sanchita, your mother, is one of the longest established so she is privy to nearly everything that goes down."

Derek Solent took over again. "So, Mister Jammy Robertson, what's it to be? Are you prepared to accept that all this was done, not only for reasons of national security but also to the substantial advantage of your family? Or are you going to tell us that you're holding out for justice for the Gillespies? You must understand that…" He was interrupted by the persistent buzz of his cellphone on the table.

"Hello, yes, Derek Solent speaking. What? Holy God! When? How? OK. I'll call you back." He didn't bother clipping the phone shut. He threw it full force against the wall and it dropped in pieces on the floor. He pulled both arms up to his head and let out a low howl, pacing back and fore behind the desk. He tripped on the chair and kicked it viciously out of the way. He turned round to me.

"You selfish incompetent bastard! You've probably killed her. Your mother had a severe heart attack. It is touch and go whether she will live. What difference will it make now if you publish your stupid story? We have lost her. I told you, she's irreplaceable."

For once in my life I was at a total loss for words. What could I say? He was right. I probably caused the heart attack and, yes, I was selfish. Was I looking for justice or just the final chapter for a story? Well, the final chapter was not quite what I'd expected. I couldn't answer Solent. There was no answer to give him. Instead I turned to Sandra.

"I'm sorry Sandra. I think I've been a bit of an arsehole."

"What are you going to do?" she asked.

"I'm going back to Dubai, assuming that is permitted by MI6 or MI5 or whoever."

"What will you do there?"

"I don't know but I can't just hang around here. I have to see her again. Her name is Sanchita, you know. It's Bengali. It means treasure."

"There is nothing to stop you from going. I will make sure that is all sorted. Will you call me when you come back?"

"Yes I'll call you. Why don't we have some fish and chips in Central Station again? Maybe we can catch up from where we left off."

"Yes, Jamie. I'd like that."

"Why don't I give you my email address? I suggested.

"I already have it."

"God, nothing's sacred. You've hacked into my email."

"Nothing personal. You were flagged up automatically when you emailed the Tarkhams."

"Well. If you've got my address, you email me and I'll tell you what I'm doing once I know. If it's OK with both of you I'm going home to look for a flight."

I went home to my PC and managed to get a flight for the next day. I went to bed but couldn't sleep. What was it I said in my opening pages?

In real life stories don't fit the standard model of beginning, middle and end. Every story is just one small piece of one long string or, more often than not, several long entangled strings wrapped together in one great intertwining sequence of events. It's not always clear who is guilty, who is innocent, who is perpetrator, who is victim even when the jury returns a unanimous verdict. The secret for a good reporter is in picking up the loose threads and weaving them into a readable text with logical sequence, conclusion and outcome. That's what the reader wants. That's what society wants. A crime reporter is not so very different from a good detective. The questions nag at you and you look for answers but often, what you find are just more questions so you lie awake at night trying to put the ends together, trying to complete the circle that insists on looping backwards taking you down Nowhere Street.

The whole world had just flipped over. I was no longer a reporter on the outside looking in. I was at the centre of the **great intertwining sequence of events** like the vortex of a huge whirlpool, a whirling mass of segments of truth and lies, of blame and denial, of reality and fantasy. I was so hell-bent on seeking truth and justice that I had met my real flesh-and-blood mother and just walked away. I was happy now with what had happened to the Gillespies, knowing the harm and hurt they had brought to MY FAMILY and yet I'd spent twenty-odd years castigating the woman I'd loved because she didn't follow my code of justice. ***It's not always clear who is guilty, who is innocent, who is perpetrator, who is victim.*** Maybe in time I would manage to ***pick up the loose ends***. Maybe I could go back and ***weave the threads together to put logical sequence and conclusion*** in my own life. For now all I could do was ***lie awake trying to put the ends together, trying to complete the circle that insists on looping backwards taking you down Nowhere Street.*** Maybe I wasn't as jammy as I thought.

Next day was no better. Getting into the airport took nearly two hours and, once inside, the security procedures were excruciatingly slow. Nearly every flight was delayed and we took off three hours behind schedule. The only advantage was that lots of people had cancelled and I had a row of three seats to myself and my thoughts. As I flew southwards towards the Arab states I wondered how I would be received by the Tarkhams. And then the realisation exploded in my brain. My own brothers were murderers. All these years I'd chewed apart all the evidence again and again, ***looping backwards down Nowhere Street.*** Now that the truth lay open before me I still couldn't take it all in. My brothers killed Iris and Freddy! And here was I wondering how they would receive me! Amidst the whirling mists I managed to make one clear decision. For now I was not going to expose them, not until I found out how my mother was and perhaps I would never reveal the truth while she was living. I had already caused enough damage.

Then I began thinking about Sandra. She was still a beautiful woman. Could we put aside our differences after all these years? Could we enjoy our autumn years together? I didn't even know if she had met someone else. Perhaps she was married. She seemed keen to meet up again. Would she email me like she'd promised? Who else had access to my email? Where would I stay in Dubai? I had rushed off without booking a hotel. Perhaps I should contact Naseer, the younger brother. He seemed more understanding the last time and he was closer to his mother but would he be so understanding now that she was seriously ill? Would he blame me? Maybe it was just a wild goose chase. What would I do if she didn't want to see me? Two women in my life and I had no idea of my future with either of them. I was shaken from my brooding reflections by a voice from the aisle.

"Do you mind if I sit here beside you?"

"What? Where? I don't know…" I mumbled. I didn't really want to share my airspace at that moment but I wasn't entitled to claim three seats.

"You mean you don't want me to sit with you?" I looked up and there stood Sandra.

"Of course I want you to sit here. I just didn't realise…Where have you come from? I didn't know they could take on passengers in mid air."

"I'm in business class, one of the perks of the job."

"Have you come to hold my hand?"

She placed her hand over mine. "I'll hold your hand if you like Jamie but that's not why I'm here. If Sanchita, your mother, is as serious as we're told, somebody has to try and pick up the pieces. Maybe she can fix it for someone to take her place. Derek Solent wasn't exaggerating her importance. We have a couple of apartments in Dubai that are normally used as safe houses and I've been allocated one. Are you fixed up with a hotel? You're welcome to stay with me."

I managed a smile. "That would be very nice. I didn't have time to sort out a hotel. I was just thinking about it, actually, and how the Tarkhams would respond to my reappearance. I decided to approach Naseer. Maybe you should start with him as well. He is closer to his mother, my mother, than the older two and I think he's more clued in on the financial side. It wouldn't surprise me if he knows all about this Hawala thing."

"How do you know all this?"

"Hell, Sandra! You haven't changed. Do you remember you asked me that question in your office in Glasgow? The answer's the same now as it was then. I don't know. It's just supposition. I'm a crime reporter."

"Why do we always manage to create sparks when we come together?" she asked.

"Not always. Sometimes you give me a soft warm glow."

"I've missed you, Jamie Robertson. You suggested one time that I should marry you and become a happy housewife. I would not have made a very happy housewife but I often regret how things finished up between us. I loved you. I don't think I ever told you that. I didn't realise myself till that night you walked out in Central Station. I never met anyone else. I'm going to retire in a few months. Why don't we try again?"

It was my turn to place my hand on hers. "OK, but let's try harder this time."

I closed my eyes and fell asleep, waking up abruptly as we thumped down on the tarmac in Dubai.

Déjà vu

We've all experienced it, that feeling of déjà vu. We stepped off the plane into the warm opulence of Dubai airport. We picked up our bags and walked out the front doors to the welcome of a limousine, this time courtesy of Her Majesty's Government. I began to recognise the landmarks as we sped into the city centre. We pushed through the logjam of 4X4s, Beemers, Mercs and buses down to the coast road of Jumeirah. This time we continued past the Jumeirah Palm and a mile or so later swung into the area of Dubai Marina, swooping skyscrapers and cool lagoons. We plunged down into the underground car park and drew up alongside the lifts. The driver took our bags, escorted us to the lift and we zoomed silently to the 20th floor. The apartment was spacious, simply but elegantly furnished with a large balcony window. I pulled back the curtains half expecting to see the Islamic Centre on the other side of the Clyde, like the view from Councillor Ahmed's flat. In fact the view was of a beautiful mosque and behind that to the left, the Jumeirah Palm and further out to the right the towering structure of the Burj Khalifa.

It was too late to go to the hospital so we had dinner thrown together from some things in the fridge. We slept apart that night, not because we wanted to be apart but because it was easier than making the moves that would bring us together. I spent most of the night with Danny O'Connor. No matter how much I twisted and turned his face was there before me, laughing at me, mocking me.

"The story is some woman found you in the bushes. I say you're from another planet. You've been playing Clark Kent nearly as long as I've been playing Robin Hood. Tell me just once in all that time that you've seen justice."

Eventually I fell asleep and woke up to a view of the morning sun glittering across the Arabian Gulf. Sandra was already up with a pot of coffee sitting on the table and some croissants she'd found in the freezer.

"I'm afraid it's Kenyan," she chirped, "there's no Columbian."

"Kenyan will do nicely. I don't suppose there's any jam for the croissants?"

She looked up, burst out laughing, walked to the window and started singing.

"Ye cannae throw croissants oot a twenty storey flat."

I walked over to join her at the window and reached out to catch both her hands. "That seems like a million years ago. Do you really think we could go back and start again?"

"No, Jamie, we can't go back but that doesn't mean we can't go forward. I don't see any point in raking over old coals. We can't go back but we can put it all behind us and start again. But that's for later. Now we have to go and see your mother. I checked around while you were still asleep and she's in the Heart Center at the American Hospital. That's across the other side of the Creek. The quickest way is through the tunnel. I know the way so I'll drive. She's still very weak but I believe she is able to receive visitors. They put in a stent."

"What's that?"

"It's a little metal tube that the doctors insert into the artery to widen it and allow the blood to flow. It's less intrusive than major surgery."

"Is there a special visiting time?"

"No. She's in a private room so we can go anytime but they suggested we should wait till after the consultant has seen her. I haven't been able to make contact with any of the sons. They are probably at the hospital. I thought we should wait till about ten then make our way across. It's not very far but the traffic in this part of the city goes at walking pace. We'll get there about eleven."

"Derek Solent called you Commander Paterson. I thought it was your rank but now I think it's just because you're so bossy."

"Habit of a lifetime, Jamie. What you see is what you get. It's the only way to get things done especially if you're a woman in a man's world and the police is still very much a man's world. I know you are here to try and patch things up with your newly found mother but I have to be more pragmatic. You saw what happened at Glasgow airport. We're all still on high alert and we need to stay ahead of the terrorists. It's a game of cat and mouse."

"OK, Boss Cat. I really should be saying thank you. I wasn't sure where to start and you've done all the groundwork before I even got up. Let's have breakfast and get ready to go."

All three brothers were huddled round the bed when we arrived. They bristled noticeably as we walked in. Masood stood up and came towards me.

"You're not welcome here. We opened our doors to you and now we have our mother lying here because of your obtuse, intransigent ideas. We invited you into our family and you rejected our invitation. Please go away. I do not want Mother to be distressed any further."

Before I had a chance to answer, my mother spoke, clear and crisp.

"Let him be, Masood. Let him come to speak with me. I want him here. Let Commander Paterson come too; I need to speak with her urgently. There are things you do not understand. Don't worry Masood. I have to do this. Give me ten minutes alone with them. I'm not asking you Masood. I insist."

"But Mother…"

"Don't Mother me. I have had a minor heart attack not a mental breakdown. Ten minutes is all I need and then they will both be gone."

The three brothers retreated reluctantly. The two elder brothers eyed us suspiciously as they walked past. Naseer, the younger, gave me a friendly tap on the shoulder.

"I'll speak to you, Jamie, before you go."

I nodded in response and approached Sanchita. She looked tired and drawn and I felt an overpowering sense of remorse.

"I'm sorry I did this too you," I said, clutching her frail hand. She gripped my fingers with surprising strength.

"No, my son, it is I who am sorry. I let you slip away a second time. I could have stopped you. I could have explained. After you left I had no choice but to call the people in London. I hope they weren't too hard on you."

"I wish I had stayed longer. Then this would not have happened."

"No. No. My son, it was not like everybody thinks. You did not cause my heart attack. Commander Paterson, please come closer. This is important." She beckoned Sandra.

"My seizure was provoked by something I read, not by you. I contacted London the moment you left and I was fairly sure they would make you see sense. What gave me the shock was a Hawala money movement, or maybe I should say two Hawala money movements. When the second one came through I had this crushing feeling of having seen it all before and the memories were not pleasant. I couldn't breathe. I thought I was going to die."

Sandra moved in closer. "Hello Sanchita. We haven't met for some time. I wish it was in a happier setting. What was it that worried you? What did you see?"

"The first was a movement of one million US Dollars from Spain to Afghanistan. That was the day before you came here Jamie. Then two days later there was a movement of one million US Dollars from Afghanistan to Spain. It did not make any sense. Why send all that money half way across the globe and then send it back again. I took a look at the details, at the names and the places. You have to understand that the people who use our system don't use their real names. Everybody has a codename or a nickname. Often it is just a jumble of letters and numbers and most are in Urdu or Arabic or an Eastern language. The recipient of the first million was the same as the sender of the second but it was not sent back to the original sender. So I looked again. I couldn't believe what I was seeing. The other two names were the same as two of the names that were in the transaction that ended in the death of my husband Mahendra. That first time there was a three way movement with Morocco in the middle"

"Good Heavens!" exclaimed Sandra, "That must have been a terrible shock. No wonder it set your old ticker pumping. Do you know the real names of these people?"

"The codenames are only known to the agent who deals directly with the customer. I know all the codes of the people who send money from here and of the people who receive payment here. I would not normally know these names if the transfer is just passing through Dubai. It's like a sort of relay. Each agent passes the transaction through an agent he knows and can trust. Sometimes there are four or even six agents involved but only the sending agent knows the real name of the sender and only the final receiving agent knows the real destination. Your man Derek Solent seems to have an unbelievable list of codenames. I don't know how he got them."

Sandra tried again, "But if you have the codenames we can contact Derek and he will probably know who they are."

"He will very definitely know who they are but you don't have to go to all that trouble. I know who they are."

"But you said…" I interrupted.

"I said that only the sending agent knows the sender. In this case the sender used our services when we were in Glasgow. It was Daniel O'Connor. The people who received the second million were that terrorist bunch in Spain. I think they are called ETA. I wouldn't know that, under normal circumstances, but Derek Solent told me many years ago. So you can see why I got so choked up when I saw the same people again after all these years and then between these two transactions you turn up, Jamie, with all your questions. It was too much. My old heart couldn't pump all the blood that my brain was needing."

"Do you think it's the same people?" I asked. "Maybe they've caught up with O'Connor and want their money back."

"But they never paid O'Connor anything, back then," corrected Sandra. "ETA never paid anybody. They were the ones who were selling. Oh, God, no! It couldn't be. If they've just received a million Dollars it could only be for one thing but that's impossible."

265

She pulled out a Blackberry and punched the little keys. "Hello. I'd like to check the weather in the Solent and Isle of Wight. OK, thank you. I'll hold."

"You're losing me, Sandra," I protested. The Solent and the Isle of White is where posh English people go sailing."

"Don't be a prat Jamie. It's how I contact Derek when he's out and about. London put a call out and get him on the line. Yeah, OK, I know it sounds corny. Anybody tapping in would know I'm calling Derek Solent but it's also a coded message that tells them and him that it's urgent and it's re-routed to him on a scrambler." She held up her hand to stop me answering.

"Derek, listen, this is important, perhaps critical. I need you to think back to the incident with the missile launchers that involved the Tarkham family. What happened to the launchers? I imagine they were intercepted and destroyed. What? Why? Tell me you're winding me up. Derek, listen. I know you're going to say it's my famous feminine intuition again but I think they have re-surfaced. Yes I know but I don't think it's them. I think it's bounced back to the other side. Look, nowadays we call them Taliban but when they were fighting the Russians we called them the Mujahideen. Yeah, I know they're not exactly the same but listen. I need you to drop everything else and get onto this one. I'm with Sanchita Tarkham at the moment. What? Yes she's remarkably well and crystal clear on what she's telling me. She has just transferred a million Dollars from Afghanistan to Spain. She says you told her years ago that the receiver's codename belonged to ETA and she recognised it again this time. That's what kicked off her heart attack, nothing to do with Jamie except he came along asking questions at the same time. And that's not all. Guess where the Taliban got a million Dollars from? Think about it. I'll tell you when you come back to me with some answers on the launchers."

Sandra snapped off her Blackberry and turned back to my mother. "Sanchita, have you discussed this with anyone else?"

"Yes, two people but don't worry. They are both safe. My son Naseer has been working closely with me on all our money matters for about a year now. I haven't cut out the other two. It's just that Naseer has a flair for money and numbers while Masood and Rasheed are more interested in developing the business. I suppose you know that it is impossible to be a Hundiwala or a Hawaladar without the recommendation of another Hawaladar. I have been grooming Naseer and he is just about ready to take over. I think my present condition means that it is really going to be more immediate."

"That is excellent. Will he be disposed to help us like you have done?" asked Sandra hopefully.

"I have already spoken to him about this and I don't see any problem. However he is a very sensitive person and I think you should approach him yourself."

"You said there were two people who knew." I reminded her.

"Well, the other one is my very good friend Mr Solent that you have just been speaking to. We haven't discussed the second of the two money transfers because I arrived here before I had time but I did contact him about the first million dollars. Did he not tell you? I thought that was why you were here."

I could tell that Sandra was thrown but she recovered quickly and produced a smooth-tongued answer. "Well, Jamie's here to see you and try to put things right between you. I'm afraid my motives are more pragmatic. You have been invaluable to us over the last few years. I know it sounds incredibly mercenary but we desperately need to keep the Dubai connection in the Hawala chain. I will speak to Naseer. I truly hope that he will help to keep us in the loop. Anyway, let's stop talking about all these troublesome things and talk about you. How long are you going to be in here? I think they like you to get back up on your feet as soon as possible."

Sanchita perked up, "Oh, yes. I'm going home tomorrow. The hospital has organised a home service and I will have a nurse on hand for the first week. I'm going to pass all the money matters over to Naseer and take things easy. I think I'd like to go back and visit Bangladesh before I meet my maker."

Sandra smiled, her beautiful beguiling smile, "I think you should do that Sanchita," smiled again and added, "but that's not exactly taking it easy."

My mother and I said our goodbyes on a much happier note than our last parting. She made me promise that I would come to see her again before leaving Dubai. We left the hospital and returned to the apartment. All the way back Sandra was silent. I tried to kick off a conversation several times but all I got was, "uh huh," or "maybe." Once we were back at the apartment she was even more distracted. She picked up her Blackberry, fiddled about and put it down again, stood up, marched around, looked out the window, fiddled with the Blackberry again and sat back down on the sofa."

"OK, Let's have it," I said. "What's bugging you?"

"I went on a training course one time, just after I started in all this cloak and dagger stuff. I learned a lot that week, a lot of things that have served me well over the years. It was an old guy who did the course. You wouldn't give tuppence for him but he knew his stuff. There were two things in particular I remember. If you have a hunch that won't go away, it's not a hunch. It's something that needs dealt with. The other gem was if you have more than one coincidence in any situation, it's not coincidence. Just shrugging something off as a coincidence may cost somebody's life."

"OK. Explain." I invited.

"He never told me. He had two clear opportunities and he just kept *schtum*."

"Who never told you what?"

She looked at me and smiled but it wasn't one of her pretty smiles. "You know what I'm talking about. I don't believe you would have missed it."

"I think I understand where you're coming from but I need to hear you say it. You need to be sure of what you're thinking without being able to say later that I put the idea in your head. Who never told you what? Spit it out."

She spat it out, "Solent!"

"Are you speaking about the place where posh people go sailing or a twisted little Cockney?"

"You didn't miss it. Did you?"

"No, I didn't miss it but you still need to tell me what you're thinking."

"I don't want to think what I'm thinking."

"OK. Let's just forget it and concentrate on why somebody's playing ping-pong with a million dollars."

"No, the two things are connected. I'm going to have to take it higher. Jamie, sit down, don't speak, don't interrupt, just listen and when I'm finished please tell me that I haven't just gone crazy."

"I'm sitting down and I'm listening."

"When we were at the airport in Glasgow trying to stop you from exposing the Tarkhams, Derek took the call about your mother and he exploded, blaming you for putting too much stress on her. He knew at that time that she was concerned about the first movement of one million. He said nothing. I spoke to him again before coming here and again he said nothing. I spoke to him, as you heard, just an hour ago and told him about the second million and again he said nothing. He could say that he forgot to say anything back in Glasgow but when I told him about the transfer from Afghanistan to Spain, surely it would have been natural to say something about the transfer from Spain to Afghanistan. I even asked him to guess where they got the money from but he said nothing. So that plants a big question mark in my head.

"Now the real crazy bit! I think they're moving the missile launchers back to Afghanistan. Why else would the Afghans send a great dollop of money to ETA? It's not for guns. They can make guns in the back street workshops and in any case ETA were never a gun toting outfit. They put bombs in supermarkets and police stations. Derek Solent says the Stingers were not recovered from the episode when we stopped the deal with the IRA. He reckons it's questionable if they're still serviceable but I don't think we can take that chance. We need to alert the MOD and the Americans are going to need to know.

I set things in motion when I spoke to Derek from the hospital but if he's holding back on something I'm going to have to go over his head."

There was nothing crazy in what she was saying but she was stabbing in the dark.

"Do you have a CIA contact here in Dubai, or somebody at the US Embassy that you know? I asked.

"Yes, I have, actually. Good thinking. They'll be more up to date on the Stingers and we need to bring them into the loop anyway." She fiddled with her Blackberry and I assumed she was sending a text message. Within a minute she had a reply. "He's going to call on the land line."

We sat waiting for the phone to ring and we both jumped when it did. Sandra answered.

"Hello Carl. Thanks for calling back. There's…What? Oh, Derek? Sorry, I was expecting a call. Doesn't matter, what have you got?" She put the phone on loudspeaker so I could hear.

Derek Solent's smooth voice purred, "Well first of all I can confirm that the Stinger missile launchers from the Tarkham affair, back in the eighties, were never traced. GCHQ are fairly sure they ended up with Hezbollah in Lebanon but it has never been confirmed. I've also had confirmation that they would be useless by now. They have an argon gas powered launcher that is triggered by a BCU. That's a Battery Coolant Unit that has a shelf life of about five years."

"So, I was wrong on that one. It's funny, I still have bad vibes. Are you sure there's no way they could do something with the batteries and get them going?"

"Slow down, Sandra. Let me finish. The answer is yes, they can, but it's much worse than that. There are still hundreds of these Stingers unaccounted for and that's not the worst part. There was word came through on the wire last week from Spain. Apparently the same technology is now used in Javelin anti-tank missile launchers. It's a US manufacturer and they have a warehouse near Malaga. Last week they had a break-in and about a hundred of these BCUs were stolen. If they find their way over to Afghanistan it'll totally change the balance in favour of the Taliban. We have to bring the Yanks in on this one Sandra."

"I've already done so. That's the call I was expecting. You know Carl Wilson. Listen Derek, do you have anything on where they got the money from?"

"Eh…Well…I haven't had a chance to check on that side of things but I imagine it has to be drugs. The Taliban don't usually get involved with drugs but if needs must, I suppose they found a buyer in Spain. I'll do some mooching around and see what I come up with."

"OK. Derek. Call me later. I'll see what I can get from Carl." She hung up and turned round to me.

"Well you heard that. He knows bloody fine where the money came from. What's he holding back? Why is he holding back? Anyway, that's for another day. Right now we need to push the red button."

The phone rang again before I could answer. It was still on loudspeaker.

"Hi Sandra. How y'doin'? What's the big panic?"

"Well after I called you I thought maybe I'd pushed the panic button too soon but with what I've just heard you're going to have to wake up the President. What do you know about Stinger missiles in Afghanistan?"

"Aw, Hell, Sandra. Don't bust a gut on that old pony. We sent hundreds of Stingers to the Mujahideen last century to fight the baddies, who at that time were the Ruskies. Your people sent over some of your SAS guys to train them up on how to fire them. They shot down about three hundred aircraft, mostly choppers. Lotsa people say it was the clincher that sent the Ruskies packing. After that we tried to buy them back. I think we offered about thirty or forty thousand bucks a piece. All that achieved was to jack up the black market price. So they got scattered around the globe. There's probably still quite a few lying around in a cave somewhere in Afghanistan. But, hey, listen! They're useless. The battery pack is only good for four or five years. We know they've got them but they're rated low risk and anyway our choppers have anti-missile flare screens. They're heat seekers. I suppose y'know that and we've got all the latest gear for deflecting them. I don't think I'll wake the President on this one, Sandra."

"And what do you know about Javelins?"

"I take it you mean the anti-tank version not the Olympic version. It's very similar to the Stinger except it's ground to ground not ground to air. It doesn't need so much punch to launch the missile but the technology's more or less the same. There's none of them in Afghanistan except the ones we've got."

"Would I be right in saying they use the same BCU as the Stinger?"

"Right on the button, Honey."

"And if I told you that a hundred Javelin BCUs were stolen last week from a warehouse in Spain?"

"I'd be worried but still not wake the President."

"So, what if I just happened to add that our Hundiwala watcher has picked up a million Dollar transfer from Afghanistan to Spain?"

"Holy shit, Sandra. You sure you got the facts right on this?"

"Our watcher knows the codenames of the sender and the receiver of the million bucks. The sender's code belonged to the Mujahideen back in the eighties and the receiver was the ETA organisation in Spain. I'm not a field operator, Carl, not as savvy as people like you, but I'd say that somebody in Afghanistan is about to pop some Viagra in their impotent Stingers. I suppose the President likes his beauty sleep but you better wake up somebody. Consider this as an official notification from the British Government to the US Government. You're now the holder of the hot potato."

"Damn right, Honey. You keep your ass covered, quite a nice ass as I remember it."

"So they say, Carl. I can't see it but I always keep it covered. I think I'm going to have to go through the Embassy here so there might be a meeting or something. You'll maybe get a call from one of our army chiefs. Thanks for now."

"Thank you, Honey. You've made my morning."

"One thing before you go, Carl. What's the current black market price for a Stinger in good nick?"

"Good nick? Oh, you mean in working order, about two hundred thousand."

"So even if they don't use them they've now got twenty million for an investment of one million. I imagine there's no shortage of buyers."

"Yeah. They can buy a few hearts and minds with that kinda dough. I think you've just spoilt the President's breakfast."

Will ye no come back again?

It was clear that Sandra was up to her ears in international brinkmanship. It was time for me to slip quietly off stage. We agreed to meet a week later back in Glasgow. She was in a hot meeting at the British Embassy when I left the apartment so there were no fond farewells. Perhaps that was best; we were still both feeling a bit awkward rekindling our lost romance. I called a taxi to take me to the airport and took a detour via my mother's house to see her again before I left. She was alone in the house except for a nurse in attendance and her Philippines cook in the kitchen.

She was delighted to see me and we indulged in a bit of what the experts call bonding. It was good to have her to myself. We talked about our likes and dislikes, a little bit about religion, cooking, sports, music, Glasgow and Dubai. She surprised me by producing her email address. I'd kind of assumed she would have no idea about computers and she boasted indignantly of how she had forced her boys to take their businesses into the digital age. I found her to be very different from the impression I had in the first moments that I met her, before I knew who she was. She was really quite a lot like Maggie. I began to realise that they probably had formed a close friendship. I could also now understand how this determined little lady had persuaded Maggie to keep quiet about her. Finally it was time to head for the airport and the Scottish side of me was thinking about the taxi outside with the meter still running.

"Will you come back again?" she asked, as we hugged goodbye.

I replied on impulse, "Yes I'll come back. Why don't we go together to Bangladesh when you are a bit stronger?

"I'd like that, Jamal. Do you mind if I call you Jamal?"

I hugged her again and said, "I'd like that, Mother. Do you mind if I call you Mother?"

We laughed as we parted and I jumped into the taxi.

Airport schedules were back to normal and the flight back home was uneventful. I was a bit trepid as I passed through the controls in Glasgow airport, half expecting to be hustled into a small room and asked what I was planning to do in Bangladesh but the airport had calmed down since its brush with Al Qaeda. I went to rescue my baby Fiat from the car park and felt like I was buying it again when I saw the charges. I felt a strange comforting feeling as I swung out into the M8 traffic. I was home. There's something about coming back home to Glasgow that just sort of seeps into you.

I garaged the car and took the stairs up to my flat, slipped the key in the door and pushed past the growing pile of soon-to-be-recycled paper. I like curry and pizzas and kebabs but it seemed like every fast food outlet in Glasgow had bombarded me with their mouth watering menus. There were over twenty, so I laid them out on the floor and did eeny-meeny-miny-mo, picked an Italian and settled for spaghetti al pesto. I sifted through the rest of the pile and found the grand total of six bona fide letters, all of them bills. I went to the living room to phone for the takeaway. The answer-phone light flashed annoyingly so I hit the button. I was rewarded with a verbal pile of garbage from six different Internet providers who thought I needed a change and lots of beep-beep-beep from callers who had hung up on hearing my out-of-town message. I was just about to press the clear-all-messages button when a woman's voice came on. It was a hard Glasgow voice with a shrill urgent tone.

"Mr Robertson, Jamie, Ah need yer help. Ah've no got anybody else tae go tae. Ye dinnae really know me but ye helped ma Mam wance. Ma name's Betty Sullivan. Ah cannae leave ma number. Ye cannae phone me. Ah huv tae phone you. He'll kill me if he knows."

She hung up and then the same voice came on again, "Aw shite, that bloody machine again. Where-ur ye? Oh Christ! Ah hope this is the right number. If yer there Jamie, please pick up. Ah really need tae talk tae somebody." She clicked off again.

While waiting for my spaghetti to arrive I dug out an old bottle of Chianti and poured a glass. I sat sipping the wine thinking of anybody from the past called Sullivan. I definitely had no recollection of any Betty Sullivan. Poor woman sounded desperate but without her number there was nothing I could do. I still had an old phone that didn't register the callers. BT would be able to give me the last caller but she was emphatic that she didn't want me to call her. My meal arrived, a very tasty pesto, but I didn't enjoy it thinking about these weird calls.

It didn't take long before I found out who my frantic caller was. The shrill ringtone pierced my thoughts. I didn't have time to do my friendly "Jamie Robertson here", before she pitched in with her frantic cries for help.

"Jamie Robertson? Thank Christ. Ah thought ye wur deid or somethin'. Where'ye been? Och, it's none o' ma business. Listen, Ah really need ye tae help me. Ah cannae take any mair o' this. We need tae get oot but they'll no let us."

"OK, Betty, isn't it? First of all, tell me who you are. I don't remember any Betty Sullivan."

"No, ye'll no remember me as Sullivan. Ma name used tae be Cassidy. Ma Mammy was Iris Cassidy. Ye must remember her. Ye helped her a lot when Freddy got shot an' a that. It was years ago but ye must remember."

"I remember Iris and Freddy very well. I know that Freddy had two sisters but I'm afraid I didn't know much about you."

"Ma sister Jane's deid. She overdosed no long efter the fire. So, it's just me noo. Well me an' Tiger Sullivan but he's as much use as a pot o' pish. If he's no drunk he's stoned an' if he's neither o' these it means he's in the clink but the silly bastard's really got us in a pickle this time. Ah cannae go back in there again. Last time ah tried tae top masel. Ah'm no a cage bird. Ah cannae dae time like he can."

"You're not making a lot of sense Betty. Do you want to come round and talk this over more calmly?"

"Gie me yer address. Ah'll get a taxi. Where'd'ye live?"

I gave her my address and finished off the Chianti while I waited for her. I got quite a shock when I opened the door. It could have been Iris standing there.

"Ye look like ye've seen a ghost." That was her hello.

"I feel like I'm looking at a ghost. You look just like her. You even speak like her."

"Aye an' ah've been hauled through the gutter by men an' aw' just like her. Ye'd think we'd learn a lesson watchin' them messin' things up but we just go an' dae the same."

Betty didn't really look like she'd been hauled through the gutter. She looked rather smart and she hadn't done her shopping in Primark. The gold that dripped from her hadn't come out of the Argos catalogue. This was the kind of lady that turned heads as she walked into a room. Poor Iris was a good-looker too but she did always look like she'd been pulled through a hedge backwards, except in the last few months before she died when she'd linked arms with O'Connor. The last couple of weeks had been a bit surreal for me. Betty Sullivan (nee Cassidy) brought me down to reality with a thump. I was back home. I stood aside awkwardly and motioned her into my apartment.

She sat down on the sofa as if she was ready for a Piers Morgan interview and fluttered her eyelids. "Ye were right," she began, "this is nice an' comfy. Ah'm mair relaxed noo."

"OK. If you're sitting comfy, let's begin. You said you couldn't go back inside again. Why do you think that might happen?"

"It's just a maetter o' time. Wan ae us is gontae get clobbered an' knowin' ma luck it's gontae be me."

"That's not really an answer to my question, Betty. I can't help you if you don't tell me what's going on. Why would you get clobbered? Somebody is making you do something. What is it and who's making you do it?"

"Mam ayeways said you was a clever clogs. Y'ur, urn't ye?"

"Answer my question, Betty. What have you been up to that could land you back inside?"

"Ye're no gontae believe this. Ah've been goin' on holiday." She giggled.

"Look Betty. You said you had a problem and I could help and I asked you round because of your Mum. I've had a long day and I'm tired. If you're not prepared to be serious I can't really help you."

"Ah um serious, dead serious. Somebody's gontae notice. They dinnae stamp yer passport any mair but they scan it in yon machine thing an' they're bound tae see the number o' times we've been there."

"Been where?"

"Lloret. It's in Spain. It's Lloret de Mar but yer supposed tae pronounce it like Yoret. Ah've been there six or seven times in the last year. Tommy, ma hubby, ev'rybody caw's him Tiger, he's only been a couple o' times. He's the catcher so he stays here."

"Would I be right in thinking we're talking about drugs?"

"Aye, ye wid. Mam telt me ye was a smart cookie. How'd ye know?"

"What were you carrying, cocaine, cannabis?"

"No, it's heroin, top grade stuff, comes fae Afghanistan."

I sat bolt upright. "Who's running the show?"

"It's a wee travel agent in Glesga Cross. The guy that organises it is Italian but he's no the travel agent. Ah think he works fur the big boss. Ye get a free hotel or apartment an' ye dinnae huvtae pay fur the flights an' aw' that. The first cuppla times it was a big laugh like, but they've started squeezin' us an' makin' us go back even if we dinnae wantae. They gie us spending money like, an' they're no tight fisted. Ah'm makin' guid money fae it but ah'm scared ah get caught an' ah want oot an' they'll no let me. Tommy disnae want oot. He's rakin' it in an he's got himsel' a big motor. All he hus tae dae is meet us aff the plane an' take the gear tae the big boys. He says that naebody ever checks oor luggage. Ah mean they dae the usual stuff aboot liquids an things but we fly fae Prestwick wi' Ryanair tae Girona an back an' ye just walk on an' walk aff an' they're only bothered aboot getting' us on an' aff the plane as fast as they can."

"So what do you want me to do?"

"God forgive me but Ah want tae tell the polis. Ah want it tae stop. Ah'm ready tae grass them up if that's whit Ah huvtae dae an' ah need somebody tae smooth the path like. Ah cannae just walk intae a polis station like. That's what ma Mam did when she punctured that wuman an' she nearly got life. An' there's wan other thing. Nuthin's tae happen tae Tommy. He's no wan o' the bad guys."

"What's the name of the travel agent?"

"Scotbrava. They used tae dae buses fae Glesga tae the Costa Brava an' Benidorm but naebody goes by bus noo. Ryanair's just a big bus in the sky an it's a hellafalot faster. Ye dinnae get a numb bum. Ah suppose that's why they Scotbrava guys started shippin' dope if their business was goin' doon the pan, like."

"OK, Betty, like I said, I'm really tired now. I'll take a snoop around in the morning and see what happens. How do I get a hold of you? You didn't want to leave your number when you called earlier."

"Ah'm no sure. It's just that Tommy might answer ma phone. We both use it sometimes. Hey, Jamie, ye gonna phone fur a taxi fur me? It's no awfy far but wi' these heels Ah'll break ma leg or sumthin"

I phoned a taxi for her and we chatted a bit while we waited.

"Ah could go a glass o' wine if there's any left in the boatel."

"The Chianti's finished. I think I've got some white in the fridge." I offered.

"Aye, that's magic. Ah prefer white."

I went off to the kitchen, returned with the bottle and poured two glasses. "Listen," I said, "I've been thinking. I've got one of those cheap cellphones that's pay-as-you-go. Why don't you take it with you and keep it in your bag. If I need to call you I'll use that number."

"That's awfy nice of ye Jamie. Yer a wee gem."

"You said you don't want to go back inside. What were you in for before?"

"The first couple o' times was fur no payin' the fines. Ye know how it is. Ye get fined fur solicitin' an' ye cannae work fur a cuppla weeks because ye know they're watchin' ye sae ye've no got money tae pay the stupit fine. Next thing ye know yer lifted and stuck in the jail fur no payin'. But that was just twenty-eight days like, sort o' like a wee holiday. The last time Ah was caught wi' a stack o' class A an' Ah got three years. It was just efter Ah met Tommy an' he stood by me an' aw' that, like but Ah nearly went crazy in that place. When Ah came oot Tommy got me fixed up wi' wan o' they internet agencies. Ah dinnae dae the streets noo. It's aw very sophisticated, like. Ah'm no a prossy. Ah'm an escort. Nae mair quickies up a back alley. It's an overnight stay at the Holiday Inn or the Marriott, two hundred a night an' sometimes extras an' ye usually get dinner an' breakfast thrown in."

"And I suppose Tommy gets his cut."

"Naw, naw. He's no like they other pimps. He's ma man. He's no ma pimp, like, an' he's rakin' it in fae the drugs thing. Ah widnae mind if he wanted a cut. Ah'm makin' enough fur baith o' us. Ah dinnae need the aggravation wi' aw' these trips tae Spain. Wan ae us is gontae get caught. Ah cannae dae time again an' Ah need Tommy but he thinks he's on the magic roondaboot."

"Well, Betty, I've been away from all this for a while and I'm a bit out of touch with who's who but I'll ask around and see if any of my old police contacts are still around. I promise to try but I can't promise any more than that, except I will get back in touch with you."

She came over and gave me a big hug, tripped on a rug and got bright ruby red lipstick all over my vintage Rolling Stones t-shirt. The intercom buzzer saved me from her exuberance. She wobbled off on her high heels to catch her taxi and I went off to enjoy my first real night's sleep for a couple of weeks. I managed to forget that my brothers were murderers, that the love of my life was out there somewhere trying to save us from Al Qaeda, that I had found and nearly lost my real mother and that I'd just had a crazy hooker wanting me to save her from the drug trafficking barons. I forgot all these things and slipped into a deep slumber.

I awoke from my deep slumber with a jolt. What was that crash? It sounded as if it had been in my own flat. I shook my sleepy head and rolled over. Whatever it was couldn't be that important. Then I heard the voices. They were coming nearer. Suddenly it seemed like my bedroom was full of armed police shouting.

"Stay where you are! Don't move! Stay where you are!"

I stayed where I was.

"OK. Sit up really slowly."

I sat up really slowly.

"Are you Jamie Robertson?"

"Yes. What the hell do you want?"

"I want you to get up slowly and get dressed."

I got up very slowly and got dressed. I was absolutely petrified. This was worse than the confrontation at the airport. When I had my clothes on they motioned me through to the living room. As I passed though I noticed that they had smashed my door in.

"Why didn't you answer your doorbell? We've been ringing for ten minutes."

"I was sleeping. I never heard any doorbell."

"Where were you last night?" My questioner bore sergeant's stripes. He kept his machine pistol aimed at my gut as he spoke. The others fanned out around the flat obviously looking for something.

"I was here. I got home from the airport about seven."

"Where had you been?"

"Dubai."

"Why?"

"Visiting family."

"How do you come to know Betty Sullivan?"

"I don't know her."

"She was here last night."

"That's correct."

"What was the purpose of her visit?"

"She asked me to help her with a problem she has."

"What kind of problem?"

"A personal problem."

"You mean she was helping you with a personal problem." Some of the other officers laughed. I didn't answer.

"Betty Sullivan is a known prostitute and drugs dealer. Which of her services did you call upon last night?" He smiled, a sly, unpleasant smile.

I didn't answer the question but replied, "Betty came to see me to ask for my help. I had never met her before last night but I used to know her mother."

He smiled another sly smile. "I never had the privilege of meeting her mother but I'm led to believe that she was a prostitute and drug dealer too."

I didn't answer. Old habits die hard. Let him do the talking. Say as little as possible and the other person is obliged to break the silence.

"You haven't answered my question," he demanded.

"Sorry. What was your question?"

"Did you use her services as a prostitute or was she supplying drugs?"

"Neither. She was just a friend that I managed to help a couple of times."

"You said you never met her before last night."

"Sorry. I thought you were asking about Iris."

"Who's Iris?"

"Betty's mother."

"I wasn't asking you about her mother."

"Yes you were."

"You're a bit of a smart arse. Aren't you?"

"I'm sorry. I don't really know how to answer that question. Is it relevant to whatever enquiries you are undertaking?"

He moved up close in a menacing gesture and pushed the gun into my belly, drawing back quickly as a plain clothes officer came out of my bedroom. The detective was carrying my Rolling Stones t-shirt. Another plain clothes officer was putting the two wine glasses into plastic bags. They looked at each other and then nodded to the sergeant.

The sly smile returned to the sergeant's face. "Jamie Robertson, I am detaining you under section 14 of the Criminal Procedure Act (Scotland) because I suspect you of having committed an offence punishable by imprisonment, namely the murder of Elizabeth Sullivan. The reasons for my suspicions are that you were one of the last people to see her alive, having entertained her at your home shortly before her death and that one of your possessions, namely a cellphone, was found at the scene of the crime."

He drew a breath and added, "You will be detained to enable further investigations to be carried out. You will now be taken to a police station where you will be informed further on your rights as a suspect. Do you understand?"

This was all unreal. Betty was dead. Somebody must have known that she came to see me and why and they'd made sure she couldn't tell me any more. I just stood there numb with shock.

"I asked you if you understand."

"No, I don't understand. What has happened to Betty?"

"We are kind of hoping you can tell us."

"I can't tell you anything."

"We'll see about that in due course. In the meantime you will please accompany us to the police station."

I didn't have much option other than to comply. My brain was racing. They had obviously found my phone in her bag or on the ground. Nobody was going to believe I gave it to her when she already had one of her own. The two glasses would show that we had been drinking together. The taxi company would say that she came from my flat. I had lipstick stains all over my t-shirt. Any reasonable person would conclude that something was going on between us especially if I couldn't offer an alternative explanation but something was buzzing in my head telling me not to say exactly why Betty was in my flat.

They took me down to a waiting squad car and, with sirens blazing, whizzed me to Central Police Headquarters. I had been here so many times over the years but this was my first time in custody. I laughed to myself ruefully as I walked in. There were quite a few sergeants over the years who would have loved to do this to me. Sandra had threatened to send a squad car the day she called me in. I wondered where she was now. I couldn't call on her for help under the circumstances. I started to panic. Who could I call on? There was nobody came to mind. Anyway, that would be a problem for later. I knew enough about Scots law to know that they could hold me for six hours before they would have to arrest me formally and let me have a lawyer. At the moment they were just making enquiries.

They took me to the front desk to get booked in. I recognised the desk sergeant, a wily old Fifer called Emslie. I didn't know his first name. He was Sergeant Emslie when I first met him as a young man and now with whiting grey hair he was still Sergeant Emslie. He was a smart copper so he must have blotted his copybook somewhere along the line. We looked at each other awkwardly, both equally embarrassed and uncomfortable with the formality of the procedure. The last time I met him we'd watched a world cup final over a couple of pints in a bar somewhere. Despite my situation his presence was mildly reassuring. After the official check-in I was escorted to an interview room and left sitting alone for about an hour.

Eventually, into the room came the detective who picked up my t-shirt accompanied by a young female detective that I'd never seen before. They say you're getting old when the police start to look too young. She introduced herself as DI Morrison and the man as DC Craig so she was obviously leading the inquiry.

"Mr Robertson," she began politely, "I'd like you to help us with our inquiries by answering some questions about last night. Is that OK with you?"

This was quite a neat way of initiating the interview. If I said OK, I was opening the door to questions I would feel unable to answer but if I said no, I was refusing to help.

"The officer who arrested me said that I would be informed of my rights when I came to the police station. Do I have the right to call a lawyer?"

"You were not arrested. You were detained pending further investigation. You will be informed of your rights if and when you are arrested and charged. At that point you may call a lawyer. While you are just detained for questioning we can interview you without a lawyer."

"As I understand it I am not obliged to answer any questions except my name and address and my age."

"You have the right to remain silent. Do you feel the need to remain silent? If you have nothing to hide I don't see any problem in you answering a few questions."

"That sounds reasonable. I'll tell you what. If you explain to me the full circumstances that led up to my detention I will try to answer your questions. Also I need your word that someone is dealing with my smashed door. Your officers broke into my flat this morning without any arrest warrant or search warrant when I was asleep in my bed."

"There is a uniformed officer in attendance at your flat waiting for a joiner to secure your door. In the early hours of this morning the police were called to the car park in Bluevale Street where they found the body of a woman. The woman was identified by her possessions as Elizabeth Sullivan. Among the items around the body we found a mobile phone. On contacting the provider we discovered that the said phone belonged to a certain Jamie Robertson. I would like you to explain how your phone came to be lying next to the body of the dead woman."

"I gave her the phone so that I could contact her."

"Why would you do that?"

"I just said, so that I could contact her."

"Why did you want to contact her?"

"She wanted to provide the police with information and she asked me to act as a go between."

"What kind of information did she want to give us?"

"I don't want to reveal that at this stage."

"That's not very helpful."

I didn't answer, waiting instead for her to continue.

"You don't deny that Elizabeth Sullivan was in your flat shortly before she was murdered."

"I don't deny that she was in my flat. I have no way of knowing how that relates to the time of her death and this is the first that I have been told that she was murdered. How was she killed?"

"I'm afraid I'm the one asking the questions. What time did she leave your flat?"

"You're best to check that with the taxi company. I phoned for a taxi to take her home. I have no idea what the time was. I was very tired and went to bed."

"You were drinking together. It that correct?"

"No, I was drinking alone when she arrived. I gave her a glass of wine while we waited for the taxi."

"You say you went to bed. I say that you followed her. What did you argue about?"

"We didn't argue."

"Did you have sexual relations with her?"

"No."

"Then how do you explain how you have her lipstick all over your shirt." She produced a plastic bag containing my t-shirt and placed it on the table."

"She gave me a hug and wobbled on her high heels. She sort of fell into me and brushed against my t-shirt. It's all covered in lipstick. It was one of my favourites."

"You're saying you killed her because she messed up your favourite shirt?"

"I didn't say that."

"So why did you kill her then?"

"I didn't leave my flat after Betty went for the taxi."

"Can you prove that?"

"Of course not but you probably can."

"How can we do that?"

"There is a very good security system in my building. You just need the video tapes to see who came and went."

"Video tapes are only conclusive if they show somebody. Just because you're not on the tape doesn't mean you didn't leave the flat."

I didn't let her draw me into an argument on videotape evidence. I let the silence hang again.

"OK. Let's say I give you the benefit of the doubt and accept your story about helping Betty. I need to know more about why she was going to go to the police. Maybe the person who attacked her knew she was going to squeal and decided to stop her."

"That thought had crossed my mind."

"Well?"

"Well, what?"

"What was she wanting to tell us so badly that she got herself killed?"

In my forty years of hard nosed crime hacking I had learned one thing. Never tell a police officer anything that you don't really have to. This young inspector was not from the drugs squad. If I told her what Betty had told me she would go blundering in and blow away all chance of catching the real bad guys. A little insect was buzzing away in my head telling me that this was connected in some way with O'Connor. I was just going to have to bluff my way out of this little corner.

"I need you to get in touch with someone in MI6." I said calmly.

The other detective had remained silent up to this point but now he jumped to his feet and thumped the table.

"Who the fuck do you think you are? Walter Mitty? Who do you think, in MI6, is going to be interested in a pathetic little tosser like you? They'd just ask the same question I'm going to ask you now. What did you do with the weapon? We will find it, you know. We always do. Do yourself a favour and tell us now. If you help us it will help you to lessen your sentence. If you piss us around I'll make sure you go down for life."

I ignored his outburst and kept looking at the DI. "The man you need to get hold of is Derek Solent. It's quite possible he's in Glasgow at the moment. Just tell him you have me in custody. In fact, if you don't believe me, just try typing my name into your central register. I think you'll find it's flagged up and you should have called them before you went to my flat." I turned round to face the DC. "We'll find out who's the pathetic little tosser."

The DI swung round and produced a laptop from the shelf behind. She flipped it open and shuffled impatiently while it booted up. She rattled a few keys and just uttered one word.

"Shite!"

"I take it you believe me." I said smugly. I hadn't been all that sure that my bluff would work. "What does it say?"

"I'm afraid I'm not at liberty to disclose that," she snapped back. "This interview is terminated. DC Craig, come with me." DC Craig toddled off at her tail and I was left sitting alone again with my thoughts.

There was a tap on the door and it opened slightly. A head squinted round the side. It was the desk sergeant, my world cup chum from days gone by. "Hello Jamie, Ah wis hoping I'd catch y'alone. Yer causin' a bit ae a stir." His broad Fife accent was still distinct from the softer Glasgow twang.

"What's happening?"

"Ah dinnae ken. As far as Ah can gaether we wernae supposed tae detain ye. We were supposed tae keep ye under constant surveillance and notify MI6 if ye came up in connection wi' ony case we were hondlin'. Ah think they're feared tae contact MI6 noo an' tell them whit they've done. What the Hell are ye up tae, Jamie? Listen, dinnae answer that. It's no why Ah'm here. Ah've sneeked in somebody tae see ye. If onybudy asks ye, it wis nuthin' tae dae wi' me."

He slipped out and another head appeared from behind the door. I jumped up with delight. It was John Sinclair my partner from Street Patrol.

"Good God, John! Where did you come from? It's nice to see a friendly face." I shook his hand vigorously.

"The sergeant phoned me, said he thought I would want to know they were about to charge you with murder. He was always a good loyal mate. He got stuck on the promotion ladder same time as me. Sometimes I think it was because of me he got stuck. He's a bloody fine copper. Anyway what's going on?"

I could hear the sound of approaching voices so I had to be quick. "John, thanks for coming. Can you see what you can get on an outfit called Scotbrava in Glasgow Cross who do free trips to Spain for anybody that'll bring back a bag of dope?" The door opened and the lady DI walked in.

"Who are you? Are you Mr Robertson's lawyer?" she demanded.

"Something like that, Love. I'll be in touch Jamie." He nodded reassuringly in my direction and strolled out before anyone could question him further.

The DI eyed me suspiciously. "I'm going to release you Mr Robertson. A squad car will take you home. Come and collect your belongings from the front desk." I decided not to make any comment or ask any questions. I went with her to my friendly desk sergeant. He winked as he passed me my things.

"Will we be seeing you again, Mr Robertson?" he asked.

"You will indeed, Sergeant. If you turn on your TV next Friday night you'll see me on the BBC. I'm on the guest panel of Question Time. I believe the general theme is police efficiency in times of high alert."

The desk sergeant laughed, "OK. Ah'll mak sure the wife records it."

DC Craig shuffled uncomfortably, uncertain as to whether or not I was taking the Mickey. The truth was I'd only just remembered that I'd agreed to do the programme. Not surprising, I suppose, with everything else that had happened. It wouldn't need any preparation but I was pleased I wouldn't need to contact them from jail to say I couldn't make it. I walked out the door smiling to myself. The DC glanced at me and caught my grin. Now he was sure I was taking the Mickey.

Photographic proof.

My door was boarded up rather crudely but I suppose it was basically secure. The caretaker of the building agreed to call a decent carpenter for me and then I had no alternative but to haul off the planks of wood and wait till the professional came. I tidied up the flat as best I could and sat down to watch the lunchtime news. Betty's murder was one of the top stories. The body of a woman was found by two beat bobbies on foot patrol in the early hours of the morning. They called an ambulance but the woman died on the way to the hospital. She had been stabbed six times according to the reporter. One man was detained on suspicion but later released. The reporter began to add some other detail but the screen suddenly went blank and returned to the anchor newscaster in the studio.

"I'm sorry," she said, "we are unable to continue with that story for the time being."

There was a shuffle at my door and in walked Derek Solent.

"Good!" he declared, "We managed to get a stop on that one."

"Don't tell me you put a D-notice on it?" I asked incredulously.

"My, my, Jamie lad. You really must try to keep up with the times. It's now called a DA-Notice. I put it on for your protection, you silly bugger. If you've been keeping up with the real world you'll know that there are now five categories of DA-Notice. Number five is specifically in place to protect the identity of members of the security forces and sometimes also those who are helping them. I assume you are helping us. How long do you think it's going to be before some bright spark discovers it was the famous Jamie Robertson that was detained on suspicion of murder? You don't really want that to be public knowledge."

"In that case I owe you a thank you."

"Never mind that. I did it for Sandra. I'm not at all sure you're good for her."

"Who the hell are you to stand in judgement? Tell me this. How come you're so concerned about Sandra and yet you tried to hide from her the fact that you knew Danny O'Connor supplied the million dollars to the Afghans."

"Because of you. You're just another snooping reporter. I knew you were going to be there in Dubai with her and the less you knew the better. I've been tracking that bastard for over twenty years. Nobody ever gets near enough to pin anything on him. He always stays a couple of steps back from the action. He's got a small army of hoodlums doing his bidding. That Hawala account has been dormant for years. I've been watching it. Why has he started using it again? Anyway I asked your mother not to tell anybody. I was hoping she would have included you and Sandra in that exclusion zone. I had no idea about this other missile launcher business."

"I thought you were protecting O'Connor. I'm fairly sure Sandra thinks the same. She reckons you should have said something before she went to Dubai."

"Yes, she's maybe right but this business works on the need to know. She didn't need to know. Anyway, enough of that. Let's get down to why I'm here. I'm told you asked for me specifically. Why didn't you call Sandra?"

"She's up to her ears in this missile thing. It didn't seem appropriate to disturb her. I couldn't think of anybody else. I used to know everybody who mattered in Strathclyde Police but I'm out of touch. You'll find this funny but I don't even have a lawyer. The last time I needed one was about fifteen years ago and he's dead. I was in a corner and I tried a bluff. My bluff worked."

"So nobody else knows about this. Good. Let's keep it that way. But listen. I have to ask you this and I need the truth. Did you have anything to do with the death of this woman?"

"No. She left my flat late last night and I went straight to bed. I was still there when the Scoobies came barging in."

"So how are you planning to explain to Sandra? She is going to find out that you were with this hooker. I suppose you weren't to know it would turn out like this."

"Whoa boy! Hold it right there," I demanded indignantly. "I wasn't with any hooker."

"You've just said she was in your flat. Are you saying she wasn't a hooker? Come on Jamie, this is Iris Cassidy's daughter we're talking about. The whole of Glasgow knows she was a street hawker. It was the family business."

"It was one of the family businesses."

"Oh, Jesus, Jamie. You're not a secret junkie? Please tell me you weren't buying drugs."

Before I could answer there was another scuffle at the door. "Hello Jamie! Are you there?" It was John Sinclair.

"Come in John!" I shouted and went to usher him in. "This is Derek Solent, a colleague of Sandra's. Derek, you maybe know John. He's an old friend. We worked together on the Street Patrol programme. He was on Sandra's team for a while." They shook hands and exchanged hellos.

"So they let you out?" asked John.

"I thought you said nobody else knew?" demanded Derek Solent.

"No, you said that nobody else knew but you didn't give me time to answer before you started haranguing me about my dealings with Betty Sullivan."

"That's what I'd like to know as well," John chipped in. "What were your dealings with Betty?"

"Oh Christ, not you as well," I protested. "Sit down both of you and listen."

They sat down and I gave them a re-run of last night's events. When I finished John heaved a sigh and leaned back on the sofa. "OK," he said, "now I can see where all this is heading."

"Well I'm really happy to here that," humped Derek, "I haven't a bloody clue where all this is heading."

John put his hand in his back pocket and pulled out an envelope of photos. "Have a deco at these. I've just run them off."

I took a quick look at John's photos, all of which were holiday snaps except one that looked like a street in Glasgow. I passed them over to Derek.

Derek scanned them and looked at both of us in turn. "Are you two taking the piss? You haul me away from serious national security matters to look at your friend's holiday photos. I don't think it's funny. There was a woman murdered last night and somebody tried to stamp your name on it. OK, she was just a hooker and a drug pusher but she was here in this flat about half an hour before she got topped and I want to know what the fuck you're playing at."

I tried to smooth him down. "Look Derek, they're John's photos. He's obviously just back from holiday and…Hold on. Pass them back here." I took the photos back and looked more closely at the one of two men sitting outside a bar on the street. "That's Daniel O'Connor. His hair's pure white, what's left of it and he's looking a bit weathered but I'd recognise that arrogant poise anywhere. Who's that with him? Bloody Hell! That's Charlie Frazzini. Where was this taken, John? Where did you get these photos from?"

"I took these photos myself. They're in a beautiful little town called Palamos on the Costa Brava. Take a look at the last photo. It's back here in Glasgow. I took it this morning."

Derek Solent picked up the Glasgow photo and studied it. "Let me see the other one," he demanded and I passed him the photo of O'Connor. He peered at the two photos for a good few seconds then stated, "This guy drinking with O'Connor is the same guy walking down the street here in the other photo. It's near Glasgow Cross. You can see the top of the Tollbooth Steeple. I'd say it's in Trongate. What did you say this guy's called? Frazzini. He was one of the players in that ice cream stramash back in the eighties. If my memory serves me right O'Connor's men were pushing Frazzini's vans off the road. Looks like they're quite chummy now. What's the connection with the Trongate photo?"

"The connection, I believe," answered John slowly, "is a lady called Betty Sullivan. Is that correct Jamie?"

"When I came back from Dubai last night…" I started.

John interrupted. "What were you doing in Dubai?"

"I was…" I started again.

"That's covered by the Official Secrets Act," snapped our secret agent Solent.

"Don't be ridiculous," I snapped back. "This is Chief Inspector John Sinclair who spent half his working life in the Scottish Police Records Office. He knows more secrets than anybody in Glasgow including yourself."

"We have to keep all this pinned down," Derek Solent insisted. "We can't have any of this being discussed in the police canteen. It'll get back to O'Connor's people before you can say coffee with two sugars."

"You're paranoid, Derek. Lighten up. John's more solid than Dumbarton Rock. If you can't accept my word on that I don't think we can move forward. If you hear me out I think you'll agree that we have more on O'Connor than you have but if we pool our resources you might get him this time."

"OK," he conceded, "but this better be worthwhile."

I started to explain to both of them. "First of all John, Dubai is not important. I'll tell you about it later. What's important is that when I came home last night and Betty contacted me she was pretty worked up. The bottom line is that her and her husband, Tommy, had got themselves involved with a gang that are hauling drugs in from Spain. It's a wee travel agent at Glasgow Cross who give the punters a weekend break, all expenses paid, in exchange for them bringing back drugs. She was desperate to get out but she seemed to be frightened of them. However she was more frightened of going back to prison and she wanted me to arrange a deal with the police where she would inform on them and get a free pass for herself and Tommy. I said I'd do what I could and sent her home in a taxi."

"Except she didn't quite get home," added John. "She was waylaid in the car park next to her flat and stabbed six times.

It seems to me just a teeny bit more than coincidence. Somebody knew what she was planning and decided to shut her up. What do you reckon on husband Tommy?

"I don't know. She painted a rosy picture of him and was anxious that he didn't get taken down but he fixed her up with a lucrative job as an escort and he's got her importing drugs so he's not exactly husband of the year. My guess is that he didn't kill her but he told somebody that he was worried about her and they closed the door before the metaphoric horse bolted. Anyway, I have said nothing of all this to the police. Sorry John, but I do agree with Derek on that point. Too many wagging tongues."

"And what have all these holiday snaps got to do with this?" asked Derek.

"That part is coincidence," answered John, "just sheer bloody, lucky coincidence. It was our ruby wedding a couple of weeks ago and the wife and I went one of these cruises on the Med. She's always wanted to go to Barcelona and we flew to Mallorca and were supposed to do Sardinia, Corsica up to a place that I can't pronounce next to Rome, Civity-something, and then Barcelona before going back to Palma in Mallorca. Turns out they switched to a little port north of Barcelona called Palamos. Well we walked off the ship heading into town and there's a lovely wee bar right on the edge of the beach. We were talking about stopping for a drink on the way back and suddenly I clocked this pair sitting chatting at one of the tables." He stopped and held up the photo of O'Connor and Frazzini and then continued.

"I took the photo because I knew nobody would believe me. They were gone of course when we came back from the town but look at this little cracker." He held up another photo and passed it to Derek.

"I know what that is," chirped Derek as he passed me the photo. It was a very plush looking motor yacht, the kind for doing your own personal Med cruise. The name on the side was *Fluir na h-Albann*.

"Do you think that's a Catalan name?" I suggested. "It doesn't look like Spanish."

Derek Solent roared with laughter and reverted to his Cockney accent. "Bleedin' heck mate. I fot you was Scottish. Even a bloody Sassenach like me knows wot that means. It's yer bleedin' Flower of Scotland." He switched back to normal English and continued. "That's Danny O'Connor's boat. It's an eighty-three foot Ferretti. It packs 2000 horsepower with a top speed of over thirty knots. It's usually parked in Puerto Banus down the south. It's all fitted out with radar, GPS, auto pilot and all the latest gadgets and we know it's used as a cover for drug running from the Moroccan coast but it's out of our jurisdiction unless the GPS packs in and it wanders near Gibraltar."

It was John's turn to laugh but he wasn't laughing at me. "Derek Solent. I knew the name rang a bell. Talk about official secrets. I know a few of your dirty little secrets. That Cockney accent brought it back. There's a whole bloody great file on you in the records office, mostly drugs related."

"I'm not particularly proud of that time in my life. I was quite a heavy user for a while but I lost some good dear friends. These people who trade in drugs just use people. The users, the pushers, the mules, everybody's expendable. I switched sides and started working for the Government. I became something of an expert on the links between drug dealing, money laundering and international terrorism. The 9/11 thing in New York blew everybody off track. All resources went into fighting the terrorists. We should have been going after the big gangsters. Now they're untouchable. At least they think they are. Sometimes they make a mistake and if we're ready we can pounce. I don't know why but I think O'Connor has dropped his guard. Tell me more. What about this photo in the Trongate?"

John took up the story again. "Well, I had these photos in my camera and I was planning to go to Tesco and get them printed off when I got a call from a mutual friend who told me Jamie was being detained in relation to a murder. So I went along to see Jamie this morning and he asked me to check out the travel agent near Glasgow Cross called Scotbrava. Well, like you say it's actually in Trongate just before it meets High Street. I was heading towards the shop when Charlie Frazzini jumps out of a taxi and goes in. So I hung around and snapped him as he was coming back out. Then I went to Tesco, got the prints and came here. Oh, and there is one other thing. About these free trips to Spain. This is not the first time I've heard about it. Some people say it's for bringing back cheap cigarettes that get sold in the bars and others say it's drugs. I reckon it's probably both. There's a hell of a whack of tax on tobacco here compared with Spain and you can take back as much as you like as long as it looks like for personal consumption."

"Thanks John," I said. "I appreciate you sticking your neck out for me. What I don't understand is what Charlie Frazzini has to do with it. He was never a gangster. I heard that O'Connor bought out his ice cream business and Charlie and Angela went off and bought a bar in Spain. What happened? Did he find a Spanish poker school?"

"You've got it in one. The bar lasted a few years and then they came back to Glasgow penniless. Angela dumped him and he went sliding down the slippery path. I imagine O'Connor picked him out of the gutter and gave him a job."

"It's always been O'Connor," said Derek in a low hard voice. "You silly fuckers were too busy chasing Gillespie but how do you think Gillespie always escaped you? You thought MI5 were looking out for him. It doesn't work that way. When you're out in the field, undercover, you're all on your own. O'Connor was the one who had the coppers on his payroll. He played Gillespie along and then set him up in the end. He's a clever bastard, a jungle animal. He stalks his prey and waits to pounce. So that's what I've been doing for the last twenty years. I've been stalking him, waiting to pounce. It looks like he's changed his modus operendi. We need Sandra in on this and I need you both to swear on your life not to utter a word of this to anybody. John, you must not tell your wife anything about what has happened today. You must not say anything about meeting Jamie or me. You can walk away now and you need not be involved further but you have some knowledge of this Palamos place so I'd like you to stay on board. Needless to say both of you will be doing this out of the goodness of your hearts. You cannot be involved in any official capacity."

"I think this would be a good point to bring John in on the Dubai end of the story," I said. "It doesn't make sense unless you know about the big money movements."

"OK," agreed Derek, "this is going to be fun to listen to. Takes me back to a conversation I had with you a long time ago."

"John, do you know what Hawala is?"

"Yes, it's the capital of Hawaii."

"No, that's Honolulu."

"Well maybe it's in one of those African states."

I looked across and he was exchanging smiles with Derek. "You're taking the Mick. You do know what it is. So you also know what a Hawaladar is?"

"Yes but they're more often called Hundiwalas here in the UK because of the Pakistani connections."

"OK, here's the big one. Don't laugh. I'm not winding you up and Derek will confirm. I found my real mother. She lives in Dubai and in one of her guises she is a Hundiwala. She has been feeding information for many years to the UK Government via Derek here. I will tell you the whole long saga some other time but for now I think you ought to know that a few days ago Danny O'Connor sent a million dollars from Spain to Afghanistan via the Hawala/Hundi channels. We assume it was to buy a substantial shipment of heroin. I think they have been piling on the pressure on people like Betty Sullivan because the drugs are going to be shipped here via O'Connor's set up in Spain. There is another part of the story that in fairness to Derek I am going to leave out. You don't need to know and it's best all round if you don't know. I just don't want you to think later that we were holding stuff back from you. It really is national security stuff and only indirectly involves this O'Connor business."

"OK, Jamie, I accept that. I imagine it has something to do with how the Afghans plan to spend the million dollars."

"Something like that, anyway, the important thing now is what O'Connor is up to. I don't understand his game. He's been strictly hands off in recent years lapping up sun and sangria while his worker bees gather in all the honey. What do you reckon, Derek? You say you've been keeping tabs on him."

Derek seemed to think for a couple of moments before speaking and he ignored my question. "So that's why she was here last night. I really did think you had something going on between you. What were you planning to do if all this hadn't happened? Her getting killed, I mean. What was she really expecting of you?"

"She was desperate to get out. As far as I understand things, it started as a free holiday in exchange for bringing back drugs. She said that there are no real checks at Prestwick or at Girona, just get everybody on and off as fast as they can to turn round the planes. So then they got her to go back and then again and again. It wasn't a holiday any more and she thought somebody in passport control might notice the number of times she went back and fore. She was genuinely terrified of going back to jail. Her husband is the guy who catches the stuff as they clear the airport in Prestwick. She wanted him to stop but he apparently gets paid well and he's been enjoying the good life. Betty asked me to set up something with the police so that she could blow the whistle on the whole set up and keep herself and Tommy in the clear."

"Well she doesn't have to go back again now," said John philosophically. "But if we manage to bring down the operation at this end our big pal O'Connor still walks away without a scratch. He'll need to set up a new route but he's been in the game a long time. He'll take it in his stride. We have to catch him on the Spanish side with his finger in the pie. I got that photo of him with Frazzini and Frazzini's obviously connected at the Glasgow end but that's not even enough to get an investigation moving. The Spanish police are not exactly the most cooperative in the world. By *mañana* he'll have slipped off back down to the Costa del Sol. This is going to need played softly, softly."

Derek Solent stood up and began pacing back and fore. He lifted his head as if to speak two or three times and then began striding up and down again. He was getting quite agitated. Then suddenly he sat down again.

"I'm going to have to remind you both that this is highly classified information. I don't think the fucking Prime Minister knows yet. Listen John, the Official Secrets Act was implicit in your previous position as Chief Inspector and Jamie this is covered by all the warnings I gave you before you went back to Dubai. I'm laying my head on the block here but O'Connor is a worm that's eating away at my brain. Fuck my pension rights, it's worth the risk. Do I have your word that nothing I tell you now goes beyond these four walls?"

I was a bit taken aback by his outburst but I understood his sentiments. "You have my word and I can tell you from many years of experience that John won't even reveal a person's name without official clearance and three signatures."

He accepted my reassurances. "We have to give John a bit of background on Dubai," he said and commenced to retell the story of the two large money transfers. He also explained the story of the missile launchers for the IRA back in the eighties, carefully avoiding any mention of the murder of Mahendra and the real culprits in the murder of Iris and Freddy. He gave a brief clinical explanation of the facts. "So, at the last point Jamie knows of, Sandra Paterson was arranging a meeting between the Ministry of Defence and our US and Spanish counterparts. There was no real problem in getting cooperation. Everybody has a vested interest in stopping the battery units reaching the Taliban. In fact not just the Taliban, but anybody in that part of the world with missile launchers to use or to sell presents a major threat to our troops and security in the region.

The bottom line is that a consignment of small wind turbines left a factory near Bilbao in the Basque region of Spain the day before yesterday with destination Kandahar in Afghanistan. They flew DHL to Karachi in Pakistan and at this moment are on the road somewhere between Karachi and the Channan border crossing into Afghanistan. There are three workers in the Bilbao factory that the Spanish security forces have been monitoring in relation to the activities of ETA so, taking a long shot, it is highly probable that the battery units are packed inside the boxes of the wind turbines. Some of the parts are seemingly very similar and unlikely to be questioned by any customs officials. These consignments have to be sanctioned well in advance and are usually escorted to their final destination in Afghanistan by NATO personnel so the people who broke into the factory in Malaga timed their raid to get the battery units and move them out of Spain fast.

Our people can't do very much till the consignment crosses the frontier and that'll be another couple of days. Why I'm telling you all this is that it's going to mean that the Spanish owe us one. If we stop these battery units reaching their destination we'll save the Spanish Government enormous embarrassment. It will also give them tremendous advantage over ETA. It will discredit ETA's phoney peace declarations and put them in an awkward position vis-à-vis the Afghans. They'll have to return the money they received and if they try to use the Hawala system we ought to be able to stop it. So all this puts us in a position where we can demand closer cooperation on the drugs trafficking than we would normally get. The only hiccup in that is the *Mossos d'Esquadra*. They are the Catalan Police. Catalonia has a lot of independence from the central government and one area, regrettably for us, is in the field of policing. They jealously guard their position and deeply resent any interference from Madrid."

"It's funny you should say that," said John. "One of the reasons I was keen on the Barcelona port of call was to meet up with an old friend, David Ferrer. Away back in the eighties, just before I moved over to do the radio show full time, I did a course on regional and national police cooperation at Tulliallan College. It was the Chief Constable's hobbyhorse. There were a number of people on the course from other European police forces and I became friendly with this young lad from Catalonia. He was a dyed-in-the-wool independent Catalan and was more interested in Scottish independence than in any kind of regional cooperation. He was also part-time DJ in a local radio station so we had quite a lot in common. We kept in touch over the years and he is now a Major which is the highest rank."

"That's brilliant, Mate," twittered Derek. "I knew you'd be a good lad to have along. I'm going to trot along now and kick things into motion. I'd like to have Sandra doing the police liaison. That's her forte. So we'll have to wait till she's free of the Afghan business but she might be able to throw some weight around while she's meeting the big boys in NATO. She can probably get the Americans to put some pressure on the Spanish. The Yanks have to be grateful if we stop a shower of missiles hitting their choppers. I have a good feeling about this. It's a pity you've retired Jamie. This could have been the scoop of your career when the security blanket comes off."

"I'm a bit like yourself, Derek," I replied. "Just taking down Danny O'Connor could be reward enough."

The carpenters arrived to fix my door as Derek was leaving so John and I moved through to the kitchen to swap notes over a coffee.

A quaint little town.

Palamos is a quaint little town nestling into the northern corner of a large horseshoe bay in the north-eastern corner of Catalonia. The bay is a natural harbour that has brought prosperity to the townspeople across the years. It has a split personality, not quite sure whether it wants to remain a sleepy little fishing town or be a modern commercial centre. You can see this on the skyline as you come in from the sea. On the east you see the old church spire and the haphazard tapestry of terracotta rooftops. Then look westwards at the jarring contrast of two skyscraper apartment towers and the sprawling, rectangular, flat-roof apartment blocks. The port is divided in three, a fishing port, a yachting club and a long quay that juts out into the sea, serving also as a huge breakwater against the occasional winter storm. Lying about ninety miles north of Barcelona its lower port charges have made it a popular stop for large cruise ships in recent years. A shorter quay next to the fishing port plays host to variety of smaller ships and pleasure yachts in summer and the townspeople enjoy strolling down to see who's in port. If there's a sailing regatta going on, you might even catch a glimpse of one of the Spanish royal family.

It's not the kind of place you'd expect to find smugglers or drug traffickers but a laxity has crept into the port area since Spain joined the European Community. First of all, the Customs Office is normally unmanned nowadays. As long as you have the correct papers prepared online, in advance, you can come and go easily. With regard to police control, every port of entry in Spain is still policed by the *Guardia Civil* regardless of whether it is in Catalonia or the Basque Country or any of the autonomous regions, but manning has been reduced to token levels and many of the duties have been passed to the regional police. However, the Catalan *Mossos d'Esquadra* don't have a permanent office in the town of Palamos. To add to the confusion most traffic movement in and out of the port is supervised by the local municipal police called *Policia Urbana*. The administration of the port including the reservation of berths and pilot assistance is done from the office of the ports authority in Girona City some twenty-five miles inland.

So, port controls in Palamos are random and infrequent. No doubt Danny O'Connor was aware of all this when he decided to move north. All of his ill-gained properties were in the south of Spain around Malaga and his yacht was registered in Puerto Banus but SOCA, the British serious organised crimes agency, have nowadays, been getting much more cooperation from Spain in trying to root out big time gangsters who have taken up residence in that strip of the Costa del Sol. On top of this the ever increasing problem of illegal immigrants from Africa and the flow of drugs from Morocco ensures that there is a significant police presence in southern waters. So Palamos, in contrast, is a very pleasant place to paddle your canoe away from prying eyes.

We skimmed the holiday rental websites and found a very nice modern flat just outside the town. It was really a base to work from and investigate O'Connor's movements. We booked it for the following week, desperately hoping that we'd get organised in that short time and that O'Connor would still be around when we got there. Sandra was still tied up in her "missile crisis" although she was now back in London. Derek Solent went down to the big smoke as well and the plan was that between them they would get official clearance and help from the Spanish authorities in the event of an arrest. John contacted his friend Major David Ferrer who promised cooperation but warned of the problems of bureaucracy between the different forces. They would all cooperate but somebody might arrive with sirens blaring right at the crucial moment.

John and I were the first to go. We took Ryanair from Prestwick and noted, like Betty said, that we were checked for metal objects and liquids but not a sniffer dog in sight. The airline personnel were much more concerned about charging extra for oversize bags than about what was in them. We touched down on time in Girona and picked up our hired car. We headed out to the coast and to take possession of our rented flat. We still had a couple of hours of daylight so we went to the port on the off chance that we might see some evidence of our quarry. The little bar next the port was closed up but we wandered into the port area past the fishing boats getting hosed down after landing their catch of the day. Sitting in the short quay was a large sailing clipper and behind that a private yacht. As we drew closer we could make out the name *Fluir na H-Albann*. What now? We debated the best course of action and finally decided that John should slip off out of sight and I should go knocking on Danny's gangplank.

I stood on the dockside shouting hellos up to the yacht. A rough looking character eventually leaned over the bow and asked what I wanted in heavily accented Scottish-Spanish.

"Que quieres, mate?"

I thought it would be more fruitful to answer in English.

"I'm looking for Danny O'Connor. Tell him it's Jamie Robertson from Glasgow."

He disappeared and within a few minutes Danny O'Connor came out and welcomed me aboard. This was definitely a class above Gurney's Bar. He escorted me through to a large lounge-dining area with white leather sofas and a mahogany table with twelve place settings. One of the crew appeared carrying a tray with two glasses filled with ice and a bottle of Glenfiddich.

"What brings you to this little corner of the world, Jamie. Have you bought yourself a retirement home? It's a nice place to spend the winter months when it's freezing your balls off in Scotland. Ah haven't bought a place yet, still looking around, but Ah've rented the loveliest wee place a couple of miles up the coast. It's an old fisherman's house right on a cute little beach. There's only a dozen or so and Ah was exceptionally lucky to get it. A guy in the shipping agents up there knows somebody that knows somebody. There's a bunch of them come and do a big paella on the beach. Ah have to anchor the *Flower* out in the wee bay and take the tender into the shore. There's a footpath going round the rocks but you can't get a car in. It's a great hidey-hole. Tell me about yourself. What have you been doing? Ah heard you had a wee run in with the Polis. Ah'm sorry about that."

"You know about that? It was never made public. I got it straightened out and it's all finished with."

"No, Jamie. It's no all finished with. Ah wish it was."

"Maybe if you hadn't been putting so much pressure on Betty Sullivan everything would still be sailing along nicely. She came to see me you know, that night before she was murdered. She was desperate to get out of your drug running holiday trips. I suppose it was one of your eager-beaver heavies decided to shut her up."

"Aw Jamie, Jamie. Why do you always think the worst of me? You jump to conclusions that are way off the mark. Betty and me were the best of friends. Ah liked the lassie. She was a dead ringer for Iris. It wasn't Betty that wanted out. It was me. We talked about it and she agreed to set it up for me. Ah told her to go and see you and pretend that she was desperate. She was to lay it on heavy and Ah knew you'd fall for it. It would have worked. You would have helped the lady in distress. My mistake was telling that silly cunt Frazzini. Ah thought he was on my side but he's even more desperate than me and desperate people do desperate things. Ah'm no sure if he killed her. He's no got the bottle but he knew what we were planning."

"You're starting to lose me here, Danny. You're trying to tell me that you set the whole thing up. That doesn't make sense. Robin Hood going to the Sheriff of Nottingham to beg forgiveness."

"Ah knew there would be no forgiveness. Everybody wants O'Connor behind bars but that's exactly what they would get. Ah want to go to prison in Scotland. It's the only way Ah can escape. Ah've thought about it a lot. In fact Ah've thought of nothing else in the last couple of months but the last few weeks just pushed me over the edge. Would you believe me, Jamie Robertson if Ah tell you that Danny O'Connor is afraid; very, very afraid?"

"You mean your mother was telling the truth. There really is a bogeyman."

"Bogeyman? Aye, some fuckin' bogeyman. You've got no idea. This bogeyman rips your insides out with his bare hands. Ah suppose you've heard of the Russian mafia?"

"Yes, I've heard of them. They make Glasgow gangsters look like teddy bears."

"No, Jamie, the Russian mafia are lovely big teddy bears. As long as you don't try any funny business they're straight down the line. Ah thought that was what Ah was getting into. They offered me a guaranteed supply of top rate Afghan heroin. They had loads of the stuff, good quality, great price. The first few runs went fine and then they started turning the screws. That was when Ah found out Ah was dealing with the Chechen mafia. They're no teddy bears. They're big grizzly bears that squeeze you till there's nothing left."

"My heart bleeds for you Danny. So you thought you'd set me up as the stooge and get me to plan your swansong. What was it going to be? What were you going to admit to that would earn you a few years in Bar-L? I imagine it was Barlinnie you wanted to book into."

"Aye, the Bar-L or Greenock would do fine for a few years till things cool down here. Ah don't fancy Peterhead but it would do at a push. Beggars can't be choosers, as they say. It has to be something they could pin on me fair and square so Ah reckoned just walking in with a kilo of magic powder in ma bag should do the trick. They would know in advance and arrest me at the airport. Ah would plead guilty and get three or four years. With remission for good behaviour Ah'll do a couple of years and by that time Putin'll be back in the Kremlin and he'll tober the Chechens. The Chechens are squeezing the regular mafia out of the game and Putin needs them to stay in power. If you want to keep your new boyfriend, Solent, happy Ah can give you a list of drug traffickers and how to catch them."

"And that, of course, would also be quite beneficial to O'Connor Enterprises."

"Och. It's swings and roundabouts Jamie. You win some, you lose some."

"Look, if you know that Solent came to help me, you've got somebody in the police keeping you informed. Why not just go through them? Why all the intrigue and special deals? What do you need me for?"

"Ah want a big spread on the telly and in the papers. The Chechens have to think Ah got clobbered for real. Frazzini was my gofer on the Scottish end and he's gone over to them. If Ah set it up with ma own people the Chechens would find out. It's got to sound like a lucky break for Customs at the airport."

"So what happens if I don't agree to pass on your very generous offer or nobody wants to play your game?"

"In that case, tell them to come with a bodybag and wait till the Chechens cut me up. Either way Ah get back to Bonny Scotland, the high road or the low road."

"This is for real. Isn't it? You really are afraid of them. Danny O'Connor shaking in his shoes. I think that would make a better story than catching you with kilo of heroin. I like the bit about you getting chopped up. I could get a front page on every newspaper in the UK with that. It could be my swansong. One last Jamie Robertson exclusive."

"It's no funny, Jamie. You and I go back a long way. What do Ah have to do to convince you?"

"Well, you could stop spreading nasty rumours about me. First of all I get accused of entertaining hookers and now you have me getting cosy with Derek Solent. If I agree to set this up for you it'll be Sandra Paterson in charge, not Derek Solent."

"God above, are you still burning that candle? You're an old romantic just like me."

"No Danny, I'm not like you. I'm not like you at all."

"But you'll get me back home?"

"I'll get back in touch with you. Do you have a Spanish cellphone?"

He gave me his number and I left without committing myself either way. I was having problems getting my head round this latest development. Derek Solent was right. It's always been

O'Connor. He's been sitting in Spain manipulating people in Scotland. Now he's got his fingers burned with the Chechen mafia and he thinks he can just scuttle off back home for protection, courtesy of Her Majesty's Government and run his operation from Barlinnie. The really annoying part was that if Betty Sullivan hadn't been murdered I'd probably have gone along with her scheme. I'd have set up O'Connor's welcoming committee without even knowing. It would have been funny if not for the sad reality of Betty's murder. It was just the sheer audacity of this man who had spent his life dodging justice and he thought he could use the system now to dodge the consequences of getting involved with people even more dodgy than himself.

I turned round to take a look at his latest acquisition, his floating hotel. There he was standing on the prow looking out into the sunset with his arms round a woman. She turned and said something to him and her face came into view. Angela McCabe! No wonder Charlie Frazzini was peed off. She hadn't just dumped him. She'd dumped him for Danny O'Connor. I scurried away before they saw me spying on them, desperate to share these latest revelations with John Sinclair.

The net closes in.

John went into a quiet rage when I told him all the details. He wanted to go straight back to the boat and challenge O'Connor. I tried to sooth his injured policeman's pride.

"Come on, John. You're being ridiculous. You can't just go and arrest him. You're not police any more, far less Spanish police. You've got no authority. He'd just laugh at you."

"We must be able to do a citizen's arrest. He's laughing at us already. We can't just shrug it off and walk away."

"Who said anything about walking away? Sandra and Derek will be here the day after tomorrow. We'll spend tomorrow planning and taking a look round. If he's talking about jumping on a plane with a kilo of heroin, that means he's got a stash either on his boat or this little cottage he's got rented. The more he's caught with, the more time he'll get. I think we should play along with his little game but change the rules a bit. Let's sleep on it and tomorrow we'll take a walk round the coast to these cottages. He said there's only a dozen and they're right on the beach, so they can't be hard to find."

"Aye. You're probably right, Jamie. What's another twenty-four hours? We've waited over twenty years. Do you know what really pisses me off? I can't just lift a phone and call the police in Glasgow. I don't know who he's got on his payroll. That's sad, Jamie. I know these guys. Most of them are top class officers but there's a handful of rotten ones that taint the whole barrel and there's others that just turn a blind eye because they don't bother any more. You've always been critical of the police. It's different for me. It's like finding out your brother's a crook."

"I found out my brothers are murderers. I know what you mean. Anyway we're going to have to contact somebody in Strathclyde. I think they should be starting to clamp down on the procedures at Prestwick. I doubt if O'Connor's stopped his operations. The free-trippers will still be carrying back little bags of smack. If they catch a few of them it'll add to the case against Danny boy. That might be best handled through Derek. He has a direct line to Customs and Border Security so we can by-pass the police for the time being."

"Aye. OK. Let's go and find dinner somewhere. This place must have a decent fish restaurant. Then we'll go back to the flat and sleep on it. Things always look brighter in the morning."

We found a very nice fish restaurant and the waiter spoke fairly good English so we quizzed him about the fishermen's houses.

"Ah yes, that's *Cala s'Alguer*. They're not really houses, just very small *barracas* but they are impossible to buy. It's really nice. You must go and see them. You have to walk to the north past a big beach called *La Fosca* and then you walk round the *Cami de la Ronda*. It's a path that goes all round the coast."

Next morning, as John predicted, was very bright, just perfect for two old city lads to go rambling in the country. We went to a bar for breakfast as we had absolutely nothing in the flat. Then we did a little shopping, a baguette, a lump of cheese, a bottle of Sangre de Toro and some plastic throwaway cups. We'd have a picnic on the beach. Our apartment was on the south side of Palamos so that added a full mile to our walk. We set off about ten, following the beachfront promenade that loops round the bay towards the port. As we headed inland through the town we could see that O'Connor's *Flower* had moved out of port. We checked our route with some locals and continued up out of the town then back downhill to the *La Fosca* beach that the waiter told us about. At the end of this beach we found the coastal path easily and started climbing again. We were both getting quite out of breath so we had a cup of the "bull's blood" and set off again. At the top of the hill we had a marvellous view out to sea and along the coast. Nestling into a little cove we spotted the row of cottages with their doorsteps right of the beach. About half a mile out was a motor yacht tied to a floating buoy, too far to read the name but I was sure it was the *Fluir na H-Albann*.

We found a bench on the cliff top, facing out to sea so we uncorked the bottle again and filled a couple of chunks of bread with some cheese and sat down for early lunch. We munched away watching the yacht and the little houses. Just as we were about to give up John spotted some movement on the yacht. A man and a woman were climbing into a tender at the side of the yacht. The tender broke away and headed for shore. We watched as it made land and the couple went into a bright blue painted door in the cluster of little buildings. Five minutes later they re-emerged each with a bag and reversed the journey back to the yacht. The deep beat of powerful diesel motors broke the calm of the morning. The prow of the yacht pushed up out of the water and it skipped the surf at full speed towards the town. Time to go down and take a look at the blue-doored dwelling.

The little beach was scruffy with dried seaweed and other flotsam and jetsam, pieces of wood and a few poorly kept boats. Both O'Connor and the waiter had indicated that the houses were unattainable but they looked like a row of old garages and ramshackle buildings, albeit in a picturesque setting. The whole place had a sort of "KEEP OUT" look although there was no such sign and there was a public footpath running alongside but no vehicular access. It would indeed be a great hidey-hole for someone like Danny O'Connor. We saw enough to tempt us back when we had the full arm of the Spanish law behind us.

By the time we got back to the apartment I had the beginnings of blisters on my heels. We did some shopping along the way and bought a roast chicken and baked potatoes from a takeaway *rostisseria*. We had dinner on the roof-terrace and chatted about old times till long after the sun had sunk behind the mountains. John's friend phoned from the Catalan police to say he'd be in the morning to assess the situation. We arranged to meet for breakfast at a *Pastisseria* on the beachfront. Somewhere around two o'clock in the morning we put the top on the brandy bottle and went to bed.

It was another bright morning with a light sea breeze as we strolled along the front to our rendezvous. I had enormous problems keeping a straight face when Major David Ferrer arrived. He was heavily built, nearly bald, with a moustache and in a black uniform with red braid. He looked like the major in the Sally Ally Band. He had a bright cheery disposition so as we shook hands he probably assumed that my smiles were just smiles of friendship. We ordered coffee and croissants and he a beer and some slices of toasted bread on which he squished over-ripe tomatoes and poured lashings of olive oil.

"I've been in contact with my counterpart in the Spanish National Police," he said, comfortably and competently in English. "The Spanish Government is anxious that we take this man O'Connor out of circulation. It's bad enough that he is trafficking drugs but funding terrorist activities is something more serious. There seems to have been a big panic in Madrid when they discovered the raid on the arms warehouse in Malaga. There were a lot of red faces when they had to tell our American friends. I suppose you know that there have been a lot of negotiations recently with the Basque separatists and everybody thought there was some progress. If your people are able to recover or destroy these parts of the missile launchers it will save a lot of face and the government will have a much stronger hand to deal with ETA. If you add to all this that we are old friends, John, then I will do everything in my power to catch this gangster. Also, I have to be honest and tell you that I have been selected for the list of the *Convergencia* party in the next elections. It would look good on my curriculum vitae if I was instrumental in catching a big gangster. It's usually just pick-pockets in the *Ramblas* in Barcelona." He seemed to manage this grand speech while stuffing his face with oily bread without getting any on his immaculate uniform.

He wiped his mouth with a paper napkin and continued, "I asked you to meet here because I want to keep this operation controlled. What is it you say in English? *Tightly controlled.* These things can very quickly become a circus if too many people are involved and I'm afraid that is one of our *faltas*. Anyway, if we try to stay away from the port, we don't need to involve the *Policia Nacional* or the *Guardia Civil*. We have a small office of the *Mossos* at the port but it's only used in the middle of summer when there are a lot of tourists. So, this is what I want to do. My brother has a second residence; I think you call it a holiday house, in *La Fosca*. Do you know *La Fosca*?" We nodded and he continued. "We will use his house as a base and from there we can walk to *S'Alguer* where your friend O'Connor has his little nest." He leaned back in his chair inviting us to respond. I let John do the speaking with his old friend.

"That's exactly how we see it too. At the moment the Scottish police don't know we're here. This afternoon we will have Commander Paterson from Scotland Yard and Derek Solent from the British Security Services. With the situation that arose concerning the missiles, the drugs and huge quantities of cash plus the fact that O'Connor is resident here in Spain, it is more appropriate to have them on board. Commander Paterson will be in charge on our side and I'm fairly sure she will want your help in searching O'Connor's house and his yacht. He thinks he's untouchable." John was obviously not going to mention Danny's latest demands until we had discussed it with Sandra.

David Ferrer couldn't hide his boyish enthusiasm. "It is going to be very interesting for me working with a Commander of Scotland Yard. What time do they arrive at the airport? I will send a car to meet them."

"Thank you Major, but that won't really be necessary," I replied. "John and I have a rented car and we have already agreed to go for them. It will give us a chance to talk on the way back and, like you have said, it is best to keep everything low key. Can you give us the address of your brother's holiday house and we'll meet you there."

"Why don't you let me show you? The streets are not all named and it's a little difficult to find. After that I'll take you back to your apartment."

The Major had a chauffer driven staff car waiting in the car park. We drove up out of town past the marina and down into the bay of *La Fosca* to a row of semi-detached houses, all of which were closed up.

"This is my brother's little home from home," he said pointing at one that proclaimed the name *Can Jaumal*. My brother's name is *Jaume*, James in English, and his wife is Alexandra. So it means the house of James and Alexandra. For the next few days it is the Catalan headquarters of Interpol. This is where we will meet."

We agreed that the next contact ought to be between Sandra and David bringing things onto an official level. He took us back to our apartment where we smartened things up a bit before heading off to the airport.

The Commander.

I caught sight of Sandra as she exited the luggage reclaim. My pulse skipped a beat. I think I must have fallen in love with the image she projected, very feminine but clearly in control. I had witnessed her weak side several times and enjoyed being able to help her but it was her "commander" look that really appealed to me. That's how she looked now. Nevertheless she dropped her bags to give me a good old Scottish hug.

"Hi, Jamie. How are you? Derek will be along in a minute. He wanted to contact somebody in Madrid and his cellphone's gone flat so he popped into the office of the National Police. We're both quite anxious to get this thing all wrapped up. I imagine you've got a car. Let's just head out and he'll catch us up." She was obviously taking command.

"I think we'd maybe better wait for him," John chipped in, practical as usual. "We're parked at the back on the second level. He'll take a while to find us since he doesn't know what car he's looking for and you say his phone is flat so we can't call him." John smiled at Sandra and moved forward to shake her hand.

"Oh! Hi, John. Good God! I didn't recognise you. It's like the old days, you, me and Jamie back on Street Patrol. OK. You're right. We'll just wait for him. It's just I hate hanging around," replied Sandra a little embarrassed.

"Well, why don't you and Jamie head out to the car and I'll wait for Derek. We met in Glasgow so we know each other." He threw me the car keys. I took one of Sandra's bags and we strolled off to the car park.

"So, how did things pan out in Afghanistan?"

"God, Jamie, you wouldn't believe it. Talk about friendly fire. Our lot are worse than the Americans. They decided to drop a squad of Paras in by helicopter. Their instructions were to waylay the shipment of wind turbines, remove the missile battery units and then let the shipment proceed. If things went pear shaped they were to destroy the whole shipment just to make sure. Well all these convoys travel under armed guard and it's all contracted out to security companies. In this case the company was Wilchester Security Services. John Shackleton Wilchester was a Captain in the Parachute Regiment till he had both legs removed by a roadside bomb. He set up Wilchester Security and recruited a whole team of ex-Paras. They now operate in Kandahar making sure that key supplies get through from the Pakistani border point. So there was a stand-off between the current Paras who were trying to stop the shipment getting through and the ex-Paras who were hell-bent on making sure it reached it's destination intact."

"So what happened?" I asked. "They surely didn't fight it out."

"Well, while they were arguing, a young squaddie slipped away and put explosive charges in the back of the truck. He strolled back to the front and told them they had thirty seconds to get clear. It seems the young squaddie's nickname is Dinah, short for dynamite. They knew he wasn't bluffing and jumped clear as wind turbines and battery units all went skywards. They managed to find enough pieces to prove that the BCUs were in the shipment."

"So where have you been the last few days? After you passed the problem over, were you not free to get back on the money movements?" I probably sounded a bit peeved that she'd stayed away but she didn't seem to notice.

"Precisely," she responded. "That's exactly what I've been doing. We really hit double tops with the BCU information and it opened a lot of doors that were previously closed. I've been talking with MI5, MI6, senior politicians, a couple of foreign ambassadors. I got the VIP treatment everywhere I went. But the best information came from a tight little bunch that don't seem to have a name and individually they didn't reveal their names. There were three, an American, an Englishman with a Geordie accent and another guy that I took to be Pakistani. They were all young guys, extremely sharp and well informed. They brought me up to speed about the flow of heroin out of Afghanistan. We sat round a table in a corner of McDonalds, each of us with our laptops logged in on the scrambler. We chatted away and for anything sensitive they sent me a mail message. It was really weird but I walked out with a lot of good leads on where we stand with O'Connor and his cronies." She paused as if she was looking for me to pitch in with my boyish enthusiasm, eager for the juicy details.

"O'Connor is linked in to the Chechen Mafia," I said. "They're a ruthless bunch who have taken control of the marketing of brown heroin across Europe. They trade weapons to the Taliban and in exchange they have the franchise to buy and sell the poppy crystals. They ship most of it in through Spain and like I said they're totally ruthless and the Spanish police are largely powerless to stop them. They just kill anybody that gets in their way. Danny O'Connor is in deep with them and he wants to get out."

Sandra stopped and turned to study my face for a few seconds before answering. "You're still a smart-arse. Aren't you Jamie? Where did you find out all of this?"

"From the horse's mouth. We had a little chat. He wants to come in from the cold, so to speak, except in this case it's in from the heat."

"You've lost me Jamie. How about you try again in standard English?"

"O'Connor wants to exchange his villa in Spain for a cell in Barlinnie. He wants to fly back to Scotland with a kilo of coke in his bag and we arrange to have him stopped by customs. He reckons he'll get a couple of years and while he's out of circulation the Chechens will move off his case. What do you think? Do you want to play pat-a-cake?"

Again she studied me for a few seconds before replying, "I think you should put that question to Derek Solent but stand clear when he answers. He wants him out of circulation, full stop. I don't think a couple of years is what he has in mind. In fact I think Derek will be more in favour of feeding your Danny Boy to the Chechen wolves. Have you discussed this with John's Catalan friend, Major Ferrer?"

"John and I thought it best to run it past you first. David Ferrer is under the impression that his job is just to rubber-stamp O'Connor's arrest." By now we had reached the car. I put her bag in the boot and was about to close the boot-lid as Derek and John arrived. Derek threw in his well-beaten Louis Vuitton and we got under way.

"Jamie, do you know Angela Frazzini?" asked Sandra.

"Of course he bleedin' knows Angela Frazzini. Jamie boy is the curator of the Glasgow ice cream wars. Angela Frazzini was Charlie Frazzini's accounts controller." Derek answered on my behalf.

I felt the need to keep my end up. "Actually I didn't know any Angela Frazzini. I knew Angela McCabe. I don't know that they ever married."

"Well, she's married now," added Sandra confidently.

"OK. OK" It was John's turn to contribute. "For the record let's call her Angela Frazzini. We all know who we're talking about. What about her Sandra?"

"Well, she's not Angela Frazzini," laughed Sandra. "She's Angela O'Connor."

"What's her relationship with O'Connor?" I shot the question at Sandra. "She's here, you know, with O'Connor."

"I know she's here. That's what I'm trying to tell you. She dumped Frazzini a couple of years ago and married Danny O'Connor," Sandra snapped back irritably. "Did he not tell you when you had your cosy little chat?"

"You've spoken to him?" queried Derek Solent.

"He wants to come home quietly." Sandra answered for me. "I don't buy it. Why would he come back to spend time inside when he's not long married to the charming Angela?"

I nodded in agreement. "I'm just telling you what he said. I've known him a long time and I used to be able to take what he said as kosher but this time I'm sure he was throwing me a line."

"Would somebody be kind enough to tell me what the fuck you're all talking about?" Poor Derek sounded piqued.

John, the liaison man, obliged, "O'Connor is in deep with the Russian Mafia and they're not as nice as Glasgow gangsters. He wants us to help stop them bullying him. We're supposed to set things up with the customs guys and he walks home with a pocketful of heroin. The quantity will be enough to ensure a jail sentence but not enough to prove he's trafficking, at least not on a big scale. He gets a cosy little hideaway in Bar-L and the Russians go home to play their balalaikas."

"No way!" shouted Derek. "I want his balls in a basket. What about this local guy, Major Ferrer? Does he go along with this?"

"He doesn't know. Listen Derek. Keep your hair on," I tried to cool him down. "I'm just passing on what O'Connor said. None of us wants to see him get away but, like Sandra, I think he's chancing his luck. He's up to something. Actually he says they're Chechens not Russians. My feeling is that we shouldn't tell David Ferrer and move in as soon as possible to raid his house and his boat. Let's see what we find and then decide which way to jump. I haven't discussed my feelings with John. David Ferrer is John's friend."

"Yes, David is my friend," John concurred, "but he'll think we're a bunch of plonkers if we suggest letting O'Connor off lightly. He's a bit laid back and maybe a bit pompous but he's a hard-nosed copper. On top of that he wants the glory. If you want O'Connor's balls in a basket, David'll do his best to get them for you. We saw him just before coming here to get you and it was agreed that Sandra and him get together to decide how we tackle O'Connor."

Sandra took command again. "OK. I'll call him now," she said, taking out her Blackberry. "Have you got his number, John?" John dutifully supplied the number and a meeting was arranged for eight o'clock next morning at the holiday-house-headquarters in *La Fosca*.

Tell me just once that you've seen justice.

Eight o'clock sharp next morning we all assembled in David Ferrer's brother's house. We were eight in total: myself, John Sinclair, Derek Solent and Commander Sandra Paterson on the Brit side and Major David Ferrer, Sergeant Jordi Garcia and Corporal Silvia Gisbert on the Catalan side. The eighth member was David Ferrer's driver. He was simply called Toni but I suspected that he was in fact a high ranking plain clothes officer. First to speak was the effervescent Major.

"Good morning, Commander Paterson. This is a privilege and a pleasure. John here will confirm that I am delighted to be working with a Commander from Scotland yard but I had no idea this Commander would be a beautiful woman."

Sandra smiled and was about to reply but Derek Solent cut in abrasively. "Good morning, Major. The pleasure will be if we catch this bastard O'Connor. The Commander is indeed a beautiful woman but I have worked with her for a number of years and I'm not sure I'd call it a privilege. She's just another plod with a few more fancy badges on her jacket a bit like yourself."

David Ferrer kept smiling as he replied. "Mr Solent, I presume. Pleased to meet you. I'm sorry, my English is not perfect. What is a plod? I suspect it is something not very nice that you pen-pushers call us policemen. Ah! Yes! Noddy! Isn't it?"

"Who are you calling Noddy?"

Major Ferrer, in his comic looking "Sally Army" uniform, began to sway from side to side and then he started to sing the "Noddy" song from the cartoon series.

"My little boy watches it every day," Ferrer explained. With the digital TV we can put it in English. PC Plod is the policeman in Noddy but I still have no idea what it means. I suppose it can't be so bad if it's on children's TV."

John decided it was time to get down to business. "Commander Paterson is up to date with our discussions from yesterday. So David, we're basically ready to make our move. It's just after eight so O'Connor is probably at the little house on the beach or in his yacht in the port. Does your Sergeant here speak English?"

"Yes, he does. What's your plan, that some of us go now to the house and the others to the boat? What do you think, Commander?"

"Yes, let's move," Sandra answered firmly, "but I think that even splitting up, there are too many of us. Let's go softly, softly and make sure we have them before we go in heavy. Jamie, you know where his house is so why don't you go with the Sergeant to see who's there. We may need the voice of authority if they are in the yacht at the port so I think myself and the major should go there. I'll recognise the name of the boat even if I can't pronounce it. Derek, I think you're so eager to clobber O'Connor you could compromise the situation. I don't mind if you go to the house or the port but stay in the car with the young officer here. I think I heard the name Silvia. Is that correct?"

Corporal Silvia nodded yes to her name but looked a bit apprehensive about being dumped with Mr Grumpy.

"Don't worry love," he reassured her, "I don't eat young officers. It's just the brass buttons that get up my nose."

Silvia's knowledge of English was too basic to understand why he wanted buttons up his nose. She just smiled coyly and said, "My car is out Mr Solent. Do you like to come? We go to the parking at *Castell*."

"Why do we want to go to a castle, love?" Derek was beginning to feel that he was being sidelined.

David Ferrer answered. "*Castell* is the name of a beach, Mr Solent. These little houses in *s'Alguer* are not accessible by car. You can walk from here but it is a shorter distance to walk if you go to the next beach. Corporal Gisbert's English is not very good but she knows what we are planning. She is also our expert with a pistol if O'Connor is armed. So, don't worry. You will be close to the action if, how do you say it? If the balloon goes up."

Silvia's face grimaced a little. She was fully up to speed on the plan of action with regard to O'Connor but she was still puzzling over the buttons up Derek's nose and now they were talking about balloons going up. She knew this part of the coast well. The winds were strong and unpredictable. It would be difficult enough if they had to call in a helicopter. A balloon would just get sucked out to sea and get carried off to Marseilles or Corsica. She decided that if they used a balloon she would definitely not volunteer.

Derek, on the other hand, was reassured by the Major's platitudes. "OK, girlie. Let's go to the *Castell*."

Sandra turned to John Sinclair. "Sorry John, you're left holding the baby. Can you stay here and start making contact with SOCA. You don't need to say who you are, just toss my name at them and they should jump. Here's my laptop. It's got a dongle so you'll get Internet. I'll log in for you and you'll have a secure connection. We'll need two of them over here to escort Desperate Dan and we need an arrest warrant issued. I don't know if we'll be taking Angela down with him but ask for one female officer too and I can pair up with her."

I went with the sergeant. "We can really get in easier from this side but I think your big-mouth friend is better at *Castell*" he said as he swung the 4X4 patrol car into a rough track through the pine woods. Within a couple of minutes we were at the spot where John and I first did our *recce* of the little cottages. Sergeant Jordi parked his car between two pine trees and we set off down the rocky path to check out O'Connor's den. It was closed up with no sign of life. I used my cellphone to call Sandra while Jordi called his boss, the Major. We agreed to stay put until they checked the port. A couple of minutes later Sandra called back.

"The *Fluir Na Whatsit* has just slipped its berth before we got to it. Can you stay there, Jamie? Let's hope they're coming your way. The Major is calling the local police. They have a fast Zodiac so we're going to follow at a distance. We don't want them to get away but neither do we want them chucking stuff overboard. Stay back out of sight and with luck we'll get them at the cottage."

We retreated to the pathway behind some bushes and about five minutes later we heard the drum of the diesel motors. The yacht stopped out in the bay and dropped anchor. Two figures appeared on deck and cast off in the small tender. As they headed for shore I called Sandra again. She was in the police launch behind the rocky headland. They had powerful binoculars, she told me, so they would wait till we confirmed it was O'Connor and then move in slowly. Before our conversation ended I was able to confirm that it was Danny and Angela. They pulled the inflatable up the pebble beach and went into the cottage. Time for the Sergeant and I to come out of hiding. He called his junior officer and told her to bring Solent along the seashore path to the cottage.

It was Angela who opened the door when we knocked. O'Connor obviously hadn't told her about meeting me. She recognised me and was visibly thrown for a few seconds. She quickly regained composure and called Danny. He invited us in cheerily.

"Have you managed to arrange anything?" he asked.

"Yes, Danny, I've arranged for the Sergeant here to search your little hidey-hole."

"That's not what we agreed," he protested, "but go ahead and search. There's nothing to find." He waved his arm round the room demonstratively. "Have you been in touch with anybody back home?"

"I've been in touch with Sandra Paterson and Derek Solent. Do you know Derek? He knows a lot about you." I taunted him.

"Awe, fuck it, Jamie. That's you trying to be the smartarse again. I told you I wanted to slip in quietly, no need for the big guns."

"Nothing but the best for you Danny. You didn't tell me you and Angela had sealed the happy bond. Is she coming back too?"

"No, she staying here to mind the shop. She'll come and visit once things are settled."

"Isn't she afraid of the Chechens?"

"You're asking too many questions as usual Robertson." I noted that he'd switched to surnames.

"It's the habit of a lifetime **Mister** O'Connor," I returned, "but I don't always get the right answers."

"Must be the way you ask the questions."

Derek and his chaperone arrived to interrupt our banter and she and the Sergeant set about searching the small house. It was sparsely furnished and didn't appear to have any hidden corners so it didn't take long to search. They found nothing. Silvia went over to the dining table which had three cardboard cartons sealed with broad coloured sellotape.

"What is in the boxes Mister?" she asked.

"Cigarettes," snapped O'Connor. He no doubt considered it *infra dig* to be questioned by a young low-ranking female officer.

"Do you mind if we open them?" asked the Sergeant.

"Yes, I bloody mind but I suppose you're going to open them anyway."

The three boxes did indeed contain packs of 200 cigarettes.

"You smoke a lot, Mr O'Connor," commented the Sergeant.

"It's not illegal," Danny snapped again.

We could here the steady thump of the approaching police Zodiac. The motors cut and there was the crunch of footsteps on the pebble beach.

"Good morning everybody!" breezed Major Ferrer.

"Who the fuck's this? Sergeant Pepper?" mused O'Connor, obviously impressed by the *sally-ally* uniform.

"His name is Major Ferrer," replied Sandra from behind, "a senior officer in the Catalan police. What have you found lads? Anything sinister?"

"Sinister?" scoffed O'Connor. "If you want something sinister just look in the mirror."

"There is nothing here, Commander," answered Sergeant Jordi. "The only thing is three boxes of cigarettes and as Mr O'Connor says, they are not illegal."

David Ferrer walked over to the table to look inside the open box. "Open the other two boxes," he ordered.

The other two boxes produced more cigarettes of a different brand. Derek Solent didn't speak. He just stood sullenly watching the process. Without a large haul of drugs or some other incriminating evidence O'Connor was going to be calling the shots. They would have to take him on a small drugs bust like he wanted just to save face. He pulled a cigarette packet from his pocket and opened it.

"Sorry folks. There's just one in the packet." He said, crushing the empty packet with one hand and putting the cigarette in his mouth with the other.

Single ciggies! That's what Myra called them. I looked at the crushed packet Solent dropped on the floor. What was it Iris said? That day at the hospital before she went on the revenge attack on Jenny Kerrigan.

"THEY PUT THE TEN WEE PACKETS IN AN EMPTY FAG PACKET."

My head felt like it was exploding.

Thank you Myra! Thank you Iris!

"Open up the cellophane wrapper!" I shouted. "I want to see inside the packets."

The Sergeant obliged, tore back the plastic and handed me the first packet inside. I scrambled to open it. Nothing! There were twenty cigarettes.

"Give me another one," I demanded. Number two produced only cigarettes. "Another one!" I pleaded. The

Sergeant reluctantly handed me a third packet. Again it held just twenty cigarettes.

"OK. Please stop," said Major Ferrer. We have searched this house and found nothing incriminating. We must now apologise to Mr O'Connor and leave him in peace. I'm sorry Mr O'Connor. I believe there has been a little misunderstanding."

O'Connor opened his mouth to reply but was interrupted by an infantile squeal from Derek Solent.

"Oh dear! Oh dear! Oh dear! What have we here?"

Derek held packet number four in his hand. He turned it up side down and out fell ten little white envelopes. Corporal Silvia opened number five and out popped ten more little white envelopes. Then packets six and seven each had ten more. Then the remaining three were bona fide packets of cigarettes. The first three, either end, were kosher and the four in the middle were filled with little packets of brown crystals.

Thank you Myra! Thank you Iris!

Angela, who had been conspicuously silent, jumped into life. "I'm sorry Danny. This has nothing to do with me. I have never had any dealings with drugs. You're on your own Danny. I'm leaving."

The Major snapped to attention. "These packets are professionally wrapped. They must have a machine to put the plastic back after they put the drugs inside. We have searched the house. It must be on the boat."

Angela ran for the door, nipped out down the beach and into the inflatable tender. She chugged the motor into life and started to pull away from shore. Danny ran after her and plunged knee-deep into the water.

"Stop Angela! Wait for me!" he shouted.

Corporal Silvia drew her pistol and squared it double-handed towards O'Connor's back.

"*Alt o tret!*" she shouted, "**Stop or I shoot!** *Alt o tret!*" she repeated and slid the safety catch off. O'Connor turned, looked at the gun and panicked. It was strangely amusing. Here was Glasgow's hardest mobster and he'd probably never faced down a gun before now. He panicked. He started to run again and flopped face down in the sea. He struggled for a few seconds and then his body went rigid. At first I thought that Silvia had shot him but I knew there had been no shots. His body rolled over and he let out a fearful groan then went still. Angela turned her boat around and came back to the beach.

"Danny! Danny! What's the matter? I wasn't going to leave you. I just wanted to get to the yacht before them. Oh, Christ, Danny! What have I done?" She jumped out of the dinghy before it reached the shore and wrapped her arms around the floating body. The Sergeant and his young lady assistant strode into the water and pulled her off. He felt for a pulse and shook his head."

"*Esta mort*. He's dead."

"You stupid bastards!" Angela moaned. "You've killed him. His heart was weak. The cold water must have brought on an attack." She splashed through the water to his side and grasped his hand. "Oh, Danny! I wasn't running away from you. You know I wouldn't do that. I wanted to get to the *Flower* before them. I could have dumped the stuff." She turned back round and spoke to anybody who would listen. "He said he had arranged to go back to Scotland and would get a by-pass operation in the prison hospital. He doesn't speak...I mean he didn't speak any Spanish. He was terrified of going into hospital here. It wasn't supposed to happen like this. How did you know about the cigarette packets?"

"And what about the Chechens?" I queried. "He was trying to get away from them."

"Is that what the silly bastard told you? No, he was big chums with them. It was probably all that Vodka that started his heart problem. They're Muslims, you know, not supposed to drink. There's two of them on the *Flower* now. They're going to have to find a new banker now."

Sandra just stood there in a daze. Solent was still murmuring, "Oh dear! Oh dear!" with a strange smile across his face.

The Major took command again. "*Sergent! Agafa el barco amb els Municipals I porta li cap al port de Palamos.*" He turned to Sandra, "I have told my Sergeant to go with the Municipal Police and bring O'Connor's boat into Palamos. We will search it there. I imagine we will find the little cigarette factory and probably a significant quantity of heroin."

"No, you can't," Angela screamed hysterically. "It's my yacht. It's registered in my name. You can't take it. That's my home. It's all I have."

"In that case you will be responsible for any illegal things that we find on board," the major answered coldly. "We came here to arrest Daniel O'Connor but we may have to be content with catching his wife. Arrest her, Sergeant, on suspicion of trafficking illegal substances."

"One moment, please," I tried to stall them, "I just have a couple of questions before you take her away. Angela, where is Charlie Frazzini. What part does he play in all this?"

"When I left him he was a mess. I begged Danny to help him and he made him responsible for the Scottish end, getting the packets of cigarettes and heroin from the punters on their flight home. Charlie never got over me going with Danny. I think that's why he killed Betty Cassidy. I think he was trying to find out what Danny was up to."

"You're saying Charlie Frazzini murdered Betty Cassidy."

"Aye. That's right. I don't think he really meant to murder her but, like I said, he's been a mess. He started using heroin and he went to pieces. Listen Jamie. What's going to happen to me?"

"That depends what they find on the boat."

"There's a pile of heroin, about a million dollars in cash and the machine they were talking about, for repacking the cigarettes."

"Well, Angela. I would say you're about to become a permanent Spanish resident but don't expect them to give you a pension. You're not going to see the Costa del Sol for a long time."

She started thumping O'Connor's floating corpse. "Danny, help me! Help me!" They pulled her off a second time, cuffed her and led her away to the patrol car.

I turned and spoke to the floating cadaver. "Well Robin Hood, you've escaped. You were right, you know. There is no justice."

There was a rumble of motors from the Police Zodiac, increasing in pitch as it headed out towards Angela's *Flower*. Then there was a deeper rumble as the yacht's engines burst into life. The Chechen's weren't waiting to say *Bon Dia*. The Zodiac climbed out of the water as its motors climbed to a high-pitched whine and despite Danny's powerful diesels the smaller boat started to gain on the yacht. They headed straight out to sea and rapidly became two small blobs on the horizon but we could still see that the Police launch was just a couple of hundred yards behind and gaining steadily. Then suddenly it spluttered and stopped, dead in the water. Angela's *Flower* veered sharp left and set course, north, towards France.

Major Ferrer snapped open his cellphone and barked gruffly in Catalan, "*Que pasa? Que? No em diguis. Ostia! Idiotes!*" He turned to Sandra, shaking his head in disbelief, "I'm sorry Commander, the idiots have run out of fuel. It's near the end of the month and they had enough fuel to patrol the port area slowly till they were re-fuelled but going really fast they have burned more fuel. We've lost them. I can call out the helicopter but they will have thrown everything overboard. We will have to let the woman go too. I was sure we would find evidence on their boat but not now. Also these Chechens will be well armed. They will fight. This is going to be extremely embarrassing for me. It will be disastrous if I lose some *Mossos* in a fire fight."

"So, that's it," stormed Sandra. "We just all go home? You must be kidding, Major. There must be something you can do."

"I can give you one hour with this Angela woman before we allow her to go free. She is in the car with the Sergeant. She doesn't know what has happened. If we don't tell her immediately she will tell you everything you want to know to save her own skin. Don't you think?"

331

"OK. Let's do that," Sandra cooled off quickly and made the rational decision.

The Major called his Sergeant and we re-assembled in his brother's house. Derek and his pretty young driver had to walk back to their car and were still walking back to the *Castell* beach when we arrived at the house. We went in and Sandra sat Angela down on the sofa to begin her bluff.

"Angela, I have spoken to the Major and we have agreed that if you can help us piece together Daniel O'Connor's operations it would be more beneficial to have you extradited to the UK. We will charge you as an accomplice and you can claim minimum knowledge. You will get a very short sentence or maybe even probation and you will escape a much longer sentence in a Spanish prison."

"But Danny has property here and money in the bank. I'm his wife so I should inherit everything. Most of it is all legal. I need to stay here to claim it," protested Angela.

"Suit yourself," replied Sandra calmly, "but I would imagine you can have a lawyer to do that. Anyway, in the meantime you could help me by answering a few questions. If there is anything you think is incriminating you don't have to answer. OK?"

"I suppose so. What do you want to know?"

"Well, Angela, the thing that puzzles me is why Danny wanted to go prison in Scotland. Why didn't he just make an appointment with a specialist and go home for a few months."

"That one's easy. He told you he was scared of the Chechens. That's rubbish. He got on great with them. It's your friend Derek Solent he was terrified of."

"Derek has been trying to catch Danny O'Connor for years. I know that but I don't understand what you mean."

"Danny went home a couple of years ago. He was attacked by somebody who tried to stab him. He was wearing a bulletproof vest and that saved him. He got a couple of nasty cuts in his bum and he couldn't sit down for a couple of weeks. Apart from that he was OK but he got a big fright."

"You surely don't think that was down to Derek Solent. Do you?" asked Sandra defensively.

"You don't know. Do you?" Angela asked with eyebrows raised. "You really don't know."

"Don't know what?"

"You know who Sam Horton was?"

"Yes, he was Danny O'Connor's main rival."

"Well, Derek Solent was Sam Horton's son. Sam was in the army during the war. After the D-day landings he was billeted in London. He had a fling with Solent's mother and then at the end of the war returned to Glasgow. He had no idea that he had a son in London. The young mother put the kid up for adoption and he was adopted by the Solent family. He grew up as Derek Solent but I'm fairly sure his birth certificate will say otherwise. When he finished school he took a university place in Glasgow to track down his real Dad. They eventually became quite close and he took it hard when his Dad died in the car crash. Everybody blamed Danny. I honestly don't know if it was Danny's men but I suspect it was."

"How do you know all this?" demanded Sandra.

"I was good friends with Sandra Horton. I was her bridesmaid when she married her first husband. We still keep in touch. I think she was a bit jealous when this guy came muzzling in on her precious Dad. Personally I don't understand why they liked him. I knew him and he was a horrible person."

"Lot's of people might say that about O'Connor," suggested Sandra.

"Not if they really knew him. He was a gentleman. He treated me like a lady. Charlie Frazzini was a pig. It was like night and day when I went with Danny. I don't know what's going to happen to me now but one thing's for sure. I'm going to miss Danny O'Connor"

"I don't understand why he was so involved, hands on, at this stage in his life. He didn't need the money. Did he?" Sandra posed the question we were all thinking.

"It's all about power and ego. Danny was happy living in Spain but he couldn't let go of his Glasgow connections. Over the years he still liked to be Mr Glasgow. Behind the scenes Derek Solent became the silent partner in Sam Horton's shady empire. Horton really was a nasty piece of work, you know. I know that Danny was no angel but at least he could speak to people politely. Anyway, back in the seventies and eighties it was all about territory. Whoever controlled the Gorbals controlled what went on in the Gorbals, or Pollock or Easterhouse or Castlemilk and it was the same in all the big housing schemes. You must remember all that business with the ice cream wars in Garthamlock and Easterhouse. There was Danny O'Connor and Sam Horton and that other thug Gillespie and lots of other little thugs and Charlie Frazzini was just trying to build up an honest business. I felt sorry for him. They were all trying to push him off the road so they could get their own mucky little vans into his territory. Jamie came to see me once asking a lot of questions and I walked out because I didn't want to tell him about my best friend's father. Maybe if I'd told him then it could have changed things but I didn't even tell Charlie what I knew. It didn't start with drugs. In the beginning it was stolen cigarettes and chocolates and aspirins and things like that. It was a great way to sell off stolen goods. The police knew it was going on and they did nothing about it except harass poor Charlie because his folks were Italian.

"Then it changed. They started moving drugs around in the vans. Things got bigger and the big Mafia boys got involved and it was all about who controlled the supply. Sam Horton gave up on pushing ice cream vans off the road when he bought the taxis. That's when he really made his move on the Glasgow drugs scene. He had half of Glasgow all sewn up and just needed a regular supply. Then Derek Solent dropped into his life like a gift from heaven. I think you know that Solent was well informed about international crime and moving money about and that sort of thing. The Horton show began to outshine the O'Connor show. They were able to by-pass the big London gangs and buy in direct. Then we invaded Afghanistan and chucked out the Taliban who had previously stopped all the poppies. So the Afghan farmers started growing poppies again big time. Now it's all about price and quality. That's when Danny got involved with the Chechens because they had tons of the bloody stuff, good stuff for half the price it was a couple of years before. They found out that Danny had a code for this *Willywalla* thing"

"You mean Hundiwala?"

"Aye, something like that."

"But why do it himself. That is the part I don't get. All his life he kept three steps back from all the dirty stuff."

"I suppose that was my fault. I begged him to give Charlie a job. When I left Charlie he was really on a downer and like always I felt sorry for him. So he put Charlie in charge of the Costa Brava operation and he messed up. The Chechens started getting nasty at that point so Danny came up here in the *Flower* to get things under control and sent Charlie back to Glasgow. Then we both liked it here. Everything was hunky-dory till Danny's heart started playing up. Then I think he kept doing everything himself just to prove he still could. You know what men are like. I think he thought of himself as a kind of modern-day pirate."

"I heard you telling Jamie that Frazzini killed the woman in Glasgow. She wasn't Betty Cassidy. She was Betty Sullivan."

"No, she was Betty Cassidy. Sullivan is still married to his first wife. Betty and him made out they were married but they weren't."

"Why did your husband kill Betty?"

"You mean my ex-husband," Angela corrected, "Your guess is as good as mine. We heard through Danny's contacts in Glasgow. If he was hoping to get back with me, it would be more likely that he'd be happy with Danny going inside, even for a couple of years. If I have to guess, and it really is just a guess, he found out that Betty was doing something behind his back and he wanted to know what. As I understand it she told Jamie that she was the one wanting out and she was prepared to shop the others. Maybe he heard this and tried to stop her. You're going to have to ask him yourself. I don't want anything more to do with him."

"Just one last question Angela. You must know a lot of Danny's contacts. Are you planning to take over his *business interests*?"

"Hell, no!" protested the gangster's Moll. "I hated that side of things. For me Danny was just a great guy who came along when I needed him. I still need him but he's gone. I don't need all his baggage. I'll take what I can get from cashing in his properties. The yacht is already in my name and it's worth a packet, if they let me have it, that is."

Sandra pondered for a while before speaking again. "You've been very frank and helpful, Angela. As they say on the telly, I've got good news and bad news. You, almost certainly, will not be charged here in Spain because of lack of evidence and I am going to recommend that you have no case to answer in the UK. There is no doubt that you have been an accessory in serious crimes committed here in Spain but the proof has just slipped away from under our noses. You are an extremely lucky lady. If the Major tips the nod, you're free to walk."

"I don't understand. What's the bad news?"

Sandra shook her head solemnly. "I don't think you're going to see your *Fluir Na Whatsit* again. Your Chechen friends gave the local Police the slip. They're half way to France by now, probably heading for Corsica. I don't think, even if you ask nicely, that you have a hope in Hell of getting it back. In some ways it's better for you. There's no way anybody can tie you to any crime now that the boat is gone. If there was heroin on it, it's been chucked overboard along with any cigarettes and the packing machine." She turned to David Ferrer, "Major, can Mrs O'Connor go now or do you need to keep her?"

"Mrs O'Connor is free to go or to stay. It is her choice. The Spanish government will try to sequester all of O'Connor's property that they can. This will be a long process taking many years. During that time nobody will be able to sell anything and all bank accounts will be frozen. I imagine you will do the same in Scotland. But Mrs O'Connor please listen well. We will not tolerate it, if you try to continue your husband's illegal activities here in *Catalunya*. I hope you will say that this is a bridge that you have crossed and will not cross back over. In the short term you are free to stay or go but there will be an immediate embargo on all of Daniel O'Connor's property."

Angela looked stunned. She just stood up, said, "Bye-bye" and made for the door.

"Don't you want a lift into town?" I asked.

She shook her head, wiped the tears from her eyes and kept on walking, nearly knocking down Derek Solent as he walked in.

"What's going on?" he asked

Sandra and I looked at each other and then said in chorus, "That's what we want to ask you?"

John Sinclair walked in at that moment and innocently interrupted, "If I understand things correctly, Sandra, our prime suspect has kicked the bucket on us and his wife and accomplice is walking free from lack of evidence. Do you want me to cancel the arrangements I've just made with SOCA?"

"No, John, not a cancellation, just a few minor adjustments. Tell them we want Charles Frazzini arrested immediately along with the owners of the Scotbrava travel agency. Tell them we need to call in the UK Customs on all flights arriving from Girona to the UK for the next seven days Everyone carrying packs of 200 cigarettes or more must have the packs opened for the detailed examination of the middle six packs. They are specifically looking for heroin. You can tell them we don't require a female officer any more. Finally tell them to expedite the extradition papers but with a change of name. Our suspect now is Derek Solent."

I walked over and spoke to the sergeant of the *Mossos*. "Can you take me back to the beach with the small house? We all walked away and left O'Connor floating in the water."

"It's OK," he assured me, "It's been arranged but why do you worry? He was a gangster. Was he your friend?"

The answer tripped out easily, "Yes, I think he was."

Printed in Great Britain
by Amazon.co.uk, Ltd.,
Marston Gate.